The critics on Antonella Gambotto

'Brilliant! Move over Anaïs Nin' *Sydney Morning Herald*

'*Dynasty* written by a young Martin Amis on speed – full of gilded aristocrats, spleen and sex' *Herald Sun*

'Gambotto's integrity, adamantine wit, and ability to cut through the most elaborate psychological defence systems establishes her as one of the finest writers this country has ever produced' Colleen McCullough

'Gambotto possesses a major literary talent' *WHO*

'This novel has it all – sex (lots and lots), adultery, murder, drugs, breakdowns and child abuse – with all the action underpinned by an obsessively passionate love story ... beautifully written, heavily descriptive, laden with caustic wit and cynicism and very, very amusing' *Cleo*

'A merciless eye for minutiae and a matador's instinct for the kill' *The Australian*

'The detail of the fiction verges on social reality – a warts and all rundown on Australian, American and UK society ... an erotic journey of self acknowledgement' *Harper's Bazaar*

'A brilliant first novel' *Cosmopolitan*

'Gambotto writes with great sensitivity and also has a keen eye for satire, which she uses to great effect' *Tatler*

'She is brilliant ... Readers will, in any case, discover this for themselves' Edward de Bono

Antonella Gambotto was born in Sydney, Australia, in 1965. She is a journalist and critic, contributing to the *Sydney Morning Herald*, *Elle Magazine*, *Australian Magazine* and others. In Australia she has published two volumes of profiles and essays entitled *An Instinct for the Kill* (1997) and *Lunch of Blood* (1994). She lived in London for seven years from 1984 to 1991, working for the *Independent on Sunday Review*, *New Musical Express* and *GQ*, winning the *Cosmopolitan* New Journalist of the Year award in 1988. She currently lives in Sydney.

The Pure Weight of the Heart

ANTONELLA GAMBOTTO

PHOENIX

A PHOENIX PAPERBACK

First published in Great Britain by Phoenix House in 1998
This paperback edition published in 1999 by Phoenix
a division of Orion Books Ltd,
Orion House, 5 Upper St Martin's Lane,
London WC2H 9EA

ISBN: 0 75380 676 2

Printed and bound in Great Britain by
Clays Ltd, St Ives plc

To Peter Wurth,
who returned to me my life.

To Alan Leslie Pilkington,
who taught me how to live.

To Colleen McCullough,
who let me breathe.

(O I willingly stake all for you,
O let me be lost, if it must be so!
O you and I – what is it to us what the rest do or think?
What is all else to us? Only that we enjoy each other, and
exhaust each other, if it must be so:)
– From the master – the pilot I yield the vessel to;
The general commanding me, commanding all.

Walt Whitman

BOOK ONE

GRIEF IS A SPHERE

I

I think my parents were bewildered by my oddity.

Conceived in the honeymoon suite of an hotel run by two penitent French fascists in an algid village near Valgrisanche, I was a child of love and not conjugal duty and thus and only thus, as my father once suggested, were certain 'vital fluids' conferred unto me. From that now-mythical hotel, the blue-white Alps could be seen through a froth of huge and creamy Sombreuil roses and it was with this realization that my father claimed to know his first child would be female. After a twenty-seven-hour labour, I was born by Caesarean section on the cusp of the hour ruled by the angel Gabriel, whom the Mohammedans understand to be the spirit of truth, the ruler of the first heaven and also the angel who came with light to the cave in which Mohammed prayed, that same Mohammed with whom I share a birthday in the northern autumn and subequatorial spring. I emerged surprised and blind and blinking and covered like a monkey in fine long black hairs. For the first three months of life, I wept continuously and then spoke my first sentence at ten. My mother's breasts were suckled by me until they bled a milk-streaked blood. I have been told these things. Only fantasists remember.

2

I was a little lamprey eel with my sucker mouth, gill pouches and special perforated head, all eyes and heart, an envoy of wonder. What was life to me then but impact? My shifting moods were dropped like jewels into the greater pool of plain being's glory: such a gift. Everything affected

3

me – content, form, depth-field of hue, every resultant feeling, every theory. Time as I understood it was too delicate for rage. There was a universe for me to know.

This was not a perspective shared by my seniors. The headmistress of one of my many schools once had me hauled with ceremony to her room. I had been caught carving the initials RH into my desktop with a compass dipped in ink. Such gestures came naturally to me; I was an incorrigible romantic. Those letters were my first conscious obsession, five strokes and a growling curve of joy, the initials of the first boy with whom I fell in love and the abbreviation for blood's rhesus factor – as it happens, mine was also my initials and my frame of mind. Two days before he turned sixteen, RH swallowed the barrel of his father's derringer and spattered that moonlit sunroom with his brains. When I heard this news, the shock impelled me to imagine his skull fracturing as neatly as a breakfast egg – there it cracked and there it fissured, exposing an innerness of firm and gleaming albumen: I willed the thing into a poem. But he was still fresh to the world when I loved him. The sugars found in fruit were equally sweet.

The gorgon who then taught me well understood the intricacies of humiliation. She was a sadist, and indifferent to my attempts to correct her pronunciation of my name. Before I was even aware that she had left the blackboard, she was beside me – howling, scowling, the size of a barn and utilizing those big brown buck teeth. Ruthless bitch, she cuffed and dragged me mewling through the class. I tripped and tripped again over my feet in an effort to match her pace. We passed in turn the rehearsing flute band, the bruised and mud-streaked hockey team and Miss Edwina Broadbeam, formerly Head of Mathematics at Bolton and Sixth Form Tutor at Lady Ellenor Holles. Degradation is the temperature of hell. On reaching the office of the headmistress, I was released, a trembling little ghost. Waited. The headmistress grew from her throne to what seemed to be the ceiling. Her eyes were large and cold, a North Sea grey. Listened to her disengaged abuse without fully understanding. She caned my palms and as I wept, informed me that an education comes in many guises. She was not wrong.

'You are dismissed,' she said.

4

Stumbling, I was marched through all the late pale strips of daylight, in which were interlaced the dust-motes (silver, gold) of those antiquated corridors. My hands were treated by the nurse, who pretended not to hear me as I begged and begged her to be gentle in my accented English. 'Please,' I implored her, '*please*.' Her face was a letterbox: square, florid with broken blood-vessels, and bisected by the mean slat of her mouth. She scrubbed each welt and grunted – as I winced and sobbed and flickered in that thick-wristed grip – her every worthless opinion on my behaviour. When she died in the rubble of a government building targeted by Irish terrorists (her letterbox-head crushed by two well-aimed iron girders), I was not sorry. By then I was an adult, and acquainted with hatred.

3

Maps of the solar system entranced me for afternoons. Darkness knew its counterpart in such mull light. I exhausted myself with cause and reason, meaning and its politics, being and non-being. Metaphors were a strong drug. I also liked to thrill myself with stories of the paranormal – headless highwaymen, phantoms doomed to walk the earth, unrequited spectral loves, griefs and obsessions carried through to other incarnations – and was addicted to the great mythologies. The mermaid was to me a figure of fascination with her lyrical elusiveness and useful tail. Those flat green weeds took her for drowned – her throat was seen to float beneath the waters, polyp-white and unadorned. Deadlocked conjecture! I would lie awake and wait for ghosts but none ever appeared. The grounds were searched for naiads, river gods, the green Megaera.

I resonated with such prayers.

My parents were very busy people, obligated to the world in their ambitions and uninclined to reinforce that Weimar number preferred by the parents of my peers. I was always permitted to read beyond midnight if I so wished. No torches necessary, nor any subterfuge. Nevertheless, such enforced individualism can lead to alienation and so to make myself popular at school (peripatetic children must develop strong charms to survive), I copied Walt Disney cartoons onto parchment with a peacock tail of felt-tipped pens. These primitive offerings were the object of much admiration and through them, I secured my social place amongst the lovely snub-nosed girls. I call them 'lovely' because I was never really pretty. My laughter, I was told so many times, was the axis of my appeal. I recall strolling down the Avenue Foch with my father and his friend. After recounting a child's joke, this man listened to my response and said: '*Il tuo riso promette.*' For years I wondered what that promise was.

An Italian child uprooted to England. Loss of history, a devastation. And like all displaced children, I was lonely. What was I doing in London and how was I expected to value its habits, history, liturgy? The many cultural adjustments were confusing. What was high tea? When adults spoke of Pimm's, what did they mean? To be excused from class, how was that phrased? These were questions with traumatic repercussions, issues over which I frowned like a philosopher. I was altered by my newest language – with the different shaping of each vowel, a different slant on each feeling and jarringly new reference points.

There is no intellectual clarity to such issues even now. I missed the lilacs of the land that shaped me. I missed my people. I missed an emotional expression I innately understood. The memory of flowering chestnut trees can still unwind my heart. And then there was the statue of that towering angel, my avenger, his cloudy wings ever-unfurling in the courtyard by my room. It is impossible to wring sense from such mysteries. How could the British compensate for such a loss? A martial race, they concern themselves with the expenditure of energy only to enforce those traditions they deem appropriate to form. England – a country my eccentric and gentle father completely loved – did not touch me; it was to me no more than badly lit Dickensian caricatures and unpaid supernumeraries from the Globe. I would have attached myself like an adoring leech to one of them but was too openly feeling to make an effective follower, leader or bully, and as a consequence, kept somewhat to myself. I often asked to be alone. My father understood this need if only because he was much the same in his desires and knew the liberty such privacy conferred. He ensured that I felt singularly loved.

4

A rural cemetery. I was one of many children playing outside the gates. Within, those marble tombs, affixed to which were glassed and glassy portraits of my paternal grandparents and burning beneath them, those eternal lights. The raised lettering of names and dates could, after a morning's exposure to the sun, brand little white fingers. Snapshots: guarded by granite, that woman by her live perambulator and that old man tremulously singing his sweet aria to all the dead. My friends and I played catch through grass as over us the shadows of butterflies drifted.

> Powdered littleness as I was then –
> a ballad of smoke,
> my floury weightlessness
> the cartilage of stellar galaxies.

Calling for me, a nanny (Jennifer) who later – much later – married an Austrian count and died at forty of misery and champagne. Reeds by a stream. Wild irises, their roots encircling those hollowed bones. A frequent image in my dreams: that one young gull seen from an old clifftop hotel on the Amalfi coast, its colour changing as it wheeled through the warm ocean haze – bright white on the slow inner loop and then a tilting silhouette of itself on the outer, pausing only to disappear as it changed wing.

These were my memories last night, uncalled and lingering.

To soothe myself, I walked out into the dark wetness of my new garden. Stared at the sky. It was a clear night, moonless, almost human in its humidity, and the oyster-clouded evening had dissolved into a yield of stars. I feel disjointed when the past returns to me – overwhelmed, darkly uncertain. I may as well have been lowered by a rope down a black well. Change can be terrible. It is my nature to preserve and as a consequence, moving house has always been a matter of anxiety and grief. Collapsed onto that lawn. As I inhaled the heat, I was the sum of gloom and fretfulness – hushed beating, unseen wings. A cricket roared. Gazed up into the ether, searching for my father in the shower of Leonids that had just become visible.

Shooting stars possess a certain grandeur for me, an almost religious significance. I see them as symbols of a pure and nervous beauty, devoid of torment, nervous in the way of any vivid thing. Even their names hum with the energy of other worlds – the Delta Aquarids, the Lyrids, the Orionids. All that splendour, and such power. The elegiac abstract. Absolute simplicity makes apparent the eternal. And I have always sought the core of things, therein their magic. In my mind, I am a Wolf Rayet star – ejecting at ferocious velocities gas shells, real caloricity. A flare of gold through the night sky can awe me for an hour. I am able to believe that meteors are the incarnations or prototypes of all great spirits, that perhaps my father is one of them, that perhaps they are his way of returning to my world. He was always one for special messages.

Why perceive a thing as separate when it can only be understood in context? His words, now mine. Separateness was not offensive to my father, merely a misunderstanding; he knew that people have a responsibility to recognize themselves in that and those around them. Related question: how is peace possible without empathy, assuming it is peace we want? This peace of which he spoke was also that which a man can find within himself. 'Bad behaviour on any level is only ever a response to fear,' he told me. 'Fear is an autocrat. All people are tender when they understand the power of their hearts.' Considered, being is a recognition of the *anima mundi*. Considered. Otherwise, life is a farce – a self-perpetuating cycle of wars and celebrations. His favourite phrase, and one always delivered with his brilliant glance: 'A member of the human race.' No matter how abject a person, how violent, how ethically repellent, they always had that passport to understanding.

He believed there was no action beyond true forgiveness.

The rulers of the Roman Empire were the first to grant citizenship and rights to those they conquered, and my father was a conqueror. His philosophical *élan* did not preclude the usual human flaws. He was conspicuously determined, and vain about his intellectual abilities. I had seen those looks of his – perceptible only for an instant, but so informed with superiority, so calm, so calculating. Despite his altruism, he could not help but think most people asinine. He was aware of the rarity of his mixture of genius and discernment and heart and application. And he loved beauty – in all its forms – too ardently. This was, perhaps, a reaction to his past. The world had not always embraced him.

My father had his enemies. His achievements made people scream. All they saw was this big, sunny building of a man – all jaw and shoulders, chairman of Queen Elizabeth's merchant bank, the legendary investor voted the world's best deal-maker by *Euromoney*, a polo buff married to a sexually exciting aristocrat. He had never had the need to talk up his own book, only flew Concorde, commissioned Tiffany's to produce his household silver, belonged to the Palm Beach Bath & Tennis Club, and owned (aside from our South Ken pile, an island off Greece, a New York brownstone, and a villa in Monaco) five thousand spectacular acres of Norfolk. I once overheard one of his colleagues hiss: 'I want to know his fucking *secret*.' This was a striking sentiment, and shared by many of his peers. There they were with their batty wives and three-star afternoon adulteries and reflux and receding hairlines and mad children shooting up in public lavatories or scoring in suburban car-parks and they began to hate my father because his very existence illuminated the desperate futility of their own. He knew what it was to have nothing and to have everything, and his conclusion was that everything was nothing without love.

When feeling melancholy, he would tell me stories of his childhood in wartime Baceno: a diet of turnips and black market sugar, the chiaroscuro of uncertainty, soldiers disfigured by battle, gunfire, heartbreak, hunger. At one point, the soles of his shoes were impossibly worn; poverty had him patch them with playing cards. 'I was the only child in history to go to school on a Royal Flush,' he liked to say. His parents were *petit bourgeois* and persecuted for their Allied sympathies. At the age of eight, his sister disappeared. He could never bear to elaborate. *I Tedeschi*, were his only words, *quegli animali*. In his wallet he carried a fading photograph with crenellated edges, a photograph I have since framed. Tame water, benign sky. Erect-backed and forlorn in pantaloons, my father as a golden child: each rib articulated, squinting at the sun and identifiable to me only by that gap-toothed smile. His sister Angelica is captured in movement – lunging or landing from a leap. Against that pre-war backdrop, her face is indistinct, there is the flavour of laughter, and her dark blonde curls are loosely upswept. The shoestring strap of her simple cotton bathing suit will never stop slipping from her small shoulder.

I was named for her.

Angelica was afraid of wolves. At night, she would call my father into her room and beg him to recite an incantation to deter these wolves from entering the house. Sometimes he frightened her by howling on all fours from the dark corridor and then repented for his thoughtlessness with an assurance and embrace. His memories, now mine. She mussed his hair with field-flowers and fought with him over the candy coal *La Strega* brought them at Christmas. Sometimes she sang: *Lo sai che i papaveri son' alti, alti, alti, ma tu sei piccolino, ma tu sei piccolino.* She often tripped when skipping and her dreams were those of every girl. When she grew up, she would be a ballerina every bit as good as Karsavina; she had read those old newspaper reports of Diaghilev's Parisian production of *Giselle*. She, too, would dance with an artist like Nijinsky and have roses, orchids, lilies thrown at her satiny feet. And here my father's voice would thicken into silence: in his eyes, a living anguish.

5

My first memory is of his mouth enunciating my name, syllable by delirious syllable. I think I was in a high chair at the time, my legs drilling the footrest, an ecstatic infantile tattoo. My father's mouth was his most startling feature and at its most powerful when he was preoccupied. He had a habit of pausing in doorways, lost in his own universe, one arm pressed to his chest, the other hand cupping his chin, his mouth absolutely still and set in a line which had as its centrepoint a darkness where his lips did not quite close; below it, the textured cushion of his lopsided lower lip. It was a sensual mouth in that it suggested or enticed the senses, in that its impact was profound: it left its imprint. Some mouths are voluptuous or full but tell only of excess; my father's was a potent soul manifested through physical means. 'Do you remember,' I asked him when I was all of six, 'when I was little and I used to let you pretend to eat my fingers?'

Certain people are impressive because they have a talent for paying attention. Through the means of a wide and welcoming smile (I am thinking of one hospitality industry witch in particular), they are able to convey the illusion of unconditional love for those with whom they deal. They are skilled at making people feel important and valued and interesting. For whatever ends, they specialize in high-beam focus. My father did not belong to these occult ranks. He was only able to make others feel that they were in the presence of someone important and valued and interesting. Without imposition or flattery, he simply projected his essence. This was not a conscious act. It simply left him in ever-regenerating rays or waves – like light, like heat. He never just 'awoke and went to work'; there was a sense of constant revision about him, a sense of expansion, an alertness to specific psychic energies. It was so strange. My father was guided, his path determined by a benevolent power. Friends have used the word 'directed' to describe him, but it is inadequate, it is not accurate. He did exist in this life but was forever jolted back to a higher vision. This quality was hypnotic, if a little inhuman. 'Do that in which you believe,' he always counselled me, 'and the rewards will follow.' However gentle he may have been, he was experienced by everybody as intimidating because he never doubted his own instincts, and because those instincts were inevitably right. He deeply trusted blood. Wallpaper whisperings of bankruptcy, Dow Jones collapse, financial meltdown, loss – these were just thunderclaps to him, irrelevant. The worst had long ago occurred.

There was a thickening of tissue on his chin – a glamorous scar from a polo fall. Some said it gave him the air of a boulevardier. I just liked its easy symmetry. When I reported that Mary Ellen Martinet's mother said it gave him the 'heir of a lardy Bouvier', my father paused for a moment before erupting in rapturous laughter. Once he had finished wiping his cheeks of tears, he plunged his fingers in my hair and called me his *cretinetti*. He would sometimes press my fingertips against the scar to illustrate the texture of old wounds. 'All heals to silver,' he would say. I now realize he was trying to tell me something of his pain. The afternoon he died I received the card he had mailed from Los Angeles the week before: *Carissima Lucciola, non mi sono dimenticato di te, sai?* No more than bad timing. This was what we understand to be God – traditionally 'the receiver of the dead' – making it known that the human mind and heart are but telescopes through which eternity can be glimpsed. With his death, a separation in me from that self I had always thought mine, that which Hipparchus called a 'cloudy star'. No longer consciously human, I became a metaphor for grief. My father had become a memory.

Loss deafens man to the exoteric world, making it so that suddenly he is fluent only in the language of the claw and madder-stained incisor: this is grief, it is preliterate and known eventually to all. That 'divine faculty' of intellect had been usurped by sorrow; love was reduced for me to the denominator of born flesh. I grieved for flesh. A hole had been shot through me. I could not but renounce my god. In that catastrophic instant, I was not brave. Orphics and

Christians are uncomfortable with skin – their belief is that the only holy element of man is spirit, his one purpose to release this spirit from his corpse. Such philosophies turn on a disregard for the temporal and thus were unacceptable to me. No more than a carcass? This was a man I loved.

> *Each layer of my skin unveils your face:*
> *it is your substance underneath mine,*
> *I have always known it.*

From thereon in, my senses would be denied my father and I grieved. I mourned him with my every breath. Districts of guilt surround the death of the beloved. Here he walked and there he stood; this was his preferred blend of breakfast tea. That indention in the armchair, it was his. The *Financial Times* had been left open at the page he had been reading late the night before. He did exist. He was a man. I loved him. These and other facts were part of him, but not the whole. They were the details of his being – enough to evoke agony, but not enough to resurrect him. All men are destined to become diaphanous. My father would now only 'be' through others; no longer autonomous, he would exist as we, his memorists, would have it. And I became one of these means of existence, his biographer, the case in which he had deposited certain private documents: it was to be a task to see myself as more.

These are cerebral anodynes. My emotions were a thing of caverns, impure ore, tremendous.

6

The unspoken assumption about life is that it will be unto infinity. My father was an evolved being, far too evolved, I thought, for the primitive suck of such intransience. He was at once a man and not a man: he was my father. It seemed obscene that he should be extinguished in the manner of a match. No mountain range is razed so suddenly; no ocean disappears over the stone wall of a night.

The Pythagoreans may have believed that the home of the soul is in the stars, but this was not a consolation. My sorrow prevented me from acknowledging a wider context. I did not appreciate the manifold guises of grace. All I knew was that the pivotal truth upon which I had based every certainty had seemingly been proven a lie and that I felt betrayed.

That simple trust I had in the world had been destroyed.

My brother Amedeo, six at the time of our father's death, was a quiet, fair and top-faced boy, a kind of mathematical prodigy and unfamiliar with the disorder of extreme emotion. There is no god to renounce at six, and so my brother renounced his true identity. His memories of our father are different to mine – generic, oddly abstracted, almost completely blocked in later life. He struggles to remember a word, his father's face, distinct events. It is too difficult. It is to hurt. To him, father was flesh of his flesh and above that, an intimidating symbol. The only male left in the family, he was prey to a dark responsibility. There are times when I see the eyes of that six-year-old boy glow through the mask of the man – in them, loss and resolute combat of that loss. Our later years were spent in search: mine, for a love that ran as deeply and my brother's, for his confidence.

The day of my father's death is recalled by me in membranophonic detail (the friction drum rubbed hard, the tambourine smashed senseless). When grief is divided by surprise, the quotient is a mechanical precision. The opening phrase? Kensington Gardens after circumnavigating the Round Pond. That duck and its fierce feathered upswoop from the water. Low sky. A winter brimming with cold possibilities. How old was I? As old as I will ever be. The afternoon was passed scaling oaks or flaking maples with Gretl Stern-Waltzer, of the distinguished German family. Her colouring was Thracian – auburn hair like a liqueur and her chemical-blue eyes were slanted, lightly lashed, near-Oriental. My eyes are too baroque to effectively demoralize; they cannot but enfold. Gretl's, on the other hand, could really frighten people.

Extreme vulnerability is often protected by a hard exoskeleton. Gretl was an unusually tall girl and very dramatic at her full height. When irritated, she summoned a defiance generally associated with adulthood. That leopard-lineage was a curse. She was motherless (suicide by poisoning – the neurotoxin acrylamide monomer) and her cock-of-the-walk father was perpetually in transit. Her response to such rejection was to feign strength and a patrician indifference; her sense of self flowed only from triumph. A natural historian, she knew all about Mussolini's newspaper *La Lotta di Classe* and had a good handle on the tenets of socialism in order to vanquish opponents in every school debate. Gretl believed in her superiority as another child would have believed in Father Christmas. Such concepts kept her wavering soul in line. And yet we laughed together, laughed so uncontrollably that we were often slapped by bitterly exasperated teachers. In the interests of schoolroom order, we were eventually placed in different classes.

We met infrequently in later years. I was based in Sydney; she had married at the sparkling age of eighteen and 'divided her time' (the expression she used) between Manhattan, Monaco, Milan, and Mustique. Our last meeting was in London. We spent the afternoon in Claridge's, her favourite hotel. She loved the *maitre d'* (with whom she flirted restlessly), and claimed the grand place brought her luck (her most romantic trysts had been enjoyed in the one gilded suite). That day she needed every illusion of supremacy. The divorce from her kinky tycoon husband had just been finalized and she was agitated, seemingly electrocuted by her otherworldly beauty, and compulsively adjusted the heels of her boots, stammered, shook her head, spilled granules of sugar and lemon rind onto the carpets and then apologized for her hysteria. New York City had elasticated her Kensington Palace vowels. Those lightly lashed eyes flashed with terror, with pain. She was that day a child, again abandoned. 'I can't take it any more, Angelica – I no longer want to *feel*.' There was a pause as she fought with her emotions. 'He took the one thing sacred to me and de*filed* it – he de*filed* it.' The cabochon sapphires on her fingers trapped the sister-light of chandeliers. 'Did I love him, do you think? *Did* I? Or did I simply envy his audacity?'

At a loss, I stroked her hand.

'My Christ,' she hissed, unnerved, 'I'm so drunk by the time I go to bed each night that I can't sleep for listening and *list*ening to the beating of my heart. These feelings, Angelica –

I don't know how much longer I can tolerate these *feel*ings. How could he –'

I held her tightly as she wept. A fortnight later, she was dead. This girl of twenty-one had slashed her scarlet arteries in the bathwater of her suite at the Pierre: *fini*.

I had telephoned her every day. I had spoken to her bored former husband (bored by her feelings, professionally remote, only half-alive within his prehistoric skin) and had beseeched her father to intervene. No-one had listened. Self-involved people make themselves busy when others are in need. The consensus was that Gretl was an adult and that she would be 'just fine'. Articulating such self-comforting statements somehow made those statements real to them, but I was not convinced. My conversations with her had disturbed me; I wanted to book a flight. But she insisted that there was little to worry about. 'Why won't these headaches let me *be*?' she asked, and then: 'I've sent you a little present.'

After her death, I received the gold identity-bracelet given to her by her mother. Her former husband's words to me the night before: 'I mean, she should just snap out of it and have a *drink*.' The autopsy revealed she had been pregnant. The father would have been that ostentatious Hollywood producer who had left her for a twenty-year-old man. Her former husband married another redhead, a celebrated Swedish lingerie model (also kinky) with an insouciant mouth and languid eyes, long and pale and smooth, usefully stupid, and who in advertising spreads was garnished with angelic laces and ribbons. He did not even send a wreath. He was too busy with his millions and his new lithe toy. He was too busy with his life.

All this was very fresh in my mind. The *New York Times* ran her obituary. She had been quite the socialite – a fixture at balls in aid of the paraplegic, at dinners in aid of the starving, at concerts in aid of the deaf. It was a meaningless existence and she knew it, but was by then too weakened by her griefs to change a thing. Capitulation to the norm was less demanding than confronting her pain. Acknowledgment of sorrow involves tiring feelings. And so to her slow death at the best tables at Mortimer's, Le Cirque, Lutece, benefits at the Whitney. In a series of spectacular ballgowns, she seduced the dry East Coast establishment. 'I sit there smiling, drinking, drinking, smiling, drinking, cracking jokes I've made a thousand times before,' she said, 'and you know the strangest thing? I no longer give a fuck whether my thoughts or actions are sincere. I used to care. I know I did.'

From what I could gather (she was unusually circumspect on the topic), the man who became her husband had outrageously deluded her. Thirty-odd years her senior, Jonas Fudd knew all the tricks. Gretl had been so young and susceptible. Tickets to the Red and White Ball in Poland, long-stemmed roses by the score, Boodle & Dunthorne trinkets, splashy weekends waltzing in Versailles, champagne, cocaine, lush hours of cunnilingus – Fudd really was a pro. He was an old hand at playing The Hero. The only indication of his true nature was his voice: it was a hacksaw, grating and serrated and designed to carve. But Gretl was suspicious of her intuition and she fell in love. The wedding, to the gratification of her family, was featured in all the right social sheets. When she turned to him for marital advice, her father said: 'You chose him, Gretl. Life is hard.'

Again: it was a slow and painful death. Fudd's fetish, she discovered, was for all the functions of the anus. His mistresses included heiresses, professionals, and schoolgirls only just over that ripe age of consent. He twice deliberately infected her with gonorrhea and then explained his promiscuity away as a by-product of her sexual incompetence. She once arrived home (Upper East Side whitestone, twenty-six-foot windows, aubergine silk-damask drapes, inferior Matisse, good Giacometti, a smattering of Schiele and Vuillard) to find her husband obediently barking on the Aubusson; above him, a sleek black latex-strapped professional wielding a crop. 'Hey, read my lips: I wasn't booked for a *ménage à trois*,' the whore indignantly declared. Gretl vomited before she reached a sink.

That Wall Street kraken broke her heart.

I still automatically search for her face in every social page, finding only the teeth and razor-scapulae of her contemporaries. The shocks of a bad marriage can be excoriating.

7

How wide the world is to a child. I could run for miles and not be indifferent to a single thing. Autumn recollections: crisp brown leaves, the crackle of brown paper parcels as they are unwrapped. Mist thickened in that late air. Shivers, a satchel, my new unlaced shoes. That hat I threw with such abandon only to lose it in the high branches of a tree. Grazed knees as we attempted to retrieve it; a surprised whoop as Gretl fell. I had recently celebrated my first communion and was still dazzled by the new magnitude of my old soul. One of my father's peers – a financial auteur and brilliant, the first of two homosexual sons to that invertebrate, Augustus Braine – had given me an eighteenth-century bone chess set. At my party, I watched him shrug at a similarly inclined friend and say: 'Child abuse is *such* a vulgar term. I prefer to think of it as the education of the young.' He left the City not long afterwards to live untroubled in Morocco, where he indulged his passions for white sunlight, black hashish and prepubescent boys. I believe he died an ugly death from AIDS. *Tant pis.* Gretl and I discussed my gown and that chess set before parting as the golden sodium lamps were lit. 'See you tomorrow,' I shouted into the deepening darkness.

Walked home in a dream dragging my feet. I was an escapist, no question: the child of people who are always in the press must find a place in which she is unwatched, unknown, and free to experiment. It was a form of entertainment then to see just how many different noises I could make. Childhood is a photic period, schizophrenic: colour and sound have real impact, which is why young children generally prefer balloons to books. Content is a perceptional evolution of form, after all. So: dragging my feet and hopping over pavement cracks. And one, and two. Buckle my shoe. Tried to visualize the Dark Ages about which I, the dark day pupil, had been taught that very day. What had my teacher said? Something about peasants, portents, peat-preserved princes. My pink-mouthed yawn encompassed all the universe. Winter approached not on little cat feet but with an invoice for all human life. And five, and six. Pick up those sticks.

A cluster of pigeons cooed from the eaves. Everywhere the tints of metal and of embers. The portly bodies of black cabs, glow-worm pedestrians. Human pace is swift in such cold weather. At the end of an elegant cul-de-sac, our house: designed by Lutyens and inspired by Wren, of the whitest Portland stone, it was so stately with French casement doors and in most every room, there was a fireplace. Through the steeply pitched roof, a double-chimney stack. On the north side of the house, an obscure coat of arms in *bas-relief* against the classical pediment. My father, a member of White's, had always been an Anglophile and this obsession – stylistic rather than socio-economically prejudicial – was reflected throughout the house. His study was decorated in the Queen Mary style. In it, a Chubb safe, a nineteenth-century terrestrial globe, and a sobering display of Purdey shotguns. Upon his desk, a detailed model of the *Royal George*, the official yacht of King George III. H.M. Bateman's framed cartoons lined the bathrooms and in the corridors, the works of Turner, Burne-Jones and George Clausen. There were lacquered cabinets, an abundance of fine mother-of-pearl, showy ciphers worked in silk, Cauldon Potteries breakfast services, all was exquisite: we were fortunate to be so privileged.

My father sometimes returned from his day silenced by the ordinary squalors of London. When the Department of Health reported outbreaks of rickets and scurvy amongst undernourished children, he was incensed. The barbaric discrepancies resulting from the English class system spurred him to publicly denounce bourgeois indifference and to forcefully involve himself with certain charities. The thought of people living on the street was not merely 'unpleasant' or 'terribly sad' to him – it was anathema. 'I find it difficult to understand,' he said, 'how people can ignore the suffering of those around them.' He was nouveau, unlike my mother.

Stamped my feet on the doormat, slid my bulging satchel along the polished parquetry. The pompous housekeeper

Catherine Chadwick (whom my brother and I had rechristened CC or, less favourably, Crater Critter for her pockmarks) told me it was 'imperative' that I see my mother. She was very adamant with that grim face of hers and so I loped upstairs, one hand gliding over the banister, swinging my plaited head from side to side, thoughtlessly impudent, my tights laddered, shoes still unlaced, staunching with my thumb and forefinger the flow of blood from my right knee and humming a ditty learned that week in the playground.

I was completely unprepared for the assault of fate.

Drawn curtains, an atmospheric gloom. Mother was hunched on the edge of her big bed and beside her, Lady Octavia Hampshire. Their silence should have surprised me, but I was busy enjoying the acrid flavour of my forefinger. Rapped on the opened door. Hampshire looked up. My dislike of her was probably lifted from my father, who was polite to her, but unimpressed. She represented that against which he fought all of his adult life: power without responsibility. Cricket games at Highclere Castle, relief balls on Her Majesty's Fleet, feigned piety at the Brompton Oratory, the Warwickshire Cup at Cirencester Polo Club – she was everywhere, the wealthy hag, and had no purpose outside that of self-aggrandizement. Our eyes locked without empathy. I shuffled my impatient feet and again rapped. A boring pause. Hampshire touched with fashionably red fingertips my mother's shoulder. Her turn was slow in that sepulchral moment.

My mother stared at me without much recognition and in a monotone, drawled: 'Your father was murdered.'

8

I do remember thinking how odd it was that she had expressed this information in English, rarely spoken in the house. My mother preferred French or Italian for their charming use of the tongue and throat. Wherefrom, then, that Oxbridge accent? The overwhelming nature of the message had perhaps overridden considerations of habitual pronunciation or perhaps my absorption of the message had rejected such considerations. Whichever, it was clarity. And so I stood, my hand now wet on the doorknob, aware of a growing impenetrability within.

Everything assumed the resonance of consciousness. The mortuary chair against the wall acquired a new meaning. My sinciput dragged my face to the floor. Other cities in my eyes, imagine. Blue sound between each glacier thought. Hampshire's face rose like a moon, some awful moon, in that crepuscular interior. I glanced away and stared instead at the window sash. My heart beat very cautiously. I was aware of it as one is conscious of a tall-case clock somewhere within the darkness of a hallway. Sore knee. Shuffled my unlaced leather feet. My flesh was tallow pale against the oakwood of the door. What had she said? Try as I did, I could not remember. Each blink of mine was a kind of thunder. The ceiling fell. That sudden torpor. A scream brewing within me and then just that sulphurous silence. Cease, ceasefire. South Ken station, I remembered, was being restored. Those lavatorial tiles! I left the room.

Native semi-metals such as arsenic crystallize in the hexagonal system and there we were, a privileged family, each member at his own point of the hexagon – my mother, Amedeo, me, my father, his existence and then death. And not just dead, but murdered: what a hexagon! This was exceptional. Where was my brother? That knee of mine would make me cry. My father's pale Sphinx cat drove her soft face into my shins. The fire had been lit and was prettily twinkling. Had he been stabbed? I sank deeply into the sofa and studied the hearth. Arctic peoples regard the Aurora Borealis as the dance-fire of the ghosts. The fragrant logs cheerfully burst. Had he been strangled, suffocated, shot? Indifferent purring by my thighs. I wished that hag Hampshire would leave. The pendulum behind me swung six times, one for each point of the hexagon. I had never realized that all flames are quite translucent. In cremation, fire is thought to separate the body from the soul. To hear such news? It was to swallow cloud: cold altocumulus upon my tongue. I would never again dream in Italian.

My father had been strolling down Threadneedle Street

after visiting the Exchange. With him, Dorian Farquarson – a close friend of his and City luminary. The two men were amongst sixteen gunned down by a sniper (modelling a .223 calibre semi-automatic Storm Ruger rifle and an Army & Navy Stores 70 per cent acrylic/30 per cent wool-blend balaclava). My father and Farquarson were inevitably the superstars of this nightmare. The general public liked to be reminded that the wealthy also died. Our funeral portrait made the front pages of the *Daily Mirror*, the *Daily Telegraph* and *The Times*: in that globally circulated photograph, I am staring from the first dimension with immortal eyes.

The newspapers outdid each other in their efforts to analyse the sniper and his motivations. One blamed the welfare state, another blamed 'the breakdown of the nuclear family', a third roped in a specialist who contemplated chemical imbalances with specious ease. It made absorbing reading. Philippe Pinel, the psychiatrist remembered for liberating his patients from their shackles, called such psychosis *la manie sans délire*. The British shrink J.C. Prichard decided it was better named 'moral insanity'. That medieval book of mysticism, *The Cloud of Unknowing*, refers to such electrodynamic emotionalism as 'monkey tricks of the soul'. There was a smorgasbord of answers to a question I had never posed.

Compelling stuff: the sniper (Sam) was twenty-four years old, never employed, the offspring of a paranoid Toxteth drug dealer and a subnormal West Indian whore, the victim of severe emotional and sexual abuse, had been on the streets since the age of ten, had been involved with car-theft, rape and GBH throughout his youth, was devoted to sadomaso-chistic pornography and crack, and when not attempting suicide, subscribed to *Soldier of Fortune*. The only thing he loved was a chihuahua he called 'Fluffy'. Sam of Green Gables. After the trial, he was escorted to Broadmoor where he is still apparently enjoying Danielle Steel's mini-series on colour television, taking brisk and invigorating morning strolls, and discussing his emotional complexities with his psychiatrist every afternoon. Poor ravaged spirit. He, too, had all his magic stolen and when a man is deprived of magic, what is there left to him but rage? I could not say with any certainty that I would have escaped his destiny given the same brute disadvantages. My wish was only that his aim had been less accurate.

I conscientiously composed this Sam a letter (which I then addressed to the Old Bailey), but there was never a reply. At the time, I did not know he could not read. The words I wrote him are still with me: *Violence was necessary as a tool for or adjunct to global exploration and the consolidation of empires, but now that the physical world has been fully explored, we must adapt to peace. Behaviour must always be modified to suit the shifting socio-economic landscape.* Admittedly, I was a peculiar ten-year-old. There was in me little desire to conform. Another thing I recall is being pitied. Pity comes in billows, and is emitted by particular alignments of the features. I never resented it, but dreamed of being in a position which did not demand it. Such delicate distinctions are important.

My mother suffered a wild reaction to the death: we were to relocate to Sydney. She wanted only to escape herself and had decided that the self in question was defined by Europe. No more proletarian unease, no more distinct winters, no accessibility. She wanted out – away from impossible emotions and headlong into the new world and its distracting difference. Her moles found us a suitable harbourside property in Sydney – not in the Eastern Suburbs, which were (she heard) 'crawling with crass Jews and all the parvenus', but on the lower North Shore, an area hospitable to her designer fascism. Our new address would be Shell Cove. Our new pet, a Borzoi. Our new home would be a sandstone house built by Irish stonemason bounty immigrants in 1845. The grounds were pampered and majestic with rare trees; from the balcony, a mantle of plush grass unrolled to the slap-slapping water. Trained to the outside walls were those same Sombreuil roses my father had loved from that hotel near Valgrisanche. She assured me it would all be perfect.

9

It was an era of discouraging upheavals. Everywhere stamped crates, finality. The Lutyens house back on the market. Train cases, hat boxes, large suitcases, stud boxes, trunks – all Dunhill black, securely locked and festooned with labels. My encyclopaediae, my collection of stuffed animals from Hamley's, all the Webb crystal, every drop-leafed gate-legged table, my toy theatre with its adjustable hand-painted backcloths, the enamelled Cartier clocks of blue and gold (those two colours associated with eternal sensibility), my Chesterfield coats and Sunday hats, Amedeo's Meccano – all was wrapped in tissue, bound in tape, routinely seized. And my father, that lapful of ashes, was left behind.

I have never visited his grave.

My throughbred *maman*, never extravagantly maternal, excluded me from thereon in. Her sorrows required an ever-ready audience and thus made it impossible for me to express my own. I had no option but to make myself as inconspicuous as possible. She made it clear that my only purpose was to help her fully exorcize her pain. For me in any way to tax her crackling nerves was unacceptable and so I learned to disappear. Invisible Angelica! I don't think I ever asked her for a thing. This is an art of sorts, and useful. I once overheard her tell a friend that I reminded her too deeply of her dear departed and therefore, of her grief. This was fantastic. Would it be necessary to revise my face in order to be loved? I store the essence of my father in my features and like him, rapidly shed my accent whereas like our mother, Amedeo – tall, so blond – has a residual Latin rhythm to his speech. His genes are matrilineal. Primatologists know that high-ranking simian females have a bias towards male offspring. All queen howler monkeys seek dinner foliage which increases electropositive readings in the cervix, those readings favourable to Y chromosome-carrying spermatozoa.

24

And it was true; my mother always loved her sexual contrasts. I was, she made it clear, a grave mistake.

Given this, I did the best I could. My emotional topography was indistinct at best; at worst, a mess and underneath it, every macrocosmic force. Transhistorically, man is held hostage by the macrocosm. A Mafia stoolie was recently so efficiently mutilated that only his hand could be retrieved. This relic was placed in a casket for the most elaborate of burials. In court, the lawyer for the co-defendant sarcastically announced that 'they held a funeral for the guy's *hand*.' He missed the point. In the stoolie's case, elaboration was only compensation: less corpse, more fanfare. Every man carries within him an understanding of equilibrium. The human race survives because homeostatic mechanisms – a series of physiological checks – monitor fluctuations in properties such as blood sugar in order to maintain functioning balance. The subconscious restores parity in a similar manner. Jung was adamant that all neurotic symptoms signal compensatory processes in the id. A void had been gouged in me by my father's death and so I, too, was forced to compensate. My mother, after all, was mad.

She trashed her previous commitments and invested all her energies into widowhood. Galvanic stuff. Grief is known to be one of the chief sculptors of the psyche. For almost forty years, a man named Joseph Cindric pushed a tattered suitcase on a trolley around Sydney's CBD. In that suitcase, his old shipwright's tools and letters from the son he lost to World War II. My mother was less constant in her mourning. Once the widow routine palled, she opted to return to girlhood. There was an icy increase in her appetite for life. She gave the weeds to charity and joined a gym. What she became was one of the marvels of the modern world and with it, made me despise her.

In the second or so it had taken that bullet to leave its muzzle and penetrate my father's heart, between the pressure of that finger on the trigger and my father's soundless roar, somewhere in that infernal compression of decision, action and consequence, I was forever altered. This was chaos. I was saturated by the loss. These, then, were my very own Dark Ages. Both parents had left me to gracefully enter their new and separate universes – Mother into that of her narcissism; Father into that of death, a spirivalve dominion. And like a baffled animal, I waited years for their return. Of course they never would, but this was not as obvious to me as some may have assumed. I would have laid my soul down as collateral security.

But question time was limited, it was all I could do to keep abreast of the ever-changing cast. Six months in Sydney and my mother was very seriously stepping out. A feminist of the Otto Weininger school, she had them all: her beaux were quite a bunch. The Mummy, Batman and the Joker – these and many more. There was Benjamin 'Big Boy' Borax, the pharmaceutical prince; Emmanuel Wiseman, the best-selling author (whom my anti-semitic mother referred to as 'Hymie Money'); Spiro Chaetes, the real-estate developer and yachting hero; Dr Richard Toole – sneeringly nicknamed 'Double Dick' – the society psychiatrist struck from the Medical Register for irresponsibly prescribing morphine and other Schedule 8 drugs (to facilitate his attempts to mount attractive female patients); Bruce 'His Grey Eminence' Lloyd-Frasier, publisher and rubber fetishist; Mark Robert Hertford, who owns most of Western Australia's cattle; Claude 'The Fat Man' Crippen, the newspaper magnate and snow-dropper; Tchaik Catheter, composer of Schoenberg-like scores and professional golfer (and married to a benzodiazepine zombie who, it was rumoured, stumbled weeping up and down the winding staircase of their Bellevue Hill villa all day long); David Dkeur (director of the 'critically acclaimed' *Back Door Man* and *The Tender Cleft*), whom my mother smacked in the mouth when he drunkenly confessed an erotic predilection for children; Sir Dominic Patapouf, the exhaustingly witty liposculpted Attorney General whose yellow squint spoke of a jeweller's appraisal, thrice divorced and the father of eight, a sexual lunatic and connoisseur of wines, who favoured 'amusing' neckties printed with Varga girls and stored his medals in a modular carousel humidor and serenaded my mother on the upper balcony as she smiled and sighed and flicked her gold-banded cigarette-butts into the ornamental pond aflame with carp below.

These were only some of the batrachian specimens on show.

They hopped and croaked and fatly flapped on the revolving stages of my mother's theatre. She was sexual, certainly, and had always loved attention. Amedeo and I were issued stern instructions by our dipsomaniacal nanny never to disturb mother when she was 'entertaining' and knew better than to break these rules. Amedeo had once caught her squealing in flagrante with one thigh hooked over the banister and I had almost surprised her pretzel-like with Patapouf and his Polaroid in the playroom.

A carved shell motif (she was obsessed by Louis XV) distinguished her ridiculously ornate bed, from which rose twisted minarets crowned by miniature pavilions. Arches of carved cherubim and seraphim appeared to gather the spidery underdrapery of lace. Needlepoint cushions, bulbous tassels, tens of invitations arranged on the Louis XV mantle, and everywhere framed photographs of Mother with her very famous friends. Spotlit on the wall facing the bed, Lucien Freud's portrait of the erotic terrorist herself (reclining on a sofa, blonde hair in disarray, thighs spread, cunt smiling, flesh a seasick green). Her dressing room was alive with shoes; she owned something like four hundred pairs. In the deep drawer of her bedside cabinet: Nembutal, Mogadon, Librium, Valium, Seconal, Serepax, Prozac, Nurofen, Ponstan, Disprin, Ural, Ecostatin, a jeroboam of Trojans, US condoms made from lambs' intestines, gorilla dildoes, KY, spermicidal gels, a diaphragm, surgical gloves, dental dams, a gleaming vibrator, eighteen-carat gold Chinese 'love balls', edible panties, discarded French-navy Tiffany's ring boxes, expired Nicabate patches, loose cents, pence, pfennigs, lire and a New York Stock Exchange money clip. On every surface, vases of fresh lilies, forced gardenias, even exotic flowers shaped like langoustines (the overflow of all her swooning stiffs). Her answering machine was always brimming with suggestive messages.

It was all quite a statement.

My mother had always been extrinsically gorgeous. Tall and slender and with saline-swollen breasts, coordinated in her movements, those ethereal curls softening the otherwise too algebraic planes of her face, blessed with a lilting alto (and 'a real peach of an ass,' according to Lloyd-Frasier), she left her sexual competitors in the dust. Beside her, they all looked like amateurs. How was it possible for such aesthetic grace to coexist with avarice? She literally bristled with delight when conversations turned to money. Her devotion was immediate to any man who had the funds and the temerity to launch a billion-dollar lawsuit. The intricacies of derivatives were one of the few things that could really make her laugh. And all, but all her men were fantastically wealthy. She said of one: 'His stomach hangs over his belt like a mailbag and he pulled down his pants and mooned at the princess, but you know, Angelica – the boy is *rich*.' Had we existed under the reign of Tutankhamen, a twentieth-century cryptanalyst would have mistaken that word for a conjunctive in our family scrolls.

All this, peripheral. I was encapsulated by my grief.

Grief is a sphere in that it can be turned a quarter turn or turned a millionth, it can be spun on any axis and by any degree and still its aspect is the same. Symmetry is nurtured by higher dimensions. This was my intellect in action and its attempts to salve. Nothing had yet healed to silver: I was raw. I was a child and I had lost my father. I lost him over and over again each morning, every long night. I lose him still. In every heartbeat, his absence and its isolating factors. And how do I remember him? On his last birthday as I stretched to kiss him on the cheek. *Buon compleanno*. Was it the Chinese Year of the Cat?

His love was fuel.

I am a blind woman recalling colour, I am the amputee who still believes that she can feel each shin. All that yearning! I was gutted: I longed for him to exist not only so that he could guide me, but so that I could love and be in turn loved by him. Forgetful wish. My father had always been that place to which I could return. I sought his voice in silence, chased his shadow through the dawn. Mourners depend on such implausibility for sustenance. It was a case of separating smoke from air and air from smoke: circular endeavours designed only to lead me to myself. Anything to distract me from the truth. My intellect reconstructed him but the experience was lost and so I valiantly incorporated that loss into my reconstruction – again, so circular. When my fabled stepfather gripped my throat and smilingly tried to choke me, all I could think of as I kicked and struggled was my father. There is such sorrow in knowing that he will never see me as a woman. There is such sorrow in knowing that he will never again share my life. There is a world of sorrow in relinquishing such love.

Grief is a sphere.

10

After three brimming years of the cocktail circuit, my mother finally threw in her gloves for an individual so demented that her choice demanded categorical respect, if nothing more. Lesser widows uncage their hearts and swim in the 'tranquil waters of decency', but my mother was too much the Newtonian for that. Force was her basic concept.

If I thought myself a Wolf Rayet star, then Aldo Belva was a Neutron: the densest state of matter known. Mother was almost genuinely impressed by his credentials – Master of Law, Doctor of Philosophy, Doctor of Juridical Studies, director of what seemed to be a thousand high-level companies, a staple of the international *Who's Who*. Aldo was a criminal barrister in every sense. He managed to remain friends with the South American heads of both the Medellin and Cali drug cartels: both Pablo Escobar and Miguel Rodriguez had played backgammon and poker in Aldo's Aspen lodge and at his villa in St Barthélemy. All black money was used by him as a cash pool to finance visible deals; in liquid terms, he was the country's richest man. When I chanced upon him testing the quality of some cocaine by rubbing it into his gums, he immediately cited gingivitis as the cause. Ugly, brilliant, mad and sleepless, he was to bring me a practical understanding of the Toltec mind.

My mother was an equally skilled operator. On their second date, she scattered white rose petals on the floor and, after dismissing the hired stylist, make-up artist and hair-dresser, spreadeagled herself in a negligee amongst the butchered blooms. I often thought she required protection from her strange intelligence. In her skull, a full measure of the purest Bosch. My father, oddly, had always been oblivious to her personal devils. To him, she could do no wrong. And Mother could summon an angelic countenance, so sincere, a work of genius: that inclination of her head, her parting lips, and then that mist slowly uncoiling in her eyes.

She was a hex.

I was only one of the many bewitched. For years, she worked me like a marionette. And my father doted upon her absolutely, his love was Schedule 8, narcotic, almost naive in its nobility. He could not see that without the baroque trivialities of the power-wife lifestyle, she would have detonated: *boom*. Such an honest explosion would have been unthinkable; she was a woman of decorum, after all. 'Poor Aldo,' she whispered to me one evening as a trembling serf performed her manicure, 'has to tolerate all those *dégoûtant* public inquiries into his work.' That sharp-eyed pause as she inspected her claws. Her frown. 'I don't *like* that colour, Marita. Start again.' And then to me: 'His composure in such circumstances should be an example to you. I have decided that you are to regard him as your *teacher*.'

Like my father, Aldo was a big-shouldered, self-made man and also a snappy dresser with his tails and double-breasted suits; his sexual impact in a dinner jacket was considerable. There end the similarities. Aldo had a lymphatic face, his nose an oedematous weight to the right and vivid with nostrils. Hair loved him. Those vivid nostrils were stuffed with fur, as were the external auditory canals of his ears, the pornographic lobes of which appeared to brush against his shoulders. On his head, a crazed mane of greying ebony and at any hour of the day, his cheeks were stippled with an erupting beard. When he stripped for the pool, he revealed himself to be as hirsute as any member of the chimpanzee family – back, shoulders, upper arms, thighs, belly, breast, thorax – why, the fur even extended to the thick phalanges of every finger. In his heart, he was of the Pliocene era. He obeyed the laws of the just-snuffed dinosaurs. And yet he was magnetic to women. During his engagement to my mother and in their Chanel couture, these masochists materialized on his doorstep clutching (with contrite expressions) casserole dishes or teenaged sons they claimed required 'a man's guidance'.

I was perhaps the only one immune to his appeal.

Men of a certain age lose the coherence of musculature and begin to resemble their less dignified ancestors: the belly usurps the clean line of the spine; the thighs slacken; the buttocks sag; the shoulders slope forward; the cheeks meld to the throat. The penis, too, surrenders. Old men are potent only in their dreams. This sexual mutiny is enough to persuade some of them to jump ship. The flagpole around which their lives formerly revolved is now flying the Jolly Roger. If my mother's nocturnal yodels were any indication, Aldo had not yet succumbed to this particular inevitability. He was still wicked enough to be interesting. And in certain lights, with his candle-wax laps of fat and mottled pelt, he could easily have passed for the king of the trolls or some prehistoric transmission into the present. His eyes were heavy, watchful, oily with intent. They slid like shadows into corners. I believe my mother gazed into them only as a means of inspecting her *maquillage*: the corneal surface was as useful a mirror as any. Perhaps to justify her choice of mate, she said: 'Aldo is so *gen*erous.'

He was not generous, but insecure; money was distributed by him as some distribute pamphlets. His ostrichskin wallet was always gorged with hundred-dollar bills. I remember the occasion on which he used one to light my mother's cigarette. This was supposedly a lesson to teach my 'parsimonious' brother that money was 'no more than coloured paper'. All Amedeo learned was that Aldo was an even greater maniac than we had at first conjectured. My mother giggled as she leaned forward, her cigarette steadily magnetized by that one note, its flames – those same flames burning the day my father died – working their reflections through her arctic pupils. And when he presented her with an engagement ring, she suffered a nervous breakdown. Gasping, she plastered one hand to her breast, emitted radio-transmitter noises, surreptitiously studied the gem and glowing, throatily cried:

'Why, Aldo, *dar*ling – it's the flawless tear-shaped 10.83 carat Graff Pink Sup*reme*!' And then she fainted.

My father's brow suggested a certain weightlessness, something supernal; Aldo's brow hung heavy, ready to pop. Everyone was out to get him. Such paranoia was lovingly encouraged by the Italian village elders of his youth. In such environments, the Evil Eye is as familiar as an aunt and always welcome. Brawls, murders, feuds, *vendette* – the boredom of rural life calls for such blockbusting entertainment. The Cosa Nostra began as such a pantomime. Myths must be acted out for the sake of continuity, after all. And my stepfather was a survivor – subject to his elders' grotesque abuses, but a survivor. A dangerous ambition anchored him. He was to rise from nothing to nothing that looked like shimmering everything: a trick of mirrors. His degrees were genuine, but as much of a front as Gotti's plumbing business. Slaughtered goats were delivered to the doorsteps of his detractors. Trouble of any description could always be arranged. When the US Drug Enforcement Administration attempted to (correctly) nail him for involvement with the exportation of seven hundred tonnes of cocaine, he simply laughed – he sat back in his chair and shook his head and laughed. As he predicted, they found his records unimpeachable, they could not touch him. He made sure his tracks were always covered. Paranoiacs are as perceptive as poets, never indifferent to their fellow men. The detail ruled him.

Aldo was famous for his powers of destruction. He left nothing of opponents – a hank of hair, a worn gold tooth, they were eradicated by his hatred. One of his methods of control was the promotion of the worst possible scenario. By emphasizing his appreciation of all peril, he also armed himself: as only he could distinguish and thus avoid all foes, he demanded power of attorney over the minds and futures of those with whom he dealt. In their control, he reasoned, the past had hopelessly collapsed so what was there to lose? The capacity to inspire fear defines all professional tyrants. Client-correspondence was often left by him on the coffee table:

Dear Mrs Victim,
Re: your trial for murder

I am taking the unusual step of writing this letter to you, with a copy to your solicitors. I have now had a full opportunity to discuss the case with no less than three defence expert witnesses, all men of great eminence and experience. They are unanimous in concluding that the account of events leading to your daughter's death as given in your police interviews and as repeated to your solicitors and counsel to date cannot be true. They all agreed with the impressive body of Crown expert evidence which says the same thing.

I must now warn you frankly that your present attitude is suicidal in the professional judgment of your legal advisors, and will lead to a murder conviction and life in prison because you will not depart from what must be, in the opinion of all the experts, an untrue story.

If you insist on maintaining your innocence, I would see myself advising you not to give evidence.

Sincerely,
Aldo Belva.

Mrs Victim maintained her innocence and hanged herself by a strip of bedsheet whilst in custody. It was later proven that what was, in the expert opinion of greatly eminent and experienced men, an untrue story was, in fact, the truth. This was of little interest to Aldo, who was busy networking at the Royal Sydney Golf Club. On another occasion I picked up the telephone extension to this, his advice to a (now monumentally successful) junior: 'What you've got to do, Julian, is establish a reputation for being a cunt. It might cost you a bit of money to buy yourself that reputation, but in the long run, it's money well spent. If everyone knows you're a cunt, no-one's going to try to tackle you. So always go for the jugular, whether it's necessary or not. Maintain your reputation. Make it clear that you can't be fucked over.'

He had frenzied himself into an unimaginable state of lunacy in his early thirties and passed a year or so molesting furniture and sparring with azaleas in a splashy 'retreat' (situated by a grove of palm trees and equipped with apple-cheeked blonde nurses in tight pink shorts). There he oscillated between arterial rage and a pitiful depression. Once he had recovered from this lapse, he set about panicking the world through different means. He wore his contacts like a perfume and never overstated his intelligence. In turn, he was both anarchic and powerfully menacing. I once heard him say with satisfaction to an immigrant conspirator: 'We *all* made it.' This caused me to wonder what it was exactly that these wonderful men had made and for whose benefit. What merit is there in success against adversity if that success is essentially an uglier form of adversity than that which it originally opposed? Not a popular question.

There was too much of him and it was everywhere. Certain politicians quaked in their imported wing-tips when he was near. He was known for having cars 'fixed' and teeth and kneecaps 'done'. His favourite hobby was lobbying. For a self-negotiated fee of four hundred thousand dollars, he once acted for a corporation whose proposal of a forty-storey building had been rejected by the prime minister. Enter Aldo. After listening to the corporation beef, he called the prime minister, who then told him that the proposed building was 'too tall'. This information was relayed to the corporation, who suggested reducing by a quarter the number of floors. Aldo speed-dialled his pal's number. The two talked tax thresholds, antiques, some golf. Some thirty minutes passed. The prime minister then (magically) approved the new proposal. After arranging to meet him later in the week for dinner, Aldo called the corporation with the news. And that was it, the sum of his labour: one hundred thousand dollars per telephone call.

'Reports show that the highest incidence of emotional disorder in children is in cases where they belong to single-parent families,' Aldo warned my mother after meeting me on their twelfth date. This was another lure and like all good marlin, she bit and flipped. It was a simple antidote to all the drudgeries of motherhood. She interpreted my misgivings as insults and I was duly punished for each one. That January, I was sent to bed at eight o'clock each night. That February, I was grounded. That March, I was barred from using the telephone. That April, I conceded to her jester's choice. The

34

show was to go on. He bought her a four-million-dollar villa in Capri and a matching two-passenger recreational hovercraft. She commissioned another portrait of herself and bought him an Old Bond Street wedding band. This pretty piece would be incongruous on him. She didn't care. Together, they were a socially incisive couple – fiercely glamorous, cool, mysterious, courted in every continent. He was all fur and force and threat, and Mother was a career beauty. She had, of course, become a zooerast. My father's death had tipped her scales. In the temple of Mendes, her jaded ancestors had practised bestiality with goats tutored in the erotic arts, and this renegade gene had reasserted itself. Dia with her stallion, Leda and her swan. It was the done thing, after all, and my mother was never one for questioning a vogue.

I I

Some six quick months after the dog-headed baboon had first parked his Maserati at Shell Cove, the union of the two was legalized at St Mary's Cathedral. Aldo was an associate of the complicit Monseigneur. This special access to the Divine thrilled my atheistic mother, who set about arranging the whole spectacle. Her gown had been flown in from Paris. A Lagerfeld original, it was no mean advertisement of his talents. An efflorescent mirage of opaque whites, it made a song of Mother's long Edwardian throat and of her hard round breasts. The bridal fashion of the time was some kickback to the Age of Chivalry – crowning the scalp, a band of myrtle or gilded laurel and the rest, an ostentatious arrangement of organza, piqué and crêpe de chine trailing substantial lengths of silken rope (with which the bride could later hang herself).

The congregation inhaled as she entered.

To have seen her for the first time in such a circumstance would have been to wonder how a woman of her age and hot-ticket experience could so convincingly portray virginity.

Stupendous, yes; also a monolith of artifice. In she whispered on the strong arm of an internationally feared industrialist, her Lalique face composed, marmoreal eyes downcast, that gown a shifting lucent mist in those everglades of hope over experience: the matron newly pure beneath the mighty and unblinking eyes of God, advancing as if in a trance induced by her *amour absolu* (who was tugging his pornographic earlobes as he awaited instruction at the altar). The ceremony was a bad dream, something like sixteen hours long. My legs were numb. The Latin drummed the roof like rain, an endless rain – the sound of which I understood to be a language, but a language I would never understand. A monstrous yacht had been hired for the orgy and once the farce had reached its climax and platinum rings had been exchanged, once the confetti had been scattered and insincere tears shed, once the radiant bride and pestilential groom had flashed their capped teeth at the *paparazzi*, we all walked the resounding gangplank.

The only child of the Vorstellung-Savoia clan, my mother was born in sleepy Strasbourg. An unfortunate collision of vehicles at the cold foot of the Alps made her an early orphan; she had been raised by nannies and stablehands and butlers on relatives' estates. These added to the golden locals and global meritocrats made for quite the international event, *carissima*. My mother's former studs attended as did Aldo's whores and divorced groupies. Fragile crystal bowls of sunset caviar, picturesque sprays of ice on the best silver, oysters, salmon, Perrier-Jouët, Dom Pérignon, Baccarat crystal (within the facets of which reflections of tall candles danced), an elaborate ice-sculpture of Pasiphaë and her white bull. Dramatic affluence. Amedeo and I watched as the guests snorted their prescription cocaine. Kinetic fireworks, music, the yacht's firm purr. My mother's glazed smile through her hands. Lunar reflections promptly swallowed by the waves and their slick slaps. Again: all eyes. The stars were in attendance. Perseus and Cepheus were valued by me for their constancy. Amedeo was wretchedly sick from the dark edge of the deck. I fed the white gulls canapés and solemnly recalled my father. Those unnaturally animated cries from within. Under a table, the movie star Julie Pulpy slowly performed fellatio on an investment banker whose wife happily lay unconscious at the feet of Washington's notorious society intellectual, Harold Fright.

It was a circus.

12

Aldo moved his Gieves & Hawkes suits and Glastonbury chairs, his monogrammed towels and Irish napery, his Nymphenburg porcelain and futuristic art into our house. From thereon in, obedience would be our only currency. We were to be punctual, pliable, we were to dress smartly every night for supper. We were to appreciate the culinary subtleties of his chef's *poulet croustillant au citron et huile d'olive* and his *goujonettes de sole*. We were to be cheerfully inconsequential – never boring she who bore us (or her mate) with the tedious dishwater of our thoughts. The opinions of women and children, Aldo informed us, were an unnecessary evil. We were never to give cheek (for fear of falling from buildings). We were to abide by the Old Testament of *la buona figura*. We were not to fraternize with the offspring of the undistinguished, Zionists, communists, bohemians, environmentalists, the poor, the faded wealthy. We were to realize at all times that we were the reflections of our guardians' capabilities. We were to make our real (but regrettably fake) parent and our fake (but regrettably real) parent as proud as parrots. Our scholastic performances would be regularly reviewed, as would our comportment. We were to avoid grazing the patience of the staff and appreciate the many bounties to which we had been born. Amen.

Remarkably different doctrines to those with which we had been raised and with remarkably different results. We both had been bamboozled and knew it. The neoclassical economic ideal of a giant mechanism is never nurturing of vibrant being. As units, we were expected never to actively perceive, remember, challenge or combine: our behaviour was to be determined. The cynocephalus had been installed and now he was to be adored and pampered and appeased. Such responses would be grudgingly accepted as basic expressions of our gratitude.

Amedeo and I performed our duties with robotic smiles for years, and then he cracked. He was thirteen years old and enough, enough. Out of self-defence, he had devolved: non-feeling and non-sensing, hard. I had been aware of his growing abstraction. It was as if he was being gnawed. He often drank himself to sleep with vodka from Aldo's panelled study. Unusual lights flared in his eyes and his fists were always by his flanks, as if prepared for an attack. On the morning of the now-legendary crack-up, Aldo had turned to him. 'Never had a girlfriend?' he provocatively asked. 'You should just accept that you're a eunuch. Don't let it bother you – some men are like that.' Only the customary criticism, customary sarcasm, customary scorn. At such junctures, Mother would always drift out of the room, patting her hair and poetically murmuring to herself. I methodically consumed my breakfast in silence, interrupting Aldo only to ask for milk or coffee or the honey to his right. Amedeo and I never even dared interarch our glances (this had been known to infuriate and was thus unadvisable). That morning my brother left the house with an abundant slamming of all doors. 'The milk has CURDLED!' Thoth screamed at Mother, who then burst into a fantasy of tears. I grabbed an apple from the bowl and left for school.

There is a limit to which a human being can be degraded; there is a limit to which a human being can be abused. Amedeo unleashed his violence on his history master during a lesson on the overly enthusiastic strategies of the Austrian and Russian commands in the early part of World War II. He pushed his chair back from the desk and stood, mechanically walked to the front of the classroom and without the most marginal change in expression, grasped the master's chair and brought it down heavily on the man's head. My brother was tall even then, with rower's shoulders and adamant hands. The master crumpled like that proverbial house of cards. Amedeo paused and then began to kick his face and torso with all his mass, until six astounded peers leapt up and struggled to restrain him.

Predictably, he was expelled in some disgrace.

Equally predictable was the turbulence at home, turbulence which took the form of Aldo blackening both his eyes, splitting his lip so that it required fifteen stitches, and fracturing his right humerus by throwing him from the balcony. A Chi'ing vase was shattered. Chairs and tables – cabriole feet kicking – were overturned. Certain priceless pieces were destroyed. Huge glossy books on Arbus and Soutine were flung at mirrors and through windows. I attempted to intervene, but was thrown mightily against the wall and broke my wrist. Unconscious Amedeo lying by the salt-water pool in his own blood. My mother – with a stifled gulp and loud low tomcat hiss – had observed the two men in her life for a Roman moment before rapidly scaling the stairs in her stiletto-heeled blue marabou-feather mules, robe fluttering. I discovered her striking an attitude by her bedroom window – left arm perpendicular to her bowed head, right hand crushing the sleeve of that soft robe to her hard mouth, snivelling, puling, bawling, begging an Almighty in whom she had never believed for his help. Outside, a massive bone-white moon was reflected in black sheets of water. The night was still and cool. An ambulance, policemen, wreckages. Misery is so easy to create.

Mother embraced the chaos. At lunchtime with her harpy girlfriends, whilst comparing jewels and discussing the newest Lotus or the best beautician, she would drink herself into a rosy stupor ('I only ever touch Krug Clos de Mesnil or Roederer Cristal, darling'). There were days she passed immobile on the sofa, stupefied by Wagner and staring at the wall. Poor Aldo! That man had forever been misunderstood. Her eyes conspiratorial over the lipsticked lip of another glass, she told me that Amedeo had behaved like an animal. My darling father had, after all, been related to some creature confined to the bowels of a madhouse. Ergo: the paternal bloodline was fertile with psychoses. Why else would such an episode have unfolded in her house? (This asked with sincere consternation.)

The psychiatrist Dr Stag (of the astrophysical fees and

Macquarie Street rooms overlooking the Botanical Gardens) was summoned to examine my demented brother. A man with a face like a peeled half-cucumber and wrapped in a cucumber-green coat, he arrived hacking and spitting into a cucumber-green handkerchief and made a show of opening the polished eighteen-carat gold locks of his Antler briefcase. A sudden cough caused him to swing around and knock the briefcase from the table. My mother started and I stared. A chemist's dispensary hit the marble floor. He and I spent the following twenty minutes chasing tricyclic anti-depressants and anti-psychotic tranquillizers under the furniture. My mother's Borzoi lapped up seventy green chlordiazepoxide tablets before anyone could stop him. The housekeeper rushed him off and crashed the car into a traffic light, killing the dog. An embossed pharmacopoeia fell open to a description of depression ('characterized by dejection, lack of hope, an absence of cheerfulness'). Stag almost concussed himself on the outstretched arm of a sculpture as he tried to stand. Greener than ever, he demanded an audience with the young madman. Three quarters of an hour with the Death Row inmate and Stag the cucumber emerged. My brother, he decided, was a borderline personality. My brother, he decided, was nursing dangerous reserves of resentment. My brother, he decided, was projecting his hostility. My brother, he decided, was unyielding, uncooperative and disturbed. My brother, he decided, was sadly unmanageable and unmanageably sad. Stag recommended medication and reached into his briefcase.

The Delphic Oracle could not have done a better job.

'*Full of rage!*' (The white thunder of Aldo's anger reverberated throughout the house.) 'I'll show that intellectually stunted son-of-a-bitch who's full of rage!' (Amedeo was locked in his room and it was silent.) 'That *bag* of shit! That *prick*! After all we've *done* for him! That little *cunt*! That *in*grate! To have hu*mili*ated us like that! You'd think he were starving in some *fuck*ing gutter, the way he carries on!' (The potent thud of some object; my mother's whimpers interpolated.) 'I've had *enough*! Do you under*stand* me? *Enough*!' (Perhaps his fist through the wall, perhaps my mother fainting.) 'There comes a point where even *I* can't take any more – where even *I* reach breaking point! Do you think I can –' (my mother urging him, sob-strangled, 'No, darling, no … please, no!') '– do you think I can *stand* this?? Seeing the woman I love des*troyed*?? Having my own life *sabo*taged?? Watching my reputation crumble under the weight of public *rid*icule?? Sitting back while my world is *ripped* –' (this squealed with a particularly theatrical intensity) '– apart by this – this – this – by this –' (he was momentarily stumped; advection had overruled eloquence) '– this little *prick*??' (An interval of laboured breathing; my mother's shaky little-girl entreaties; the loud pulse of an admiral's heart.) 'I wouldn't piss on him if he were on *fire*! That *cunt*! That little *cunt*!' (A pause.) 'That piece of *shit*!' (And then the trickle of regrets and his hoarse bravery.) '*No more* …' (Another pause.) '*No more* … I can't take any more …'

Injuries sustained in battle. Once his had healed, Amedeo was spirited away to the West Point Academy or some such US institution which rewarded community-minded murder. He never again saw the sandstone Shell Cove mansion. Life was kinder to him at a distance from Ms Vorstellung-Savoia and Aldo Belva. After graduating with respectable results, he was enrolled at Harvard for a degree in politics and economics. Another respectable graduation and then head first into the world of trading and broking through the New York City firm of Lynch, Burne & Hurt. It was not long before he was earning something like twenty million dollars per annum. The shy mathematical prodigy had turned. It appeared he was promiscuous. It appeared that he took drugs. It appeared his sexual preference was as yet undecided. He appeared in all the papers (our family is closely allied with the news). He disappeared for lost weekends. The eastern seaboard of America is infinitely suited to such glamorous dissolution.

He and his friends frequently drove their elite cars whilst eight or more times over the legal limit. If chased by the police, they would dump these vehicles and report them stolen the next morning. He lost millions on the gaming tables of corrupt Nevada. The women he chose were tough, stupid and beautiful and presented each other with breast-augmentation vouchers on their birthdays. His closest friend, Anatole Kitcat, was almost caught by police in a seedy

Boston flat at 5 a.m. one morning with the overdose case he had (or so my brother told me) wanted to 'screw'. The usual wild night and then the girl vanished into the bathroom. Kitcat, his 'balls blue' and 'wired on coke', broke down the bathroom door. The girl was on the floor with the syringe still dangling from the hollow of her arm. Kitcat's first thought was not for her welfare, but of the press. Imagine if those reptiles got hold of this: UNCONSCIOUS 17-YEAR-OLD BLACK JUNKIE FOUND BLEEDING IN THE ARMS OF CANDY HEIR!

My brother moved in damaged circles.

In many ways, he was no better than his awful friend. Amedeo created his own hellish adventures. He was briefly linked to a coke-addicted model who had indulged in a little 'high-level hooking', most notably with the arms-dealer Gaza. The couple split after (another) smashed-plates-and-left-hooks argument and, derailed by drugs, this girl rang Gaza and babbled something about my brother having a contract out to kill her. Amedeo came home from work and found his answering machine loaded with thick Arabic threats. Gaza's goons were on the case. Nauseated, he rang Kitcat who then rang his 'eminent and experienced' brother-in-law, Lord Firkin, the rangy and deranged English MP. Firkin, a righteous opponent of the press's, 'villainous intrusions into the lives of decent and upstanding men' and pious Anglican (also involved in shady dealings with Gaza and other lawless warthogs), rang the arms-dealer and had him 'call off the heat'. Amedeo was saved. The model was murdered for wasting Gaza's time. For years, she surged screaming through tar-pits to my brother in his dreams. Kitcat, who was to marry a contessa and mature into a toad-faced senator with hair-plugs and a taste for black transsexuals, comforted my brother with these words: 'Shit happens.'

Poor Mother was 'reduced to tears' by her son's antics, and poor Aldo – hung, drawn, quartered by his stepson's bold misconduct – just managed to hold 'his head up high'. Courageous man! Amedeo's one ambition in life, my mother said, was to make their existence intolerable. '*Spite*,' she hissed, 'is all he lives for!' She became pregnant only to miscarry in her fourth month after opening a magazine to a full-page spread of her son french-kissing the muscular scion of a family made rich and butch by cattle. O, the tragedies that fate dealt the undeserving! 'Life,' she managed through the tears she wept on the many occasions they had guests, 'can be so *cruel*.'

For a month, she and her husband considered adopting a replacement from Romania. There would be certain advantages to such an act. Firstly, motherhood would impart youthfulness to her; secondly, they would publicly be seen to be unprejudiced; thirdly, it would overshadow the negative coverage they had received as a result of Amedeo's self-induced calamities. Eventually, it was decided by the caucus that such a genetic lottery would be fraught with too many aesthetic risks. Imagine a hairy little hunchbacked troll frolicking amongst the Renoir sketches!

They instead invested in another Borzoi, which my imaginative mother christened Fiat II.

13

My existence was thus textured. The potent solitudes of adolescence were only magnified by such volcanic irregularities. I was so softly spoken that I caused those around me to feel deaf. All elbows and evasive eyes, I was a frightened fieldmouse. My nights were governed by Paraqlitos, the Angel of the Sorrows of Death, and with his presence, a recurring dream. The setting: a misty midnight landscape. The plot: I stood on the banks of a motionless cold silver river, a river in which I could never see myself reflected. Kneeling, I would slowly wave my hands over the surface of the water and still the moon would shine right through them. And from the corresponding bank, a woman's moan. Looked up and there, in a pose identical to my own, was my *Doppelgänger* staring back at me with my lost lamp-black eyes. A typically schizoid bifurcation of identity or better yet, that classic 'split' of which analysts like Stag the cucumber are so enamoured. My fellow cast members were less poetic with their woes. Aldo was ever-reptant and still squiring mother to functions in his ever-tightening dinner ensembles. And mother's stoned social routine was to become all the rage. It inspired the haystack-chested editrix of *Vogue* to devote an entire issue to the art of yearning. Mother was touched; such acknowledgment evinced from her a certain luminescence.

I continued to perform well academically, finding the work an engrossing diversion from family dislocations. My concentration (the ability to focus upon the head of a pin while the world was imploding) was considered 'extraordinary'. Was I planning to follow in my stepfather's paw-prints and become a pillar of society or was I planning to write the definitive treatise on being? 'Because,' as one kind mistress said, 'the world is your oyster. You can do anything you want on condition that you put your mind to it.' I put my mind to it each and every night. Mine were fevers of escape and validation, aches and regrets, unwanted memories: insomnia. At three, sometimes four, sometimes five in the morning I would still be alert, wary of sleep and the vulnerability to attack it imposed.

Sweet bird of youth. I was sixteen and already fractured when Aldo crept into my room one night. A paradigm of paternal concern, he gingerly closed the door behind himself and waited patiently on my seventeenth-century Persian carpet. His shower-damp hair dripped onto the shoulders of his thick white bathrobe and his eyes leaked meaning. I had some instinct that all was not well with my world (pitching and tossing as it was through unsettled seas), and was not as surprised as I could or should have been when he eased his rump onto my mattress, assuring me that he fully understood my sadness and how I must miss my murdered dadda and how upsetting my hormonal changes must be, little treasure that I was.

> It began with a headless study and came
> to the desperate fulcrum of her dress between his teeth.
> That concentration fused
> the resurrection of her peeled, unspeakably beautiful
> cleft cunt.

44

Gradually, he moved closer. I studied him, horribly mesmerized by his song. He glanced at the floor. I was really
something, had he ever told me? *Really* something. Why, it
seemed like only yesterday that I was a little snot-nosed kid in
plain white cotton underpants and look at me now! A
woman. He felt that he could be straight with me, no need to
play the role of adult: I was an equal and equipped to
understand. His pause was loaded with desires I didn't want
to understand. There was – there was a touch of Mother
about me but I was more *access*ible, less – let's be straight,
Angelica – less *cold*. Those rank bowlfuls of breath. That
posy of strong black hairs at his throat. His slackening
bathrobe belt. Those fat cigar-stained fingers on my quilt.
Perfectly still, I watched him in the way all prey observes its
predator.

'Let me give you a *big* hug,' he whispered, his intentions
lifting each syllable into the *castrato*'s highwire domain.

I smiled an automatic smile and stammered that it it would
not be it would not not would not be it not would be
necessary.

Closer still: 'I may be your stepfather, but I'm also a *man*.'

And before I could breathe, he had smeared those fat cigar-
stained fingers over my breasts and slid them down over my
vulva, his fat cigar-stained tongue deep in my mouth.

Perhaps he expected me to respond like Anais Nin, who –
after boffing her dear old dad – left the room with a silk scarf
between her legs to catch the bubbling flux of semen. Perhaps
I was expected to recline smiling and lasciviously purr: 'Feed
me your cock, Aldo, my emperor.' It was the first time I had
ever known the emotions that fuel homicide. A woman
regularly molested as a child by her stepfather recently
murdered her two sons. The English ganglord Ronnie Kray
was known to simply kill those he thought 'over-familiar', a
textbook response to early sexual abuse (the victims of which
react dramatically to the trespassing of certain boundaries).
Recognition: enemy. Object: expulsion. Youth is only ever a
prison to some. Aldo's face to me in that instant was a thing
of holocausts. I sensed in him a slender, tentative, lunatic
smile; I sensed in him the red lucidity of the insane. A
revolution brewed within and kindled in me fire. Spat out his

tongue. Slapped his mouth hard. Sluggard absorption: had I dreamed this indignation or had the assertive act been real? His hand rose to his cheek as if through water and an expression of real terror lit his eyes. I knew then and only then that it had really happened.

Some said it had been modelled
on a panel of Christ, a flaking pietà
whitewashed in days only Magdalen remembers.

That slap echoed around the room. Previously muted, my breath came at me in blowtorch flames. Aldo had not expected this response, he was accustomed to capitulation. Smarting with fear, apologizing in thin frantic hisses, spinning promises of Handel concerts and pretty dresses, he was absolutely cowed. That warlock's bathrobe fell open and exposed his wen-splashed belly and its mangy fur. His boxer-shorts (a size too small) were crushed by the opposing forces of his gut and upper thighs. The fly opened, exposing a slain gastropod. Such sloping shoulders, shaking jowls. I recall my feelings – wild and defiant, seismic – more accurately than I recall the wording of my odium. I had learned a thing or two of threats from him and he had proved (as Mother had predicted) a very competent teacher. Repeatedly touching his stinging lips, he was astonished and stared at his fingers as if they had been lacquered with his blood. Flurry of towelling and the door was quickly closed.

Unable to cry out or weep, I sat shivering in bed, attempting to soothe myself with the mechanical activity of rubbing my thin arms. And how it was possible to be betrayed. I was a perceptive animal, but this was of little relevance. No child is a small adult for the adult is the evolution of the child. Subtle distinctions. I was so dazed. I felt as if I had been killed.

It can be said that I was raised in an environment of sexualized mortification.

Aldo's work was not affected. Normal responses had never been his bag. Pink-ribboned briefs and countless millions were that which engaged him. He was charging unheard-of sums for unheard-of victories. Justice has always been secondary to force, and thus force cannot be abolished; it can only be understood and then, if possible, harnessed or countered. He was rarely at home. Mother began seriously abusing prescription drugs, a sport which cancelled certain social arrangements. No matter. The big man was also a brave man, and undertook such crucial networking on the arms of smiling socialites and their daughters. In circles such as theirs, marriage is understood to be a socio-economic grouping ratified by ministers and priests; it has little to do with soul-shaping love. Compartmentalization is all such people comprehend. And Aldo's mistresses were never vulgar, always of a catwalk height, buoyant with private incomes and decorous enough to shade their faces when the *paparazzi* loomed. Mother knew that what she pretended to ignore inspired groundswells of pity in others. Her life was no more than Platonic shadow-play.

My response to the whole shebang was to develop eating disorders and anxiety attacks and to be hospitalized for a Mogadon-overdose in my seventeenth year and briefly go (as they say) off the rails and, oh – it was all much of a muchness, that time.

I do remember waking after my stomach had been pumped. My throat was sore and the curtained-off ward was loud with recovered heroin-overdose cases wheedling and screaming for methadone. As two bodies were wheeled out, one nurse collapsed onto her knees, her arms victoriously raised, her pelvis strongly proffered. After months of waiting, she had been offered a position as a windsurfing instructor at a resort on faraway Phuket.

Closed my eyes and slipped back into a dream.

It was as if I were bound to an eternally revolving wheel in my own special hell. There are only so many ways in which a being can express despair, and I was just getting the hang of it, after all.

14

Fuge, late, tace. On graduating from my chi-chi school, I was awarded the expected certificates and breathless commendations. I was – in the unlikely case that anyone had failed to notice – a 'marvellously gifted girl', and 'disciplined'. It was all very nice and ultimately meaningless. To escape my mother and Aldo, I moved to familiar London, whereupon I almost immediately became engaged (father-seeking missile that I was) to a novelist twenty years my senior. We lived together in an affable and tolerable arrangement for a number of predictable years. I completed an honours degree and PhD in astronomy, astrophysics and theoretical astrophysics and published a widely admired thesis on the ambiguity of the second dimension. My fiancé, meanwhile, polarized the literary world with two best-selling novels. We were a wrongly envied couple.

Relentlessly self-referential, his mind a shrine to his ego, William Grieve was a gifted urban miniaturist who specialized in the vicissitudes of sex and class within the parameters of East London. He was the little god of the English literary scene, king of their lexical slagheap. A compact man, he had the skull-heavy dimensions of an infant. His face was a substantial affair, each feature attractively vulgar, and it struggled out from magazine covers, brow-powerful, nicotine-grey. The neatly trimmed goatee at which he tugged like a firm teat gave him the air of a suburban Mephistopheles. Generally inert (half his life was spent brooding on the toilet), he controlled his countenance to create the impression that most everything bored him to tears. 'Oh, *fuck*,' he'd drawl in that affected Anglo-American burr, 'not another goddamned *party*.'

On Thursday evenings, we paced the aisles of clean lit busy Marks & Sparks, loading our trolleys with continental cheeses and smoked meats, Greek olives and designer tortellini. On Saturday afternoons, we played chess (him fierce, one thumb between his lips; me playful, watching him overinterpret my every move). We read D.H. Lawrence's poetry to each other in our nightshirts. We debated discursive subjectivity in the press, the spontaneity of the psychoanalytic encounter, Natticz's transitional perspective of Wagner, the new historicists, Wittgenstein's philosophical problems with the works of Shakespeare, Ian McEwan and his bias against and attraction to Churchillian depression, Koestler's promiscuity as a metaphor for pre-war social fragmentation in Europe, Balthus as a manifestation of Freud's id, the role of the Polaroid camera in Dennis Nilsen's murders, the opposing attitudes of Orientalism and Utilitarianism to British India, Beuys' use of the blackboard and its repercussions on state education, Bertrand Russell's declining interest in formal logic, the socio-economic history of East Timor, William Blake and the auric colour spectrum, questions of homosexuality in contemporary South American fiction, Bataille's impact on the perception of the omelette and its aphrodisiac potential, the figure of the *puer eternus* in Mann's work and its formative influence on the ideals of the Weimar Republic, and the psychosexual symbolism of fourteenth-century footwear.

We furiously attended performances of Pirandello's works at the National Theatre and vacationed in the Virgin Islands. He had his hair washed, dried and styled at Sweeney's in Beauchamp Place. I was regularly massaged, steamed, and marinated in grey mud. We did the rounds at the Groucho. I read the *Independent*, he subscribed to the *New York Times Book Review*. He belonged to a society dedicated to saving Eastern Bloc novelists from prison. I sent away for periodicals from the American Center for the Advancement of Objectivism. He made certain I was entertained and I patiently groomed his grandiosity. We consulted a marriage guidance counsellor who told us that his sense of inferiority manifested as cruelty and that I had no self-esteem. He sipped Stolichnaya in the 400-foot dining room of the Athenaeum. I attended the salons of divorced women desperate for love. We dined with crushingly important cultural figures – anthropologists and actors, balletomanes and bishops, philosophers and billionaire philanthropists – at Scott's in Mayfair, Le Caprice, Le Gavroche, San Lorenzo, and the Ivy.

We were entertained by prominent Democrats at the Jockey Club in Washington DC and frequently dined at the Kennedys', where we were seated always by Zuber's 'Scenic America' screen and where we were expected to favourably comment on the Hepplewhite table design and the Seal of the Commonwealth of Massachusetts in the library. We were guests of Vidal's at La Rondinaia, which overlooks the Gulf of Salerno. There my fiancé was propositioned by the world's leading short-story writer. He had been admiring the Morris rocking chair facing the tufa and ceramic tile fireplace in Vidal's bedroom when Charles Chichester-Charterhouse entered and, after running his palm down my fiancé's back, said: 'I've always rather fancied tiny clever men.'

I selected shirts for him to wear on television (no checks or stripes which made him look like bad op-art) and listened to his hysterical accounts of inter-editorial treachery and cultivated a big warm special smile for anyone who had the power to advance his fulminant ambitions. It was a time of freedom conferred by masks.

We met at a soirée held by one of my mother's friends, a big frog in the academe who had written a 'ground-breaking' book on the New Physics. The setting was a Chelsea Embankment split-level apartment overlooking that incongruous golden pagoda and the phlegmy Thames. In the corner, a crippled concert pianist was playing Messiaen's *Oiseaux Exotiques*. A celebrated Norwegian fauvist wearing a snapdragon in his buttonhole introduced my future partner to me with a flourish of white spectral hands.

I was still frail from my hospitalization and more than a little disorientated. This daze must have been apparent, for William grasped the opportunity like the sexual imperialist that he had always been: all coos and soothing platitudes, affectionate little pats on the buttocks, much grave assent, select references to Tolstoi and the 'coarseness' of the Age of Reason, dark intimations of impending nuclear disaster, his little fingers eloquent through his unfashionably long hair, fetchingly batting his feathery lashes, stroking that absurd goatee and pressing me not to believe anything I may have heard about him. 'I have the most regular life of any man I know,' he said. While I did not make the common error of assuming that his speech – by dint of its style – had substance, I still listened.

'It's not often,' he murmured as he filled my glass for the fifth or sixth or seventh time, 'that one meets one of your calibre at these in*ter*minable do's.'

So bright and yet so innocent! So beautiful and yet so haunted! Why, I was like a flayed angel with my unspoilt eyes and 'big bruise of a mouth'! A very *ang*el! 'Stendhal –' (luxurious exhalation here) '– would not be sufficient to do you' (his lips fluttered on my inner wrist as he fixed me with his lugubrious stare) '– *jus*tice.'

He informed me that a young woman such as my good self (bright, innocent, bruised, et cetera) should not submit to Society so very quickly. It would de*plete* me, all this sycophantic patter. He told me that I should be in bed (his bed). He told me that if he weren't so advanced in years (a veritable mastodon, it was so unfortunate, this business of ageing) that he would fall *blind*ly in love with me. I had no idea, did I? No idea at all. How could I? I was so young, I had no point of reference. Oh, but it was tough, it was terrible, it was excoriating, this *curse* of the artist. And to think of the nobodies who annoyed him with their nominal brains, the despicable, the *en*vious (one of his favourite words – he really relished it, rolled its syllables over his palate with his thick pink tongue, lengthened the sibilant) *vul*tures who preyed upon his *art*. Why, it was enough to make a man jack his lot in and get a job hosting a game show. No-one, but *no-one* (did I understand? was he making himself clear?) suspected the ecstatic spirit which flew, unchained, within his heart.

Clasping the organ in question, he surveyed my breasts. My *God* – had anyone ever told me that I looked like something out of Modigliani? Like something plucked from the – the – the – what *was* it precisely that he was attempting to articulate? Like something plucked from the *mem*ory of his optic fibres or the essence of his choleric fevers or a figure from his dreamscapes, *Christ*! He passionately shook his head. How in*ade*quate words were! It was a wonder he still bothered with them. 'You don't understand, do you –' (I did) '– when I tell you that men are impressionable creatures, infinitely naive and far more susceptible to a woman's power

51

than she could ever guess. A man can be *woun*ded by beauty – *woun*ded.'

Inhaling as if to inhale the whole of me along with his oxygen, he turned his long-haired baby-head away so that we were both staring at his perfectly shod feet. 'You just don't under*stand*,' he sadly said. 'You are too young. You are too gorgeous – I look at you and feel as if I have to rub my eyes. And I, I am just too goddamned *old*.'

This last word was so acrid in his mouth that I shuddered and pocketed my hands.

He pulled himself together. Straightened his back. Poured me another glass. How could I be so heartless? How could I be so heartless as to play the ingénue when obviously I was *toy*ing (bored, one gilded paw extended) with his injured pride?

I stood with the mathematical precision of the polite inebriate and watched. This routine was familiar. Associates of Aldo's had regularly itemized their inadequacies (many) in the hope (far-fetched) that I would be so overwhelmed by pity that I would divest myself of my virginity (fat chance). Conquistadors must feel themselves to be marvels of sophisticated guile. The capacity of their victims to be profoundly hurt is attractive to them as they perceive emotional damage to be their signature. They brand the young as farmers brand their cattle and with an equal lack of feeling. William was something like this, he had left corpses in his wake. I could see that he was indifferent to my responses and concerned exclusively with his desires, the pressing fingers of which were stunting the spin of his strange little spirit.

But I was jet-lagged, drunk and flattered by the literate attention and besides, I think I no longer really cared about a thing.

He drove me to his dilapidated Georgian home, supplying me with a monologue of such conspicuous clarity in the car that I realized the words were too familiar to him; he slipped too easily into the language, was too inventive with his phrasing. This inventiveness alone suggested that he was paying more attention to the presentation than to the content. The subtext was as polished as a ceremonial canoe. His voice dreamily visible in the chill, he told me of the 'embarrassingly cheap' estate in Gloucestershire he had bought with the monstrous advance for his next three novels, and of its gardens (designed by Clough Williams-Ellis) and the yews (clipped into twenty-two-foot plinths). There were white marble fireplaces and framed firescreens embroidered by the wives of nineteenth-century literary lions. Duncan Grant was responsible for the mural in the bathroom. Clematis romantically climbed the terrace balustrades. Cranesbill geraniums exploded 'like tufts of heaven' in majolica pots arranged on many of the window sills. By his bed, mounted spheres of angelskin coral. It was so restful. It was so beautiful. He had just fallen in love with the place at first sight. He knew that I would, too. He could just *feel* it.

Parking like a maniac, he switched off the ignition and sat anxiously beside me, breathing noisily and fiddling with the keys. The ghostly powdery phosphorescent snow stifled the urban soundtrack and returned me to memories of my other life. I recalled a Saturday with my father: Hatchards in Piccadilly, a cool lemony late September sun. Bookshops are much like cathedrals in their dense hush. Ten poetry books for the birthday girl and Frege and Hume for her father. His coat, so black, so ravishingly soft, its wool smell a secure fragrance beside me as we walked. Luncheon at Albany with a widowed lepidopterist and his two daughters (the neurosurgeon Ada and the arachnologist Jacqueline). There were scones and there was cream and fresh salt-butter and a brilliantly red preserve. There was the plaque announcing that Gladstone had lived there. There were generous pots of seasonal shrubs. There was my father's smile and his extended hand as we left – *dai, Lucciola, andiamo, vieni* – and then William tapping my shoulder and asking me if I felt well. Momentarily baffled, I stared at him and shook my head. He clucked so reassuringly as he unclipped my seatbelt. I remember that cold stumbling through the snow, the steps, the paint flakes on the corners of the doorframe, stamping my feet, words and more words.

15

O nce inside, once he had lit the fire, once he had eased some Billie Holiday into the CD player, once the lights had been dimmed and the Bollinger poured, William rolled me my first 'joint' (courtesy of his local dealer, the Mercedes-driving Rastafarian psychopath, Winston). He assured me that it was so light as to have no effect at all – merely a formality, Angelica. Yawned helplessly and warned that I would fall asleep. Positioned himself next to me on the sofa. Hummed along to 'I Cover the Waterfront' as he passed me the joint. Held my stockinged foot and slowly massaged it. His eyes licked at the corners of my lips.

As he exhaled, his head vanished within a cloud: Magritte. I took a 'drag' (his lingo) and gracelessly coughed. Took another; coughed again. I was able to hold the third in with bulbous cheeks. Held the fourth in, no problem. Heard myself say: 'The first known galactic supernovae were seen in – were seen in Lupus in 1006. And … then … in, um … in 1054 in Taurus … and then in … was it 1572 or 1575? One or the other. At any rate, they were observed in Cassiopeia. And then … then … um, then … did I mention Taurus? I did? Excellent. But there were more. More supernovae. More supernovae in Serpens. Fifteenth century. Which is interesting. I think so, don't you? Because I do. Think so. Supernovae in Serpens. Supernovae *every*where.'

William narrowed his eyes with pleasure and murmured: 'No supernovae in here.'

This made me laugh so violently that I rolled onto the floor, where I lay hiccoughing and holding my belly. Still smiling, William helped me back onto the sofa, sensuously stroked that stiff goatee, murmured words of love, and offered me another joint. My world gradually flattened to a strip – a baseless world of journeys with no destinations, pale roads wreathed about paler hills, explosions of monstrous roses and then William's face as huge and stupefying as an Egyptian temple. I was out of my brain.

The realm of the quantum overtook me. Such an experience is more about gluons and heterotic string than it is about emotion. This was science – a laboratory episode by the light of my cranium's twenty-watt bulb: parapunitive, infra dig. My vaporous underthings hung suspended from the crimson lampshade and his nasty socks, underpants, and discoloured vest had been thrown on the floor. We apparently 'made love' the whole blistering night. I apparently reached a transcendent state (multiorgasmic, a convulsing screamer). The only aspect of this carnal encounter I recall is awakening the following afternoon with a mouth full of plankton and then peering through a headache (one hundred kilograms of a C_4 explosive – nitrate 002, perhaps) at my William. His hair was a metallic gloss across the chalk-striped pillowcase and he mumbled: 'I love you.' With my eyes, I followed the dome of his forehead and then listened to his subway breath. In years to come I was to recognize this sensation of emptiness as a disguise for terror or confusion, but at the time I really thought myself capable of feeling nothing.

It was an ignoble introduction to the world of genital liquors but I was used to disappointment. I had learned not to hope too hard for fear of having that hope smashed or rubbished or otherwise violated. I think I hoped in secret; I retained a small measure of optimism, preserved it from the prying and sadistic, the clumsy and the stupid, and the face I presented to the world was one of candid ignorance. Socratic irony, by Jove! I remained with William not out of love, but out of respect for my own need for stability. At that point in my life I had no overview of my emotional structure – various inhibitions disconnected me from my true feelings. Nothing seemed like the result of anything else. I had temporarily abandoned my father's all-is-one philosophy. Only retrospect imposes a pattern or plan on life, making it seem as rational as a novel. From the standpoint of the present, the future is always a derangement of ambitions. And William was kind enough, he was gentle enough, he was self-absorbed enough not to intrude too much upon my inner world. We were both spastic in matters of the soul.

16

William had laboured all his life for love and this labour had embittered him. His father's response to any articulated want or need was always mockery. Dismissal of the basic right to respect poisons any spirit, however originally ebullient.

Grieve Senior (whom William supported) had retired from his brass-goods stall on the Portobello Road at the age of fifty and now wasted all his days reflected in a pint of bitter at the Silent Woman, an establishment which catered to the Hogarthian in all its patrons. His repertoire of jokes concerned the reproductive organs, the Irish, Jews, blacks, and the reproductive organs of the Irish, Jews and blacks. When William withheld funds in protest against his alcoholism, Bart made certain that he was photographed for the Sunday Sport grossly naked in a wheelchair, his legs warmed by a ratchety tartan rug. 'Wot wos it oi done to 'im to make 'im 'ate me loike vis?' he begged the sympathetic female reporter. 'Awl oi ever done wos luv 'im an' now 'e leaves 'is awld dad to manualtrition! Oi got t' get ver bus t' ver ospitool fer awl ver medersins instead of 'avin 'im care fer me loike any udder son. *Will 'e 'elp me?* Not on yer nellie! 'E's too busy livin' it up wiv awl 'is fancy laydies in ver Ritz.'

These threads or ropes of filial duty were a noose around poor William's neck.

The memory of his mother was less distinct – a faint fragrance of menstrual blood and whiskey, nail varnish, frying fat, fish and stale chips, the suggestion of a hawkish face, that full moon he swore he could remember from his tattered bassinet: this was Mother to him. And her words: what had they been? Only the feeling behind them remained with him, and that was anger. 'Holding onto the memory of the dead,' he once said, 'is like cupping water in your hands.' She had abandoned him weeks after his gory breech birth. His father still spoke of the horror of being subjected to the spectacle of her vaginal stitches ('Dreadfuwl, my son – just *dreadfuwl!'*). William's bawling soon became too much for her and she attempted to strangle him by slotting his big head between her thighs and squeezing. Auntie Wanda intervened, there was a scandal and then the elderly *prima gravida* disappeared.

At the age of seven, on a wet afternoon after school, William was told of his mother's death. 'Yer muvver's wiv ver littool angels, son,' the old soak stammered as he gushed proof tears. His escaped wife had been stabbed to death by her belligerent boyfriend somewhere in Newcastle at four or so in the morning after brawling with her rival in the loading dock of a semi-demolished department store. Her corpse had been discovered with its arms around a headless mannequin. Despite such a childhood, William managed to establish his place in the world. 'Thank *Christ* I never had a sister,' he would say during his daily funk, 'because she would have been *completely* tonto.'

Extreme emotional deprivation is always the precedent to extreme ambition, and William was to evolve into an embarrassingly oleaginous social climber. From that loading dock in Newcastle to *Burke's Peerage*, he was set. Aristocratic girls – however homely, however deformed – invariably gave him erections. He wooed heiresses, suffered tachycardia in the presence of minor royalty, attempted show-jumping only to break both arms and fracture his pelvic bone. He studied the history of polo, cultivated nasal vowels, practised arching his left eyebrow and wandered the streets of Pimlico for hours in the hope he would be seen by the relevant (who would then assume that he was servicing a well-born beauty and/or her stately mother). He was famous for his squishes on greater writers and wrote them obsequious mash-notes. They became his pen-pals, his big mentors, his new dads. He pored over the social pages, desperate to find his image in the colourful crush of emeralds and pinstriped cravats, and every night he prayed that the words 'William Grieve dazzled the crowd' would be set in eight-point type beneath his published (and absurdly flattering) photograph.

After he managed to plough the young wife of an impotent earl, he was overjoyed to discover that photographers had recorded the whole sordid event. He was all over the front pages and for all the best reasons: bum in the air and looking with shocked eyes over his shoulder. He had arrived! When his friends rang to console him, he said (with evident strain, through gulps): 'I simply can't *tell* you how hu*mil*iating this all is ... I'm afraid I don't know what to *say*.'

Awarded a scholarship to Trinity College, Cambridge, William sweated out a first in history and dominated the Gray Society with his sonorous opinions. He was later ejected from the college after being discovered defecating from a window and in a huff, moved to an unheated second-floor flat in Girton. It was whilst working as a literary critic for a minor journal in London that he disgorged the first of five thick novels (*Trust, The Dangerous Game, Dancing in the Dimness of the Afternoon, Hypocrisy* and then *Betrayal*). The latter was a 'runaway bestseller' and blacklisted by feminists for its lavish descriptions of gang-rape and the dismemberment of schoolgirls. His female characters belonged to three and only three categories: the Bad Girl (who was killed because she liked to fuck); the Good Girl (who was killed because she didn't like to fuck); the Average Girl (who got to live because she had always been fucked). He played one note (his lyre 'tuned in a sty', as one critic put it), but he played it well. There was no reader who could not relate to his simplistic gumball archetypes.

William was no Pythagorean; in him, there were no esoteric principles of harmony, there never was celestial music. That understood, he worked on fame. His dustjacket portraits were an art-form in themselves. He practised posing for them before the bathroom mirror – adjusting his chin, lusciously pouting, lowering the dense beam of his slinky eyes, cultivating mystery. After I once teased him about this affectation, he changed his pose to a Rodin, all goatee and forehead and the illusion of intellectual intensity. Just before his death, he had again amended the way in which he wished to be perceived: an emphatic studio light accentuated his high cheekbones and in one tortoiseshell hand, a copy of *The World as Will and Idea*, two of his fingers obscuring part of the title so that it read *The World as Will* (which was, essentially, the way he saw it).

To the greater public, he was an existentialist wandering the nuked landscape of love. To me, he was a simple wimp. That marvellous intellect about which he bragged was, at best, a hop or two from varsity mediocre. This did not stop gullible cadet journalists tearing their blouses open after an interview and asking him to sign their breasts. Senior journalists – gay, married or divorced – slipped their business cards into his pockets, some of them scrawled with quite unbelievable requests (all of which he wryly showed me). Fame harnesses the energy of others with sheer awe. 'Kissinger,' he said, 'was right, my love. He really was.'

17

My own imago sank quickly into the swamp of his imagination and emerged distorted and embalmed: I was transformed by him into the soulless and seductive celebrant of heartbreak, for whom the Great Harlot of the Apocalypse was the prototype. The mistress of Louis XIV, Mme de Montespan, served a similar purpose in that she allowed the moral to triumph in an orgy of self-righteousness. She was framed with accusations of occult practices, bizarre sex, infanticides, untold blasphemies. Similarly coloured, the goddess Ishtar. Lions who dared love this nymphomaniacal deity were impaled on stakes. And then there was the popular Medusa, her scalp rich with phallic symbols and remarkable for her ability to convert living matter into granite with one ocular zap. William tuned his receptors to such dark gods, finding in them every justification for his misogyny and determinism. He was convinced of the lost, corrupt and hopeless nature of humanity, its one redeeming quality the ability to recognize its inherent purulence. This was a colour-by-numbers philosophy, easy enough to conjure in a bad mood. It also required an appealing salesperson. And so who better than the Machiavellian who loved cathouse couture?

Franz von Stück had also paid his bills by trading in Freudian archetypes.

William presented the black-bound galleys of *Juanita Dark* to me with trembling hands. An ugly row. I believe I aimed the atlas at his head and knocked him out. On regaining consciousness, he clutched at the heels of my slippers and bawled: 'If I use people's lives in my – in my writing, I'm just using my own, which is the only one I've *got* ... and if I use you, my darling, it's because whether you like it or not, you're *part* of my life. No-one can control the slant things take on the page; I can't apologize for the ugliness you see in the world I create. I love you, darling! *I love you!*' And here he began to sob so horribly that I could not but pity him. The book was to be the usual financial success, but I knew that no matter how hysterically he posed by his typewriter (index finger glued to pumping temple, eyes ravaged, chewed thumb cupping jaw), he had trouble mustering beauty. It eluded him, dissolved before his scrutiny. His paragraphs were inadequate bars, he could not lure it. Ultimately, his sensibilities were those of a thriller writer. And more than anything else, this killed him. He knew in his heart that his work was substandard.

At times I would become aware of him studying me – I would be rinsing a plate or stretching my back or lathering a stubbled armpit in the bath and he would be there, thrice removed, like a wheel within a wheel, his eyes convex surfaces through which the relevant data was osmotically processed, his nostrils effortfully vibrating. When the distance between us was negligible, William became anxious and stepped backwards neatly into observation. It was his means of allaying the tensions that intimacy induced. In his eyes, the world was a gutter – but there you go, some of us were looking at the stars.

Platitudes and unthoughts, easy generalizations – these were his working tools. He was (after twenty or so years) bored stupid by letters, but had no other training and so chained himself to that which would inevitably sell, the formulaic. Never a Byronic hero 'shaking his fist at the skies', my William was a queasy newt awaiting his dictation. His soul was closed to the real world and its disorder, its complexity, its spiritual grace. Beneath his barbed carapace, an expanse devoid of temperature and pigment, ambivalent waves, seasonless skies, a dream of noise. And I appealed to him because he thought that I did not appreciate these things. He loved me for my show of ignorance, for my youth and my money, for the seemingly vapid journey of my eyes across his face. This was, as I have before mentioned, the blank countenance adopted to discourage thought-control. I had the rare gift of making him feel that he, the word-king, was back on the throne.

Lucidity and wit did not save him from loneliness. William had no *feel* for people – no overview, all the wrong questions, no answers, little logic, no generosity of perception. Added to this was his defensive arrogance. He was the kind of man who stubbed his toe and interpreted the act as a metaphor for the decline of Western civilization. When interviewed, he expounded on the rigours of his intellectual labours; his afternoons disappeared, he said, in a *brouillard* of French studies and comparative literary analyses and Russian history (and they believed him). In reality, William only ever wrote until one or two in the afternoon, jogged to the local hellhole of a pub, played pool, drank lager, extravagantly foraged through his nostrils in an attempt to retain some 'street cred', staggered home, and either did the Swim to 'Sergeant Pepper's Lonely Hearts Club Band' (eyes closed, mouthing the words) or watched imported pornographic videos by the dozen.

By the time I arrived home, he was on the verge of screaming for lack of company.

The critics regularly taunted him into labyrinthine rages. These were carefully suppressed from all but three intimates (his rummy father, his only friend and literary agent Mortimer Schicklgruber, and whichever woman was acting as his psychiatric nurse). Throwing the newspaper at me across the table: 'Oh, just *read* this trip, will you? What a *prick*. What a self-serving *fuck*. I bet you he's sitting there in his two-inch cubicle at *The Times* going *tee-hee-hee*, that balding bug-eyed pederast. I bet you he's just creaming his Oxfam tweeds thinking: oh, *goody*. How I love to cut my undergraduate fangs on literary insti*tut*ions.' A Gregorian pause. Then: 'That dumb asshole. Couldn't fight his way out

of a prep-school spelling bee. That *fuck*pig. That *freak*.' A
sneer of cardinal magnitude (eyes slitted, upper lip gradually
furled). 'And don't – don't for a *mom*ent think that I don't
know why he did this – oh, no; oh, *no*.'

Here he would perform a small and muscular pirouette,
landing with his feet in the Number One position and with
his fingers splayed over the table. His heavy tongue would
slide over his lower lip as he prepared himself. 'His *ed*itor and
I had a little run-in over a lady at Cambridge. This scabrous
Newnham tart assaulted me one night after a party – I mean,
Angelica, I was *wretch*edly drunk, com*plete*ly crocked,
discrimination gone to the dogs – and took my cock in her
mouth and sucked it for the better part of the early morning.
We may have shagged, who can remember? I mean, how was
I to know that the oik – who was from *Leicester*shire, I might
add – was in *love* with her? For Christ's sake! I didn't study
fucking *philo*sophy! I would have understood his *pique* had I
cribbed his notes, but *cunt*? That's *ever*ywhere. I *told* him I
was sorry – I *tried* to set the yokel up with Arabella's sister,
but he wouldn't hear of it. Arabella's sister! Not just an
amazing fuck, but destined to inherit half of Scotland! And
that is what this review is really about – not my book, but
that oik's *pride*. And all over some *fuck*ing nobody slapper.'

A small and satisfied pause. And then the explosion, each
word – a damp dark vapour – rising from his bowels to be
ejected in a single noxious plume of gas. 'I mean, Angelica,
can you be*lieve* this trex?' A pitchfork of fingers slammed
down on the paper. '"William Grieve should, if only for the
quality of his prose." Oh, *brill*iant. Oh, the *wit*. The work of
a prodigy! Prismatic *gen*ius! That fuckpig. That son-of-a-
syphilitic-bitch.' A sudden relaxation of his features. 'Perhaps
I should interpret this – this *mas*terpiece – (indicating the
feature with his chin) – as an *homage* to my sexual prowess.'
Significantly sly blue glance. 'Not a bad way to look at it, is
it, darling?'

And before I could even turn to register the title of the
piece, William would leap into my arms, all tongue and livid
pelvis.

Certainly, I must have been affected by his theorems, the

curving gorges of his greed. Certainly, I must have suffered blackly, flattened to a kind of disc beneath his strong sarcastic spirit. William could be very cruel, he could be underhanded, a real thief. His peculiar little body and its spring suggested many angers. But – and here it is, the rationalization – he was also a funny man. During an unusually vigorous bout of sex, I somehow somersaulted from the edge of the bed and smacked one of my front teeth with my kneecap. *'My tooth!'* I cried. *'My tooth has been dislodged and will go black!'* William sat back on his haunches and quietly said: 'That's all right, darling. I have some correction fluid in my study.'

Seemingly empty of compassion, he still managed to convert his skewed perceptions into the surprise of laughter. Such contempt could be infectious.

18

His stupidity in emotional matters was legendary, it was almost poignant.

After a decade of promiscuity in his twenties and to infuriate the titled tootsie who had left him for a regional poet, he married Patricia Cow, a woman he would later refer to as 'the cleverest man in Britain'. Cow was seventeen when, in 1978, he met her at the Club des Allonges in St Tropez. He remarked on her subtle handlebar moustache, she emptied her fluorescent cocktail down his shirt, he was hooked. 'She had that certain *je ne sais quoi,*' was how he justified his disastrous choice to me. The truth? William had become obsessed by her immensely pendulous breasts, two structures which dazzled him with their 'paradoxical barbarity'. But Cow, despite her barrel-scrape of an IQ and cupcake nipples, was a perfidious individual. This 'Birmingham-bred lass' (who had abortions performed *'in lieu* of contraception') quickly adjusted to William's neuroses and his income and she quickly learned to play his game.

In desperation, driven mad by her incessant yacking and

superpresence around the house, dying a slow death in the compost of her bushy sex, buried alive beneath her bosom and weakly quacking, William arranged for her to contribute a column to a tabloid newspaper. He felt that such an activity would help her develop what he described to his associates as 'a more socially acceptable attitude'. His intuition was, as she would have said, 'right on the money'; from thereon in, Cow stopped gobbing in the claret of their amazed dinner-guests and flashing her labia majora at commuters on the tube.

The treeless topography of the Docklands soothed her. Nature upset her if only because it was beyond improvement, it was autonomous, the antithesis of the artifice she so adored. It had no need for her; she could not profit from it. Its effortless leaves and stems and blooms just made her want to spit. At one o'clock every afternoon, having snorted a line or two of relatively clean amphetamine and hypertyped her column, she would sprint out of the building and into the rain or sleet or mist or watery grey sunshine and cry a cry of jubiliation, oblivious to all but that surge of power.

She flourished before her word-processor. Therein she found a courage that eluded her in direct confrontation. Through her columns, she was able to communicate with her people – the impotent, the wrathful, the narrow, the reproachful. She had discovered a conduit for her contempt and cranked out reams of compellingly horrible prose, prose as compelling as transcriptions of conversations with Ted Bundy prior to his frying, prose which not only demeaned its reader by its syntactic incompetence but which, in its popularity, reflected a disturbingly vigorous resurgence of fascism in the junked suburbs of Britain. Her column was referred to as 'the anus of the Fourth Estate', its author as 'a parasite gorging on the tragedies of the oppressed'. Flattered by the intelligentsia's consternation, Cow accelerated the sensationalism. Her editor (the Gucci-clad, Perrier-swilling, Ferrari-driving Neville 'The Smiling Assassin' Mothersole), after having received one shoebox packed with poisoned horse-manure too many, decided to publish her photograph in conjunction with her thoughts in order to redirect the public's hostility. 'Let 'er take the brunt,' was how he justified his decision to his cringing deputy, Rick Scunge. 'We'll sell 'er to the public as the biggest fuckin' bitch ever to get a byline.'

I once and only once saw her – at the Groucho, sullen and surrounded by her coterie of castrated lower-middle-class subeditors and queens. She was in black, short black, unwisely short. Her hair was bleached fright-white and crewcut, her eyebrows were unkempt and black, her thighs blue-veined vintage cheese, her nose was hooked as egregiously as the handle of an old umbrella. She had been slim but the amphetamines she snorted or injected or sprinkled on her black pudding every morning destroy the most robust metabolism. And that psychic void? She was infamous, she was rich, she was fat, but the fact that she was known as an intellectual mote eventually aggrieved her. Inflated wage-packets were no longer sufficient; she now wanted respect. Wearing sunglasses, a necklace crafted from the skulls of laboratory mice, black lipstick and a distressed leather jacket, she appeared on *The Big Breakfast* to discuss her new plans to write 'literatewer'. And she did try. Her magnum opus, *Sucking Very Big Cocks*, was reviewed by the major critics and sold respectably.

Alas, William and Pat divorced. Senior District Judge Nicholas Gamble set the legal seal to the divorce by pronouncing decree nisi at the hearing in the Principal Registry of the Family Division at Somerset House, London. Seven months later, William married the daughter of a Portuguese nobleman – a tall and wide-assed woman with a head like a wingnut who, in Cow's vivid words, was (also) 'stacked like a friggin' chimney'. Such exaggerated secondary sexual characteristics appeased William's frenzied primary appetites. He clung to her breasts like a monkey to a palm tree in a simoom. This marriage lasted three years, whereupon the troubled Aurora Maria Velàzquez took the unprecedented action of suing her husband for mental distress.

This was a lawsuit filed outside marriage, above and beyond the call of divorce – this was black magic, this was metaphysics, this was business.

As a result of being subjected to William's 'violently improper conduct', she had developed a rash of borderline psychoses. Of course he cross-claimed in defamation, alleging that her accusations to friends and doctors were actionable as they brought him into 'hatred, ridicule or contempt' and were demonstrably untrue. Ill-advised William! The guilt he experienced over the coital act ensured that he associated it with horror. According to Aurora Maria (who, as if to prevent her brain escaping, wore her long blue-black hair wound in a plait around her skull), William found all 'normal' sexual practice 'boring' and 'proletarian'. He was unresponsive to her attempts at 'traditional' stimulation, his senses requiring serious jolting in order to function.

His second wife, who had been forced by her condition to resign from her valued position as a data processor at the London School of Hygiene and Tropical Medicine and was now stuffed to the gills with lithium carbonate, stood in the Queen's Bench Division of the High Court, one hand unnecessarily raised throughout her testimony, and woodenly catalogued each and every peculiarity of his to which she, the victim, had been so recklessly subjected. Unreasonable demands?

William had insisted on wearing a black leather mask with a zippered mouth when she performed fellatio on him ('He – he – he looked like that awful man from *A Clockwork Orange*,' she said by way of explanation). He had demanded (down, dog!) that she perform enemata on him with equipment he had purchased from a pharmacist in Tooting. He had demanded her participation in 'golden showers' whilst on a lecture tour of Denmark (an act he apparently claimed was a metaphor for Scandinavian drama). He had sexually assaulted her with a 'Double Dong'. (The Judge: 'I beg your pardon?' Her silk: 'A "Double Dong", my lord.' The Judge: 'And pray tell, what is a "Double Dong"?' Her silk: 'A double-headed dildo, my lord.' The Judge: 'Go on, go on.') He had tied her to the bedposts with postal string on their honeymoon and penetrated her with jellied eels and a salami which he then feverishly enjoyed with their guests over dinner. He had tape-recorded himself with three black whores and forced her to listen to the tape after she told him she was depressed about their marriage. He had slapped her face when she refused to masturbate over magazines celebrating the expression of breast-milk. He had participated in a sexual floorshow in Bangkok and then goaded her by dismissing it as 'research for (his) fiction'. (The Judge: 'Re*search*?' Her silk: 'He claimed that his protagonist was a sexually perverted adulterer, my lord.' The Judge: 'Continue, continue.') He had attempted to seduce her seventeen-year-old sister by asking the virgin adolescent if she had ever 'made it with a dog'. (The Judge: 'Would you be kind enough to repeat that?' Her silk: 'Mr Grieve asked Ms Velàzquez's sister if she had ever engaged in sexual congress with a dog, my lord.' The Judge: 'And why did Mr Grieve do this?' Her silk: 'I believe Mr Grieve was researching the response of a seventeen-year-old virgin to such a question as he wished his fictional dialogue to have verisimilitude, my lord.') He had threatened to mail pornographic photographs he had taken of her to her family if she did not sit in the bathtub suckling her own breasts while he stood over her and madly masturbated. (The Judge: 'Was the location of any significance?' Her silk: 'Yes, my lord. Mr Grieve liked to keep his perversions sanitary.') He had demanded that his wife emulate the maidens of Babylon, who in the temples of Venus were taught to contract the anal sphincter 'in order to grip and milk the penis'. He had exposed himself on a public thoroughfare in Cardiff and waved his member at his wife demanding that she 'genuflect before (her) one and only master', lest her one and only master resort to concubines in his frustration.

When asked why she, an otherwise capable and respectable woman, had submitted to such emotional and physical abuse, Aurora Maria Velàzquez dully replied: 'I really can't say. Smart women, foolish choices, I suppose.'

William came close to suicide. His every thought was of knives, of poisons, of beckoning clifftops. Near the end of the trial, he actually jumped from a second-storey window (having left a note for the mailman, the paperboy, paid the electricity and telephone bills, and removed his reading glasses), but only broke an ankle and grazed his hip.

Once the whole debacle was over, he relocated to the island of Bali for two years where he could be found swaying, etiolated by marijuana, amongst the giant papier-mâché deities carried through the streets on public festivals. His father happily answered the *Sun*'s calls and explained that his son's 'evelator (sic) dun't go ter ver top flawer'. Schicklgruber issued a statement to the press: his client was wooing his muse in the South Seas and would be unavailable for comment until that time when he felt 'sufficiently cleansed of the venoms injected in him by the envious'. Writers did not live by the same rules as the rest of us, Schicklgruber sternly reminded the world. Writers were the mouthpieces (or perhaps the word he used was 'fieldphones') of God, as distressing as that may be to the average philistine. 'Writers,' he intoned one night during an appearance on *Wogan*, 'are not like you or I; they are the torches in the long, dark tunnel of the soul.'

After a year, the callous British public relented and William's book sales tripled. Schicklgruber was able to secure a two-million-pound advance for a novella of his entitled *Bitch*. Another year passed and William returned – tanned and victorious and as bored as ever to sign copies of his novels at Hampstead bookstores.

Having mastered an important lesson in inter-personal warfare, William, from thereon in, confined his bizarre sexual inclinations to his fiction. Out with the flagellant deviant and in with the dutiful lover! I experienced him as remarkably easy in his erotic tastes, plebeian, even. Super-involved with all the frivolity and froth of the soft-core arena, my William deeply admired satin panties, patent-leather boots, sparkling garter-belts, long gloves, rouged nipples, and the unsteady escapes of pantomime virgins. He liked me to strut around the billiards room in a scarlet basque and four-inch heels, with my hair in a roll and my eyes smudged with kohl, blowing cigarette smoke in his face and sneering whilst he panted as he valiantly pulled his penis. For years I equated sexuality with theatre. He really was a fetishist. He loved me to describe my underwear to him over the telephone. When I visited friends, he would call me up to whisper: 'What colour panties are you wearing?' To which I often exasperatedly replied: 'Discoloured grey Y-fronts, William.' Late at night, he wanted me to soothe him, to rock him, to alleviate all the preposterous demands of his intercontinental fame, to compensate for all the wounds inflicted on him by older and wiser women, and to convince him that sleep was a blessing and not a foretaste of death.

I was the votive candle lit in his honour, barely cognizant of my existence outside his.

19

In a nineteenth-century Russian mood, he once dropped to my feet in Beak Street and said as he looked up at me from the filthy pavement (ignoring the drug pusher who was, at a distance of a metre, kicking a drunkard unconscious in the gutter), 'I know I look like fucking shit and you're a goddess, but I'd like to formalize our union, Angelica.'

I quickly looked around to see if we were being observed and when I saw we were, I hissed: 'For God's *sake*, William – get *up*!'

He shook his head and instead began to kiss my shoes – not once, not twice, but persistently, his lips suctioned to my shoe leather. I lightly kicked him, but this only increased his strange ardour. Belly-down on the pavement, his hands gripping my black heels, his baby-genital crushed against the cracked concrete, in a field of yellowing newspaper-sheets and chocolate wrappers and banana peel and dog faeces, he repeatedly kissed the toes of my shoes until I shouted: '*All right! ALL RIGHT! I'll marry you!*'

He suddenly stopped and lifted his head a fraction to stare at my stockinged ankle and then swallowed. I noticed his hair was thinning considerably at the crown. There was a slight flutter in his voice as he gazed up at me and groaned: 'You preside over my life, Angelica.'

Our evenings soon merged into a continuum of clever nothingness, the most exemplary being my twenty-third-birthday dinner at Bibendum. William was surprisingly handsome in his dinner jacket and I was in black silk velvet, my breasts emphasized at his request, my throat encircled by his gift of pearls.

William: (ignoring the waiter, very loudly) 'On top of your virtues and attributes – that *mouth*! that *face*! – you really are divinely articulate. In me, divinity has absented itself ... but you, *you* – your ankles, your wrists, that Valentine-shaped bottom ... I want to be reincarnated as your trousers.'

Angelica: (opening the menu and scanning it) 'Wouldn't it serve your ambitions better to be reincarnated as the jockstrap of a Booker judge, darling?'

William: (lighting a cigarette and smiling) 'Your breasts drive me *mad*. Those shadowy declivities, the fullness, that softly dropped weight –'

Angelica: (staring fixedly at the menu) 'Do stop, William. You're beginning to sound like Flaubert. Now, I think I might start with the *Escargots de Bourgogne*. Haven't had snails since –'

William: (through smoke, very aware that he is being recognized by other patrons) 'Since you last had snails, darling. Of course, love is always the Self's most urgent quest ... but how do these things *really* turn out? After the anagrams and the hang-gliding, after the dinners and the breakfasts, the nature rambles, the sunsets, the six months of hysterical sex – *then* what? Where does one go from there? Either you split up or you marry.' (Pausing to tip ash in the champagne bucket.) 'Marriage, in most cases, just happens because there isn't any *alter*native. It's something men do to get through the second half of life.'

Angelica: (still staring at the menu) 'On the other hand, I may just go with the salad of *foie gras*, French beans and artichoke ... although the *Risotto alla Milanese* sounds rather good, don't you think?'

William: (dragging on his cigarette, foxily) 'When I think of you, only Neruda's lines come to mind:

> The street
> drowns in tomatoes:
> noon,
> summer,
> light
> breaks

in two
tomato
halves,
and the streets
run
with juice.

Angelica: (distracted by the noise, glancing at him) 'What was that?'

William: (with a sardonic expression) 'Sometimes I do believe that you don't listen to a *word* I say.'

Angelica: (returning to the menu) 'And who could blame me?'

William: (draining his cigarette butt of nicotine) 'Oh, Christ. Not your period. Say it's not so, Angelica.'

Angelica: (with menace) 'Don't patronize me, William.' (Patiently, after a pause.) 'I'm definitely having the snails.'

William: 'You're miffed because it's your birthday and you think you're getting old. I was *just* thinking aloud. Why do you crucify me every time I open my mouth? You'd think I were some kind of dotard on a park bench, *drool*ing down his shirt ...'

Angelica: (exhaling) 'Don't start, William.'

William: (defiantly, but with humour) 'A *drool*ing dotard playing pocket-billiards in public, soiling the trousers he has belted with a length of string ... awful, but so true. That's how you see me, isn't it, my queen of death?'

Angelica: (very slowly) 'William, it's my birthday and I'd like to enjoy myself, if that's all right by you. Do me a little favour, will you? Stop preening for the people at the next table and pick up the menu. You might be interested in the smoked wild salmon.'

William: (lighting another cigarette) 'You don't love me any more. That's it, isn't it? My empress, my goddess of marble, pure and virginal.'

Angelica: (gripping the menu) 'Come to think of it, the Baltic herrings *à la crème* might be more your speed.'

William: (through smoke, vaguely offended) 'That was a quote of Turgenev's.'

Angelica: (looking up without expression) 'What? The line about the Baltic herrings?'

William: (rolling his eyes) 'No, not the line about the *Baltic herrings*! The line about the goddess of *marble*.'

Angelica: (returning to the menu) 'Really.'

William: 'You just don't love me any more. You secretly want to return to Australia to get yourself some nine-foot beach hugie.'

Angelica: (controlling herself) 'Not this, William – *please* not this.'

William: (ensuring that the couple at the next table are watching him) 'That's it, isn't it? You just want some nine-foot beach hugie on your arm. Or a thug. You want to writhe topless at a disco with some bulging thug shoving his hand into your hotpants.'

Angelica: (voice trembling) 'I really don't know what I'm doing here. You're fully capable of having conversations with yourself.'

William: (drawing on his cigarette, leaning forward, deliberately) 'You want a biker with a three-day growth going down on you when you have your period. You want to be gang-banged by a gym full of steroid-happy bodybuilders in sweat-soaked Lycra jockstraps. You want to marry a man who swings from a tyre. You want to be molested by a tribe of Ubangi warriors with monstrously engorged members. You just don't love me any more, do you? I'm not quite "wild" enough for you, am I? I was warned by Mortimer that you loved danger too ardently to make me a good wife. I'm simply not enough of a "rad" or "groover", whichever term it is that your coevals apply to sexually desirable love-objects.'

Angelica: (deeply inhaling, placing the menu over her plate) 'Do you *con*stantly have to assert yourself through sarcasm? Are you constitutionally incapable of having a normal conversation? Do you *al*ways feel the need to create a combative atmosphere? Are we going to spend the rest of our lives sitting around sounding as if we're drafting the script of an Albee play?'

William: (with a patrician expression) 'There are worse fates, my darling. What bothers me is that you have – in your quaintly convoluted way – accused me of not being *nor*mal. Not normal! I have *nev*er been so denounced by a woman! *Nev*er! You revile me! Look at this face, Angelica – come

72

now, stop feigning indifference, look up, you beautiful incubus; come on, stop sulking – yes, yes, that's right – look at this face. Is this the face of a madman, darling? Come on, answer my question. Is it? No, that's right, it isn't. Wherefrom, then, your extraordinary argument? You have never understood me, never. I sometimes wonder how it is that the knowledge has not infiltrated the Nazi compound of your mind. It is *oth*ers who are abnormal, who are – how shall I put it? – *ton*to. I am a paradigm of virtue, of regularity, of sanity! I should be exhibited to psychiatric students to illustrate the better extremity of mental health. Why will you never learn? Angelica, you are a rotten little tyrant. So frail, and yet so powerful ... so *dom*inating, and yet so vulnerable ... so au*thor*itative, and yet so gentle ... an idol to be worshipped. I kiss your feet, my darling.' (With mild consternation.) 'Don't make that face, Angelica – you enjoyed it at the time.' (Returning to his oratory.) 'You were born to be a cult figure amongst higher tribes. A deity carved in –'

Angelica: (dully) '– marble, pure and virginal. Turgenev.'

William: (smiling, with a throat-emphasizing inclination of his head) 'Oh, don't for a *mom*ent think that I don't remember what it was like to be your age, that era of contrived cuteness. Not normal! You have a hide. As if I could ever be anything but elevated from the moronic conflagration of humanity. As if there were any hope of me being anything but estranged from the pornography of modern consciousness. Do I look like Norman Mailer? *Christ!* Next thing, you'll have me married to Vanessa del *Rio!*' (Shaking his head.) 'As if the average jug-eared cretin could share anything with me aside from oxygen. The concept of the collective unconscious, my dainty little atomic warhead, was only ever the wet-dream of an intellectually impaired old mystic. Discerptibility is the only reality. *Difference.* Diversity. Divergence. Dissociation. And the world thrives on its unworkable differences because they create the friction or fission necessary for life.' (Pausing.) 'Don't look so suicidal, darling. It's your *birth*day.' (Lifting his glass, victorious.) 'To my one love!'

The Waiter: 'Are you ready to order, madam?'

Angelica: (relieved to be distracted) 'Yes.'

William: (with hostility) 'No, we're *not*, thank you *so* much.'

Angelica: (to the waiter) 'You'll have to ignore him, I'm afraid. We *are* ready to order.'

William: 'But I haven't *decided*!'

Angelica: (coldly) 'I am *ready* to order.'

William: (with sudden tolerance and warmth) 'You irresistible bolshie, you.' (To the waiter.) 'The lady will have the *soupe de poisson, rouille et croûtons* followed by ... let me see, let me see ... followed by the *pot-au-feu* of ox-tongue with beetroot, horseradish and celeriac *purée* and for dessert ... for dessert ... skip the dessert. I have decided to put her on a diet. Her breasts are far too voluptuous for any man to bear. They have been known to inspire vicars to kick holes through stained glass windows.' (Pausing to chuckle.) 'Ah, and she'll also want some mashed potatoes. And I shall have whatever's marvellous on the condition that it isn't fish or chicken.'

The Waiter: 'Very good, sir.'

William: (gravely) 'Do try not to overdo her potatoes, won't you? The last serving had the consistency of vaginal discharge.'

The Waiter: 'Very good, sir.'

William: (deeply sighing) 'I mean, I was asked to review that dreadful new Chinese place for *GQ* magazine and the kindest comment I could muster was that their entrée tasted like fried handkerchiefs.'

The Waiter: 'Anything else, sir?'

William: (silkily, now ignoring the waiter) 'Not to mention those grey things in their won-ton soup. Boiled goat testicles, I promise you – and not just *boiled*, but boiled for many, many years.'

The Waiter: (bowing) 'Sir.'

Angelica: (watching the waiter leave) 'You *amaze* me. You utterly *amaze* me. Why I allow myself to be *treated* in such a –'

William: (dismissively) 'Yes, yes, yes, darling, I've heard it *all* before. Don't test my patience. John Updike and I were actually discussing patience in relation to the creative process this morning. He and I – well, Angelica – intellectual equals. Great man, great man. He was suffering the usual *crise* over

74

the relevance of his artistry. "William," he said, "William, I'm not sure if Angstrom really *works* as a character in the context of –" '

Angelica: (lightly frowning) 'Ångström?'

William: (peeved at the interruption) 'Yes, Angelica – *Ang*strom.'

Angelica: (thoughtfully) 'How very clever.'

William: (rolling his eyes) 'Yes, darling – in*ord*inately clever. Now –'

Angelica: 'You do know what it means, don't you?'

William: (lighting another cigarette, exasperatedly) 'What *what* means?'

Angelica: 'Ångström.'

William: (inhaling smoke) 'Of course I know what it means! It means *noth*ing! It is the name of his most famous *char*acter! A resonant name, but absolutely –'

Angelica: (with subtle satisfaction) 'How very odd. And here was I, under the ridiculous impression than an ångström was a unit in which to measure the wavelength of light.'

William: (nervously) 'A wave ... length ... of –'

Angelica: '– *light*, darling. Remember subtext?'

William: (embarrassed) 'Well, of course! I mean, *ev*eryone knows *that*. I just thought you meant *as*ide from that – *that* meaning ... *ev*eryone knows that Angstrom means a unit of light ... length.'

Angelica: 'A unit in which to measure the wavelength of light, William, not a unit of light-length.'

William: (scrambling) 'Where *was* I? You forced me to digress. Ah, yes – marriage. My first marriage was a byproduct of reactive depression, nothing more. My second marriage was naught but a cold compromise between the individual and time. I was all of a raw rose fluster, and I made a *very* serious mistake, oh yes; a *very* serious mistake. One of the few. Ah, the harsh glare of retrospect, how it shames me! I did not aim for love, Angelica. I did not aim for *love*. No, I did not aim for –'

Angelica: 'What was that for which you did not aim, William? I'm not certain I heard you the first thousand times.'

William: (index finger dancing) 'Ah – ah – *ah*! You must listen. That is your most preposterous – perhaps your only – failing, my darling. You never listen. If you listened, you

75

would learn much about yourself and your place in the world, which would or perhaps wouldn't be a good thing. Ignorance as bliss, and all that. I may be a vile old polyp to you, but very few are fortunate enough to extract any seriousness from me. I am professionally glib, if expressed in the form of pomposity. I am a very sly and tricky dog, a remarkably elusive fish. You will remember these words. In years to come, you will reiterate them to my biographers or perhaps insert them in the novel I inspire you to write. But for now, you must simply *listen*. The young, my love, should be all ears. Ears and breasts. Wisdom springs thereof, all that. But don't forget the breasts – I ado*re* your breasts. Now, where was I? Ah, yes. Of course, of course. The second half of life. I state the rock-bottom case, just to give the stark perspective. The old guys who abandon themselves to youthful love – I used to think that they wanted two lives, I really did. Now I have come to understand that what they want is two *youths* – one in the bag, one on the Other Side. It is all *sav*agely compelling. But with you, my frowning little yuppie triumphalist, it isn't even a matter of youth or desire or appeal: *you are my vocation*.'

Angelica: (staring at him) 'I hate you, William. I wish you were dead.'

William: (happily) 'You don't *hate* me – you're just con*fused*. The boundaries of your emotions overlap. Remember those Venn diagrams you drew in prep school? You were raised by reptiles. All your life you have suffered a crisis of meaning. You have looked to the world around you for your ideals and have found nothing. The mandatory imposition – rather than natural discovery – of ideals confuses the young. In you, love and anger unpeacefully coexist. All that money, your murdered daddy ... of *course* you feel confused! And that is where I come in. I exist to unravel your cares, to carry that baggage of yours, to *teach* you.'

Angelica: (crisply) 'Do you think, William, that if I leaned across the table and stabbed you through the neck with my butter knife I would be jailed for murder or would they give me a reprieve on the grounds of the insanity to which you have reduced me?'

William: (ashing his cigarette on the floor) 'Oh, stop being so dramatic!'

Angelica: (indifferently) 'If I did, you wouldn't have any material.'

William: (after a phlegmatic sigh) 'Do you know, Angelica, that I yesterday heard a young woman speak, in perfect seriousness, the following words: *everybody please check the bags*, she said, *cause there's a couple what ain't been taked yet*. I swear to God, Angelica – those were her words. And *that* is what I have to tolerate most every day. Rampant stupidity. I don't know why they just don't cut out the middleman and pull my fingernails out with burning pincers.'

Angelica: (glancing in the direction of the kitchen and after a long pause) 'I do wish they'd hurry up with the food.'

William: (stubbing his cigarette out on his butter plate) 'I could reverse the vasectomy, you know. We could have a little daughter. Calliope. Clytemnestra. Andromeda. Aria—'

Angelica: (staring to his left) 'I'd rather die than bear your child, William.'

William: (cooing) 'Lovely pale pink nursery. Nabokovian pink. Little cutie smiling away at me in her cot. With my profundity and your verbal celerity. A little daughter I could dandle on my knee. She'd grow up to be the president of the United States, Angelica. She could arrange for my face to be on the one-dollar stamp.'

Angelica: (shaking a cigarette from his packet and lighting it) 'They say that fifty per cent of heavy smokers are killed by their habit. Which gives you a one in two chance, William. It's an ugly death, but it would stop you talking. I could study patterns in star clusters while you lay beside me, breathing from a hole in your throat.'

William: (gazing at her admiringly through smoke) 'Every time I look at you I think the same thing, which is *Jesus*.'

Angelica: 'That's uncharacteristically sweet of you, darling.'

William: (suddenly) 'Did I tell you about the *Observer's* shoot? A room full of publishing tarts and a Canadian – *withoat a doat it's about* – that *acc*ent! So there was this Canadian wretch with a camera and me, under a heavy fire of lights … you can just imagine it. An un*qual*ified nightmare. I was practising my glazed stare – the one editors so love, you know, because they mistakenly interpret it as intelligent. It's what they want and there is nothing I can do to change that.

Those boring imbeciles. They're all so desperate to be my friends. They *all* want to be processed through my imagination, emerging as far more interesting than they could *ever* be in real life. Christ! And that journalist, you know the one I mean – that good ole boy with sizzling eyes, you know, back-slapping and one-lining ... come on, Angelica! *You* remember! That dope-addled Yank. The one who fucks typists in public toilets. The one who was seen disappearing into a New York cold-water walk-up with a transvestite hooker. Come on, come on! *Surely* you can't have forgotten him! We met him at Alessandro's for dinner ... crashing tie? voice like a nasal spray? talked about Liberia and the diseases of the large intestine all night? Oh, anyway, he was in my face all afternoon: *Mister Grieve, pardon me? ... Mister Grieve, how so? ... Mister Grieve, as an American* ... I felt as if I'd been trapped in an elevator with the love child of Bill Clinton and Howdy Doody. *Oh*, Angelica, the things I *do*, the things I *do* ... I'm using up my *life* this way. And what a miracle! Our food has arrived before the dinosaurs reclaim the earth!'

20

One polar morning I stood in the kitchen, blowing on the window pane and writing the word EXIT in the condensation with my finger. There was a thick crust of ice on the sill; a dead pigeon lay on the pathway. The sky was a dark roseate grey. In William swept, his hair slicked back with water, eyes bloodshot, trailing his imperial dressing gown. He stood before the other window, his palms flat on the wooden benchtop, staring out at the devastation.

'Sometimes,' he said without addressing me, 'I feel as if I just can't take it any more. All around me, death. *Death*. Look at that pigeon. Christ. I look out the window and there it is – the metaphor for my life.' A crosspatch pause. 'Can you remember where I left *The Anatomy of Melancholy*? I spent three *hours* last night looking for it.'

'I'm leaving you,' I said, turning to look at him.

'Wonderful,' he absently said. 'Wonderful. No *Independent*. One snowflake, and those work-shy yobs are back on strike. I now have to sit down to the *Guardian* – a good newspaper, admittedly, but one that requires the term of a natural life to read.' He sat down at the table. 'Make me a coffee, won't you, darling? My mouth tastes like J.B. Priestley's prose.'

Slowly blew on the glass. 'I'm leaving you, William.'

'*Hushhhhhhhh* ...,' he coaxed. And then: 'Have you *seen* the front page?'

'William –' and it occurred to me that my words were unnecessary, that they were unheard and would remain unheard.

'I don't believe it, I just don't believe it.' Intense, absorbed, almost emotional. 'These spastics just can*not* be serious.' Rubbed the back of his neck with difficulty. 'Myth of decline. Myth of decline! What reconstituted – I just cannot be*lieve* it.' His words filtered to a murmur and he shook his head.

Looked down at my feet. The toes somehow seemed alien to me, unfamiliar; it was as if I were inhabiting the body of another. Lifted my head to gaze at the man who believed himself my future mate and felt as if I had been bruised, as if I had tripped or cut myself or collided with a wall. What had once been comfortable had become insufferable, and in remaining with him, I was defeating that for which I now knew I stood.

Redirected my attention through the window. Over these hours and days and weeks and months and years I had become aware of an energy within me and with it, an awareness of its being constrained: common confinement. William glanced at me, glanced at the newspaper, glanced at me, glanced at the newspaper, cleared his throat, glanced at me and then, resigned to my intransigence, decided to make his own coffee. Still holding the paper before him, he walked over to the counter, activated the kettle and then heavily leaned against the bench, intently reading, the sole of one hirsute and prominently boned foot moulded to the tarsal area of the other, losing himself in typeface until the kettle boiled. This kettle wheezed and spat and spat and wheezed until I could no longer stand it and so through my teeth said: 'William – are you *deaf*? The water's ready.' 'Unh?' he asked,

79

and swivelled around. 'So it is, so it is.' Once he had stirred coffee into the billowing white steam of a mug, he held it with both hands to his blowing mouth, his elbows on the table, his eyes still following the print. The steam extended its tendrils over his cheeks and temples and finally dissolved into the stalest kitchen atmosphere.

Rubbed the silk hips of my nightgown and stared at the dead pigeon. Its elegantly graded feathers were matted with blood. That band of iridescent violet feathers around its throat, the white crest on its beak, its curled red claws and opaque open amber eyes, its breast: once so beautiful, and now just decomposing. The creature had been attacked and then abandoned to its grave of plain snow-salt there in the shadowless garden. Pressed my warm cheek to the glass. It occurred to me that all predators felt in some way threatened by that which was soft or swift or which could fly; it was as if beauty liberated was an insult to their strength or a reminder of their own deficiencies; it was as if by killing it, they somehow triumphed over their own fears. All hunters are at heart so envious, so insecure, so trapped.

William suddenly opened his mouth. Mess of teeth. Tongue, liverish. The poisoned well of his oesophagus. He relieved himself of some dissonant wind, one buttock artfully lifted from the seat. In that moment, he was no more than an object to me, a slide smeared with bacilli. Grunting, he scratched at the sandpaper of his chin. So ordinary. Who could have guessed what was to come?

He was to die a few years later in his bath – abominably inebriated after a night of whoring and brandies with schnapps chasers and rectal chilli, having been scooped from the sawdust floor of an all-night 'Western' motif bar by the equally inebriated Schicklgruber and in a screaming heap delivered home, he swallowed ten Halcion tablets (thinking they were laxatives; he was plagued by chronic constipation). In an effort to sober himself, he ran a bath and then, after urinating a river of liquid butterscotch, tripped into that infernal bath and drowned. The tap was still thundering twelve hours later, which is when the police, alerted by neighbours alarmed by the Orinoco flowing down William's front path, broke into his house and discovered him floating prone, his wet shirt greedily trapping pockets of air, his famous face a Francis Bacon, trousers undone, those powder-blue Swiss underpants (with that decorative fly he found so amusing) unhygienically streaked, a smashed bottle of Stolichnaya by the fungus-throated toilet, the bidet beside it filled with thumbed pornographic magazines and tubes of masturbating-facilitating hand-cream and the 876-page hardback critique of Bellow he had been reviewing for the *Washington Post*. Some weeks earlier, he had sent me the only poem he had ever submitted for publication:

> **For Angelica**
>
> *Algid sister,*
> *juncture of root and vapour –*
> *O, daughter*
>
> *Lucifer.*
> *This glacial ache, dull swab*
> *of sorrows:*
>
> *how we are defeated.*
> *From marrow*
> *with the ghost of you*
>
> *I surface to a kick;*
> *to have nothing left intact, my love,*
> *but the indifference of my intellect.*
>
> *O, guardian,*
> *my heartless visionary –*
> *this carapace of blades is all that love is.*

William's publisher was his messenger of death ('Awfully sorry to bother you, Angelica, but I'm afraid I have some *rather* unpleasant tidings ...') The following weeks were agonizing. I would be thinking of unrelated things and suddenly find my head in my hands, and the tears, and the tears. We had shared years. It was a loss.

The obelisk-collecting Schicklgruber later wrote me a letter suggesting that I was to blame for William's death. *J'accuse*! 'After you left him,' the thing read, 'he sought refuge in women who looked like you, he could no longer sleep, his writing lost its electricity, he felt he had no reason to live and so searched – as if for the mythical and ultimately treacherous genie – for your love at the bottom of a bottle. Because of you, Britain has lost its finest author. Be it on your head, you MURDERER!' Heartbreaking rubbish, and so typical of Schicklgruber's inflamed brain. He required a target for his frustrations after losing hundreds of thousands of pounds through one of the four Lloyd's Gooda Walker syndicates. I corrected his spelling and his syntax, drew a red felt-tipped pen over his clumsier similes and returned the edited missive to him with an Alcoholics Anonymous pamphlet. And what absurdity. I never again heard from the pufftoad, whom I watched describe me as a 'dramatic, arctic bitch' on *Oprah* some months later.

But that grim February morning, I felt only contempt. In faultlessly forging his signature on a cheque the previous evening, I realized I had – in some terrible and inexplicable way – become too much him and in that, not enough myself. The chair legs ached across the floorboards. Soundlessly left the room. The house was what real-estate buffoons refer to as 'sprawling'. He would not notice my absence for hours. And so I dressed, packed two suitcases, caught a cab to Heathrow and was booked on the next flight to Sydney.

William finished reading the *Guardian*, called for me, shuffled disconsolately around the place, made himself another coffee, warmed a croissant in the oven and then decided that I was purchasing that Hermes scarf I had told him I 'rather liked, really' at Harrods.

2 1

Safe in that aircraft. Remembered, as I was fed macadamia nuts and sparkling mineral water, the New Year's Eve William and I had passed passionately kissing beneath the statue of Eros in Piccadilly Circus, a statue that was at the time securely gagged and bagged for detailed repairs. I recalled the melting ice-crystals upon his lips. 'To awaken to your face for the rest of my life,' he had whispered. Stared out at thirteen thousand miles of world – at the Arab lands, at their dunes, selenian; at those Indian mountains; at the flickering necklace of Singapore; at the gritty scarlet cartilege of the Australian deserts and through, through to the blue robes of the glittering Pacific – the iridescent, the irreplaceable, the irresistible – loving her wild white spray, the tropical curvature of her shores, her corals and the shallow lulls of all her greens.

22

Still have a photograph of William, a dog-eared snapshot smudged with strawberry jam. In it, he is smiling with all his failed tea-coloured teeth, his bad humours a bad memory, lolling like a pasha in a honeysuckle haze. To his immediate left, a jar of Melatonin to preserve the youth he never had; to his right, a stack of physics texts; atop them the sculpture of a mourning girl I had given him and which he treasured, really treasured. There is a rug of English sunlight over his naked little feet. He is wearing a loose moth-eaten shirt and old unbuttoned jeans. His hair is tousled, his goatee tinged with wildflower honey in that fading light. We had just finished making Sunday love. During his climax, he had moaned: 'Do – you – think – that – if – I – sank – into – your – mouth – I'd – ever – get – out – *alive*?' (This delivered with comically contorted features.) There is in me a small reliquary of love for him. There are still days when I retreat from the moment and telescope back, back into that time when I was familiar with his lips, his fingertips, his sultry bitter breath, far back into that time when I did not value that which was within me, when I thought that he was all I had.

23

The years that followed were insular: I enclosed myself within each day; I shelled myself with calendars. At the edge of my consciousness, the distinct presence of sadness, spiritual ills. I was dismayed by myself, certainly; I was as startled by my impulses as if they had been generated within another. Where was the source of these important waves of feeling? All I knew was that I existed in an infaunal world, a damp and glutinous realm, sunless and far above me, what seemed to be a universe of water. Swells of obscurity would often interrupt the flow of my discourse and leave me standing, lips frozen on the brink of a forgotten word, my thoughts a broth, eyes suddenly arrested by an inconsequentiality – a button, say, or an inexpertly ironed lapel; from this, a waking reverie – shimmering mental spheres, the byways of remembered phrases, faces: in these I would lose myself and my perplexed observer, who would (invariably) report me to a friend or an associate as 'cripplingly shy'.

One morning I received a psychedelic brochure in the mail along with my telephone bill, a letter from the Courant Institute, a yellow paper flyer promoting a laundromat (run by a slim and shifty cretin married to a sour skeleton some three hundred years his senior), and a romantic note from an English astrophysicist on holiday in Prague. After a fantastically paranoid introduction, the psychedelic brochure detailed the three phases of social reaction to crisis:

I. The first is Superficiality, in which the threatened population will react by adopting some shallow sloganeering ideals to which, however, it will not attach any serious ego investment. This is a passive and maladaptive response, maladaptive because it fails to identify the cause of the crisis, and therefore the crisis and its sister tension persist.

II. The second phase of the reaction (since the crisis continues) is Fragmentation, in which panic begins to strike, social cohesion breaks down, and small social groups try to protect themselves from the crisis at the expense of other small and fragmented social groups. This, then, degenerates further into the third phase, Dissociation.

III. In this phase, the victim turns away from the source of the tension and slithers into a world of internal migration, introspection and obsession with self. Superficiality is thus paired with Synoptic Idealism as its opposite; Fragmentation with Authoritarianism; Dissociation with Evangelism.

Plucky stuff, and worth preserving if only because its author's frenetic concern for the future of mankind paired with my own mystic's indifference as its opposite (I was a Phase Three Girl, after all, and long entrenched in my classification).

24

A serious quandary: such cynicism may have been my means of self-preservation, but also disparaged my essential nature, which has always been – if not docile and temperate – then tender, touchingly tender. But survival is the ultimate goal of the sentient and therein the twist (of sharp green lime, of lemon). Damage defines the survivor and once damaged, survivors learn to regard that sentience they must protect to be as threatening as its metaphysical alternative for without sentience there is no pain, and this is where Hamlet's fabled question becomes the summary of the human condition: ambivalence and its despair, ambivalence and its excitement, ambivalence as a homeostatic mechanism – all exercises in acute consciousness.

On the surface, I was very mild, a kind of elegant librarian; within, I was lubricious and conspicuously calculating, labyrinthine in my wants, sharply (again, that lime!) erotic, a complicated being and strictly classical in application. My grid was one of limbs and unfolding vulnerabilities. My way was Bacchic – immediate, celebratory, physical. I was a specialist, certainly, and my refined sense of emotional sadomasochism was not secret.

I once walked, agonized and in a thin red woollen dress, through the dewed apple orchards of Worcestershire in the birdless hours of the night, lamenting the loss of some now-blurry love (hair black, his mouth the colour of blood through water), weeping and shivering and stumbling and cat-sneezing, softly beseeched by Evesham's timeless ghosts, the hills around me rising like drugged giants through the lacquer-black shadows, the moon a keyhole through which a palace courtyard blazing with torchlight could be glimpsed, those little apples cobblestones beneath my feet and not a human sound – not a whisper, not a sigh – to be heard for miles; and then I fell asleep in a wet meadow where the silhouettes of marble sheep could be distinguished through the chilling silky opalescent mist. I also dined with gargoyles, kissed villains, knew sensual senselessness with rogues and always liquefied before beauty. A less romantic memory: that haddock-eyed Division Director of a Debt Markets department who, over dinner, warmly remarked: 'You know why I admire you? Because you stick to your regiment.'

My regiment incarcerated for shell-shock, I was left alone, not yet fully comprehending the words inscribed in the leaf of my father's favourite book: *ignoti nulla cupido* – the unknown is not desirable just because it is unknown. I unthinkingly continued and only increased my momentum. Anything to dull the pain.

The (hypothetical) point between the (hypothetical) conscious and unconscious is understood to be the (hypothetical) self, and this self was for me the self that I expressed sexually. Sex was the only realm in which I felt I really did exist as during it, my every quality – corporeal or otherwise – was engaged; it was the one river in which I saw myself reflected and in that reflection, suspended as it was between the vacuity of air and the dense liquid it animated, I was not merely an *à propos* of surface tension but the synthesis of space and water, my identity a fusing of the elements – naive art, knowing nature; for once, precious. So I was not all a tempest. But I did have my lovers and my bothers, both eclectic and dear; I knew of arousals and brute swoons, essentially mucilaginous sentiments.

I was certainly searching for something.

25

With one lover I flew to Cairo, suffered severe food poisoning in a Hilton suite with panoramic views of the pollution, admired in the busy museum dedicated to Auguste Mariette the shrewd-faced and large-eared 3,000-year-old mummy of Ramses II, and was called Nefertiti by brown children hawking beads outside the Valley of the Kings. Gagging and grimacing, my lover and I climbed steep ladders through the pungent narrow tunnels (in which the desiccated guides would freely micturate) of the pyramids. I stood like a statue in sandstorms, my skin protected by a fine silk veil. I wore my hair in beaded cornrows and rode a moody camel over tired dunes. Animatronics of memory.

We sailed up the Nile and on the yacht won a fancy-dress competition – my lover as the slave-trader with me behind him (wearing ankle bracelets and with a basket overflowing with dates balanced upon my head). We sailed past El Minya, Abu Tij, Girga, Dishna. We stayed at the Winter Palace in Luxor and idly played chess and chequers at the base of its dramatic staircase. The Winter Palace was also where I caught the illiterate maids squealing over the sexual lace in my suitcase. And when my lover read Shelley's 'Ozymandias', I could only think of my stepfather:

> Half sunk, a shattered visage lies, whose frown,
> And wrinkled lip, and sneer of cold command,
> Tell that its sculptor well those passions read
> Which yet survive (stamped on these lifeless things),
> The hand that mocked them and the heart that fed.

In the Temple of Luxor, ogled by tourists and archaeologists and devotees of defunct North African religions, the tremendous head of Aldo/Ramses. On his stone brow, the Uraeus of the Cobra Goddess. Looking at it gave us both the creeps and inexplicably subdued, we left. The next day I bought from a hunchbacked merchant in his dingy cluttered stifling store a lapis lazuli carving of the great monotheist Akhenaten, whose god Aten is represented as a burst of sun with rays terminating in human hands. One night my lover turned to me in bed, his eyes lunar in their emphasis, and told me, in the low and mesmerizing voice that precedes sleep, that in the Valley of the Tombs much of the artwork had been destroyed by a damp and saline exudate and that only fragments of winged figures and the three grossly deformed sons of Horus could be seen. 'Such sacred monsters,' he whispered, 'have flourished throughout history.'

Another lover and I travelled to the Cape York Peninsula – through Rockhampton and boring Townsville, pausing only to sail by sloop to Orpheus Island and the invisible border of the translucent blue Magnetic Passage and then back, back to the mainland and then north and north again, through low clouds of soundless sandflies and russet dust, along crocodile-rich rivers and tall humming reeds, by swamp, by rock, past canefields burning red and black and hell-orange in the endless boiling afternoons. We lay like flamens to the sun-god on arcs of blinding white salt-scented sand; we cut our feet walking on tough brown palm fronds; we sucked sweet milk from holes he bored in coconuts; his skin was punished by the unrelenting light. He deeply entered me beneath the surreal fan-leaves of a Guadeloupe Palm in a cool and serpent-laced rainforest, and then we bathed naked in clear green pools of icy water in which unnamed fish gathered in schools.

At an airless coffee-shop in some suburban small-town shopping mall, a coffee-shop in which the table-legs were of different lengths and the floors laminated, in which the walls were papered with *faux*-brick and all the sugar bowls plastic *rocaille*, in which the somnolent waitresses wore mermaids' combs in their opaque bouffants and on their feet broad rainbow-coloured rubber thongs, we overheard an exchange between a bald fat sweating man and his mail-order bride, a tiny Oriental showpiece.

'Does birdy go tweet-tweet?' he asked.

'No, only other birdies go tweet-tweet,' she said.

'I want you to tweet-tweet,' he ordered.

'No,' she said, 'no tweet-tweet now.'

His throat flushed with anger. '*Go tweet-tweet!*'

'Tweet-tweet,' his Confucian canary whistled after a miserable pause, 'tweet-tweet.'

At night, my academic lover kept me awake with his queries about the Best of All Possible Worlds, theories of meaning, Sortals, Counterfactuals, Atomic Propositions and his dreams of the shared future I knew would never in a thousand years eventuate. But he was feeling very spiffy; he had just returned from England, where he had successfully spoken at the Oxford Union in favour of the motion 'the manufacture of mordant genius is not possible'.

Mordant genius was only one of his obsessions. Like many men, he invested most of his energy into self-importance and regularly bragged of his intelligence quotient (a respectable, but hardly extraordinary, 150 points) and of his manly daring. Example: as an adolescent, he had dislocated his shoulder when his surfboard had ricocheted into the air and landed on him. 'I had to paddle back to the shore with one arm,' he gurgled with pride. 'The rip was terrible. I almost drowned. Just one of the many occasions on which I cheated death.' This nagging shoulder-injury added to his propensity to grill like a hotdog in the sun cut short his wildman's surfing life. And for all his athletic and intellectual feats, he was as capable as an ape is of developing intense fetishitic relationships with the inanimate – namely, his motorcycle. 'There is nothing, but *nothing* like the feeling of power I get from a bike,' he said. 'When I'm racing, I feel as if it wants my arms torn from their sockets; a spell of fifteen minutes can transport me. When I charge and the road seems an inch from my face, I feel like I can conquer the world.'

I was to discover that this urge for conquering worlds was very popular with men. It could amuse them for hours, sometimes occupied them all their lives.

We bought fresh hamburgers leaking rich butter and crisp

lettuce shreds and glutinous red ketchup from stoned vendors behind fat-filmed counters in hibiscus-bright hamlets. We ate hot thick salted chips from oil-spattered newspaper-cones whilst meandering along twilit beaches, seagulls wheeling in the lilac air and the sea a mirror over which the day surrendered to a universe of stainless stars. We fed each other the moist white flesh of crabs and lobsters, cracked open plump pink shrimp and uvular oysters in open-air hotel restaurants, outside which from greased chains swung signs hand-painted with the legend: ALL YOU CAN EAT FOR $13!

My lover left me in a *cabaña* to fill the tank of his Ducati 900SS and returned some fours later, his white T-shirt carmine and his upper lip maintained by fifteen stitches. Two rednecks had assaulted him after he had asked them to reconsider dumping a urine-soaked sofa and two hundred empty beer-cans by pristine green bushland. In Casualty, the city-bred intern sighed and advised him to repress his social conscience whilst in the area. 'Around here,' the young doctor explained, 'manhood is defined by the conscious brutalization of limitations, which are perceived to be feminine in nature.'

The waters of the north are unparalleled and once my lover's lip had healed, we swam in them most every day and returned to the neon and the tarmac feeling almost human.

I then left him. Recriminations, the usual resignation. My attitude to love was too experimental to allow for any real development of intimacy; I was too frightened and too numb, too careless with myself, unknowingly dishonest. It was less debilitating to have a mask rejected, certainly. And so I absorbed their needs and wants, half-losing myself in the process and in turn, resenting them for that half-loss. To Kunz, sex was perverted in the absence of love; to me, this was the norm. Mathematical formulae are no less accurate for want of compassion in their computation. And how could I have known differently? This was my way, what I had come to understand as interaction.

26

When dealing with abstractions or symbols, the shape of the abstraction or the symbol is irrelevant and so I chose as my next sexual partner a young woman. Her name could have been Saskia van Doete, she chain-smoked menthol cigarettes and wore round rimless glasses, she was all arms and legs, a vibrant spider. On her left deltoid, the fading blue tattoo of a fruit bat in flight. With her disproportionately long thighs and defensive sense of self-deprecation, she intrigued me. She rarely combed her hair. She suffered anxiety attacks in parking lots. She bit her nails, never wore a brassiere, slept fitfully, knew all there was to know of Tudor history, named all her potplants (Edgar, Bradley, Paul, Sebastian, George Felix), was born on a kitchen table in New Mexico the fierce day Congolese insurgents repelled government troops near Lake Tanganyika, had a manic-depressive sister and a brother who had died at birth and a weakness for persimmons. When she found a small screw on the throw rug and long before anything had taken place between us, she rotated it between her thumb and forefinger and then turned to me with a dazed and humorous face. 'Is this what you're after?' she asked me through a teasing laugh.

She studied epistemology and had lived for three years in the garden flat owned by her aunt an avenue parallel to mine. I would find her ironing shirts in the late afternoon, the steam rising to her Dutch cheekbones from the hissing cotton, so flushed with sweat, her fine black hair like a mantilla over her impure brow, her eyes drugged with the strangest cravings. And as I sipped endless cups of tasteless black coffee, she told me of her every sexual fantasy (basketballers, eskimos) and chuckled from her fur-lined throat, sweat trickling into the hollow of her pronounced clavicle, occasionally brushing from her face that hair with a slow trembling hand, her bare big feet impatient.

When listening to me speak, she had a charming childlike

way of crossing one long arm over her chest. She wore long patterned cheesecloth skirts through which her plain black underpants were visible and beneath them, the full swell of her unknown sex. The laces of her supermarket tennis shoes glowed in the dark. On Wednesday mornings, she studied Greek. She told me she had always been an atheist. Her father was in jail for armed robbery and rape. Telling me this, she shrugged and changed the subject.

One Friday afternoon she was all helplessness, disorder, bony wrists. She kissed my cheek. She blushed. Stepped back. With effort, gestured nonchalantly towards the coffee-table. 'Bought you some roses,' she bravely said, 'they're over there; the only scented ones that I could find. Thought you would like them.' Slight faltering. Gnawed at her thumbnail. Suddenly turned her back to me. I walked over to that bowl of roses and sank my face into their fragrance. Half of them had fully bloomed and hung wantonly open. I stood and looked at them, barely aware of her heightened chatter or the clatter of cheap china cups.

'Join me for dinner,' I said without looking at her and an hour later, she followed me home, that bowl of sexual roses rocking in my arms.

Set the bowl by the bed. Ordered Chinese. Lay on the floor with all the windows opened to the summer night and talked. She drank sloe gin and then grew serious. Her candid glances, those bare big feet drumming a camphor chest. She paused forever, closed her eyes, said she was drunk, said she no longer knew what she was saying, said I was so beautiful, said she had been in love with me for months.

Outside, the shadow of a bat soared into the foliage of a camphor laurel.

Opened those sloe-gin eyes of hers for my reaction.

I was motionless, an exhalation of the night.

On her knees – slowly, trembling – she approached me with all the liquid sugars of her mouth. Flowed into me. There was no resistance. We made love on the floor by the bed, cloaked only by the scent of those unforgettable flowers. Her sex was a revelation: gluttonous, as contoured as those persimmons she loved. I kissed and again kissed that tiny mole on her full pubic mound; I slid my lips over her perineum; I twisted my fingers in her dark fur. Seven days later, she was killed on impact on the pedestrian crossing of that intersection sloping into Greenwich by a white van with no numberplates. Another early winter.

The second of my two female lovers was another matter. An anarchic establishment beauty from an old Australian Catholic family, she was the archetypal fast-mouthed bullion-and-bellies trader and a sucker for cruel men, self-loathing, alcohol and drug abuse. In the inbuilt mirrored wardrobe of her serviced CBD high-rise apartment, thirty-one identical charcoal pinstriped bespoke suits with matching heels. She was acutely sensitive to sound, this sensitivity developed over years of sifting relevant information from the stockmarket's cacophony, a sensitivity evident in the gun-quick inclination of her head and sudden frown. She had bedded one half of the exchange floor and rebuffed the other. The language she spoke was never mine.

As she chopsticked sashimi onto her sharp pink tongue, she attempted to seduce me with the following: 'I was waiting to be filled – waiting for the double O's. I rang Chicago and asked: *who's standing front of me?* and the Anti-Christ said – the Anti-Christ being this sleazebag who fucks around, gets home to his dumb wife at three, changes the hands of the clock to ten, wakes her up to ask her the time, waits until she looks at the clock and tells him ten, kisses her, waits until she falls asleep, then readjusts the hands to three-fifteen, what a prick – the Anti-Christ said: *you've got a couple of Jane Russells right in front of you, pal.* So then I paid up – I paid two – it went down, they rang me with the fill, and I asked: *what the fuck happened to the Jane Russells?* And the Anti-Christ said: *she's gone down on somebody, Deep Throat.*'

In her sleep, she would buck and grip me with the friction of her nightmares, hissing, *dollar/yen, you fuckhead, dollar/yen!* or, *deutsch bucketing, my backside's done!* With her at all times: her three-thousand-dollar digital mobile, her electronic organizer, her pager, a vial of scarlet amphetamines, a sheet of five milligram Valium, her Chanel No.5 atomizer, a dazed passport-booth photograph of me. She would spray herself an asthma attack, consult her organizer, pop a pill and dial the world direct.

There were nights she unexpectedly materialized upon my doorstep, rigid with the urge to part my thighs. She purred in bed, narrowed those sesamoid eyes, groaned in French that I was never, but never, to leave her, sometimes I worried that she would snap in two. Her pager interrupted every tryst. She cooked me fish soup, picked me violets, died a thousand times in sexual ecstasy and cooed sweet nothings in my ear. She was frail and pale and graceful. Her achromatic nipples never hardened, a genetic flaw. Her fluids were oddly chemical and sometimes profuse; she would dip a manicured finger within herself beneath any number of tablecloths at any number of five-star restaurants and then – brimming, glittering, heavily breathing – offer it to my stunned mouth. Indigestion was not to be dismissed. But I was for a time transfixed by the gay insanity of her exceptional and slanted silver eyes. Such lunacy was not uninteresting.

Those sharp pinstriped suits were her salvation. When she disrobed, all was desperation for a love it was not possible for anyone but a parent to entertain. And I was in a private bathysphere; her face was only one of many presences smudged against the glass. But such devotion! With an undertone of heartfelt madness and at least once a day, she would insist: 'I love you so much I could *eat* you.'

To touch her was to dip my fingers into a mirror and find that my reflection adhered and autonomously responded, having assumed a mysteriously new life of its own. The blatant narcissism of the exercise appealed to me. Primary difficulty? Roles. Both traditionally feminine, we were monsters of affected consideration. Allow me. No, allow me. I insist. No, I must – allow me, please. We nearly came to blows over who should empathize or soothe or who should rearrange the chairs. She finally explained to me that as I was her intellectual superior, it was only proper for her to assume the role of nurse or chic assistant and so she baked me fragrant pies, attempted to educate herself in matters of cataclysmic variable stars and in the spare time her demanding work allowed her, darned my tufted sports socks and resewed all my buttons.

The stories of her father were as grossly poignant as my own. Electra to Electra, we would sit facing each other over vats of warming Chianti and slowly cooling tagliatelle on otherwise lambent evenings, chilled by our chilling reminiscences of childhood. Her parents were a Spartan pair, lovers of war. Woks and Wedgwood plates, lampshades and Waterford crystal, plate-glass windows and even the family dog, good Christ! – all smashed, ripped, hurled, or crippled. Her father had affairs with waitresses and lithe young shopgirls; her mother mated with pool-cleaners and the fitters and turners she seduced verbally in local bars: blue-collar workers manned their warship. My lover's only purpose had been to play audience to their Wagnerian battles and reconciliations (which led to further battles and reconciliations and so on and so forth, *ad nauseam*).

So sad, but not enough to keep me.

Worried by the fact that I accepted her passion *cum grano salis*, she eventually resorted (as mad lovers and obsessives always do) to threats. 'Angelica,' she would whisper, those silver eyes silvery slits, 'were I to suicide because of your indifference ...' Such hypotheses made me study her most carefully from the corner of my eye; such hypotheses made me realize that any extrication from her pretty tentacles would have to be executed with a surgical finesse.

Sensing my waning, she flew me to Venice for a vulvate vacation. Together we admired the public clocks, the huge unfurled flags, carnival millinery and the green diseased lagoon. There she bought me a Versace handbag, Prada 'essentials', La Perla lingerie; there we lingered over the necklaces in black-and-gold Cartier. There she bought herself sackfuls of lipsticks in all shades and densities, leaving their traces on green-tea bowls, half-eaten *panini*, the bone stem of her customized toothbrush, on my throat. Dying of apathy, I kissed her in a *caffè* over curdling *caffelattè*. She hunted me down stinking *calli* to make certain I was not telephoning other lovers from public telephone boxes. 'Do you still love me?' she asked me on the hour, every hour, every day. She tried to fondle me in *gondole*. In one of the small toilet cubicles of Harry's Bar, she stripped and then lasciviously asked me to lap her pointed breasts. She bribed the fortune teller sitting at a table in a pool of midnight seawater to tell me we would spend our lives together.

In St Mark's she led me by the hand through the West

Atrium, under the Dome of the Pentecost, past the Crucifixion Mosaic, under the Dome of the Ascension, under the Dome of Christ-Emmanuel and to the Pala d'Oro where, surrounded by the timeless and the exquisite, with that hotly coloured map crushed in one fist and with both fists crushed on her hips, with a furious noise and tarnishing of those precious eyes, she snarled: 'Angelica, I've had it with these saints and sanctity – let's just go back to our suite and *fuck*.'

At the base of the Giant's Staircase, a few feet from the moist green shade of the Arco Foscari, she fell to her knees and struggled to insert her head beneath my skirt. Sansovino's handsome sculptures – helmeted Mars to our left, Neptune without trident to our right – were the only witnesses to our romantic spat (I slammed my new Versace handbag on her head and told her to leave me *alone*). Days later, having recovered from the most monumental sulk, she decided that the *terre verte* shutters of the Calle de Mezo were to be reproduced for the windows of the oppressively architectured Eastern Suburbs villa she had purchased (against my wishes) as a 'little love-nest'. She then slipped her arm through mine, batted those eyelashes and snuggled closer as I frigidly withdrew. No more than behavioural homeostatic mechanisms, her unconscious pursuit of balance.

The ardour of the local *pappagalli* did not distract her from her mission (that is to say, making herself indispensable to me). Her little freckled nose shot high into the air when those enthusiastic and sexually arrogant men pooled their fingertips and made lush *moues* and cried: *ma vieni qui, adorabile! bella – vieni qui!*

She called me her witch, tracing with a single cool white finger the scar across my belly (souvenir of ruptured spleen). My philosopher-king had never in reality been the speedway hero of his dreams. The accident that ended our affair had been too rapid for accurate assimilation and thus my recall can only be impressionistic: the Prince's Highway, burning glass, wrenched flesh, a madly turning wheel, the body of a stranger on the asphalt, blood, the sun one acidic white scintilla then another. The other party, a father of three and lecturer in particle physics, was permanently paralysed. His skull had been torn clean from the first cervical vertebra, causing a massive blood-clot to press against his vulnerable brain-stem and flood his brain with cerebral fluid. His wife, after being confronted by the vegetable that was her husband, became hysterical and had to be restrained by buxom nurses from attacking with a vengeful madness my bruised lover, who was sobbing with all the abandon of the damned.

To cut a long story short: my batty girlfriend predictably slashed her wrists (horizontally, not vertically) when I left her (in a puff of coloured smoke), but was saved from an uncertain death by her aromatherapist (due that afternoon to loosen her tense shoulders). She survived to make (more) millions and marry a sullen starving would-be Shakespearean actor who, before leaving to find himself nubile young men every second Saturday night, made a practice of blackening both her eyes. In later life, her sight disintegrated to the point where she was almost blind and then she finally divorced him and retired to her property in the fire-plagued Blue Mountains with a mastiff.

27

Alone at home, I wasted countless evenings wandering from room to room to room, as if in mourning or awaiting the return of a beloved soldier. Listlessness, and for so many years. I sometimes felt as if there were nothing left to say, as if the heart just sometimes sickened, some distant star of love remaining.

Life struck me as a senseless exercise in tolerance. How long, after all, is it possible to maintain a charade of meaning? The interest I had in contuinity was feigned, was forced. Psychically, I felt annulled. This was a period of nicotine hues, of cigarettes smoked with one shoulder pressed to the cold glass of a window, of sunlight suddenly spilling onto the floorboards of a dim hallway, of silence. And every day, fingering those same worn pages of my memory. I could find nothing in myself but want but could not find the energy to convert that want into a quest. My wish was to be liberated from myself and beyond that, I did not care, I did not care, the devil take me.

I attempted to socialize, but sorely failed. The company of frauds and idiots can set my teeth on edge. I remember three of these in particular (for reasons known only to that capricious agent of the dark subconscious): the divorced mother of three young children, the witless sister of a fellow research scientist, and the sports master of an exclusive girls school. The divorced mother, a woman of thirty who bore an extra decade in her eyes, whose thin dry skin sagged in brown folds from the corners of her nose, voluptuous in youth but now haggard and resentful and exhausted, punished me over a three-hour luncheon. 'My fourth book is now in reprint, you know,' she said. 'I'm *terri*bly lucky to have the children, all that warmth and support, you know,' she said. 'It's not that I'm cynical about men, but I just need my own space in a relationship,' she said. 'Of course, no man worth his salt is ever interested in young women because they have no brains of which to speak,' she said. I had been shovelling *carciofi* and *frittata* into my mouth and heatedly nodding at her every fatuous comment, but when she said, 'You know, Angelica, I like a partner to be more intelligent than I am,' I cracked and, holding her snaky gaze, replied: 'So do I, but I can never *find* one.'

The witless sister of my fellow research scientist was not weathered, but equally unbearable. That trattoria at which we dined was owned by an overflowing ark of Cantonese and through their quacking, she shouted: 'I see my body as a REWARD. My boyfriends have to EARN it. They're never after my BRAIN, so if they want my BODY, they have to, you know, agree to the DEAL.' The deal in question involved first-class travel, sumptuous hotels, swaggering furs, truck-loads of hothouse flowers.

And then the sports master, a pal of an acquaintance married to an outstandingly gifted businesswoman. Jealous of his wife's achievements and eager to restore the balanced distribution of sexual power within his marriage, he struggled to court me. 'I *really* like you, Angelica,' he said. 'No,' he said, 'I mean, I really *like* you.' 'You know something?' he said, 'you have a mind like a steel *trap*.' 'You're quite stunning,' he said. 'I've been thinking,' he said, 'and it occurred to me that we should have an affair. I promise I won't get too involved,' he said, 'just a physical affair … with respect, of course; a *lot* of respect.' 'You're a classy woman,' he said, 'a really classy woman … but with the common touch. Ever considered a career in sales?'

When I read him the usual script (awfully flattered, you're married, impossible, awfully flattered, no), he unloaded his retarded friend into my lap and when I also rejected him, never spoke to me again. This pal of his, a retired decathlete and sentimental teacher, was dulcet in essence but suicidally stupid. His conversation concerned pole-vaulting, muscle-groups, his glory days, corporal discipline, nutrition and the many, many fascinating gears on his new bike.

Not long after this evening, I was again sitting disconsolately on Beulah Street Wharf (bare legs dangling over the jetty, palms flat on the splintering grey wood and staring across the water at the skyscrapers). Suddenly beside me, a heavyset man in his late twenties, a man with twinkling blue eyes and jet-black hair, with the immature paunch of a barfly-in-training and whose thick hairy calves reminded me of the hull columns of great grey offshore rigs, on which algae richly bloom. His smile was artless and he displayed his ruined palms for my inspection. 'Was painting m'boat,' he said. 'Got paint with fibreglass hardener all over m'hands. Can't get it off. Was thinkin' of draggin' 'em behind a bus.'

As he laughed, I saw that his teeth were even and superbly white and that beyond them, there was only darkness.

28

Futility is a dangerous sensation. Amedeo felt he required Grade A drugs with which to face it. He could believe himself a sultan when high on cocaine. Before his income appeared to justify this fantasy, he simply said: 'I'm not in an executive enough position to feel human.' My means of distraction was to stare at the ether; in doing so, I was rendered insubstantial by my very awe. A liberation. Phosphoros, with her great promises of hope and Hesperos, there to sustain the world through every night. Ceres, Pallas, Vesta, Juno, bright Hygeia: remembered as transparent spheres and resulting from these memories, questions which transported me into a consciousness beyond sorrow or flat human defeat.

A smart lover remarked: 'There are times when you make me feel a piece of equipment in a gymnasium.' Others were less perceptive. I recall photographing the partially eclipsed sun in its ascent from a beach near Puerto Escondido in old Mexico – a real spectacle: it could have been a symbol torched by unknown gods. Those sands had been my refuge. I had escaped the persistent attentions of the unlovely Stanton Dean Thug. This slobbering gorilla mistook my (somewhat indiscriminate) sexual attention for intellectual admiration, assuring himself that I let him share my bed because I was astounded by his (putative) grasp of astrophysics. In part, I was to blame for this misinterpretation of intent; to snare him and perhaps as an homage to my skewed mother, I had feigned delightful ignorance (the silverback is partial to such displays of submission and can be seen regally picking his nose at his inferiors in documentaries). Despite the incongruity of our union, it was a pleasing episode. I don't think we ever left the bed.

Thug was an indefatigable and talented – if unsophisticated – bestial realist. A zealot for fellatio, he would stand on my bed like the Colossus of Rhodes, one hand steadied by the wall and the other on his hip, grinning with guileless anticipation at what was to come (that is to say, him). He was also pathologically vain. His bathroom was a shrine to the cosmetic – toners, cleansers, gels, oils, creams, treatments, balms, foams, sprays, the finicky equipment of beauty professionals, shampoos, conditioners, mud-packs, deodorants, vitamin scrubs, colognes. On weekends, fantastically naked but for striped football socks and the pale green cream of an exfoliating masque, he would fill my apartment with his awful bonhomie, listening to himself recite poetry, rearranging my furniture, chiding me about the standard of my domestic order, unpeeling a banana. 'What you need, A, is a man like me to take care of you,' he would magnanimously offer as he waved half a salami or a rolled newspaper. 'Little thing like you – not the most practical mind in the world, let's face it. Girl like you needs a man like me to take charge of things. A lord and master, if you like.'

That big body, those stupid cubits of glorious flesh – so warm, a kind of home. After reaching a chest-beating climax, he would exhale a smile and murmur: 'I'm *very* intelligent, you know.' There were in him angelic qualities known to the beasts of every field. With his imposing shoulders, dumb-guy gait and elementary broken-nosed face, he looked of unprepossessing stock: the offspring of a boxer handsome in his youth and a naive blonde girl, perhaps, or the son of a hypothyroid military man and his squab bootee-knitting wife. The adolescent Thug and his subhuman friends had excelled in forming 'brown-eye pyramids' (a repulsive proletarian obsession involving the clambering of half-naked men atop each other on all fours in formation, so that the family photographer beheld an upwardly diminishing series of sticky damp recta and testicular sinews of varying hues and lengths.)

At every available opportunity, he would vigorously – and with a strong jaw-jutting masculine intensity – scratch what he referred to as his 'nuts'. I forced an agreement: from thereon in, he was permitted to only scratch these nuts of his at home or in a lavatory (and not in restaurants or whilst strolling down the street). 'I've been waiting all my life for a woman who appreciates my brain,' he said. 'It's not every man who has such an impressive portion of meat and two veg,' he said. 'Watch who you're describing as having an "ox-like" build,' he said. 'I want to smack your bottom because you've been insolent,' he said. 'You have to understand, I'm a bit unnimble,' he said.

Sadly, it was not long before he developed all the early indicators of paranoid schizophrenia. He began to insist that he was from the Pleiades. He had been sent to Earth, he said, by aliens as a prophet. The Nazis were alive and well and playing croquet in underground polar bases. He and his leaders would soon be water-skiing on the Moon. Bertrand Russell had pioneered the creation of AIDS as a device to control world population. The CIA, the Catholic Church, the medical profession and the government of the United States of America were conspiring to create a New World Order which would be run by a 300-strong ruling elite known as the Illuminati. Marconi had developed Tesla's original designs of electrically driven solar-energy-powered flying saucers after World War II. The present day city of New Berlin had a population of two million *Supermenschen* engaged in human genetic engineering. The hundreds of thousands of children missing in America had been abducted by the Nazis for the gulag of underground Frankenstein factories for 'batch consignment' slave labour on the Moon. President Clinton and Pope John Paul II had both approved Soul Engineering – soul transplantation, technology-assisted walk-ins, time regression.

'Think about it,' my lover reasoned. 'Where have all those celebrities with strange deaths gone? James Dean? Elvis? Marilyn Monroe?'

As a child, he had been severely and repeatedly beaten by his father and my theory was that part of his brain had finally disengaged. So the only answer was Mexico, really. One minute longer and I would have been passing the hat around for the local madhouse. Mexico was colourful enough and, like Cairo, overpopulated and foully polluted. From its alleyways of rabid dogs and ailing children I flew to Port-au-Prince, where I paid to watch a voodoo spectacle in which a foaming, coffee-fanged fanatic bit the head from a poor struggling chicken. This performance had its emetic effect, and that hawk's esurience for blood encouraged me to leave long before my scheduled departure date.

In Sydney, I accepted a part-time position as a research scientist at the Anglo-Australian Observatory. For three days or so every six months throughout my late twenties, I visited azure-and-violet Siding Spring Mountain, where on volcanic rock of a thirteen-million-year vintage is situated the Observatory's telescope. Otherwise, my time was spent both on research and developing new instruments. Broad division stellar astronomy, *mon amour*.

The man with whom I worked, Dr Septimus Dream, was a Nobel Prize-winning eccentric, a specialist in the field of cataclysmic variables. Comparatively, my area of binary stars was far less glamorous, but still challenging. The observing programmes active around me: lithium-deficient halo stars, the extragalactic distance scale, polarimetric probing of red-giant winds, faint quasar luminosity function, the eye of the Tornado nebula. Celestial poesy, and a world away from that which so eroded me. I enjoyed writing occasional articles for newspapers and scientific publications and was regarded as an authority on certain stars – in particular, the Algols, pulsars and beta Pictoris, a single star embraced by a cloud of gas which appears to be an embryonic planetary system.

The study of such things imbued in me a faith in life.

29

While I was engaged to William (whom Aldo had always referred to as 'that little English faggot' or 'Jane Austen'), my mother and her husband had relocated from Sydney to Westchester County in the prodigious state of New York. They purchased a grand old estate not far from the extremely particular Westchester Country Club, where Aldo exorcized select demons through the gun club, networked on the golf course, and where my mother swayingly partook in tennis matches and ritzy tailgate picnics.

Nearby Greenwich was a wealthy town, loved by many for its tax concessions and the home of certain great investment firms. Aldo had decided to stitch up large amounts of foreign money by creating a special tax structure in the Dutch Antilles. He knew some guys, he was looking for some fun. The law had become a grind for him. Wanted a change and so arranged it. My brother remained in New York, where he was about to suffer the first of innumerable cocaine-related seizures. 'I'm a drug pig,' he conceded on the telephone, 'but as long as it doesn't affect my work, who *cares*?'

The nights were killing. I slept or did not sleep like one haunted by an atonal loss. My soul, like all enchanted souls, was perpetually alert; I no longer swallowed sleeping pills as they reduced my life to one vague hangover.

It was as if some apple-knuckled witch or warlock had cursed me. I would lie awake in bed, hopelessly aware of my very existence – the colubrine nature of limbs, of the dorsal arrangement; the exact fall of flesh from the fertile pelvis; that ability to supersede the physiognomy during heightened emotional states; the fervours of love and its ribald blueprint in every cell; the memory of evolution – spores, fins, glistening gills, the tail suggested by the coccyx – all of it spectacular and so profoundly ordinary. Such thoughts obsessed me. I felt as if I were being annihilated by my own consciousness. Such awareness, solitude, the suppression of urges so intense they made me feel that at any minute I could have flown apart, exploded, my soul a cracker-shower of scintillant blue stars: these things combined became a burden. Simplicity eluded me. In the early hours of the morning I would listen to the owls, those two-eyed vivisectors, their vigils of unrest twinning my own. There were conflagrations behind my eyelids, wars, incredible songs. A stern god had commanded me to examine, reconsider, edit, constantly devise new paradigms. It was a prison of perception, certainly. There was in me always the suggestion of a sonar – an ear tuned to the universe, a mechanism of ultimate industry: I was my own timing device.

It gradually became obvious that the prospect of losing control unnerved me. This sparkling consciousness, then, was only a fear of being invaded. I had not for so many years felt safe. My poor spirit hovered over chasms. I really needed help, but did not know where to begin looking. It seemed to me that there would never be any help to be had.

I suppose the only real sustenance I had during this oppressive time was a dream. Its costumes and sets were periodically redesigned, but it fundamentally remained the same. I dreamed of an important love. I dreamed of a love upon which I could to some extent rely, a thing of solidity and worth, true, wholesome, so erotic. I dreamed that some day, somewhere, somehow, someone would emerge from the complicated colours of the world and announce himself a miracle: my complement. The idea of a productively intense emotional commitment absorbed me; I had grown bored with the macaronics of obsession. Obsession is only ever an interaction with one's neglected needs and nurtured deficiencies, never real communication. It is also the behavioural mode most prevalent in this emotionally neglectful culture, an interesting reflection.

To illustrate: I recall meeting in the changing-rooms of a South Molton Street boutique a victim of this general neglect, the sister of a girl whom I had known at my first English school. A fraying blonde with bloodshot eyes, haggard and sterile, she was a relic of the days when the practice of promiscuity and ingestion of psilocybin mushrooms were considered to be intellectually liberating actions and not exercises in psychopathology. Her chainsaw monologue: circular, self-referential, mindless, delivered on the edge of paranoid hysteria; a monologue concerning the man or men who had beaten and betrayed her, the various minor celebrities with whom she had snorted cocaine and then coupled in the toilets of elite nightclubs, parties and partings, weddings and woes, art and injustice, her fading looks and irrelevance, and that stale champagne breath of hers, carbon monoxide in my face. Children are not legally permitted to drink alcohol, its premise being forgetfulness; thus it can be said that children must wait for adulthood to forget their childhoods through champagne.

And like so many others, she was compensating for lost time.

This love of mine, this complement, as yet had no discernible facial features. The Magritte cloud had its purposes. He was tall, I knew; such knowledge is stored in blood, is stored in bone. The image of one's truest love is secreted in forgotten dreams. I knew him able to distinguish the coloratura through the elegy and that there was a tempest at the core of him, a sexual liquid, good intention. And he was able to withstand my strength.

Weakness was of no use to me. I wished for an equal, for a man capable of formulating his own laws and with the discipline to implement them, a man who could not be scorched by the hottest faith and who was as engrossed as I was by emotion – his own and mine. *How do you feel*: words rarely heard outside the rooms of medical professionals and words I had been hankering all my life to hear. *How do you feel?* And that was it, my heart's desire purpure: a man of distinctive processes, of kindness, a man as honest as a knife.

In essence, I wished for a magician. The scent of him was already with me, a suggestion of it through my every dawn as if he were already close or fast approaching, the suggestion of white ash and columbine – and then it disappeared.

My lustfulness was not indicative of any lack of magic in me, rather the only way in which I properly expressed myself. It was my idiom. Although I was no longer the angelic wreckage William had seduced in that ostentatious Chelsea apartment, I still retained the flavour of virginity – a smatch of cool theory, some twang of inutility. Certain men were besotted by these very things and wanted only to corrupt or own – as one would own a goldfish or a grove of orange trees – my oddball purity. Others were violently attracted to my shadows; emotional disorders were their daily fare. They demanded psychoses, a gorgon, sabre-toothed fucking, bloodshed and curses, oestrogen poisoning, the lascivious snap of the *vagina dentata*. In the era which produced the formal moral visual code, the Hollywood director Ernst Lubitsch conveyed sexual arousal in his silent films by focusing on appropriately suggestive objects (the roaring train, a sad banana, dessert silver heaped with ravaged figs, a drain). I was not dissimilar in my methodology.

All hubris, detritus.

To have been able to extend a fourth-dimensional hand through any of my lovers' breasts and found the labour of a heart synchronous with my own: a foolish wish, perhaps, but also mine and true to me.

BOOK TWO

A LYCANTHROPIC GOD

I

My mother swapping lipsticks and narcotics with her girlfriends; Aldo thickly discussing capitalization strategies and incremental increases in net productivity and the propylaea of his mistresses with his associaties; my brother ploughing cheerleaders and the next morning, whilst licking every trace of cocaine from his hand-mirror, commanding his assistant to call the previous night's cheerleader to arrange another date; my father, nowhere. These factors added to others were the precedents to change.

There had to be new worlds – green and map blue, lake-braceleted – to love.

2

An unassuming advertisement sandwiched between an article about a serial rapist and a minor celebrity's weekly column in the local paper brought me to the modest sock of a questionably blonde divorcee. For the first time in my life, I wanted to understand this world that surged outside my windows, and had decided to shuck privilege by plunging into the educational experience of 'sharing a flat'. The arrangements to have my own apartment rented out had been concluded. Knocked twice, very efficiently, and between the preparatory backslide of my knuckles and their third purposeful rap, she wrenched the door open, the resulting influx of air almost causing me to fall into her arms.

'You must be Annabel!' she sang.

'Angelica,' I corrected.

'Angelica, yeah – 'course!' She gestured as if swatting at a fly.

'Caroline,' I said.

She smiled. 'You're early but that's fine, no problem.'

Shadowed the buzzard, trying not to stare. She made two cups of tea from two tea-bags pulled from a jar labelled TEA. She stirred in four teaspoons of refined white sugar from a jar labelled SUGAR. The milk was poured from a jug on which was painted a brown smiling cow. She chattered happily as she served the libation. And what a lovely suit! Where *did* I get it? And wasn't it *chilly*? She tensed her swimming champion's shoulders and went: BRRRRRRRRRRRR! If only the nights were as warm as the mornings! If only the mornings were as hot as the afternoons! If only the afternoons were as cool as the evenings! She brightly paused and then indicated with dyed and cruelly tweezed eyebrows the new Victorian-look table-lamp she had snaffled at a Victorian-look table-lamp sale. What a bargain! You'd almost think it was the real thing. With evaluative rapidity, she blinked over the lip of her cup and recrossed her legs. Her white high-heeled shoes had been recently resoled. Her tights were a shade of pink I had never before seen. Her snug skirt was so brief I could see the harsh scarlet of her panties through the hose. She compulsively smoothed her hair, still holding the cup in its vibrating saucer.

I smoked a cigarette: this pleased her. She felt free to indulge. It was like being a leper these days, really – just like a bloody leper. You'd think we weren't getting cancer from nuclear fallout and car fumes every second of the day. She suddenly raised an index finger. Speak, memory! Some nutter on Chalk Farm station platform – you know, like this (she crossed her eyes and let her tongue loll), *actually tugged the fag from her mouth in front of all the other peak-hour commuters and called her a filthy C-U-N-T!* Talk about dying of embarrassment. And what about the bloody British government, emptying institutions of these lamebrains! No wonder she had emigrated. And besides, the weather was much nicer here. Fluidly, her eyes moved along my body and stuttered only on my diamond ring. Settling back into the two-seater sofa, she was distracted by silent calculations. She then sat up. She wanted to divine my domestic aptitude. I lifted my head, half-excited by the horror of her, but also wary. Paused. Tapped my cigarette into a clown's face ashtray and steadily gazed into her eyes. Said nothing much to the effect of something. She paused again – a hydromagnetic charge in the air – and then expansively flipped open the cigarette packet for another puff.

'Should show you 'round then, eh?' Her words escaped from the filter of her cigarette and as she lit it, the birthmark she obscured with thick foundation on her left cheek became apparent.

Placing her lighter by the new table-lamp, she stood. This tasteful living space that I saw before me was her very own. Co-director of a slobs-and-slags dating agency specializing in tick-the-box questionnaires and disco nights on hired barges, she had dragged the company up through the economy by its unwilling ears. And what was love if not an anodyne for fiscal miseries? That market never bottomed; there would always be a demand for love. And as for the supply, well – that was where Miss Brine stepped in. A few years ago she had tried her unflatteringly venous hand at a mail-order pornographic videotape business: it was a lark and lucrative, but then with this and that and the taxation department – not that it was my concern now, was it? Just a mess, a *mess*, a bloody mess.

Which wasn't to say it hadn't been the best time of her life. She waved the hand she had tried at a mail-order pornographic videotape business at the bathroom. I slowly nodded as she expounded on the aesthetic agony behind the arrangement of hotel soaps on the window sill, and after she had she pointed out the dusted tropical plant in its wicker basket by the heated towel rack, I felt it only proper to examine – with a selection of carefully approving expressions – the miniature teddy bear propped up by the enamelled tissue-box on the cistern. The bear's name, she admitted with some torment, was Napoleon. Napoleon le Teddy Bear what had been given to her by the Great Love Of Her Life (a Parisian personnel consultant she had met during a sweaty game of catch-the-egg at Club Med somewhere in the radioactive South Pacific).

Her voice suddenly softened and she leaned against the white tiles of the wall, passing the bear from one hand to the other. In a trance, she told me that she would never forget the human crotch-to-buttock chain the group of revellers had been asked to form. 'The G.O. (*gentil organisateur*) asked us to swivel our hips and then thrust them while shouting: FIRECRACKER, FIRECRACKER, BOOM! BOOM! BOOM!' Here she sighed (very long sigh). And then: 'That guy what gave me Napoleon was right behind me, and every time he finished swivelling and began to thrust, he would lean close to my ear and ask me if I liked aubergines.'

Again, she sighed. 'And this,' she sadly said, indicating the cistern with her desquamated elbow, 'is Napoleon's Waterloo.'

The room I was to inhabit was a reasonably sized cube of pink air overlooking the square lawn. As I looked out of one of the two windows, I saw the reflection of a flying ibis from the Botanical Gardens in the closed upper window of the house next door. Before me, citrus-green and orange G-string Lycra leotards hung dripping from the clothesline. The instructors at the local gymnasium, she told me, were ever-so-good, especially Ludovic, who was (and here she girlishly minimized her shoulder-girth and made a stupid little noise) just *scrummy*.

Otherwise: cheap pink carpet, plasterwork, all doors painted a glossy white. We passed the cane bookshelf and its popular astrology books, bodice-rippers, guides to stress relief, film-star biographies and beauty manuals (no dictionary). I was still nodding, a contender. She chewed on a tasty hangnail as she dismissed the living room (seen that, hadn't I?) and escorted me to her den of sin. The centrepiece was a Victorian-look king-sized bed heaped with lace pillows and a small red stuffed synthetic satin heart. Dried flowers, plaster plaques. In the corner, a hat-stand festooned with camisoles and French knickers and beribboned basques. The dressing table was crowded with framed photographs (some dire mongrel leaping for a stick, his shining phallus perfectly in focus; a broken colliery town set on a shore of cinders, rusting car-parts, and beer-cans; humiliated mules, their lice-infested ears protruding from the brims of straw hats bunched with plastic fruits; the regional manager of an accounting firm with a rose between his teeth; Brine fellating an empty bottle of *spumante*). Pressed to the wall, a handsome wardrobe. She quickly kicked the trunk of the vacuum cleaner back under the bed as she closed the door behind us.

I followed her into the kitchen, enchanted land of elves.

She unnecessarily displayed the boring contents of her cupboards, made inane references to cast-iron saucepans and detergents, straightened a print of Miss Muffet on her tuffet and yanked open the door of the refrigerator, inside which was: the brown smiling cow, a tank of purified water, a jar of crusty chutney, cheap Chablis, a few disgusting cheeses, an opened can of 'Diet Farmhouse Vegetable' soup, a cling-wrapped bowl of cabanossi, three bruised peaches, half a greying head of lettuce, a black tomato, ten bleached eggs, a gnawed mass of nameless pâté on a saucer, a molested chicken roll (its ingredients printed in microscopic lettering on the wrapping), two tubs of sugarless raspberry yoghurt, a wizened passionfruit, six bottles of nail varnish, a 200 ASA Kodachrome film, a leaking blue plastic bag of chicken livers, and half a squeezed lime.

With her hands behind her, leaning on the aluminium sink, she nattered (at a speed which suggested that she hoped I would not register any information which could be used against her in the future) about the bond and rent and gas and electricity and telephone and water and chores and extras and laundry and shopping and overnight guests and the two twisted lesbians upstairs. The lesbians? Oh, yeah – it was enough to make you sick, what with all these perverts carrying on. Carrying on? Well, yeah. Just carrying on – nothing in particular, mind you, but just *things* – you just could *tell*. She picked at her teeth with the painted white acrylic fingernail of her little finger, pouted at the subsequent damage to her manicure and then, with the professional sparkle of a failed mail-order pornographic video entrepreneur, she chirped: 'So when can you move in?'

Shrugged and muttered something about Tuesday.

'Great!' Her teeth were the picket fence circumnavigating a neglected rural rectory. 'Annabel,' she said with feeling, 'I know we're gonna have a real *laugh*.'

3

Ah, Caroline Brine – with your aversion to bohemians and homosexuals, students and 'foreigners', with your lacerated womb and scullery rat's brain, with your phosphorescent dildoes and potted African violets, haunted by the ghost of your aborted baby and contaminated by envy, you freckled, you artificially tanned, you stupefyingly bland and vicious mediocrity – even after all these years, I still detest you.

'Know what I mean?' she was saying, having finished with the turkey-talk. 'The others who applied were all just barking. One was a darkie – stank to the high heavens, just revolting; another said he shagged is girlfriend in a specially designed coffin and did I mind; and the other said that she was an artiste – which was absolute bloody rubbish, of course. She just glued broken plates to a piece of board and threw red paint at them.' Inelegantly, she struggled into a box-jacket studded with brass buttons. 'When I was married to Stan, we never had these problems. Lived in the nicest little cottage in Chipping Sodbury before moving to Piddle, in Dorset. Our neighbours there were always nice. But you get all kinds in a big city. Can't even leave the door unlocked in case some granny killer breaks in and buggers you before chopping your head off, spray-painting rude words all over the walls and then stealing all your money.' She thoughtfully paused. 'Mind you, the pubs here are a lot more fun.'

The 'girls' were waiting for her at the Café Olé. She shook my hand, asked me if her mascara had smudged, and smoothed what was left of an unruly eyebrow with her thumb.

'See you Wednesday, then,' she said.

'Tuesday,' I corrected.

'Yeah, whatever – see you then, I gotta go.' She slammed the door behind us, overtook me at a cracking pace and then vanished with a flourish around the corner.

4

Saturday and its chore-virtue. With my furniture in storage, my books boxed, my clothes in tissue and cellophane, my astronomical equipment cased and my soul *in extremis*, I made the unusual decision to attend a society crush. I had attended thousands of such events with my mother in my teenage years – shifting archipelagos of tight black dresses, broken accents, pretentious conversations and good gold. And this was a very serious invitation (gilt-edged, hand-delivered), issued only to high-level types (obscure professors, drug-loving painters, literary bankers, successful playwrights, concert pianists, crazed novelists, real and artificial beauties, advertising hucksters, heirs, professional killers).

The hostess Dorota was a supple and covertly bisexual Polish Catholic sculptor with skeletal hands and great black sucking orbits and a thing for intellectual girls. Her shatteringly dull husband (or 'Horse', as she mockingly called him) was a financial systems analyst, a valiant student of the advanced topological conceptions of Riemannian geometry and its application to economics, a sickly onanist given to wearing open-necked shirts and smoking weekend marijuana, a reformed cocaine-addict and lover of yachts and thorough-breds and meditations on tantric sex and who, despite his suggestive sobriquet, had considerable difficulty in 'getting it up'. *Plus ça change*. The consequential frustrations of the situation were manifested through their perfunctory embraces and the tinny manner in which they applauded each other for performing the most basic domestic duties ('Isn't Horse a *gen*ius?? He watered the plants all by him*self*!').

Perhaps to compensate for this half-life, Dorota collected noisy people. Their perpetual drama distracted her from marital tensions and generated in her a warm amusement. She was powerfully pretty when she smiled. Her parties were famous for their exchanges of information. The modern world was wholly intellectual in outlook, after all: art, music, literature – from the bitty Kandinsky to the dissonant Glass, from the limited Beuys to the nasty Sartre – disdainful of harmony, of the heart's detail. I had no wish to be collected, but she was difficult to ignore. Those overt black eyes! She really persisted. Wearing me out with her melodious telephone manner and beseeching little notes, she chased me as ardently as the most obsessive beau and eventually, she caught me. Arrived early and depressed. Positioned myself on one of their state-of-the-art gunmetal stools and watched Horse help shred smoked salmon for the buffet. In his cool grey scaly tones, he asked me how I was feeling and as I expressionlessly told him, his pale earthworm fingers slipped in between the ocherous and bloodless sheets of flesh and as if digitally programmed, he nodded at regular intervals, unhearing, concentrating instead on the distribution of fresh fennel and listening for the footfall of his wife.

Dorota materialized in a snakeskin sheath and spike-heeled shoes, her black hair fanning out behind her like a cape. Her every noise was practised and appropriate ('My *dear*! And how *love*ly to see you! How long *has* it been? And what a *charm*ing ring! From another of your innumerable swains? You drop-dead doxy, you! Come give Auntie Dorota a *hug*!' et cetera). She then wandered about the kitchen, criticized the preparation of food and when the injured Horse defended himself, berated him for spilling the salad dressing, quickly looked at my legs, patted him on the cheek, danced away from his emerging arms, squeezed my cold thigh, praised my artful sense of presence, applied her liquid gaze to my mouth, swore brutally as Horse's ageing Rottweiler shoved its muzzle into her cunt, rearranged the show of waratahs, offered to manipulate my 'tight' shoulders, and laughed a shower of tourmalines when the doorbell chimed. Sped to the door.

Phoney after superficially interesting phoney trickled in. The room suddenly seemed suffocatingly overcrowded; it was as if the walls were closing in. Horse oversaw the serving of the wine and water and I stiffly stood by a framed seventeenth-century Flemish damask napkin depicting unicorns and deer, hunters in pantaloons and rearing stallions. Stared at the costly and obscene lithographs and at the famous actor who stumbled in, already stinking drunk. She knocked a Portuguese ceramic sculpture from its plinth and then stood, dangerously swaying, her eyes widening to marigolds as her art-dealer lover apologized for the mishap. Dorota flowed amongst them like a stream of patterned water – '*Dar*ling! *An*gel! *Lov*ed one! *Kit*ten!' – while her husband furiously rinsed two Holmes & Edwards oyster forks in the sink.

Through the crowd and through the crowd and still that dark ephemera.

Discovered a half-lit niche and hid there, clutching in one hand a glass of ice and sparkling water. Two hours at the most and then I would proffer my excuse of a migraine. Pooled on a sofa and with their backs to me, two of the country's professional socialites – the pinch-faced blonde formerly married to the ore king, the buttocky redhead formerly married to America's most successful plastic surgeon.

The Blonde: 'I rang Gabriel this morning. I'm interested in having a look around the highlands for a little … cottage. I wanted a little place to go to on weekends, so I thought I'd give him a call and ask him for some advice, but … he definitely is *tot*ally strange. Francis was saying that he's *never* direct … like, Francis asked him what his handicap for golf was and Gabriel said – oh, he said something which didn't mean *any*thing. He couldn't give Francis a direct answer.'

The Redhead: '*Ser*iously?'

The Blonde: 'Francis said that he doesn't have any friends, either.'

The Redhead: 'Well, you know why, don't you? He's *tot*ally paranoid. Do you know that when he drove me back from his property - after spending twelve hours with me – when he drove me back – I'd taken a bag to pop my jods in, and we got into the car –'

The Blonde: 'What exactly *hap*pened that day?'

The Redhead: 'Well, nothing much –'

The Blonde: 'Are you sure about that?'

The Redhead: 'Well, I mean, it's not as if –'

The Blonde: 'I think he's incredibly insecure.'

The Redhead: 'He's not like Jeffers because Gabriel is honest, but there's something of –'

The Blonde: 'Oh, he's not, apparently. He's not honest.'

The Redhead: 'How do you know?'

The Blonde: 'Well, Francis just said that he's – he's – he's not honest, so ...'

The Redhead: 'That doesn't seem fair.'

The Blonde: 'Well, I don't know – I mean, look, I don't know him well enough to say.'

The Redhead: 'I just think he's astoundingly rude.'

The Blonde: 'I don't think he's rude, but he still hasn't returned Francis's call. I've left him a message to call me. It'll be interesting to see if he gets the message –'

The Redhead: 'Oh, he gets *all* his messages. And you know another thing about Gabriel? He *never* answers the phone. He always gets his –'

The Blonde: 'That's not strange.'

The Redhead: 'No – at *home*. He never answers the phone at home. He gets that Venezuelan housekeeper to –'

The Blonde: 'Well, I understand that ... I *hate* answering the phone.'

The Redhead: 'Paranoia! When we got into the car at the end of the day, I could see him peering in my bag to make sure I hadn't *stolen* anything.'

The Blonde: 'Well, what does that mean?'

The Redhead: 'He doesn't trust *any*body.'

The Blonde: 'But that means he's not trustworthy himself. People who are really paranoid about things like that are really dishonest themselves. I *really* know that. Compulsive liars and thieves are always projecting that onto others.'

The Redhead: 'He was trying so hard not to be obvious about it –'

The Blonde: 'Sure you're not imagining it?'

The Redhead: 'Positive. Absolutely positive. It got to the point where I *al*most suggested that he frisk me to make sure I hadn't tucked one of his commissioned bronze sculptures into my panties.'

The Blonde: 'Same feeling you get in some shops, you know? You just don't feel like looking any more because they're looking at you as if you're about to steal something.

Well, at least you know not to take it personally; you know that he's obviously got some incredible ... *block* ... in his personality. Francis said it was no wonder he doesn't have any friends.'

The Redhead: 'None that I know of. He's *so* lonely. The loneliest man I've ever known. But he doesn't let anyone *in*. He doesn't even let anyone *close*.'

The Blonde: 'Chelsea's after him.'

The Redhead: 'What? When did this all happen?'

The Blonde: 'Didn't I tell you? I can't *believe* I didn't tell you! She separated from –'

The Redhead: '*No!*'

The Blonde: 'Mmmmmmmmn-huh. Found him in bed with his –'

The Redhead: 'Not his secretary!'

The Blonde: 'His astrologer. He's been *totally* strange since he went to that ashram last July. So she's on the prowl for a meal-ticket.'

The Redhead: 'She is just so ... fat. I'll *die* if she gets Gabriel.'

The Blonde: 'No chance. I don't think he wants anybody. Every woman in this town has tried to bag him. Every woman in the *world*. He had Cordelia Frankincense after him forever.'

The Redhead: 'Cordelia *Frank*incense?'

The Blonde: 'Yah. One of the richest girls in the world. And soooooo beautiful. He didn't want a bar of her. Said she had a brain the size of a pea.'

The Redhead: 'Well, Chelsea's *gross*.'

The Blonde: 'She *has* gained around the hips, hasn't she?'

The Redhead: 'Totally gross. And she looks so *old*.'

The Blonde: 'She looks her age.'

The Redhead: 'That's what I mean. You should give her Michael's number.'

The Blonde: 'Michael?'

The Redhead: 'My ex-husband. He'd rip her hips off and sew on some tits.'

The Blonde: 'I thought you meant *Michael*.'

The Redhead: 'Which Michael?'

The Blonde: 'My little indiscretion.'

The Redhead: 'Oh, the one Francis doesn't know about?'

The Blonde: 'Mmmmmmmmn-huh.'

The Redhead: 'Whatever happened to him, anyway?'

The Blonde: 'Oh, it just all ... you know, it just –'

The Redhead: 'I wonder if he'll return your call.'

The Blonde: 'Michael?'

The Redhead: 'No, Gabriel.'

The Blonde: 'Well, I don't see why not. I mean, I'm certainly not interested in him. I just want his advice on highland properties. I thought he could show me –'

The Redhead: 'Are you sure you're not interested in him?'

The Blonde: 'Not my type. We have nothing in common. Nothing at all. I mean, I hardly know what to say to him when I *see* him – he's just so *to*tally strange. You know what these super-brilliant men are like. Furtive ... minds. You never know what they're thinking. I really think Gabriel's an Enigma. A total Enigma. I just want his advice. I mean, I can't even *imagine* us together. Can you imagine us together? He's just too weird. I mean, he's such a *loner*! He never turns up to anything. Always accepts invitations and then doesn't ... Francis told me that he'd agreed to go to a big luncheon at the Shark Pool for – for that man, I can't think of his name. So, anyway, they had, you know – those place-cards with calligraphy and everything and Gabriel just didn't *show*. His chair was empty all afternoon. The only empty chair at the table. So that proves what I was saying before. He's a real Enigma. And anyway, he loves riding and I love skiing and he refuses to ski any more, so ... I mean, he's quite handsome and charming and ... no, I'm not remotely interested in him. Strange you should mention us being together, though, because a number of people have suggested that I ditch Francis and make a play for him. I mean, I suppose I could learn to enjoy riding, but I don't think so. And hills make me feel so middle class. I prefer the mountains.'

The Redhead: 'If you prefer the mountains, why do you want a cottage in the highlands?'

The Blonde: (after a long pause) 'I thought I might start – I thought I might start, you know – '

The Redhead: 'Start what?'

The Blonde: 'Start – start studying some ... intellectual ... things ... oh, look – *I* don't know! Stop asking me all these questions! I'm not *after* Gabriel! He's all yours ... that is, unless Chelsea gets to him first. I mean, you can *have* the man. Take him! I just wanted his advice on property. I need somewhere tranquil to expand my *mind*.'

5

A lifetime passed. My third glass of ice and sparkling water. The eighth cigarette. I felt as if I were completely immaterial, a thing of esoteric doctrines, nonexistent. The blonde and her redheaded friend had moved over to the table and were discreetly picking at the salmon. At the other end of the room, the wife of a property developer, her lacquered bouffant a kind of wicker basket, was insanely laughing at something said to her by her Swedish gigolo. And then, just as I was about to disappear into my own sense of implausibility, a brown voice suddenly beside me: 'I was raised to believe that a man should never display any emotion aside from anger – whether that anger was homicidal or not was never the issue. It was the only acceptable emotion. Sheer aggression.'

I slowly turned to face the voice. Standing confidently to my right: a chunky brown-skinned man with brown hair and brown eyes and a brown mouth and wearing a brown jacket and a light brown shirt and brown pants and dark brown loafers and holding a large glass of brown beer. His smile was crooked.

'The name's Howard,' he amiably said. 'Howard Brown. Lecturer in Men's Studies at the University of Technology. Dorota's husband is one of my students. Howard Brown.' I shook his hot wet butcher's hand. The crooked smile remained. 'I was raised,' he resumed, 'to believe that real men fucked women – as many as possible, as often as possible, and as conspicuously as possible – and that's what I did. That's *all* I did. I was an ex*treme* conformist. Total rigidity.' He paused for a mouthful of beer and then smackingly swallowed it. 'Our society produces men who have an experience of emotion that is bipolar: elation or depression, with little in between. No subtleties. No room for the refinement of any concept. Our society produces men who believe that if they stop performing – even for a minute – everyone will jeer at them and leave.' Admiring his own sagacity, he stroked his thigh with his flattened palm and smiled without exposing his teeth.

'I was raised,' he continued as he stared through my eyes, 'to believe that if I was not a winner, I was *per se* a loser. I could not under any circumstances come second. Nope.' He shook his head. 'Nope. When I look back on it now, I see the perception of manhood with which I was raised as being so utterly simplistic that I find it hard to believe that my forefathers were able to keep it up without just dying of sheer boredom.' That lipless smirk. 'I simply don't understand why my father didn't one day just stop breathing because his life was so utterly *boring*.'

Spiritual stasis: I blinked, confused and dismayed by everything and everyone and by Howard Brown, who was still beside me and droning, a breastplate of sweat slowly forming on his shirt-front. '– *vast* areas of experience that many other men had access to, even though they were just like me in terms of what they thought it was all about,' he was saying. 'For me, it was a matter of discovering my own identity. There was a time a few years ago when I virtually could not get through a day without seeing some poignant thing that reminded me of something of which I'd been deprived by my father, and working up tears as a result. It can still happen to me now, but the stimulus has to be something more central to my existence ... more to the core of me, but yeah: once a man is capable of shedding tears, the madness which preceded them dissipates. But I mean,' and here he jammed his little finger in his ear and squelchingly rotated it before suppressing a belch, 'I mean, it's not like things are as they were before except I sometimes cry – far from it. For years, I went through numerous days when I considered ... I never got to the point where I *seri*ously considered ...'

He courageously inhaled and then, with a buccaneer's defiance, tipped the last of that brown beer down his systematically working throat, his forearm tensed and his low forehead varnished with perspiration, and closed his brown eyes and stood there – sturdy, placid, resolute, his brown neck the trunk of a protected oak. Opening his eyes not to look at me, but in the interests of adding to the impact of his oratorio: 'I never did get to the point where I *seri*ously considered suicide, but I did think about voluntarily entering a clinic staffed by doctors trained to deal with the intricacies of acute male crisis, a problem endemic in our society. And why? Because the acknowledgment of sensitivities previously considered antithetical to masculine identity cannot only seriously threaten the average man's sense of gender, but also opens a real can of worms as far as experiencing extreme emotional pain is concerned.'

I lit another cigarette and exhaled so that the smoke – warm after circulating like a wish within me and tinged a blue in which translucent fibrils trembled and were lost – rose from my lungs like a reversed wave in which I imagined myself spinning, a pale and slender spool, pared of air and then I would be fluidly unconscious, nothing but the shadow of a pearl in a dreamed ocean.

Beside me, Howard Brown was still talking.

He was, by now, ecstatic; confession liberated him from any pretence of interest in those around him. '– want to know when the change in me occurred. Well, let me see. That's right – it happened in the underground McDonald's outside the Hoyts cinema complex. I'd just ordered a Big Mac and – no, it wasn't a Big Mac ... I'd ordered a Quarter Pounder, that's right – a Quarter Pounder and a large serving of fries and a chocolate thickshake and one of those apple pies that look like an outbreak of cystic acne ... these details are significant, I feel, and in themselves a pertinent comment on popular culture ... and I was standing there, just about to take the plastic tray with its little sheet of paper decorated with drawings of Ronald McRapist – which, if you look at it in a cultural sense, is essentially what the character is – so I was standing there, looking at my Quarter Pounder and at the one disturbingly crushed chip that was hanging like a broken arm from the yellow bars of its cardboard box, when I suddenly saw – as if in a movie – The Void.'

The immensity of this recollection filled his voice with a real gravity. 'I suddenly saw – as if *struck* by lightning – and that is no exaggeration – I suddenly saw my life flash before me and then I panicked. I understood that I had never really been myself, but that I had been acting out the role ordained by my father, whose own role was ordained by his father, whose role was ordained by his father, *ad infinitum*. I realized that I was not a man, but an actor reading the script of a character he had been told was a man. I was just a miasma – a miasma in trousers, a miasma of misconceptions and inherited perceptions. Brown fog. These realizations were occasioned by the fact that I'd been living entirely in my head for my whole life with nothing of the heart to sustain me.' He paused as if expecting an ovation. And then: 'I eventually stopped thinking of the world in such a way that I could only see myself as this unique colossus striding through it, indifferent to the ordinary nourishments that ordinary little people require. I finally learned to communicate.'

That crooked smile returned. From the pungent foam streaking his empty glass, he looked to me. 'It's been a real pleasure to meet you, Ms …?'

My voice was new to my ears.

'It's rare to meet a woman who understands the difference between the particular and the universal,' he decided with unique charmlessness. 'I've really enjoyed talking to you, but as my partner – who is suffering from pre-menstrual tension – has just walked in, I feel that I should go and be supportive.' Again, that hot wet butcher's hand.

I watched as his chunky brown back was reabsorbed by the crowd, the palm clutching my glass of melting ice now numb.

The expression I had sustained for him was one I reserved for those in need: the essence of listening. Where another would have shoved his puling face into the nearest tureen of borscht, I remained – if only externally – cool, calm, and culpably collected. I had been left standing, my right hand a petrified claw, it was as if my head were vibrating with the stuff of a thousand meaningless exchanges, and for an intensely frightening moment I thought that I had lost the ability to breathe and felt unnaturally light-headed, my knees so weak, and had to balance my shaking hand against the wall and then, when I thought I was in danger of bursting into wretched tears, composed myself and pushed past two guffawing corporate troubleshooters to hurry up the stairs (where I could hide, where I could hide).

Bad Vietnamese prints of rice-fields. In the centre of an otherwise empty room, Horse's Shapemaster Toning Table and an exercise bicycle, over the handlebar of which hung tangled a pair of headphones. That cacophony of words! Unwanted information sometimes had the effect of making me feel as if my unlatched soul was sailing away until it paused, pellucid silk, rippled by the winds over Reunion, beneath which a huge plume of magma infernally slurs.

Dorota had left her bedroom door open; of course I was not paying attention and walked straight in, convinced that it was the bathroom. Opened my eyes. In the place of the bathtub I had been expecting, Dorota's bed: a stadium designed for internationally acclaimed athletes, square and hard and deep, its sheets satin and immaculately made. This marvellous bed and I were reflected in an immense oval mirror and with us – appropriately enough – a widescreen television on a black metallic trolley stacked with pornographic videotapes for which the entrepreneurial Brine would have bartered her brain.

I shut my eyes and leaned against the door so suddenly that it slammed against the wall.

Like all those whose one means of survival was the ability to escape, I had an uncertain grasp on the moment and often lost the present to the past. In a recent letter Amedeo had described an impulsive visit to Mother's estate. Having been detained by a driving conviction, he arrived at midnight. Dogs sporadically barked in the distance, pines rustled, the moon was swallowed by a Central Casting cloud. Adjacent to the most accessible back door, the television room. Quietly and through the darkness Amedeo walked and then he froze. Through the window: Aldo and Mother on the sofa, concentrating very hard. On the screen before them, a naked woman in her thirties was in the act of sexual congress with a pig. *A pig*. No metaphors were necessary here, no symbolism was required. Amedeo reported the hog as being appropriately libidinous and not without the occasional intelligent expression. Its penis 'looked like a corkscrew' and the naked woman's performance consisted of:

A) submitting to the pig's embrace,
B) agreeing to be filmed whilst in the pig's embrace, and
C) loudly moaning and feigning an epiphanic rapture in response to said pig's embrace.

Aldo's eyes were 'stinging with interest' and Mother's marabou-feather-slippered foot was nervously vibrating. Minutes passed. My brother stood observing them as if paralysed. And then the romantic couple exchanged unromantic words, words which led to Aldo reluctantly replacing the farmyard frolics tape with one entitled *Night Nurses*, an opus in which the actors were exclusively bipedal. *Night Nurses* was the story of a lascivious nurse with mocha nipples, a depraved nurse with a depilated pubic region, a monstrously breasted nurse who carried a glass eye in a tasselled purse, and a startled (if easily enthused) patient in traction. The tale opened with the patient in traction allowing the lascivious nurse with mocha nipples to Sellotape his mouth shut and then kiss him. My mother appeared to be perplexed by this action and asked her husband to explain. Aldo sighed and shrugged. 'She must like the taste of plastic.'

Minutes passed.

Mother suddenly snatched the remote control device from her partner as the patient in traction was about to ejaculate and fast-forwarded the tape. Aldo placed his head in his hands. Mother threw the remote control device at the screen and screamed something about one of his mistresses. As dogs sporadically barked in the distance, Amedeo stumbled back through the rustling pines and then, under a moon swallowed by that Central Casting cloud, he barrelled back to New York City in his Ferrari 512TR, his hands 'uncontrollably shaking' and his vision blurred by tears or fears or homely pain, stopping only at his dealer's penthouse for eight grams of uncut Bolivian cocaine.

Grief is a sphere and still a sphere to all the privileged; by definition, even private laws have limitations to their efficacy.

Starlight and roses: back into the corridor and through the second doorway to my left and into the whitest of palatial bathrooms, where I slowly and repeatedly splashed my face with cold water. All I wanted to know was the sensation of cold water against my skin and nothing more; with its implicit activity, premise of differentiation and identification of object, perception was too complicated a process. Patted my cheeks dry with a bathsheet. Returned after a time to the pandemonium downstairs.

Howard Brown was animatedly boring a young woman in black. The blonde and the redhead had cornered a young heir and were in the process of overwhelming the boy with their nylon hair and polystyrene breasts. A few advertising wheels were snorting cocaine by the unlit fireplace. No longer Frank Sinatra's 'Swing Easy', but the Beatles' 'Abbey Road'. The volume was enough for war. Sat down on the carpeted stairs, by a filled crystal ashtray. My stockinged knees felt bony and too small as they rubbed against each other and my head hurt and I lit a cigarette. Stared at the unrecognizable portrait of Dorota on the opposing wall. The artist was a grateful abstract expressionist who had been made to understand the advantages of sensory consciousness by Dorota's intelligent fingers, and also talentless. This dizzy girl may as well have painted one of those seascapes in which a score of aroused stallions with nostrils the size of Sicilian lemons and insane manes highball their way through an apocalyptic surf in a typhoon. Below the portrait, a woman with an impressively pointed nose and a slack pink mouth was snoozing on a sofa, her gold lurex Moschino up around her thighs. Exposed, the thick 'control brief' bands of her expensive pantyhose.

Settled my chin into my kneecaps and sullenly looked out at the room.

6

Across from me, an enormous rectangular mirror, its cornices gilded serpents and fourth-century BC Hindu monkeys and gilded berries on gilded and unlikely boughs. This mirror was so polished that its reflection was as brutal as that star at the heart of every block of ice. Such blue. I squinted, smarting from the smoke, from my own headache. Remembered reading of a man who, after plunging his tomahawk into the back of a ten-year-old boy's neck and then sexually assaulting his showering mother, dragged the woman into her bedroom and attempted to strangle her. As he turned, he saw himself in the mirror of her dressing table and it was then and only then that it occurred to him: 'I can't do this.' Reflection often imparts the greatest truth. I stubbed my cigarette out into the ashtray on the step beside me and in doing so, displaced three lipsticked butts, a crumpled business card and a small masticated piece of yellow chewing gum.

Looked out across the room.

In the mirror, a man facing away, shouldered as if yoked, his height almost defying the frame. I stared at him closely. His brow and jaw were broad, his eyes slow-flowing, trickling over surfaces, through the walls of the inconsequential conversations. My tongue was dusty with rare sugars, and I swallowed. He was densely muscular and tan, his throat a living sculpture, powerful, the warmest isthmus. In his face, the impressions of a hard lifetime. His lower lip was full and dark, his nose perfectly aquiline. The pale wine in his glass reflected green in that mirror there beside him and reflected, his skin had an agate cast. He held the fragile wine-glass stem between his thumb and long forefinger and his wrist was thick and still. As I watched him, there was in me only a sense of the aquarium, as if I were swimming towards him, weightless, that subaqueous slowness, my tongue a pulse, my cunt a tongue. To have in that moment lapped him as I would have blackstrap molasses; to have in that moment kissed his lips, and then again. Glass suddenly divided me from all but him. Beauty. That ice-white dress shirt, the sleeves pushed to the elbows, his elbows chafed, on his left wrist a watch – exquisite, but with a sharply cracked face.

In me, phosphorescence: the newest fluids in my arteries, my mouth a mammal.

His worn blue jeans hung frayed over dark and hand-tooled boots. A light awareness of being observed. It was as if he knew, as if he were accustomed to attention. Silence: that slow full rush of thermometer warmth. Shifted my thighs and thick between them, nectar. I was all liquid, strangely conscious of my infinitely opaque responses – so lolloping, so slow. He suddenly ran his fingers through his hair, locks of which fell loosely over his broad forehead. His skin glittered with the lightest sweat. There was a heavy vein – a vine of blood, red blood – that ran right down over his defined forearm. An eloquence about his form, about his stance, about his arrogance, an eloquence that found its audience in me. Beauty. I knew, I knew as I continued to absorb him. It was as if a hand – hot and so scented – had been clamped over my eyes: blind sex. There was that sense of the aquarium and its sensual distorted lentor, but also peril. Minutes ago, there had been a circus around me and now him, now only him. Again, that glass, that membrane! The slow slant of his cheekbones and my own devouring spirit in its stealth. His length, his breadth, his density. Lividity, that full wide mouth. No smile; he dismissed the greetings of however many others with a nod.

I lit a cigarette and watched him through the undulatory veil of smoke, of warm blue smoke.

That half of him in the mirror could have been a portent: composed and in its foreground with his back now squarely to it, he was glancing calculatedly around the room. Rapidly ashed my cigarette. My eyes were smarting. Fascination in me can become a drowsy cannibalism, wherein even evil is delectable: I can be hypnotized. Stared at him and through his beauty then discerned a shield. This, then, was the potency of the arcanum; such secret qualities are the pivot upon which all the erotic turns. This may or may not have been my attempt to refine my understanding of matter. I could not say when or where or how I had before encountered him but I knew I had. And then: a sudden mental image of him in the white bed of a hospital, delirious and sickening, so close to death – I heard him calling me and calling me, there was the perfume of driftwood, and then it disappeared.

That cigarette between my fingers was a tower of forgotten ash. Turned to bury it in the ashtray and then returned to my hypnotic object. Unsuspecting: I was burned alive. Our eyes met in that mirror and I shot my look away. Breathed so deeply, felt my sex contract. Human experience is said to be retained in the retina but his were impossible to read, they told me of nothing but his unwillingness to be so known. The look itself: direct, congested, in it a flicker of what may or may not have been an inexplicable anger, absorbent, in itself a duel. Tacticians are professionally cautious with their every expression; by such individuals, security is never assumed, only proved. A long scar cut down from his hairline to the midpoint of his brow. The human organism has the means to clear the memory and desire is the most intoxicating of those means. My heart was torn from me and I suppressed my terror, my excitement. Glanced back at him and met – just for an instant – that same direct stare, green as the flames of torched acetates.

Felt occult as I looked away, as if I had been penetrated by an unseen blade.

7

To save myself, I closed my eyes. Deliberately slowed the beating of my heart and focused on hearing only my breath. And then, from his dark and hand-tooled boots, my look slid up along the broad length of his thighs. He was standing in front of me and I was wiped clean of personality.

'It's hot tonight.'

'Is it?' I nonsensically asked.

'Different metabolisms perceive temperature differently,' he said. His pupils were a fighting black and very still. Clean skin. The first two buttons of his ice-white shirt had been left undone. The hollow of his throat was pulsing. He gestured carelessly. 'Do you mind if I sit down?'

I shook my head and moved to the very edge of the step, in the process knocking that filled ashtray over so that it shattered on the polished parquetry. He was the only one to notice but that only made it worse; poised like a child or creature hunted to its unprotected home and seared by shame, a childlike shame, I stared down at the map of ash and fractured crystal, unnerved by my own mundane incompetence.

Offering me his empty wine-glass, against which his lips had rested: 'Use this instead.'

Without lifting my head, I murmured my embarrassed thanks. Shook another shaking cigarette from the trembling packet. Could not, I could not bring myself to look at him, it would have been to feel. There was a pause and then, with a surprising swiftness, he crouched to offer me the light of my own lighter. My knees were suddenly apart and he somehow seemed to be between them as he drove that flame towards my mouth, and I could not have said why or how it was that the house around us and its many guests receded to a heat-shimmer and then disintegrated in the manner of those initially lucid and ultimately elusive thoughts that precede deep sleep and then are lost, but it was so; and it seemed to me that he and I had been encapsulated by a feeling that I could not or did not want to understand and as a conse-quence, we were not just enclosed in a strange new and wonderful silence, but were active on a plane of conscious-ness where nothing is what it appears to be and yet all is right, for there was us and only us and then that whipcrack of a flame. It startled me.

Time had deferred to temperature and I was dazed, I was astounded. Fire has its own polemic. Lifted my blur of a hand to cup the light. The flame then vanished without spark and he slipped my lighter into his pocket. Prometheus thieving the fire. Released from his displosive scrutiny, all I knew was my desire. Had he pushed my thighs apart right then and there, his sunned skin dark against the tallow pallor of my own nocturnal flesh, and plunged two of his thick fingers thick within me, I would have felt it apt, so natural. These were full sensations and as ripe as pears. One of his arms was resting on his knee; the other behind him. Thighs inflexible.

'You're an intimidating-looking woman,' he said, his gaze drifting into the distance.

'Am I.'

'You are.'

I paused and then, through an uncharacteristic chuckle, said: 'I remember once opening a game of Scrabble with the word ingénue.'

His smile was sudden, fantastic, solar, winning – a ravishing display of interestingly discoloured teeth. 'You're English?' he asked.

'Italian,' I replied.

'Then why the accent?'

'Lived there,' I said. 'Lived there for years and then I left.'

'And now you're here.'

'That's right. And you?'

'And me?' He smiled. 'I think I may be here, too.'

'I can't place your accent. Where are you from?'

Holding my gaze, unreadable: 'Oh, here and there.'

I smiled. 'A funny answer.'

'Possibly, but also true.'

I smiled. 'Golf handicap?'

Holding my gaze, unreadable.

'I'm joking,' I said quickly, and looked away. 'It's just that you remind me of the man that blonde over there was discussing with her friend before you came.'

Holding my gaze, unreadable: 'You know them?'

'No,' I said, 'just overheard them.'

'Poor man,' he said. And then: 'I like that mouth of yours.'

Silence: that slow full rush.

'It is,' he calmly said, 'a kind of mutilated orchid.'

I could not speak.

'Suddenly tense,' he said.

Tremblingly ashed that shaking cigarette and cleared my throat. 'I am.'

'I see.' A tendril of light hair over that scar. 'So tell me why.'

'Just temperament,' I said, and forcefully inhaled two lungfuls of blue smoke and then forcefully exhaled them.

'Golf handicap?' he asked.

I smiled. 'I'm sorry, I just get jittery in crowds.'

'We were doing so well,' he said, 'and then you spooked.'

I smiled. 'That's right,' I said. 'I spooked.'

'Let's start again.'

'You have discoloured teeth,' I said.

'You are too kind.'

'Please, don't misunderstand me –'

'I wouldn't dream of it.'

Tremblingly ashed that shaking cigarette and cleared my throat. 'I've always liked discoloured teeth.'

'How fortunate,' he said.

Poised like a child or creature hunted to its unprotected home and seared by shame, by childlike shame, I stared down at the map of ash and fractured crystal, unnerved by my own mundane incompetence.

'Even as I child,' I tried to explain, 'I liked discoloured teeth.'

'If I were you, I'd quit while I'm ahead,' he said, and then I saw that he was smiling.

Tremblingly dropped my cigarette into the wine-glass and as the bulb gradually clouded with cold smoke, I said: 'I read an article in the paper about a man who lit a fire in a backpackers' hostel. There were six deaths. He stayed to watch them die. He stayed to watch them die, he said, because he loved the sound of human screams.' The cold smoke unfolding slowly from that wine-glass distracted me and so I sealed it in its bulb with my damp palm. 'His – his lawyers claim that he suffers from Korsakoff's Syndrome, which compels him to lie.'

'And the lie?' he asked.

'The lie?' (Through the trembling filter of another cigarette which he so swiftly lit.)

His eyes were clouded by cold and slowly unfolding smoke. 'What did he lie about? Didn't he *really* love to hear the sound of human screams?'

'Do you know,' I said, forcefully inhaling two lungfuls of blue smoke and then forcefully exhaling, 'I can't remember.'

A pause. 'That's some piece of information,' he said, and then slowly took a sip of wine. 'In fact, it's right up there with the time a systems analyst warned me that if I stand too close to a leaking microwave oven, my testes will explode.'

I laughed, but remained seared by shame, a childlike shame, and stared down at the map of ash and fractured crystal, unnerved by my own mundane incompetence.

'You can take your palm off the glass,' he said. 'That cigarette was suffocated long ago.'

I quickly looked down and retrieved my palm and then all between us was stale smoke, cold and unfolded.

'You find it difficult to conduct a conversation with a stranger?' That stare of his, green as the flames of torched acetates.

'I do,' I suddenly said, 'I do. And nor are you of any help.'

Calm interest. 'Presumptuous?' he asked.

'So arrogant,' I said, inhaling forcefully two lungfuls of blue smoke and then exhaling.

'A flaw,' he said. 'Forgive me.'

Tremblingly dropped my half-smoked cigarette into that newly clouding bulb of glass. 'All right,' I said, 'let's start again. Tell me something of yourself.'

'I am,' he said with ease, 'phenomenally dull.'

I looked at him but could not read his eyes. 'You know,' I said, 'I don't believe you.'

'Understandable. It's possible that I, too, am suffering from Boris Karloff's Syndrome.'

'The lie?' I asked.

'Do you know,' he said, 'I can't remember.'

I smiled but tremblingly shook another shaking cigarette from the now-rattling packet.

'Let's start again,' he said with false decisiveness. 'An inane question, but also of some relevance: do you have a lover?'

'Engaged to be married,' I said, and waited for him to light my cigarette but he was strangely still.

A pause, and then so casually: 'To whom?'

'Irrelevant,' I said.

He remained still. 'And where is he tonight?'

'London,' I rapidly answered. 'On business.'

A slight and dangerous smile. Another pause. 'A shame,' he said.

Ferocity: 'And why?'

'Because,' he said, 'I wanted you.'

Silence: that slow full rush, blind sex. I swallowed. Slowly he reached into his pocket for my lighter and then again, that driving light. I forcefully inhaled two lungfuls of cold cloud and then exhaled, poised like a child or creature hunted to its unprotected home.

Third supple pause. 'Your field?'

'Binary stars,' I whispered.

And then, as if to himself, as if articulating a sequence of thoughts: 'Eschatology is the doctrine of finality. The means as the end. The limitations of linearity. Cosmogony, on the other hand, hinges on continuity and association. All is water. Hope as a maxim.' He stopped to glance at me. 'You are an optimist,' he said. 'Unusual.'

Unnerved, I felt my sex to be a slow unfolding bulb clouded by smoke, the smoke of green torched acetates, and I was poised: a child or creature hunted to its unprotected home and then that nectar, secreted with each beat of my thickening pulse.

Almost absently: 'You want me to tell you something of myself. A reasonable demand. Strangers can be frightening. I weighed twelve pounds at birth, which almost killed my mother. After examining me, my father asked her if it were possible to have me drowned.' Almost imperceptibly, he shifted closer and I saw his jaw slightly contract. His hair was thick and its warm gloss suggested edibility – russet and strawberry, honey, wheat, raw sugar, milk. And then there was the nape of his broad neck, and its fragrance of vanilla.

'Your cigarette,' he said. 'You've burned the carpet.'

I looked down and there it was: my wound or his and only one of many.

So unsuspecting. Suddenly felt the pads of his strong fingers on my exposed inner wrist and startled, turned to look at him. Silence: that slow full rush, blind sex. I was reminded by his eyes of Albrecht Dürer's self-portrait – something of a white hand pressed to tender fur and that unearthly quality, ever-unfolding. My wrist, against which the strong pads of his fingers pressed and thickening between my thighs, real nectar.

Fourth pause. And then: 'Tell me, are you a victim of Karamazov's Syndrome?'

Tremulously: 'No.'

'Then why,' he slowly asked, 'did you lie to me before?'

I looked away, my tongue a pulse. 'How did you know?'

'Too many years of practice,' he demurred. More potently: 'Don't lie to me.'

Poised like a child or creature hunted to its unprotected home and seared by shame, a childlike shame, I stared down at the map of ash and fractured crystal, unnerved by my own mundane incompetence.

'I am so sorry,' I said haltingly. 'Let's start again.'

So gently, so gently that the sensation was almost negligible – as if dreamed, as if it were occurring to another or in the past, the distant past, as if it were a ritual of the realm of silks and silken wisdoms – he closed each of his fingers around my exposed wrist and with his thumb, began to slowly stroke its blue-and-white translucence.

After a torched pause, he said: 'Your skin is quite transparent.'

We watched his thumb so slowly stroking my pale skin and thickening, a real nectar there between my thighs and deeper still, where the contractions were a pulse – that pulse, desire: my heart. No longer regular, his breathing and then our eyes met: inexplicably full, unearthly, ever-unfolding.

Difficult pause.

'New start,' he said with false decisiveness. 'I once spent New Year's Eve in a New York City meat-market district salsa bar, where I met a cardiothoracic surgeon who told me that she had that day – through sheer miscalculation – killed a patient on the operating table. Bryn Mawr girl, black sweater like a second skin, a scarlet skirt, so short.' Tight little exhalation. He looked down at his thumb so slowly stroking my pale skin. 'We talked,' he said, 'until four that morning.'

'No more?' I asked.

'No more,' he said. 'Just walked her home and roamed the cold streets until dawn.'

'Liar,' I said.

'The truth,' he said. 'I never lie. Just walked her home. She was, I think, spectacularly drunk. Not long afterwards and for completely unrelated reasons, I toyed with the idea of throwing myself from the 35th Avenue overpass of the Clearview Expressway in Queens, but decided against it and instead flew to Libya.'

The caloricity and pressure of his thumb melted my skin so that it was not blue-and-white translucence he was stroking but red blood, but bone: my home, marrow. My sex contracted and then again, that nectar spill and then again, my thoughts a green glass bulb clouded by smoke. Physics is the science of mathematical description and of measurement, of cold quantification and thus lost to this occult erotic process: it was as if I had been penetrated by an unseen blade.

His voice was both an orchid and an oxymel as he then said, '*Outside.*'

Blind sex.

8

Inhaling, his chest steeply rising, he stood and extended a strong hand for me to tremblingly climb. I followed him in a strange new and wonderful silence through all the pointillist faces, my skirt a black silk pendulum, its sexual oscillation a whisper against my thighs.

I followed him down through the garden, beneath low arches of dead apple limbs and ghostly roses, around us both the rich white opiate of a Yoshino Cherry, past boughs freighted with jacaranda blooms, my high black heels catching in knolls and in a fever, followed him. A hidden courtyard. Hushed: the flickering of lights cast otherworldly hues throughout the ivy. Wet flagstones. That pale gold crush of kumquats at our feet. Exigent greens. A sudden blue outpouring of starred sky. He stooped to cup a fall of moist wisteria, bringing it to his lips and drawing deeply of its lilac essence. The night was tropical; it had been hotly raining. Salt sweat, humidity. He rose with his broad hands along the length of me – my calves, my thighs, my hips, my waist – to cup my breasts. Bruised breathing, fear.

My ache: his broad face then against my throat and he inhaled me, he inhaled me with my flesh tenderly between his teeth, and then again, that nectar spill. I could so smell myself, I could so smell the bestial fragrance of his hair, my own desire and then his fingers through me ruthlessly and then I buckled in his grip, my mouth a mammal. Kissing my cheeks and licking at my burning flesh – that sacrifice to the cunt's holocaust – he pressed his parted lips to my closed eyelids and then down hard over my mouth: we kissed.

It was as if I had been penetrated by an unseen blade; it was unlike that which I had ever known; it was more than a simple revelation; it was a terror in its potency.

His fingers through the silk-flesh of my arms and with a simultaneous inhalation, we both withdrew our mouths and in white silence, looked away. Bruised breathing, fear. I felt as if I had never known another. His hands were almost imperceptibly trembling. Demolished, we both swallowed. I knew that we had reached the gates of an enclosure we had been waiting all our lives to flee, and now the prospect of such liberty was almost threatening. Between my thighs, thickening nectar and with one trembling hand, he found it and therein dreamily sought depth and then dominion, my sexual oils absorbed by his dry palm.

With his other hand still gripping my frail arm, he kissed my mouth and then again and then more fully, my back so arched against that ivied wall and in that arbour of flickering fairy-lights and moist wisteria, we kissed again: stars burst, I heard them – beta Pictoris had been lanced and gushed, a sulphur-gold through soundless indigo, and I was his.

Two of his fingers thickening my tender sex, the dry palm of his hand absorbing my salt oils, he could not stop; with his other hand, he pushed the pale silk of my blouse aside and exposed to his hot mouth my breast, and through the friable white lace, his jaw working, he suckled me and as his tongue moulded to my thickening nipple, he widened my wet sex with his thick fingers to amplify the liquid friction: my eyes and mouth were open but I had been rendered dumb and blind, and then he pushed – as he would have a peach – my breast from its lace cup and rapturously sucked it, thickly sucked it, his jaw an occult erotic mechanism in itself.

Stretched to a wet gyre by his fingers, my oiled cunt and how I rubbed it hard against his palm, his working palm. Illicit mysteries: I let myself dissolve over his hand and far above us, stars particular and brilliant or perhaps they were imagined, and the moon – serene, insane, a smoking lamp. That sky, a night-blue kingdom: Ceres, Pallas, Vesta, Juno, bright Hygeia. I felt his cock – that flesh of Orpheus – swelling against my thigh and then I was bewitched. Below our feet, those crushed sweet pale gold kumquats and around us both, exigent greens.

My hands were pressed damp to his back and his thick fingers slowed within my cunt – that tenderness that I had ever owned but only wholly known through him: between a woman's thighs, the delicacy of the universe and origin not only of real love, but of the world. My head, that glowing lantern and my thoughts, a green glass bulb clouded so slowly by unfolding smoke. My nipple thickened in his mouth and then we kissed and then again, our tongues entwined. He brought that hand with which he had so thickly pierced me to my lips; his fingers glistened with want's adhesive, nectar, glandular oils. With his broad pelvis, he ground me hard against that ivied wall, my breath lost in that storm of moist wisteria, and slipped those glistening fingers over my tongue and then I slowly and lasciviously suckled them, and then again, and then again. He watched me openly, his face serene, insane, a smoking lamp.

Beauty. His eyes were the green flames of torched acetates, he unbuttoned his blue jeans and with a tug, pulled out his heavy cock – that silken supple length and breadth – and watching me, his glistening fingers suckled by the mammal of my mouth and watching me, he bumped his cock against my stretched wet vulva until it was, in part, absorbed. That hidden gyre of mine, where the temperature was my desire for him and only him, it swallowed all his breath. I felt his thick foreskin unpeel – the skin of that same peach he had before pushed from its lace – and then he was as naked as he would ever be or perhaps I only dreamed it.

His hands so careful and so broad, he lifted me until my thighs were full astride him and we kissed again and then again, our tongues entwined and suddenly he penetrated me wholly and I grunted and I grunted and then felt myself fall open to him or apart and then unfold, my flesh a smoke: I had been rendered dumb and blind and in that golden instant, amplified to that which I had never, but always should have been. Such beauty. His eyes so tightly closed and then his mouth sought mine through the wisteria's drunken perfume and far above us, the desperate loveliness of all the blue starred sky and so imploring him, I could have died, I could have died, I may have entered a white decade: all the world was lost and then regained and then with a convulsive overflow of feeling, I came so deeply that I felt I had dissolved to a hot syrup over his cock, over his tongue, a syrup burning through his fingers.

He kissed the journey of each cry from the base of my torched thorax to my lips and then he arched and arched again and hard within me, discharged his heat and other lives, his fertile milk, a heart made fluvial. I was all breath or breathlessness. That sky, a night-blue kingdom: Ceres, Pallas, Vesta, Juno, bright Hygeia. Still holding me fully astride him, he slumped a little and then pressed his open mouth to my soft hollowed throat. There was the plashing of light rain, blood-warm and trickling down over our eyelids and our swollen lips, between my breasts, over my nipples and my doubled belly, down the plane of his back so that his shirt adhered in hot moist patches and I kissed his tender temple and again, and again. The sticky plug of him within me: human, African. Our kiss was one slow tongue unfolding. His fingers trembled against the silk-flesh of my thighs. Tight little exhalations. My home, marrow. And there with him in that tropical rain, I wholly spread over his cock – surrendering both to him and to myself, my heart a smoke, my lips caressing his wet cheek.

It was as if I had been penetrated by an unseen blade; it was unlike that which I had ever known; it was more than a simple revelation; I knew it for a treasure, that which was within me.

Around us both the ivy glistened, otherworldly and vibrating with lightening drops of rain. So open-mouthed, our kiss. He then so slowly pulled himself from me, releasing his fluids: my bare thighs burned with all his albumen. Such beauty. Below the crush of silk over my hips pulsed his new kingdom, my ripe cunt. Other gods within me as he then sank down onto his knees and pressed his open mouth against me there, against my bruised full vulva, his tongue a smoke unfolding and his eyes so tightly closed, his hands drained of their strength by my torched skin.

Delirium, my heart.

Lapping his come from me, so suckling the soft pale folds of fucked wet cunt, so suckling my every tender flange, that hot penumbral membrane and his tongue thick with my oils, he moaned. Beauty. Through the wisteria's drunken perfume, the desperate loveliness of all the blue starred sky and so imploring him, I could have died, I could have died, I may have entered a white decade: all the world was lost and gained and then with a convulsive overflow of feeling, I grunted and I grunted and I came so deeply that I felt as if I had dissolved to a hot syrup over his tongue, a syrup burning through his mouth, the syrup active in Reunion.

That white shirt sticking to his back in patches and his hair adhering russet to his temples in wet strands, he rose to kiss me on the lips and with that kiss, delivered unto me his seed so that both open mouth and swollen cunt were salt and dulcet with him, and then I staggered and he caught me. One of my hands was well entwined within the ivy and wisteria; raindrops traced the blue lacework of veins down the transparent length of wrist and arm; and then his moan, muted by our soft kiss.

A moment's breath.

'I have to go,' he whispered.

That slow, full rush: blind sex.

Drunkenly buttoning his blue jeans and pushing in wet strands his hair from both his temples, he then stood and stared at me. He remained strangely still, and I could only breathe and breathe and look at him, only at him. Insane, serene, a smoking lamp. He stepped forwards to ease my skirt over my licked vulva, to ease my blouse over my suckled breasts. My nipples were so pale in that low light. With his sex-scented fingers, he then touched my lips and held – with grace, with a dark tenderness – my face and stared into my eyes: his stare direct, congested, in it a flicker of what may or may not have been an inexplicable anger, absorbent, in itself a duel.

Our kiss was lost in its own drunken perfume.

Around us both, the voice of rain.

'You don't know who I am,' I whispered back, each word slurred by the slowed pulse of my tongue.

Holding my gaze, unreadable: 'Oh, yes I do.'

'And how?' I asked, and when he did not answer, paused. 'Well, you may know my name, but I don't know yours.'

His smile was no more than a shadow. 'Lagen,' he said.

Wet light slid down each green shuddering leaf. 'Lagen?'

A strange stillness.

'Lagen?' I again asked.

'Gabriel Lagen,' he murmured, and then his smile transformed into an expression I could or did not want to understand, that shadow through him like an unseen blade. He dipped his mouth to mine as if drinking from a pool. Last

kiss. And then there was his footfall and the darkness
flickering with otherworldly lights and then that sky, a night-
blue kingdom: Ceres, Pallas, Vesta, Juno, bright Hygeia.

And you could part my soul at this hour
like a paler curtain.

Slumped heavily against that ivied wall and slid – wet light,
bright sound – slid down to those wet flagstones, surrounded
by the pale gold crush. Blind sex.

It was so late. The cab was all cigar-smoke and vinyl.
Shivered with tiredness. The traffic on the Harbour Bridge
was slow. Ahead, patiently blinking orange lights. Eight
ruined cars, brutally strewn across three lanes. A madman
screaming: 'NO! NO! NO!' An open ambulance and in the
distance, two others driving away. My driver's thick red
neck, craning. His Slavic curse. Shattered stars of glass across
the asphalt and some twisted steel. A broad tarpaulin over
corpses and seeping from the green darkness beneath it, one
reproachful thread of blood. Certain destiny. Over the white
lines, bloody tyremarks and floating like pale tissue in night's
formalin, the disturbed faces of policemen. Another siren.
From the suspender cables, harsh light-shafts in which
persistent silver filaments of rain could be discerned. The
madman silenced, there was a sobbing girl wandering around
in a blue drifting ballgown, and then she suddenly collapsed
over the broad tarpaulin.

9

A woke as if through veils in my old bedroom to
Gabriel's eyes.
        The morning light was strong and hot across the
floorboards. Rainbow lorikeets screeched from the trees. My
every movement echoed in the emptied space. Outside, the
sky was a paint blue. Slowly sat up. Sensations folded and

folded again into each other, and such purity. That blissful absence of analysis. Closed my eyes and basked in that strong hot light. Gabriel's lips on mine and then he disappeared.

Next door, the linden-lined avenue's one prodigy already at her piano and her music, it was absolutely beautiful.

As promised, the two removalists arrived at ten, the two halves of a pantomime mule: one tall, one short; one fat, one thin; one happy, one maudlin. They took their cups of coffee from me and then nursed them as if they were two aching teeth. Appropriately idle chatter about packing crates and masking tape and the pristine Greenland-white sofa they had moved through the red panic of its owner only the week before.

My existence had been shifted; now in the orbit of Miss Caroline Brine of Irony Avenue, Neutral Bay, I could but make the best of a bad deal. Her ghost rattled its metallic nail-files and nine-carat gold-plated jewellery at me from every room bar my pink cube. What had I done? I did not wring my hands but seriously considered doing so. With grim alacrity, I unpacked those crates that had not emigrated to locked storage. Properly arranged my new bedroom. Opened the windows overlooking the cursory garden. Another Lycra leotard crucified there on the line, its reversed gusset indelibly stained. I was to discover that Brine's menstrual blood not only had the consistency of glue, but the eye-watering tang of cheap insecticide. A faded cane basket of pop-coloured pegs had been left on the white plastic garden table (the moulded hole in its nucleus oddly pathetic). A breeze ruffled the domesticated palms. What had I done? I would grow used to it, I would adapt. By the end of the following week, Caroline (part of whose gums, I strangely remembered, had been removed) and I would be sipping nice iced tea beneath the beach umbrella (inserted through the table's moulded hole), our thighs glossy with banana oil, in complementing Lycra leotards.

The last book placed upon the shelf and the last towel assiduously folded, I read a letter from drab London's BBC. I had received it that morning with a letter from a Brazilian paramour (interesting) and a bank statement (boring). Lit with steady fingers a preparatory cigarette. Smoked it. Then read: *Dear Ms Botticelli, Alethea Mediocrity and I are currently working on a programme which explores the relationship between fictional characters and real people.* I liked that 'real'. 'Real people' (a phrase which demands an imperial quota of gravity), the collective term for both 'real women' and 'real men', their respective knitting needles and Mack trucks loaded with compressed hydrogen at the ready. *This programme is due to be broadcast as a documentary for BBC TV early next year.* And here the despicable typeface reared up at me, a smiling cobra: *You might have something to say about William Grieve's characters in* 'Betrayal' – *in particular, the character Juanita Dark. If so, might you be prepared to talk to either myself or Alethea about it – no shock horror exposé, we guarantee!!!* Three exclamation marks, one for each prong of her pitchfork. I could see her so clearly, this terrible tart, with her flame-streaked hair and handbag full of leaking pens, ordering Notting Hill spritzers in a garrotted Midlands twang. *Sincere regards and hoping to hear from you soon, Fiona Flake.*

Incredulously, I read the awful thing again.

A BBC TV documentary! Oh, yes – oh, absolutely; and filmed in the sparkling white refracted light of the Opera House, how apt! And with me as myself, musing loosely on William and twiddling a straw, authoritatively expounding on the impact of life on the enchantment of art and perhaps vice versa, plaintively explaining (in my Chanel sunglasses and a charming thong bikini) what it is to have one's essence distilled into the popular scent of a fictional character. A fictional character! My life had been that of a fictional character. I wondered sometimes if of the two of us, Juanita were not the more real. And so I telephoned the brave Flake at her Battersea flat (like the good girl she was, she had supplied her home, work, parents' and boyfriend's telephone numbers in order that I not be deprived of the opportunity to interact with the matted voice behind the flyscreen of her words).

It was dawn in England, and cold and damp and horrible.

Initially somnolent, Flake soon snatched the oars of our exchange and fiercely rowed.

I was crisp, as the passionately disorganized Dark would never have been. 'Ms Flake, I am extremely flattered that you considered me for your *Forum* documentary, but I'm afraid I have no wish to comment on the matter.'

Snap crackle pop of intercontinental static. Her alert dismay. 'You were – you were engaged to William Grieve, weren't you?'

Simplicity itself: 'I was.'

'Well, don't you think – I mean, as ridiculously intrusive as this may sound, but it's so – it's so im*por*tant for students of modern literature and for our – our, um, our *understand*ing of culture and the arts in general and even psychoanalysis, and – um, and the nature of inspiration and so ... on, to – I mean, what I mean is that it's quite essential for us to be in touch with – with the, um, the total *impetus* of the creative spirit or – um, um – to, um – would you mind awfully holding on for a tick? The cat's – the cat's – oh, *Robes*pierre! Do let go of the cord! I *am* sorry, Ms Botticelli ... the cat *will* play with the telephone cord, silly thing – and now, where was I? Oh, yes – that's right, that's right, yes: the creative spirit's impetus, and what we – that is to say, Alethea and myself – ostensibly, what we would like to do is – is, um – to, um, to –, (her train of thought chugging its cargo of dull coal up the cloud-shrouded mountain) – get some *idea* of what it is precisely that artists mean when they speak of a "muse" ... am I, um, making any sense to you at all? You're our only lead aside from Schicklgruber, and he's – Schicklgruber is ... well, he's –'

'A moron,' I offered.

'Yes, well, he's not quite *access*ible to our audience, whereas I feel that you would – from what I understand – have more of a *hand*le on – oh, *do* let go of the cord, you miserable animal! – where was I? Oh, yes – an absolute *hand*le on depth and perspective, literary technique and intellectual breadth, and in particular, the concept of the narrative as a kind of stranglehold, if you ... know what I mean. I mean, you and Grieve were terribly ... *close* ... which is, of course, a statement of the bloody obvious! And the abuse of – of the contemporary idiom was a specialty of his, if you will; and I do believe that it's so very necessary to illuminate the artist's relationship with reality as ... um, as ... as I can't really say that too much is understood about any of it, really ... which is absurd. I, myself, refer to it as a form of deliberate and imprudent ignorance, because it *is* – you agree, I'm sure; because the artist's distortion of reality to complete a cycle of – a cycle of – let me put it this way: the way that writers in particular take the world around them and –'

'Shaft it to serve their own pernicious ends?'

She was startled. 'Well, not *exactly* – although I must say, Ms Botticelli, that yours is a perfectly valid viewpoint, but ... I meant, perhaps, something more along the lines – something more along the lines of, um –'

'Betrayal?'

She laughed with practised insincerity. 'How very witty, yes, but I mean –' (madly rowing) – 'I mean, it's *terri*bly important that the "man in the street" has some comprehension of the workings of the minds of the great ... if only to enrich his own l–l–life ... and artists like Grieve or Strindberg or Mann, you know, pivotal stylists and, you know – um, they're – what I mean to say is that they're – aside from their genius – they're no*tori*ously cryptic and ... mysterious, despite the apparent nakedness of their works ... but what I really was alluding to were the many *layers* of reality they perceive ... we're not trawling for scandal, you understand; we're simply trying to apply psychoanalytic techniques to art in order to – to really get to the *guts* of creation in order to – to – to discover its link with – with – with mysticism ... so that it's possible to, um, perform what I believe – and what we at the BBC believe – to be a sacred –'

I was impressed. First thing in the morning (a slug in the kisser from nowhere) and she performed this well. A born robot. It would have taken me a number of a powerful coffees and a carton of cigarettes to even approximate this astral degree of garbage.

'I really do not wish to comment, Ms Flake – I trust you understand.'

The receiver returned to its cradle.

Let them think what they want, it was nothing to me any more.

10

Sagged in the shower, lost in that dreamworld of steam. Grinning frogs, shell-shaped soaps, my soaring hum. Rinsed the dust and the sweat from my long hair and let the scalding water pelt into my mouth. At ease: the pink cube was now fully furnished and in it, my restored antique Dutch bed. Towelled myself dry and heard Brine's Triassic racket from the other room: the tyrannosaur in its agitated arc behind the sofa, its great back to the wall, its tail entangled in the undergrowth of vermilion drapes, and Caroline – clutching a club, her manly walnut-coloured legs akimbo – hopping from side to side, rabid for blood, the shrunken heads of former flatmates thudding against her breastbone, panting for that moment when she could skin the monster alive and ferociously fry it up with a sack of chips for dinner.

'*Just me!*' she screamed. '*No need to worry!*'

Her howl of greeting was returned. Slipped into a black silk dressing gown, my hair in a Hollywood towel, and walked into the kitchen. She was standing outside its linoleum perimeter, *I'm OK – You're OK* perched by her hip on the second shelf of the bookcase, the staleness of the day about her, chewing, fidgeting, limp-haired, a cheese-and-pickle sandwich distorting her ambrosial smile, and a whisper of salmon lipstick across the cracked tiles of her two front teeth. She tightened her eyes (a Mandelbrot effect). 'A cuppa tea?'

'Coffee, thanks.'

A lifetime's silence.

The interlude of children and their toys next door.

'Nice robe,' she said, tucking the last of her sandwich down her throat with a single finger.

She was wearing a transparent black nylon blouse ornamented with cordate buttons, beneath which an elaborate black brassiere and the deflated sun-speckled meringues of her breasts were visible. Her legs were unevenly shaved, her knees were perforated shopping bags, and the heels of her open-toed black patent-leather shoes were tortured, inwardly curved. As she reached through me for a cigarette, I conspicuously gagged on her perfume (a dormitory laundry basket).

Watched her as she lit up and with one arm across her breast, blew out a dissolving cylinder of smoke. What a day it had been! She plugged the kettle in, that cigarette glued to her salmon lipsticked mouth. What a bloody day. Her every movement was exaggeratedly delicate and executed with big freckled limbs. Oh, this *woman*! I should have seen her. A bloody Crufts' champion and there she was, her money on the table, wanting to be matched up with an aristocratic type or the like. A snowball had more of a chance in hell, but what could she do? *What could she do?*

Sighing smoke, she detached a tea-bag from its twin and then unscrewed with a hefty gesture the brown lid of the coffee jar. On and on and on. As if an aristocratic type or the like was ever going to shag a thing with a head like that. Oh, yeah – oh, *very* likely. With the thumb and index finger of her right hand crabbed, she sucked every last microsome of tar from the butt of her cigarette. Squinted at me. Screwed the butt into an ashtray. Yeah, sometimes the dating business was just – just bloody unbe*lie*vable. Sighing again, she stirred a kilogram of sugar into her tea and then my coffee with a teaspoon crested with the word MAJORCA in metal.

I was immobile in my chair, my black silk robe a black silk pool between my thighs.

Handed me my cup of coffee and sat down with an elongated exhalation. Efficiently, from the secret drawer beneath the tabletop, she produced two laminated coasters on which were depicted two surly grey koalas in the crotch of a dead tree and slid one beneath each cup. 'Rings on the table, otherwise,' she explained, and then politely pursed her lips to blow the hot steam from her tea into my face. Slung across the latest issue of *Singles Monthly*, her car-keys and their brass BOSS keyring. 'Phew, it's hot!' she said, and sipped her tea. Satisfied sigh. Each sigh was visible, in it strange particles, dead air.

My own boredom. The sparkling spring evening. Slow breathless arabesques of synthetic lace at the kitchen windows. Peasant warmth. Such shallow shadows across the black-and-white linoleum. A lazy lull. And then she suddenly stood and smashed the lamp-switch, having decided that it was 'getting gloomy'. From that lamp, a smoked-ham glow.

'So,' she brightly said, 'I see you've moved in OK.'

'I have,' I said. 'All is unpacked.'

'Home sweet home!' she said with a detestably false wink.

'Oh, yes,' I said, 'it's home sweet home.'

'You'll feel as if you've lived here forever in no time at all,' she said, 'just wait!'

'Already do,' I said.

She paused. 'Room look nice, then?'

'It does,' I said. 'Exceptionally nice.'

'Mind if I take a peek?' she asked.

'Feel free to peek,' I said.

She peeked. Returned. Sipped her tea. Then, piously: 'Lotta books.'

'Yes,' I said. 'I like to read.'

'Yeah, books are interesting,' she said. 'But what's that black thing on a tripod out the window?'

'A telescope,' I said.

'You're not a Peeping Tom, are you?' she asked.

'I'm not,' I said. 'You're thinking of binoculars.'

'Oh, yeah,' she said. Her pause. 'So what d'you need that for?'

'Because,' I said, 'my eyes are too weak to discern certain stars.'

'Ah huh,' she said. And then: 'My husband used to have binoculars.'

'A Peeping Tom?' I asked.

'Oh, no – not *Stan*. He liked to study birds,' she said. 'A real oncologist. Sat in the garden, watching sparrows and the like through his binoculars.'

'I see,' I said.

'Can't say I saw the thrill in them myself,' she said. 'I had a budgie once, but it wasn't very interesting. Just made a bloody noise all day and kicked seed onto the Axminster.' Sipped her tea. 'A dog is Man's Best Friend,' she said, 'but birds just fly around.'

'They do,' I said.

'Know what I mean?' she asked. 'Just fly around and poop on people's windscreens, that's what birds do.'

'Yes,' I said, 'I do know what you mean.'

'Like a dog can play with balls and guard the home and save the kids from drowning in rivers and is intelligent,' she said, 'but birds –'

'Just fly around and poop on people's windscreens,' I said.

'Yeah, they really do,' she said. 'Just never really understood Stan's interest in them, really. Funny.' She sipped her tea. That pause. 'Innit funny how you can be married for seven years to a man and then at the end of it, you might as well be strangers?'

'It is,' I said.

'Like he could be a pedestrian,' she said, 'just anybody.'

'Somebody on a bus?' I ventured.

'Yeah!' she said. 'So you've been married, too.'

'Oh, no,' I said.

'Engaged?' she asked.

'Just once,' I said.

'To who?' she asked.

'A writer,' I replied.

'Famous?' she asked. 'That is, if you don't mind me asking.'

'I don't,' I said, 'and yes, he was.'

'His name?' she asked. 'I might've read him.'

'Will Grieve,' I said.

Her pause. And then: 'Never heard of him.' Sipped her tea. 'Stan and me weren't rich,' she said, 'but things were cosy. He was in sales. I don't think I ever *really* loved him, though.'

'Even though he was in sales?' I asked.

She shook her head. 'The only time I ever was in love,' she said, jabbing her thumb in the direction of the bathroom, 'was with that French guy.'

'Napoleon's ... father?' I ventured.

'Yeah,' she said, 'only ever him. He was ...' here she sighed and glanced at those slow breathless arabesques of synthetic lace, 'just *such* a scrummy guy.' Her pause. Sipped her tea. 'Though his English wasn't very good, Goblessim; all he knew was twenty words.'

'Just twenty words?' I marvelled.

The brown goose honked. 'Just twenty words,' she said. 'Funny, innit?' And with a certain comic aptitude: 'So he used to say things like, *hello, woman! dinner today, room-service tomorrow?*'

'A regular card,' I said.

'A *scream*!' she cried. 'He was a scream. Tarzan, I called him. He had no idea he was so funny. Couldn't understand why we all fell about in hysterics. Goblessim, but he made me laugh! Best week of my life. Real tummy-giggles.'

'So you were Jane?' I asked.

'Oh, yeah,' she said. 'Romance, you know. I miss it, now.'

'Understandably,' I said.

'Awful, innit? When it's gone, I mean,' she said. Her pause. 'Most romantic guy I've ever met. Put flowers on my head while we were walking down the beach. But then all those French are so romantic. In their blood, you know. You've seen the films.'

'I have,' I said.

'Just so romantic,' she said. Her pause. And then, in an aggravating little voice: '*Moi aussi! Moi aussi!* ... whatever that means. He used to say it all the time.' Another pause. 'I wanted to keep the baby, I did, but he said no.' Sipped her tea. 'I had the termination on the last day of the financial year. Wrote me a letter from Paris, he did. I got a friend to translate. Said he already had a girlfriend and a baby and couldn't be responsible for ... another one.' Third pause. 'He said that what it was between us was True Love, but that sometimes Love didn't work because Truth got in the way. Which is right, I guess.' She stared for a moment at the bottom of her empty cup. Courageously: 'But I have no regrets.' Replacing the cup atop its coaster, she lit a cigarette and then, after exhaling another dissolving cylinder of smoke, said, 'Sometimes I wonder, but, if it would of had his eyes.'

A long and difficult silence.

The rat-scratch of her fingernails upon the table.

Air and its laniferous full volume; a certain inutility in such warmth.

Clearing my throat: 'I'm having an operation tomorrow.'

'You're *what*?' (Sincerely startled.)

'An operation,' I said.

'What kind of operation?' she asked.

'A cystoscopy and diathermy to the Skene's glands.' I stretched my legs. 'Routine.'

She smoked her cigarette through a squint, the freckles on her nose suddenly bunched. 'Right,' she said. And then, with trepidation: 'What ... where are the – the Skein's glands?'

'Mouth of the urethra,' I said.

Exhaling: 'Right ...' That marinated sea-slug of a tongue was back between her teeth. 'So it's like they'll be down –'

'There,' I said, 'with scissors and a fish-knife. Precisely.'

She grimaced. Folds of smoke issued like steam from the deep cavity between her now-protruding lower lip and her now-exposed front teeth. 'Better you than me,' she said.

'Not wrong,' I said, and stood.

'Scissors and a fish-knife,' she shuddered.

'Not to mention the hacksaw, bucket of vinegar, sharpened knitting needle and oyster fork,' I remarked.

She stared at me without comprehension and then screwed her cigarette into the ashtray. 'Well,' she nervously said, 'break a leg!'

I smiled. 'I'll try.'

Left the room.

Six hours or so later, I stared up at the ceiling's bone-yard shades. The sheets were clean and redolent of sunlight. All the world was snoring. A sudden and profound disorientation, that anxiety again. What was I doing, sharing an apartment with that fool?

The fool in question was propped up by pillows in bed, snug as that bug in its rug, watching one of a thousand interchangeable late-night movies as she devoured with her filed canines a wheel or three of cheddar cheese and pickled scrota from the jar. Every time she opened her door to 'retire to the little girls' room' for what she delicately referred to as a 'pee break' (one hind leg shakingly raised above the seat), all was the music of recorded car accidents, police sirens, collapsing bridges, people trapped in burning buildings, aircraft plunging into mountains, ocean liners sinking, New York City detectives loudly demanding: *'Is this the scene of the crime??'*, rural psychopaths threatening to knock some curious adolescent's head from their shoulders with an axe, urban psychopaths leaping from baths with a tomahawk, children mourning the mother they had lost to the latex-and-fibreglass jaws of a rampaging and totally implausible Japanese monster (*'Mommy! Mommy!'*), maniacal lawyers arguing a settlement, neurosurgeons screaming for a scalpel, young women smackingly savoured by mechanical sharks, martians abducting pregnant receptionists, executions, demented lords or barons torturing virgins in their castle dungeons with hat-pins or heated tuning-forks, little boys and girls vomiting as Satan possessed them, gunshots, razor-blade enhanced brawls over heroin deals, and the clanging tonalities of local rednecks as they advertised whitegoods or swampland or manchester sales. Entertainment. As the toilet gaggingly swallowed her secretions, Brine tunelessly hummed 'Que Sera, Sera'. Her footfall shook the universe as she returned to her bedroom.

Closed my eyes and then Gabriel's mouth over mine, as it had been every second of the day since he had left me.

11

Through a passage as narrow as a vein in the wrist, my consciousness broke open to an image of: sandstone boulders tumbling down into a lurching sea, flame-flowers forced, a greenhouse made of liquid glass. I was kicking. I was kicking against banks of mud – the mud of drugs, blunt punch of anaesthetic. Erotic confusion. The nurse and her soft *it's all right, now; it's all over; you're all right*. Her voice: a basket of loose serpents, docile, diamond-eyed, their argyle skins like stockings glimpsed between a low hem and a heel. Above me, the lights of the recovery room were polar, bright and unforgiving, but I was down amongst the molten substances of dreams – my father, I had sensed him near me for an instant, I had sensed him near me and then I was weeping against the starched weave of the sheet, my gown unlaced, one breast exposed, the nurse adjusting it, more of her words, her strange selenian face right over mine and then the slow injection of cold pethidine: that long needle releasing acids in my muscle, such an axis of pure pain. The

metallic aftertaste of anaesthetic – nausea, bold nausea. A
steel bowl placed beside my mouth and then my moan.
Retching. My blood dipped below eighty and I was inconsol-
able, so feeble, weeping against the starched weave of the
sheet. Those fading lights – tankers anchored at a distance
from the reef, their cargo of crude oil a black reality. Oh, be a
fine girl and kiss me: the mnemonic for the spectral classes of
all stars in order of descending temperatures – O, B, A, F, G,
K, M. My father, I had sensed him near me for an instant and
then I was so weakly sick. Bold nausea. The nurse, her words
lost in that unforgiving polar light, her hands suddenly
multiplying around my face: flame-flowers forced, huge
sandstone boulders tumbling down into a lurching sea, that
greenhouse made of liquid glass, and then I saw that both
sides of my bed were barred, those bars bright ropes of
mercury. I had been caged. I read the sign tacked to the wall:

VENTILATOR AND TUBING
BLENDER
PULSE OXYMETER
BLACK BAG
STETHOSCOPE
SUCTION EQUIPMENT
SEDITION RELAXANT
NARCOTIC
ECG MONITOR

And I lost consciousness.

12

Hallucinated for the first thirty or so hours on my
return.
It was as if my sanctuary from the world – that
empire of reverie in which desires and aspirations reign – had
been invaded or denied to me. Vaguely recall a wild and
irrational burst of giant hailstones through the open windows
and scattering across the floor, where they melted as the sky

cleared to a bluish blush. The stars and their incomprehensible perfection were only another drug. Old Leonids were pouring into another field of vision, and Mars was in conjunction with the Sun in the traditionally occult constellation of black Scorpius. Such a conjunction was a clarification of or emphasis upon the nature of masked violence: death, obsession, arcane knowledge, passion, pure warm streams of blood. Few compromises there. Venus joined Jupiter in the eastern sky at dawn, and then there was the return of Faye's comet to the perihelion, its heart a concentration of real gypsum white.

That nasty little garden of Brine's was sublime in darkness. Shadows ate the clumsy shapes of chairs and tools and of the sagging clothes pegged to the line. Left: only the plutolatry of pure conjecture. The lawn was rarely tended and was thus rich with sticky buttercups and clover-flowers and wheaty weeds with ornate bronze serrated heads. Chewed one and stared at the jacaranda tree that scented each night with its presence. The wooden fence-palings were shawled with Morning Glory vines, their daylight blooms a deep real use of form, their petals' nervous textures designed to withstand such stormy pigments. Smoked cigarettes even out there: adjunctive behaviour is the term psychologists use to describe a soothing activity that accompanies another task. Around me and beyond my understanding – gossamers from secret looms. I was, in part, restored by such abstractions. My surrender to the world, inspired by the aforementioned Scorpius, Circinus, Lupus, Crux: incomprehensible perfection.

Half-asleep out there one early morning, I recalled the tale of the god Shiva and his wife and their ten-thousand-year embrace. Standing guard at the door and the only witness to their sexual ardour, a white bull sworn to secrecy. Restrictions of any description inevitably grow to feel oppressive. The white bull broke his vow and as he spoke, blossoms fell from his white lips and were gathered by sages, who then composed the prototexts of lovemaking whilst meditating on the petals. And in that darkness by my mouth, a buttercup and as I licked it clean of gold, there was just Gabriel.

13

Another dawn painted by Fragonard. Another sultry afternoon. Beyond that long depressing week and into Thursday night: nine, ten, eleven, twelve. That glass of water from the tap. Twelve thirty-three, and then a slow quarter to one. Brine had dematerialized during my need, which may not have been a bad thing; her presence could have finished me. So: patiently lay perspiring in the sudatorium of my Dutch bed. Stared at the door, the walls, the floor, the ceiling, every book, my Questar catadioptric telescope. The heat was merciless, my sheets were wet. All the world was gilded by the fullest moon, her opalescent syrups spilling in from both the open windows: mother-of-pearl pools there on the dim and dreaming floor moved imperceptibly over the surface of each piece of furniture. My enervated stretch from toes to fingertips. Faraway vehicles and their purr. Two crickets alternating in their song. The caw of a lost bird. By the mysteriously fluorescent and fading numerals (ancient battery) of my digital traveller's clock: one thirty-five and its unwanted consciousness and then the telephone.

Surprised, I reached across myself for the receiver: 'Hello?'

Torched pause. Tight little exhalation. 'Battalion,' he announced. 'Glee. Icicle. Lace. Cello. Angel. Lit – which, as you know too well, means "bed" *en français*. Belittling. Antibiotic. Coil. Billion. Biting. Toll. Eagle. Bent. Logical. Globe. Italian. Agitation. Alibi. Act. Collegiate. Collect. Illegible. Entice. Tale. Cage. Lion. And best of all – allow a man his puerile amusement: I can't be illogical.'

Torched pause. My heart. 'You're not doing a bad job,' I said. 'Nothing you've said makes any sense.'

His smile was audible. 'You don't understand,' he said, '*I can't be illogical*. It's an anagram of your name. Two letters missing, but it's close enough. Angelica Botticelli: I can't be illogical. Concise, don't you think?' Another tight little exhalation and then, with humorous *gravitas*: 'I have developed an impressive theory.'

'Educate me,' I murmured, pressing the receiver to my lips.

'My theory,' he said, 'is that we are no more than the sum of the anagrams that can be made from our names.'

'Give me a moment,' I said. A pause torched by my calculations. And then my mimicry: 'Which means you are banal. Banal and bare. If your middle name were David, you would be rabid. So: bare, banal and regal. Which means that you are near, agile and that you lie. Are you an aria? You are a general. You range, you reel, you could be big. A brain. An eel? You like to brag. This system works. You have a gall. You seek the Grail. Stranger still: algae and labial. Bail, nail and glare. *En français*, a station: *gare*. And large. That's very curious, you know – both large and big are in your name. Another stunning combination: glib angel. And what else? Braille, which means that you can only be read with fingertips. Whose fingertips?'

'Educate me,' he murmured, pressing the receiver to his lips.

'I don't know, but can only hope,' I said.

'A lion in her cage?' he asked.

'A biting eagle,' I replied. 'A victim of Italian agitation.'

'My alibi,' he said.

'Your crime?' I asked.

'Seeking the Grail.'

'That's not a crime, that's punishment for high ideals,' I said. And then, pressing the receiver to my lips: 'Where have you been?'

Torched pause. 'Oh, here and there.'

I sighed. 'Your standard obfuscation.'

'Perhaps,' he said, 'and here I am with you at 2 a.m.'

Torched pause. 'Not here,' I said, 'but there.'

His voice was loved by me and so uneven as he murmured: 'Ten minutes or so.'

'Ten minutes or so what?' I asked.

'Not here,' he said, 'but there. I'll see you then.'

And he was gone.

With the precision antithetical to dreams: the flipping of the fading and fluorescent one-five-nine into a two and its two elemental noughts and he was there, a half-lit presence on the fire-stairs and of that rare stuff, reverie. My wrist was no more than a pour of wax as I pushed back strands of hair from my hot brow. Inaccessible through logic, the midpoint at which our fascination for the other met. Slowly he eased both of his big elbows onto the sill. His forearms were so beautiful. That scar bisecting his forehead was, in that light, invisible. In the band of shadow cast by the painted white meeting rail, his luminous observant eyes were gold. He stood there looking at me with a strange intensity and I could not help, I could not help but think that he was just another of my incurable hallucinations.

'You're here,' I said with some uncertainty.

'That's right,' he said, and then I saw his smile. And softly, so softly that it was almost inaudible: 'Dress. We're going for a drive.'

I watched him turn away from me so that his back blocked all the sky from one of my narrow windows. Naked and perspiring and on unsteady legs, I stood. Faraway vehicles and their purr. Two crickets alternating in their song. The caw of a lost bird.

'You do exist,' I whispered.

Without turning, but with a gradual inclination of his head: 'I'm real enough.'

'For what?' I murmured.

He did not answer, but returned his head to its original position. The sky before him was completely cloudless, its rich blue punctured by hard bright stars. A breath away from his warm throat, I could so smell him – that suggestion of white ash and columbine and then it disappeared.

'For what?' I again asked.

'I'll tell you in the car,' he said.

Watched him slowly walk away.

14

Tenderly turned the lock, opened the door, crept out into the mauve communal hallway and through the double doors' rectangular glass inserts watched Gabriel's shadow drifting through great lakes of lunar light. Stepped out and was then led by destiny down the garden path. Behind me, homely clumps of puce Impatiens, a sunburnt plaster gnome, the ridged big rubber barrels of garbage bins and those swathes of lace fading against Brine's window-panes. That avenue was for the first time magical to me: a theatre-set unpopulated, prepared for the first act of a play. The eye-blue cross-bar of a bicycle lay diagonally shimmering in a driveway. Through the grand window of the house opposite, a china cabinet could be seen in the elegant gloom – each of the panels of its arched-top glass doors imprinted with an image of the moon, so that the end effect was that of sixteen pearls or strange white fruits suspended in nocturnal ether. From the empty central business district, a certain orange glow. Gabriel had disappeared and then with effort, I discerned him deep within the shadow of a branching linden, his right arm territorially across the black roof of a Bentley Continental R. Metallic racks had been affixed to it and roped to them, a pale Xanadu surfboard, its nose curled in the manner of a Persian slipper. Fragrant with expectation, that night air. The slim ghost of a cat vanished beneath the belly of a car. It was enough for me that he was there, I could not have asked for more. Over the Bentley's black hood, distorted reflections of the both of us and elliptically reflected over the windscreen, that same full moon which had been multiplied by all the panels of the arched-top glass doors. Inhaled. Below me, pavement squares cracked by the bursting roots of trees.

And Gabriel, opening the car door for me from within.

15

Scent of leather, scent of salt: that dark and bestial-skinned interior and its tumultuous impact on me. On the back seat, a varicoloured Mexican blanket and a crumpled wetsuit and its frank human shape. Somebody's former life in neoprene. I could not look at him, it would have been to feel. Trapped beneath the windscreen-wiper: the newness of a maple leaf. It was as if my dress were no more than a vapour and my sex thickened with oils. How was it that with him beside me, my every movement seemed mechanical? Coughed and looked down. His broad brown feet were bare. Again, those frayed blue jeans and the sexual proximity of each wide thigh. His plain white stretched T-shirt and beneath it, his hot breast and within that, his heart. The fragrance of his sweat was an intoxicant and for a moment, I did not move but pictured with wild eyes his two axillary concavities, so curved: smooth-textured and thick-ened by russet-blond hair, each shaft encrusted with the body's salts, those salts expelled by every pore, his every pore, and then I only saw my tongue flattened against his skin and then experienced his flavour – white ash and columbine, and then it disappeared.

Belted myself in and then tremblingly pressed a button so that the window slid down to its brim. Waited. The muscles of his thighs suddenly tensed and as they did, my sex unconscionably swelled and rhythmic against its slick, the engine's hard vibration. He seemed to be awaiting some response from me, but I looked straight ahead and said: *just drive*.

The avenue unpeeled itself from my awareness in dim strips that were not unlike old photographs and then we were in motion.

Neutral Bay by streetlight, under stars: boutiques modern-ized by geometric mannequins, bookshops, restaurants, a florist's window overwhelmed by its arrangement of Bird-of-Paradise flowers. Concentrated fiercely on the view. Passed that penthouse gymnasium and its frontage of stick-figures synchronized to flash in turn, creating the illusion of gayest momentum. Swallowed with difficulty, a difficulty I saw him note. And easing into me from the right, his words, indigo-low: *you have been on my mind.*

Lights and more artificial lights, a residential vale of neon-tinted trees. A noiseless ambulance turned into Military Road and overtook us.

I'm taking you to Whale Beach, he said. *All surfers know it as the Wedge.*

I glanced at him. That long scar absorbed the light and filtered it silver, the colour to which all heals. His septum flowed in graceful lines. The pores of his brown skin were open and glittered with the lightest sweat. And quietly, almost an afterthought: *I've been away. Sometimes I get so tired of my work.*

We reached the tar swing of the Spit; on either side of us, a sequence of glimmering yachts and their backdrop of opaline bushland. A landlocked rowboat and a white brick restaurant advertised by a blue awning. The Bentley's upswing into the road which leads to every northern beach – at the peninsula: Avalon, Bilgola, Whale and Palm. My hair was swept in strands over my mouth and with one hand, I plucked them from my lips. So inhaled the heat and closed my eyes. I could not look at him, it would have been to feel. Opened my eyes and instead stared at all the milk-bars, at the lit car-showrooms, at the department stores, at the cinema complex, sailboarding centres, surfi'n'ski outlets, stared at the red-roofed houses and their yellow lawns, at the hamburger heavens and at the pizza hells, the windswept intersections, at all the tall black spiked generic beachfront pines and I could hear the ocean's foam restlessly sigh and hiss against the cliffs, over the shores.

You haven't asked me what it is I do, he said, his big hands easy on the steering wheel.

Turning my face away from that hot wind: *and why should I? Do you believe it would make any difference?*

His laughter was gentle and low.

Far into that enchanted night, my stare.

Agile and near.

I could be some kind of criminal, he said, *or stand for that which you despise or pity.*

In him that aria – the general commanding me, commanding all. His glance was braille.

My spirit reeled. Turned to look at him and turned away. *My analysis?* I asked. *You are torn between conservatism and real anarchy. How do I know? The Bentley and the Xanadu. Very basic observation, Gabriel. Neither fish nor flesh; you are both and neither. How would I describe you? Let me see. As a reactionary and an idealist longing for integration. Am I being aggressive? If I were, you wouldn't care. You've never in your life taken a gamble you couldn't win.*

His smile was slow, but one of strange pleasure. That warm and sweating throat. And then, with unexpected vulnerability: *do you really believe fundamental change is possible, or do you think superficies are all that can be changed?*

A drunken couple in their drunken twenties cross the sober road – she was rippling with red laughter and his short brawny arm was tight around her waist.

Impatiently, I answered: *A rhetorical question. Tell me instead of the ocean.*

On reaching the other side of the road, the red and rippling laughing girl stumbled and fell, and as her knight staggered to help her, she was all tears and thighs there on the kerb, her dress torn so that her floral underpants were on display, and then she vomited Auerbach's palette and in it, fell asleep.

Gabriel smiled without feeling at this bald performance and returned his attention to the road. *The ocean,* he mused through an exhalation. And then, with a tenderness that was abstracted but still touching, he said: *in water there are no mistakes, only directions. Do you understand? To our right, the sea – the moonlight carves a canyon through its heart. Truly; look: a canyon of reflected opalescence. I never lie. Why? Because there is no point. Lies complicate existence. Despite this, no-one has ever wanted me for my own truth. My whole life has been one long unwitting lie and it is seen to be desirable. I am, to put it bluntly, an example to my fellow men. There are myths in which we are all taught to believe, and imperviousness is one of them. There are myths to which we all subscribe – money, success, power over peers. If a man is dead within those myths, nobody cares. Mythology is no place for a human being. And yet we are conditioned to desire that which cannot be attained. And why? Because it creates an environment of struggle and when struggling, man is too busy to grieve for that which he has lost.*

We rapidly passed thirteen streets and then stopped beneath the glowing flower of a traffic light. He did not look at me, but instead stared out at that carved canyon and its opalescence.

Survival is an extremist, he said, *in that being and non-being are its two concerns. The one philosophy of all the elemental is dualism. And as if to spite nature's sovereignty, man has created a world of interjacent greys; when there are too many shades or variables, man is confused and thus meaning is sacrificed to the painless allure of minutiae.*

He inhaled and frowned at the coastal view before him and then his glance, the greenest flame.

In the ocean, he continued, *I feel that I am of the world and not just in it. The sea is one of the few arenas in which responsiveness is not only justified, but mandatory; without responsiveness, survival in the ocean is impossible.*

Again, that frown at the coastal view before him and his glance, the greenest flame. Opaline bushland reared on either side of us and behind it, that opalescent canyon carved through water by the moon.

All that is required of me, he said after a pause, *in my everyday existence is control, and that control is well rewarded. Denial of the psyche's wants and needs is that for which every ambitious man now strives. And to what end? To be applauded and rewarded with trite compensatory objects which increase his value in the eyes of those similarly limited – a car, a green estate, a ring. The symbols of feeling have come to seem more meaningful to us than the feelings themselves. This appears to be a player's trade, but in reality, creates nothing but a self-perpetuating appetite which comes to justify itself. We want and want and beyond that, only more want. Only the deprived desire with such urgency. That sense of peace promised is never found because peace can never be externalized, and the resultant frustration of each man is wreaked upon the world around him – aesthetic and emotional brutality, depravity of action and thought, the withdrawal of all social contribution. And that great new god our children are being taught to worship, technology: no more than the incarnated cry for communication of a mute civilization. Do you understand?*

The Bentley angled and we turned into a low steep road. Pale oleanders brushed and snapped against the body of the car, so that the hood was asymmetrically adorned with those toxic and lemon-butter scented flowers. Black gravel and its crunch beneath four tyres. Gabriel eased the car into silence and then slowly withdrew the key. The fragrance of his sweat was an intoxicant and for a moment, I did not move but pictured with wild eyes his two axillary concavities, so curved: smooth-textured and thickened by russet-blond hair, each shaft encrusted with the body's salts, those salts expelled by every pore, his every pore, and then I only saw my tongue flattened against his skin and then experienced his flavour – white ash and columbine, and then it disappeared.

My heart was burning and my mouth was dry.

The ocean's call.

Do you know, I whispered, *that I feel as if I've known you all my life?*

Slowly, I turned to look at him: direct, congested, in me a flicker of what may or may not have been an inexplicable anger, in myself a duel. He smiled, but in a way I could or did not want to understand.

You're naked underneath that dress, he said.

And then his broad brown hand and its paradoxically motionless arc to my full breast – motionless because the arc seemed to have existed before Gabriel had moved; it seemed to have existed as a Platonic truth; more than predestination and because of this, possessing an hallucinatory lustre, it seemed to be a universal absolute: a gesture-groove outside time and accessed perhaps through what was pure desire.

My sexual exhalation as he felt my breast was not his name, but a release.

I can hear your heart beat with my palm, he said, and kissed me: one slow tongue unfolding.

The air around us was so aromatic with cunt-oils; I rubbed my breast against his hand; he grunted and his eyes darkened and suddenly withdrew his mouth from mine. The thickness in his throat was a white kind of fear and I was in that moment no more than a component of his stare.

Let's go, he murmured, *let's get out of the car.*

Handed me the jar of perfumed wax and from the back seat, tugged that blanket. Left the wetsuit behind. With bare feet, I stepped out onto the gravel and could only watch him as he unroped the board from its metallic racks and then slipped it beneath his broad right arm.

Beside each other we walked over the straggling grasses, beneath the low and scaly boughs of pines, that hot sand a kind of flesh between our toes. Fresh sweat in rivulets ran down my throat, between my breasts, in aromatic darkness down my inner thighs. Pale silk-chiffon was sticking to my ribs and to my back's wet sway. The heat was sexual and I inhaled, I so inhaled. Gabriel paused – that long board beneath his arm – to look out at the water and its canyon of reflected opalescence. That alteration in expression: square chin lifted, eyes narrowed. Low whistle and his unknown smile.

A filthy set, he said. *It's pumping.*

On either side of us, raw upswept bushland: three porch-lights shone in the blind wilderness. Graded and ancient, its black base stacked with sandstone books sprayed white by the sea's lacework, that curvilinear cliff to our left. Slow slush of tide, the water warm as human blood and shifting and again shifting with it, splinters of driftwood. Transparent jellyfish along the shore. The moaning heartbreak of a distant ship and then a gull's cracked cry. My exhalation, that release. The scent of resin is so sharp. Gabriel's smile evaporating to a gaze: it was unreadable. Unsaid words between us and his breathing, deep and significant to me. The form of dunes quietly resonates in the subconscious. Gabriel lay his board down and spread the blanket on the sand. Then sinking to his knees and powerfully fanning the fingers of one hand, he wiped from the base of his throat hot sweat and as he did, said: *sit by me and listen to this night.*

16

Pumping. Dichromatic creases of moonlight on the water's lip: quartz and silver, shivering and splitting in each fraying smack of spume. *An eight-foot swell,* he said, *left-hander's coming off the rocks and peeling down the beach.* The dreamy hiss of offshore winds. Glassy conditions. The waves rose slowly from the fulgent ocean to the sky and cracked down crystalline, black as the body's soft arcanum. Rahab, the Angel of the Sea, was twice annihilated for refusing to conform to Divine authority. Lay down upon the blanket and so inhaled the heat, the fragrance of his sweat, the ocean's call. Embedded in the sand were miniscule white shells, the pearly fingernails of debutantes.

Gabriel turned and for the longest time gazed into me. Languidly, he leaned over and unbuttoned my light dress and as he did, he counted just below his breath to seven. One nacreous button for each tone of the musical scale. One nacreous button for each of the planes of nature: the physical, the astral, the mental, the Buddhic, the Nirvânic, the Paranirvânic, the Mahâparanirvânic. One nacreous button for each of the heavens, each heaven ruled by its own prince. Gabriel rules the first. Inhaled. Raphael rules the second. Exhaled. Dalquiel rules the third. Inhaled. Michael rules the fourth. Exhaled. Samael rules the fifth. Inhaled. Zachiel rules the sixth. Exhaled. Cassiel rules the seventh.

So inhaled the heat, the fragrance of his sweat, the ocean's call.

Spread on that blanket under his fingers, I looked up at the moon. Ancient religions decreed that her craters were evidence of battle with supernal enemies. On the western shores of the Mare Imbrium, the Bay of Rainbows. Mare Orientale, Mare Frigoris, Oceanus Procellarum: the sky's waterless seas reflected in the airless ocean.

Around that moon, a numinous halo in which so many stars were captured.

On his knees before me, his hands flat on his broad brown

thighs, his torso tensed: Gabriel – ruler of the first heaven and the general commanding me, commanding all. He was so still. His shadow fell, ample intangible, over my naked pelvis. Range, eel and glib. His green gaze was another form of heat against my sex and then my vulva further thickened; I was obsessively aware of its plump folds, its oils, its yielding and tender protrusions. However primitive, it is an expression of my soul as significant as any word or thought or feeling. So slowly, I widened my pale thighs so that his gaze could fully enter me, and then again. Regal and labial. Bail, nail and glare. And in that moment, I wanted only to give him all. Human, female, hollowed and filled: and this was how he made me feel. Mare Orientale, Mare Frigoris, Oceanus Procellarum: the sky's waterless seas reflected in the airless ocean.

Around that moon, a numinous halo in which the both of us were trapped.

Grail, large and big. His strip was languid and intent – that T-shirt and those jeans discarded, such unnecessary skins. And on his knees, naked beneath that moon, he was all that I could ever have imagined and then more; revealed, his solid and provocative male sex, its russet-blond fur, the peach-flesh of his foreskin and still holding me, his gaze – its chrysoprase profusely bleeding gold and in that gold, hard shards of jet: one of two colours outside the chromatic scale and the most intimate. Naked, he eclipsed that hot horizon. Arms a wingspan, shoulders flexed, the base of his broad throat glistened with sweat. The ocean's call came from within him and I could hear it. Still holding me in his green gaze, he lowered his lips to my vulva and then barely kissed me there. I closed my eyes. That impact of his mouth against my cunt. Shuddered. Pulp of his tongue against the smoother pulp of genital. My heart was no more than a syrup in his mouth and like a gyre, I widened: blue light around us both like that emitted from the burning leading edge of the veil nebula, where the most violet collisions occur. Taking my perineum in between his teeth, he tenderly nipped it. I had been rendered dumb and blind, and my remaining understanding was all glandular.

Those words of his murmured against my cunt: *you smell like sand beneath a bonfire, your scent is that of ocean floors*

– I've been there, pinned by waves to those dark depths, pinned to the point of death by water. Just like silk, he breathed, *you feel like silk. Your scent is that of ocean floors, the point of death, a sunken ship, the mosses live on sunken treasures – oh, my Angelica.*

I moaned. Agile and near. There was the suddenness of his dominion – succulence, my pulsing sex. Deeply within me with his tongue, he pressed each thumb into my flesh as if to transcend mass by force. Human, female, hollowed and filled: and this was how he made me feel. I liquefied against his mouth, that full dark mouth. Around us both, a blue light like that emitted from the burning leading edge of the veil nebula, where the most violent collisions occur. The ocean's call. Slowly he spread my buttocks and his tongue was in me thickly there, within my darkness, all the pure: Mare Orientale, Mare Frigoris, Oceanus Procellarum – the sky's waterless seas reflected in the airless ocean.

Around that moon, a numinous halo in which my heart dissolved.

My grunt as he so deeply entered me with his torched tongue and then those words of his murmured, murmured against my cunt: *you smell like silt, you feel like silk, your taste is that of mosses live on sunken treasures. I want to know you where you are the most unknown. I want to be your home, marrow. Such silk, this sex. I want to be familiar with your sin. I want to understand your lies. You never really show your hand. You are a spirit of the underground. I want your skin to sweat my name. Such silk, this sex. I want your skin against my lips – oh, my Angelica.*

Three of his fingers thrust within my sex and webbed with its syrups. Such senselessness and in it, a Platonic truth. *Come hard for me*, he whispered, *come hard against my mouth.* Exhaling and in flames, I was now his. I ground my cunt against his lips. His hand had stretched me to a gyre. I was all oil and gasped at this, a lurid beauty, and so senselessly. Those words of his murmured, murmured against my cunt: *Angelica, you murder me. Angelica, you make death sweet.*

Immensity in bouts of three: my cunt contracting – more a giant nerve axon, its stimulation leading to the synchronous contraction of my skin and in that moment, I finished with the self I used to call my own and was the sum of my sensations. My hoarse white cries, that Vedic hymn, his murmuring: all of the sea. And then my spine, a fulgent wave from water to the breathless sky and cracking down, so crystalline. Red blood, that subtle fuel, and that blue light enveloping the both of us like that emitted from the burning leading edge of the veil nebula, where the most violent collisions occur.

His mouth suckling my vulva and I could not stop coming against its pulp, those fingers of his hard within me, I was pierced: there was in me a haunting natural ascension from the physical and past the astral to the mental – all the pure. Such senselessness and in it, logic like that which I had never known. Spiritual capitulation. I would never, but never, forget a word he said. The momentum of his tongue and fingers eased and then he paused to barely kiss my sex, and then again. Mare Orientale, Mare Frigoris, Oceanus Procellarum: the sky's waterless seas reflected in the airless ocean.

Around that moon, a numinous halo in which we were both locked.

My open lips brushed hot against his throat as he levered himself over me. Such tenderness, that which I had never known. I had been rendered dumb and blind, and my remaining understanding was all glandular. Beyond his curvilinear shoulder: the lunar Apennines and the Caucasus Mountains. West of these mountains and far out in Imbrium's lava plains, the craters Archimedes, Aristillus, Cassini, Autolycus. Our kiss was one slow tongue unfolding and its fragrance. As he withdrew his mouth from mine, he stared with those chrysoprase eyes into my shadowed own, and then I saw in them a flicker of what may or may not have been a certain agitation. The ocean's call. A gull's cracked cry. Suddenly still, Gabriel closed his eyes and with some difficulty, exhaled. One of his arms cradled my back and my own hands tremblingly gripped his scapulae. Agile and near. Inhaled my heart. Slowly, he eased his two unyielding thighs between my own and slowly, oiled the big head of his sex against my vulva – back and forth, back and forth, his peach-foreskin unpeeling and then my moan.

Those words of his so softly murmured: *I'm going to fill you, my Angelica.*

In him, the levanter and in his eyes, gold, chrysoprase and

jet: one of two colours outside the chromatic scale and the most intimate. That burning breath of his against my lips. Dipping his cock within me gently, he so slowly pulled it back. Cunt suck. Dipping his cock within me gently, he so slowly pulled it back. Cunt suck. Our conjunction in this traditionally occult constellation: a clarification of or emphasis upon the nature of masked violence – death, obsession, arcane knowledge, passion, pure warm streams of blood. A 10,000-year embrace. Dipping his cock within me gently, he so slowly pulled it back. Cunt suck. Those words of mine so moaned against his lips.

Look into my eyes, Angelica, he murmured and then I looked within him – cunt contracting, heart a giant nerve axon and so carved, a canyon of reflected opalescence through my soul. I saw myself contained within his pupils, those doubloons: my face in climax held within his eyes. My image was now part of his – a supernatant cameo preserved between his lids. Dipping his cock within me, he so slowly pulled it back. Cunt suck. Those words of his murmured against my lips: *spread your thighs further apart, I want to feel you split, I want to feel myself enclosed by you, spread yourself open.*

The ocean's call. I spread my thighs. His flesh emitted light as blue as that emitted from the burning leading edge of the veil nebula, where the most violent collisions occur. That general commanding me, commanding all. Between my thighs, thickening nectar, those slow, slow plumes of slurring magma. Resting his weight on the arm cradling my back, he slipped his other hand between my legs. His fingers traced the lips of that elliptical slickness and palpated every flange, slid thickly past the head of his big cock and thickly into me. So slowly retracting his fingers, he then rested them upon my tongue and blindly, I suckled them. Suddenly he bore his weight down hard against my breasts and without a sound, he pierced me – a canyon of reflected opalescence was thus carved. My hoarse white cry was no more than a gull. He turned his throat in agony, in pleasure, and I kissed it with an open mouth.

My heart, contained within the moon's numinous halo.

Shaking, my hands clasped to the nape of his neck and then I bucked and met his plunge. I was impaled. He ground against me heavily, his cock bursting with syrups and so thick, so thick that I was rendered dumb by come-momentum: he had stretched me to a wanting scream and then I could not stop, I could not stop, my shaking hands were clasped to the nape of his hot neck and burning, I then bucked and met his plunge. It was as if my mouth were welling with nectar – pure as the mouth of a sucking calf, pure as the mouth of a hunting dog seizing its prey, pure as the beak of a bird severing fruit from a tree: the mouth of a woman during lovemaking. My cries were no more than the ocean's call and Gabriel, Gabriel, Gabriel. That sudden intensification or realignment of his energies and with his eyes closed and his jugular filling, he discharged himself within me. The chemical had become mechanical and then sublime. I held his sweat-filmed flesh. The heat he radiated was a halo and I was captured like so many stars in it.

From the hyoid arch which controls the apertures of the face, my name in the italics of his heart: *oh, my Angelica.*

We lay against each other, deeply breathing. Essence and force had come together in his look: these were the eyes beneath the eyes he usually wore. Slowly, I clasped his face and kissed his mouth, his broad brown cheeks, the lids of his observant eyes, his broad scarred brow. My fingers were trembling. Such tenderness, that which I had never known. And fully spread apart, my thighs: between them, all glandular oils, his will, the possibility of incarnated union. A lake of flame had been accessed within me. This feeling was no more than a Platonic truth, completely independent of us both: we had discovered pure desire.

Gabriel paused, and then rested his weight on that big arm cradling my back and lifting the other, curled a dark lock of my hair around his finger and then kissed it. So exhaled. I looked within him, past the chrysoprase and jet, through what perhaps was his one viaduct into the universal spirit. He kissed the edges of my wide soft lips. The ocean's call. My hands clasped shaking to the broad nape of his neck. Such heat. Beyond his curvilinear shoulder: the lunar Apennines and the Caucasus Mountains. West of these mountains and far out in Imbrium's lava plains, the craters Archimedes, Aristillus, Cassini, Autolycus. Inhaled my heart. The burning leading edge of the veil nebula had never known such a blue light. And then those words of his, murmured against my mouth, and thickly: *oh, my Angelica.*

Thoughts were collected by me in coloured formations but then dissipated to a sigh. Gabriel withdrew his cock from me thickly and his syrups – warm and opalescent – gushed from my sex. Such tiredness. Again, he kissed my shoulder and again, his lips a drug. Suddenly overwhelmed, I looked into his eyes – gold, chrysoprase, hard shards of jet: one of two colours outside the chromatic scale and the most intimate. There was an echo of his sex within me and its milk. The ocean's call. I closed my eyes and listened driftingly. The air suggested a seraglio in its scented warmth. In chiffon folds on either side of me, that rose-burdened silk dress. Vassago is the name of the good spirit invoked to find a woman's deepest secret and he was present, for I felt his sway.

All in me had risen to the surface of my skin and from each pore, Gabriel, Gabriel, Gabriel.

It seemed to me that he was standing in the sky, that board beneath his broad brown arm and with the other, he then helped me stand.

Gazed at the interlocking of our fingers and said, as if to no-one but myself: *my mother's rings are quite superb, but I have never seen her hands unadorned by gold or platinum or jewels. Imagine that. I've never seen my mother's hands naked.*

We clambered over boulders hacked by time and over wide cracked slabs of prehistoric sandstone. Adhering to the rock, thousands of tiny tough seasnails, some populating julep-shallow pools of minute crabs and purple urchins. Rich green mosses sucked lugubriously at our soles. Waves smashed against those sandstone swags and then slipped back, leaving clear plasma. Between my thighs, fresh sweat and that sea-breeze. Brushed his lips against my own and turned and walked to the sandstone's worn brink. He faced the water, waited for its motion to subside, pressed that board to his broad chest and suddenly threw himself into the ocean. The sky was blue seen through a garnet glass; the full moon was vanishing, a footprint in a field of falling snow. His biceps flexed and rippled as he paddled rapidly out to the break. *A filthy set*. The Xanadu sank just below the level of the water and rhythmically, it dipped and surged as the first wave unrolled slowly beneath him.

Years may have passed.

Waves green as those torched acetates convulsed behind him from the shelly floor – gaining solid shoulders, gaining brute momentum for that one release, and this was Gabriel's environment – the rolling quarrels of water and its unpredictable serenity, the sky above as variable in hue and temperature as the human heart. Lifted a slow hand to my eyes. In the liquid distance, light was reflected by the ocean in patches of pinkish glittering lentigo. Sweet on my tongue, all the residual sugars of arousal. Long strands of hair latched to my lips and with one hand, I brushed each of them away as I gazed out at that hot ocean; life had begun as an alloy of sunlight, methane, carbon dioxide, ammonia and water. Pearled lines of light so creased each crested wave – the voice of oil, the voice of every slap. Inhaled that salty air until all was delirium.

The set's second wave gorged on its volume and erupted into an improbable wall, and Gabriel – from his prone position, broad back primed – suddenly leapt onto the Xanadu and gouged the roaring cliff of water, his board carving the lip and sailing – parallel to the dim and hissing foam – into the morning's outstretched palm: tensed, contained, he then inclined his head, twisted his hips and jolted his left arm and its rigid fingers to the sky, raising his right arm to a strongly sinewed angle, and the board's white nose pierced and split the lip of water, causing him to vanish in a dream of warm white spume. He emerged vertically, with a brief balancing fanfare of arm-gestures and shook that wet blond hair, dropped back his big shoulders, and then his arms were raised in the salute of victory. Years may have passed.

17

That Saturday: jewelled light and tropically hot and further disintegrating in it, the bleached kitchen curtains. My dressing gown a glade of shadow. I sat and drank weak coffee as I read the newspapers. Mood ruined: Brine. Cocooned in that shapeless old bathrobe, she shuffled in felt slippers to the kettle. Bloodshot eyes. My stomach tightened and I blinked away tears of rage and pure frustration. I inhaled shakily, shaded my face with one cool hand, and hunched over the newspapers and sycophantic tribute to the 'key stylist' of modern British literature – the late, great, and much-lamented William Grieve.

Brine muttered about the glare and I ignored her.

That hacking, so intolerably prolonged.

I clenched my fists. Unclenched them. Breathed. I turned the page.

'Know what I mean?' she was asking. 'Bindi – (last domestic victim) – was a really good friend. We used to go out almost every night.'

My pause. Looked up.

She was slapping her slipper against the linoleum, and then yawned like a horse. 'Anything good in the papers, then?'

The letters swam before my eyes. Inhaled. 'British fish,' I said, 'are changing sex as a result of the contraceptive pill's oestrogen in female urine flowing into rivers formerly polluted only by lead and mercury.' My pause. 'A bingo king obsessed by his faithless ex-wife arranged for her to be strangled.'

Again, that hacking and the kettle's scream. Brine slammed her cup down on the counter, aimed a tea-bag, and poured in the boiling water. Jiggled and dangled. Hacked again. (She had the previous night eaten a pack or two of filterless French cigarettes.) With a practised hand, she tossed the drained tea-bag into the 'tidy', added milk to her hag's brew and then blowingly sipped it. Shuffled in those felt slippers to the dining-room table and frowned. Her ash-dry forehead ruched. 'Rings on the table,' she scolded. Hungover, she slipped a coaster beneath my coffee cup. The freckled pouches beneath her eyes were streaked with old mascara and her hair was an explosion in Kansas. Another dainty hack. Slurped at her tea. She watched me pretend to read an article about a woman who lost custody of her ten-year-old son after hiring a stripper for his birthday party.

Long pause. 'So ... doing anything today?'

'Just reading,' I fake-casually replied.

'Uh-huh,' she said, and again slurped at that steaming and gravy-coloured tea.

I turned the page. Three adolescents in Atlanta had been charged with murder. They had, over a period of twenty-four hours, tortured a disabled pensioner with seven knives, a barbecue fork and table salt. The victim passed his last hours pleading with his frenzied tormentors to kill him. Transhistorically, people have only ever extended kindness to those they think human and transhistorically, humanity has been a synonym for shared ideological beliefs and never a physiological affair: real faith in sin is the mother of victimization, and the victimized will atrophy unless helped or by others be destroyed.

'Might go to the beach with Mandi,' Brine mused as with one chipped nail she picked at the cracked tiles of her two front teeth.

I turned the page. Four teenaged girls in Indiana had bludgeoned, sodomized and then incinerated a twelve-year-old peer. Their reasoning? The twelve-year-old was thought to have 'stolen' one of their boyfriends and was thus declared deserving of frenetic sodomy with a tyre lever, having her thighs slashed with a knife, and being doused with petrol before being set alight. Transhistorically, people have only ever extended kindness to those they think human and transhistorically, humanity has been a synonym for shared ideological beliefs and never a physiological affair: real faith in sin is the mother of victimization, and the victimized will atrophy unless helped or by others be destroyed.

'So,' Brine plaintively asked, 'you wanna come?'

I scowled, exhaled, looked up. 'Pardon?'

'The *beach*,' she said in an insistent tone, 'd'you wanna come with Mandi and I to the *beach*?'

'Thank you,' I said, 'but no. Must read.'

'Shame to spend such a nice day inside,' she said, and again slurped at her tea.

Next door, children were shouting – '*Mine!*' '*No, MINE!*' – in the trampled disaster that was their garden (a lawn of urine-coloured grass, blackberry bushes, a young mulberry tree stripped of its limbs, that bed of dehydrated rosemary, healthy green weeds, a crop of colourful Meccano). Their dog mournfully howled. A hundred klaxons battled for supremacy at the nearest intersection. Brine stood and shuffled to the sink. Sloppily ingested a tub of sugarless raspberry yoghurt as she leaned with one elbow propped up by the refrigerator door.

And then: 'Sure you don't wanna come?'

I shook my head.

It took her all of three minutes to strip and reappear in a white nylon bikini, sunglasses, high-heeled clogs, gripping a basket in which she had shoved a towel, sunscreen, and garish blockbuster (the cover of which featured a woman Brine would never be in the early stages of ravishment by a man Brine would never attract).

'See you later!' she cried, and then with a wave was gone.

Lay down on the floor, slaughtered. The white ceiling had been stained by nicotine. Reached up for my packet of cigarettes and lit one and then angrily inhaled. *What had I done?* The neighbouring children had been frogmarched inside and now there was only the invective of their mother as she berated the sexually frustrated family dog. There seemed to be a sudden deficit of air. Across from me, a minute cockroach scaled one of the table-legs and with the edge of the ashtray, I methodically crushed it and then scraped its winged remains from the blond wood and onto the carpet. Remembered that tables are only seemingly solid; in actuality, they are predominantly empty space. (Had Brine been aware of basic physics, she would undoubtedly have asked for a fat discount from the table's salesman.) Idle conclusion: humour relieves the stress of sense and sex relieves the stress of love. And Gabriel? Perhaps that occult conjunction of which I had been dreaming with wide-open eyes had been nothing but a farce, a mechanistic farce;

perhaps my system was only the sum of its love-starved parts, those parts programmed for deprivation. Depressing thought. Pensively stubbed my cigarette out in the ashtray and lay back on the floor where I remained for hours, just remembering.

18

During my hundred years of solitude with William, I had been plagued by bouts of fierce cystitis. On the recommendation of Kitty (a former Miss Orange County and wife of an *idiot savant* quantitative analyst who earned over half a million pounds a year), I became the patient of Dr Huysens, of the candycane white-and-maroon Harley Street (which my fiancé referred to as 'the valley of the shadow of death'). We had met at a Fulham Christmas party – an event starring a gargantuan roasted turkey, impeccably dressed in watercress and crisp white paper tennis socks, and a richly baubled jugged fir tree. Beneath one of its branches (a ceramic interpretation of the Baby Jesus in his manger dangling to my left), I shook Kitty's soft pink hand and engaged in the traditional female exchange of powerlessness over hair and hips and husbands. Kitty (a touch-sensitive musical bow in her blonde hair) parted the weighted branches to maximize the impact of her perfect face. 'You have gotta see my doctor, Huysens!' she exclaimed in response to a complaint. 'His obstetrics package deal is only nineteen hundred and fifty pounds, and he is a genius, a real star.'

And so I did.

Huysens met me at the door of his Victorian rooms in a spotted silk bow-tie and shallot-coloured double-breasted suit, his collar-length locks superbly coiffed. These seraphic ringlets flatteringly framed his face and lightly bounced whenever he inclined his head. The discord of traffic from the Marylebone Road was muted by the double-glazing. Huysens noticed me looking around and smiled engagingly. Big dairy teeth. Mean little lips. '*Ms* Botticelli!' (Delicately resting his fingers on my shoulder.) 'And *what* a charming name! *Do* come in!' (Batting his eyelashes.) 'Kitty called to warn me that you were gorgeous. I must confess, I *do* adore those Fulham Americans – so bright, don't you agree? And so astute, despite their seemingly inane chatter.' (Waving his hand.) 'Sit down, sit down, sit down. I've had the *plaisir* of seeing you from afar on various occasions – in particular, Tiggy Dum-Dumfries' birthday party at the Ritz, to which – and do correct me if I'm wrong – you wore an unforgettably black gown.' (Slyly grinning.) 'My wife Amanda never fails to point you out in all the social pages, and now that you are here before me in all three dimensions – although a woman like yourself undoubtedly has four – I am more able to empathize with my wife's fascinated envy: a sorry plight, and one so typical of every woman's middle age.'

From my clawed chair, I stared across the desk.

On the wall to his right, his family (three miserable porkers in boaters and a pilchard-wife); on the wall to his left, an aerial portrait of his Irish castle ('Quite beautiful but chilly, much to my wife's chagrin'). Behind him, framed degrees from Cambridge University and St Bartholemew's Hospital Medical College. His desk was narrow and of a pinkish wood I did not recognize; on it, neatly stacked papers, an elaborate computer terminal, and another framed photograph of his family. Clasping his hands, he gazed at me with a sudden intensity.

How could he improve my life?

As I catalogued my ills, he made concerned and understanding noises and nodded. Steepling his hands, he rested his mean lips upon the tips of his long fingers, a gesture which widened his eyes and their perilously creamy intent.

'You need a *kinder* man,' he said. 'This Grieve of yours is no more than a semi-trained wolfhound. You might find an affair would save your life.'

Butterflies soared within the spacing of his words.

His pause was in itself a meadow.

Eyeing me steadily, he led me to the annexed examination room (made intimate by kilims and primitive sculptures). A bone density machine provided an element of medical reality. What skin I had, what grace, what wit! His touch was fluid and his voice was no more than a nutrient for those starved of affection. 'A woman is like a *flower* here,' he cooed as he surveyed my sex. Allowing one hand to drift over my naked thigh, he sighed and then abruptly stepped back to the door. 'You are the kind of woman who will drive men mad until you're forty.'

Only until forty?

Back in the clawed chair and attentive.

'I keep all my patients' records here,' indicating the computer. And, given that you belong – if only by proxy – to the world of literature, there is something I feel I should tell you.' Laying those palms flat on the desk, he filled his eyes with decadence. I was bewitched by the dramatic performance of his throat. 'I am,' he finally managed, 'a *poet*.'

Staring at the rain pelting against that one window behind me: 'I – I have never told *any*one this before, but I feel that I could tell you anything.' Slight pause. 'You have a certain quality – some indefinable aura of compassion, Angelica ... you don't mind me calling you "Angelica", do you? It's just that I feel – I feel –' He squeezed his eyes shut and squeakily exhaled. 'I feel as if I *know* you.'

Biting his lip and looking me directly in the eye: 'I cannot find it in myself to with hold *any*thing from you.' He forced a blush and delivered unto me a bashful grin. 'I – I have always written ... poetry. I won a number of silly little literary prizes at Harrow, meaningless things. My poems are nothing, really – just the embarrassing work of a dilettante, I'm afraid.' His fingers lit expertly on the keys as he searched for an appropriate work. '*Ah!*' he cried. 'Here it is, here it is. Now you must *promise* not to humiliate me.'

I promised; he punched a key; the printer began its vibrato. We stared into each other's eyes as the long poem stuttered out. A high-pitched sound indicated that the printing was complete. Huysens athletically sprang from his chair, theatrically ripped the paper free and handed it to me. 'Before my father forced me into medicine,' he breathed against my cheek, 'I wanted only to become a poet-warrior.'

THE MOON AND STARS MEAN NOTHING TO ME

The moon and stars mean nothing to me.

They twinkle like the suspicious eyes of strangers on the tube.

They reach across the ether like the outstretched arms of beggars.

I only want to tear the sky to pieces.

The moon and stars mean nothing to me.
They sparkle like the evil eyes of schoolboys on detention.

They are utterly pointless, and nothing like your fawn-like grace.
They spin and mock me like callous jesters.

When I think of your legs wrapped around me like a familiar scarf.
I want to destroy galaxies with the power of my desire.

The moon and stars mean nothing to me.
To think of your flaxen hair. To think of your tinkling laughter.

To hear the screaming of my heart, more tortured than ever
without you.
And the owls are hooting in the yews.

What does it matter that our love can never be.
I only want to kill God.

O, Fate! Despair is within me in the mirror!
My wife is like a leech. I hate her.

You must go on without me. You must climb the shivering volcano
with another.
How this prospect makes me squirm and suffer.

My soul floats out of my body and into yours.
I seek your face in my hands. I want to slap myself.

The years before you were a desert infested with Arabs and
scarabs.
Those years have been cremated, their ashes in the urn of loving
you.

The winds spit at the cold planets.
The seas lash at my heart like whips.

Nights of marriage, nights of bondage.
Nights without you are absolutely frightful.

I remember our kisses in my rooms.
Your seamed stockings were as sheer as my veneer of respectability.

But your destiny must, like a bee or some bats or a satellite,
Fly unhindered by me through the stormy night.

'So,' he jauntily said, 'what's your prognosis?'

Folding my hands, I nodded as I slowly and silently reviewed every possible response ('You certainly pissed up a storm with this one, old man.') After a pause punctured by partial exhalations, I cautiously said: 'It's strongly ... evocative.'

The avalanche was not unexpected. 'How extra*ordinary*! That's what Piggy – my old English master – used to say*! Strongly evocative, my boy!* How extra*ordinary* that you should use pre*cisely* the same words! Absolutely extra*ordinary*!' His throat fattened with pleasure. 'Must admit, though, that I'm *rather* fond of the bit about the seamed stockings. Took me *ages* to write – absolute *ages*.'

'It doesn't show,' I said, gravely referring to the evidence.

Suddenly vulnerable, he swallowed. 'You ... *do* like the bit about the seamed stockings, don't you?'

For a moment, I was paralysed – my left hand flared, my lower jaw extended, brows purled, heart wholly tapped of oxygen. And then: 'Of course, of course ... but it was the ... desert metaphor that struck me – that struck me as –'

He leaned forward. 'Blindingly original?'

Another pause. '*Lyrical* is the term I would be inclined to apply to it,' I said.

His wounded glance. 'You don't like the stocking bit.'

'No, no, no,' I hurriedly said, 'the stocking bit is terribly ... expressive, but it was the desert bit that struck me as – in particular, the bit about Arabs and scabbards –'

'*Scarabs*,' he corrected.

'Scarabs?' I nervously asked.

'*Lyrical*, you think,' he mused. '*Lyrical*.' Opening the first drawer of his desk, he rummaged around and then his hand re-emerged wrapped tightly around a fountain pen. 'You are too kind, you are too kind.' His ringlets danced a little as he smiled and shook his head. 'Perhaps,' he said, 'Piggy was right – I *should* have been a writer. You're not the first to notice that I have The Gift.' It was apparent that he had been told a thousand times by senile aunts that his dimples were charming, and the resultant vanity was evident in his eyes. 'You know, I would appreciate it terribly if you kept the poem, Angelica. You would be doing me a *great* honour.' And then, as if remembering the pretext for this stretch of psychodrama, he made himself officious. 'I suppose I should fill out your prescription?'

The rain was passionately cracking against the window, its sound that of the most rapturous applause. Would he now stand to take a bow? His pen flowed easily across the pad, and then he signed his name as if signing an autograph. '*This* should fix it,' he trimly said. 'Augmentin, 375 milligrams; Trimethoprin, 200 milligrams. I trust you to precisely follow the instructions. And whatever else you do, don't under *any* circumstances resort to those NHS butchers. Each and every one of them was personally trained by Eichmann.' Paused to collect his thoughts. And then: 'And I'd like you to return to me in a fortnight. Hopefully, all will have been resolved. In the interim, *do* counsel that creature with whom you live to treat you with a touch more care. Poorly endowed men always feel they have to compensate for their lack of length and girth by hammering – which is, as you well know, not only counterproductive to pleasure but terribly *pain*ful. As they say in Earl's Court: *it's not the size of the wave, but the motion of the ocean*. Or so my secretary tells me.'

After politely laughing, I turned to look behind me at the rain and he was suddenly before me, planting on my lips a moistened kiss. '*Au revoir, Angelique*,' he murmured, 'until we again meet.'

Sadly, we never did.

19

Days later: the bus was varicose with schoolchildren and office workers gripping bags of catfood, tense new mothers, shrieking infants, and the homeless mad. I was shoved against the glass partition to the immediate left of the sebum-smudged pole and to the right of the door, the blade of some arthritic crone's umbrella (in this weather?)

wedged in the crease between a buttock and wet upper thigh, a rotting gouache of peanut-butter sandwich at my feet. With clouded eyes, the driver fixed the asphalt haze ahead. I had been travelling for twenty minutes and not a soul had left the bus. The thing would be transformed into a colony of hell, roaring for all eternity around the city and stopping only to add to its burping population. Near me, two tanned gibbons in badly cut business suits reviewed their modest lives.

Gibbon One: 'Saw Jo the other day. D'you know she used to be three stone heavier?'

Gibbon Two: 'Yeah?'

Gibbon One: 'Yeah, really.' Pause. And with concern: 'She looks really rough these days.'

Gibbon Two: 'Yeah, well, she doesn't get much sleep. Always out at nightclubs.'

Gibbon One: 'Yeah. She's the kind of girl who would look good if she dressed a bit more nicely.'

Gibbon Two: 'Yeah. A nice sort of dress and some sleep would do her the world of good.' Pause. Politely: 'You know, I rang the bank the other day and this girl answered. Funny how some girls sound like real stunners on the phone.'

Gibbon One: 'Yeah?'

Gibbon Two: 'Yeah. That happens sometimes.'

Gibbon One: 'Reckon!'

Gibbon Two: 'Yeah. Lindy's a bit like that. We had breakfast last week.'

Gibbon One: 'Yeah?'

Gibbon Two: 'Yeah. It was nice. Funny girl. Cute.'

Gibbon One: 'Yeah. Amazing how cute some of them sound on the phone, but then when you see them, in person they're not as cute.'

Gibbon Two: 'Reckon!'

Gibbon One: (After a pause) 'Yeah ...'

This chorus of meditations and affirmations concluded with an abrupt halt, the passengers soaring forwards in a damp mass of flesh and damp apologies. Stumbled and smashed my forehead against the glass partition as the crone behind me lurched into her own lap and simultaneously thrust the point of her umbrella deep between my thighs. The door unfolded its transparent wings just as abruptly and with the same sadistic aptitude he had used for braking, the driver pulped the accelerator with his black boot, the brute (a hiss of teeth visible between his lips), and then the vehicle loosed its thunder.

20

This thunder had become a feature of my life. I wished for nothing but control. Easier said. I think I was really after an apartment in the universe of blocks, a universe in which all was geometry – a Euclidean paradise, unchanging and precise: a world of hard and shining surfaces, in which there were no fluid forms or mergings, in which all remained distinct, defined, denumerable – in short, I was afraid of my own heart.

As a fevered child, I had hallucinated a carnivorous Cyrillic alphabet, toothed logarithmic spirals, dodecahedrons with the power to absorb a human soul: a horrible experience, and I recall crying to be rescued from these, the villains of numerical theory. The individual still held a greater interest for me than the general; in this respect, I was more artist than scientist. As a result, a certain confusion reigned. Late in the afternoons, I would lie in the long grass and yawn uproariously as red or yellow ladybirds navigated the air-flow. Through shaded eyes, I would watch dragonflies pierce the many levels of sunlight; I would observe the world and think. Sometimes I dozed and in my every dream, a ceiling of green water over me. I often thought that in another life I might have drowned, my former bones a friable sash dropped to a plunging slow black floor of scalloped weeds, but willingly – for love, perhaps.

For love.

21

A vibrant southerly, its many voices trapped like threats of vengeance in the rattling window stiles and jambs. I lay on the floor reading and listening to the telephone ring. It rang only for Brine, who would man the kitchen extension (a maddeningly inconvenient metre or so from my bedroom door), receiver crushed to her bat-ear, one hand systematically smoothing the plastic cord, and in her stiff hair enormous salon-pins (emerging like antennae from her scalp). Brine would gnaw at her fingernails, littering her seersucker tongue with flakes of nail-varnish and calcium. These conversations could continue for hours and, judging from her responses, were fundamentally interchangeable: it was always the one conversation held between Brine and the externalized other half of her mind. I was less loving of symbolic exchanges, but limited by a similarly astigmatic sense of otherness: at night and after hours of trying for sleep (awful grey hours, endlessness), I felt that I had grown horns, a hump, a tail. My skin stretched until it felt like a scaled tarpaulin and my incisors devolved into tusks.

The spectral haruspex who haunted me divined from my hot entrails doubt, she divined loss.

Brine had been out forever and returned one night at two or three or four. Exploding through the front door, she thundered sobbing through the flat and into the bathroom. In bed, I sighed. There was a certain rhythm to her misery. It was not difficult to visualize her face (maraschino eyes, melting cosmetic features, exaggeratedly sad mouth). I listened to the clatter of her heels on the tiles, to the bap-bap-bap of the toilet lid, to her drilling micturation and its spring trickle of a stop, to the cistern's sudden storm. And then, as in a soap opera, the telephone wailed. Those big transvestite's feet thumping.

Heard her grapple with the live receiver and in response to some entreaty, cry out: '*No*! I don't wanna discuss it now!

I'm too – I'm too – I'm too hu-hu-hurt!' (Fresh volley of sobs.) '*How could you do that to me*??' (Her outraged pause.) 'How *could* you?? I would never do that to *you*! *I thought you were my friend!*' (Her pitch was psychotic, inhuman, unbearable.) 'I can't – I can't *believe* the way you carried on! No, that's right – I won't! *NO!* I won't … I said *no* … I'll speak to you – *don't* … I'll speak to you – I said *I'll speak to you tomorrow* … no … no … of all the things to say! I just couldn't believe my ears! I can't … that's right, you did … that's right … and I – yeah, that's right, you're not telling me something I don't know … I was … yeah, exactly … you did … you bet you did … of all the things to say! And I'd told you in – yeah … exactly … and he – no, now he won't because of … no, he won't, he won't, he won't … how would *you* of felt if I'd … yeah … how would *you* of felt, eh? … yeah, if I'd of done the same thing to you?? … you *ruined* … no, you did, you *ruined* my … that's right … you bet I am … you bet I am … no, I won't … *no* … I said I don't wanna – *no*! I'm *tired*, that's why! … no … no … I don't – I don't care! You ruined – no, he won't, now … *I'm gonna go to bed* … I couldn't care less … I'm going to bed now … I'm gonna – no, I won't because I don't *want* to – no … no … I'm going to bed right now this minute – good*night*!'

Goodnight.

The hu-hu-hurt Brine smashed the receiver back into its cradle, thundered back into the bathroom, urinated like a moose, slipped to the floor with a large jar of cold cream and screamed, crackingly sobbed, slammed the vanity cupboard door open, in her frenzy knocked ten thousand bottles of lotion onto the tiles, violently cursed, slammed the cupboard door shut, and once she had adequately bandaged her bloodied hoof, retired to her frilled lair where she soundly bawled until dawn.

22

The following day I reminded myself that triviality rests in abstraction from human interests, and so attended the local premiere of an art-house documentary about creative sexual practices. This masturbatory garbage starred a reclusive former pornographic queen who now posed as a professor of the libidinal arts, a bovine prostitute who – in an effort to demystify her noble and therapeutic calling and during a sell-out tour of her didactic infra-red show – inserted a speculum within herself on stage and invited the audience up for a 'Public Cervix Announcement'. As the more enterprising members of her fan-club sank their sweating heads between her thighs, this permed sociopath delivered the soothing emetic of her commentary – lecturing (in a frothy and teeny-tiny voice) on the simplicity of feigning arousal, orgasm, sanity, et cetera. Later in the opus, we were introduced to her 'favourite sexual partner' – a tattooed hirsute hermaphrodite with withered breast-pods, pierced nipples, gelatinous buttocks, a harelip, and an ersatz penis stiffened by the insertion of a wooden or plastic implement into the relevant surgically engineered flap of flesh. This favoured dualistic sexbeast, oddly appeased by the clinical flavour of his/her demonstration, stared into the camera and said (with a disturbingly ironic undertone): '*Hi, Mom.*'

Brine had evaporated (no doubt out repainting the old town) by the time I returned. She had left most of the windows open as she was convinced of the effectiveness of her one security measure: an active radio left on the sill. I boiled some milk and drank it by the window near the sofa, mesmerized by the decaying fence-palings which separated our brick block from the palace next door. At random intervals, artificial light would fill their bathroom and through the frosted glass, strangers of varying sizes could be seen performing their distorted and mechanical ablutions. I stood in darkness by that window for an hour, without cohesive thought or motivation, sad as I had ever been and holding that cheap china cup like an imploring effigy.

Night brought disturbance. I dreamed of leather hands, each phalange affixed by a screw, each lunula fashioned from steel, struggling to force open my bedroom window: always that one dream of insanity, a ribbon of white light along the conscious edge of a long blade, that blade plunged back into a darker psyche.

Too frequently, I awoke shouting.

Too frequently, I feared to be asleep.

23

A story for the little ones arranged before the crackling fire, their rumina, reticula and psalteria decocting their dinner of turkey and plum pudding to the allegro of sleigh bells outside: at the age of sixteen – when I was bulimic or anorexic or suicidal – I was selected from the national GPS swot pile to attend a three-week course for gifted adolescents at a Seventh Day Adventists' holding in the desperate nothingness of western New South Wales. Bald hills, dead plains, infernal winds. At midday when the asphalt souls of the streets rose to a haze, when all the local housewives (rollered locks in checkered cauls) 'took a nap', I would walk those hazy streets and ponder the possible early family environments of every authoritarian personality (dominant father, submissive mother, children denied expression of vulnerability and sexuality and aggression, children deprived of affection and encouraged to project their suppressed feelings – that is to say, aggression and vulnerability and sexuality – onto those they had been taught to regard as their foes).

My mother had at the time temporarily relocated to Europe, our housekeeper was in traction (a genuinely disambiguous car accident – she was plastered), Aldo was 'away on business', and Amedeo had been left 'to his own devices' in the Shell Cove house. I may as well have been on the lava plains of the Mare Imbrium, preoccupied as I was with the work of Robert Browning, criminal psychology, Occidental Decadence, and conditional deterministic time.

And so my brother, who had been taught to fear intruders, slept with all the lights on and the dog locked in his room. The undomesticated Fiat defecated throughout the house, ruining many of the precious carpets and certain treasured medieval tapestries. On the third day of his sentence, Amedeo left the iron prone on the upholstered board for half an hour and almost burned the house down. On the seventh day, a sewage pipe exploded, flooding the driveway with faeces that remained there until Aldo returned (to boil them for breakfast). On the the tenth day of his sentence, my brother decided to clean the pool. At that age, he was still eager to express his need for approval. Instead of pouring the hydrochloric acid and chlorine in separately, he thought he would 'save time' by mixing the two. Had it not been for our nosy neighbour (an ebullient Confederate that minute returned with her third husband from their second honeymoon amongst the rutting elephants of Kenya), Amedeo would now only be a memory. She discovered him just after he had inhaled the noxious fumes (convulsing in the shade of a spreading Camperdown Elm, a bed of bright papilionate flowers at his feet).

There was some trouble when the authorities attempted to contact our jetsetting parents. Aldo was very displeased; on his return, he lashed the boy so thoroughly with his Cartier belt that for a week, he limped and could not sleep. Arabic cultures are not the only cultures in which the anger of the father is believed to be that of God. Mother refused to discuss the incident. Her couture expedition had been interrupted, her husband was enraged, she did not want to know.

Through their lack of love, through their lack of applied affection, through their lack of compassion, through the surfeit of their compensatory greed and ambition, through their insecure self-aggrandizement and defensive indifference, through their lack of respect for others, my mother and her husband had distorted two young lives and they were accountable, yes; they had polluted pristine waters from which others would drink.

My stepfather needed a target: man, woman, child, law, corporation – it was all one to him, all that mattered was an acute aim. These facts were irrelevant to my mother, who felt his presence was essential to her sense of femininity and social standing. I was unfeminine enough to force the issue when Aldo pinned my brother to the wall with a chair. Amedeo, guilty of stealing a twenty dollar bill from my mothers' purse, was dragged from his bed by our stepfather who punched him and then pinned him like a starfish to the wall. Aldo's words (I paraphrase): 'You *dumb* little cunt! You fucking *faggot*! I'm going to fucking *kill* you – do you *under*stand?? I'm going to fucking *kill* you! What do you think this is – a *welf*are hostel? Do you think I'm going to sit back while you suck me *dry*?? You *piece* of shit! You *useless* fuck! Live off me like a leech, is that what you think you're going to do??'

And so on and so forth, a music by which to waltz. My suddenly-deaf mother (modelling a chic straw hat, champagne satin mules and a Versace one-piece) was positioned by the cast-iron balustrade of her bedroom veranda, seemingly hypnotized by the sun-speared harbour. I cried out that Aldo had gone mad, he had gone mad; I cried out that Amedeo was bleeding, he had been hurt; I cried out that we had to call for an ambulance and the police – Amedeo had been badly hurt, blood was running from his mouth.

She comes at you from the ink and the chemical
infra dig, a full page frontal
of fractures and breakfasts and sodomy:
the animal liberties of modern marriage.

There comes a time in every love
when the word made flesh
becomes a theatre.

She is more the stuff of ghosts every time you look at her.

My mother's voice only lightly trembled as she spoke. 'Aldo's just tired, darling,' she whispered as she mechanically adjusted the black strap of her bathing costume, 'he's been working far too hard. This Calvinistic ethos of his is *très ordinaire.*'

24

Early on in our marriage, Brine and I had agreed to alternate the household duties and it was my turn to lug that pail and its greying mucilage. Abstergents, toxic sprays, the elimination of certain vital spiders. At my own apartment, I had employed a busty German woman, but here at Flat Number One, 666 Irony Avenue, I kept my promise to experience life in all of its mundanity. What had I done? Tugged on flesh-coloured latex gloves, my long hair loosely braided, and remembered – in one of those quaquaversal bursts of graded irrelevance – Brine's breakfast wisdom (dispensed over the table some five days ago): 'Can't say I like women what act like men,' the cretin had mused through a jawful of fat-free-sultana-sweetened bran flakes and a cup of sickeningly sugared tea, 'know what I mean? I think that being a woman means looking nice and smelling nice, even if you're not going anywhere special. I mean, I even put on perfume and nice knickers for when the man comes over to mend the fridge. Which is how it should be. Nature. Women were made to make themselves pretty for men, don't you think?'

I certainly did.

But enough of my sarcasm; we had a houseguest. Absorbed by my thoughts and recollections, I was kneeling by the toilet (both arms plunged into the soapy bowl). Looked up. A rough block of a man, the tips of his nude square pink toes resting upon the metal strip which separated the white tiles from the acrylic carpeting. His heavy arms were laced with amplitudinous blue veins, his lower lip was plump and hung as if detached from his weak jaw, his eyes were prominent and set in creased and purplish sockets. Congenially hung-over.

Well, well, well! I must be Angela. I looked busy!

His tar-cracked laugh and then he coughed so violently I feared his lungs would slap out onto the tiles beside me. His abundant paunch was the colour of a plucked chicken and speckled with strange growths; it spilled over the knotted cotton sarong Brine always wore to those relaxed rum-and-coke kind of evenings at downmarket yacht clubs. Rubbing his palm over the dense black stubble of his cheeks, he smiled. Would it be all right, then, if he took a shower? I paused and slowly pulled my gloved hands from that frothing bowl. Cautiously nodded. (Who was this fool?) He crossed the bathroom's threshold, minimizing his use of space (in deference to me, the little lady), and applauded my great and shining talent for interior design (I did not bother to correct him).

Stood and crab-walked past him, lugging my pail full of scum.

Once he had lathered and rinsed his eyeballs and unimaginably forested perineum, this man lumbered out into the dining room and remarked (whilst vigorously drying his receding canine hair with Brine's appliqué hand-towel) on my focused drudgery. Looked a bit pale, I did. On my knees with a sponge, I stopped scrubbing the kitchen's black-and-white linoleum tiles and weakly smiled. He suddenly and thickly clapped his hands. Felt it necessary to go and greet 'the old bag'. A quarter of an hour passed. Our hero returned from Brine's wing with two new love-bites and brandishing his shirt like the national flag. Where was the ironing board? I glanced at him and winced as menstrual cramps spliced and respliced my pelvis. Indicated and then lied: 'You look like you had an enjoyable evening.'

Surprised by this courteous claptrap, he swivelled around. The iron's flat and black-streaked face reminded me of the door of a country church. Wasn't like that at all. Bumped into the old bag down the Olé. First time in donkey's. And then it all got out of hand. I knew how it was: a few too many Bloody Marys and then, *bingo*! Anybody's. Trimly tipping an imaginary glass to his lips, he winked and then again, that excruciating expectoration.

Felt faint. Rested my cheek against the refrigerator's cool white door.

Was I all right?

When I replied that I was due to bleed, he shuddered vividly.

The kitchen had been cleaned and now I was scheduled to vacuum every nook and cranny of the awful place.

Stood outside Brine's door. That radio I so despised. Drawers opening and closing. Her high and tuneless hum. I knocked. Her voice: the rustling grasses on which slender nymphs so slowly combed their golden hair.

'I need the vacuum cleaner,' I said, my lips pressed to her bedroom door.

The fact that I was not her man worked well against me. *'Well, you can't have it now!'*

Lord, please have her die beneath the crawler track of a preposterous tank. My pause. And then: 'Caroline, I'm feeling a little ill. Can you please leave it outside your door?'

'I'll leave it – (shrill) – when I'm good and READY' (shriller). Slammed drawer. The radio announced the imminence of a tropical storm ('the price of a perfect summer day, Sydney').

Knocked again. 'Caroline,' I asked, 'could you please leave the vacuum cleaner outside your door?'

In response, she petulantly punched or kicked the wardrobe door and then resumed her humming.

What had I done? I did not wring my hands, but considered doing so. Instead, I flew back through the living and dining rooms, past the whistling Yeti (who had graduated from the iron to the biscuit barrel marked biscuits) and into my room. Beat the mattress. And suddenly, there seemed to be in me a kind of revelation, a moment in which I was no more than a concentric shattering of glass, a moment in which I was both less than myself and more than my environment, a moment of ingenuity, of inhumanity, of madness and the purest unassailability: beyond logic. And then the telephone began to wail. Clumsily grasped it.

'Hello?' I asked, my heart too loud.

Gabriel: 'You sound harassed.'

'I am,' I said.

Softly: 'In what way can I change that?'

'Don't do this to me,' I heard myself say through tears, 'don't make me think that I can rely on you, please don't. I have to go. Goodbye.'

Replaced that slippery receiver and then wept.

25

Brine and her swain were bickering on the other side of that wall against which my bed was pressed. It seemed that he had better things to do than accompany her to Darling Harbour to watch touring Croatian gymnasts balance swords and kingpins on their noses. Beside me on the floor, a book lay opened at a photograph of the Crab Nebula – in it a pulsar: the remnants of a star destroyed in AD 1054.

Ache in my upper back and dull throb in the winged base of my skull.

Outside, the thunder cracked like a live element in water and I could not stop weeping. In tears, protein. In tears, necessity. There was a sudden avulsion in the stratosphere – an acropolis toppling from a bulbous and unsteady cloud. The whole world echoed with its violence. And I was soothed by this turbulence, soothed by the wetness and the heat, that hush after the downpour, the pure clarity. My secret needs bowed to such climactic phenomena and it was true: I was confused and required a profound release. The rain fell like a heap of metal from the sky. My mind may have desired a Euclidean paradise, but my heart sought chaos, instinct, sensuality, this storm: it was a paradox with which I had wrestled all my life. Again, the thunder cracked like a live element in water. The sky was dense with marbled cloud. To be washed clean of doubt, to be renewed. I closed my eyes.

26

Another hour.

Cranked open that back door and stood outside in the fantastic rain. Stood on the landing of that five-step stairwell and looked down to my right at the weed-strangled strip between the mean bricks and the fence. An unravelling tennis ball rested against the wooden palings and discarded beside it, a plastic toy spade. Menstrual cramps spliced and respliced my pelvis and I tremblingly inhaled. Against my skin, the pounding rain. The air was sweet with the perfume of flowers – campanulate bluebells, radiate daisies, spathiate lilies, their milky innerness stained only by golden pistillary powders. The dog next door began to howl and then there was a curse and the dog winced.

Above me, thunder; above me, the sumptuous black antagonism of cloud. Glanced back down at that discarded spade. Originally vibrant, it had faded in the sun to an enervated pinkish-gold; half of its blade had restlessly been chewed.

Suddenly sensing movement, I looked up.

Gabriel was leaning with his right arm hard against the wall, his face shadowed. Each of his fingers bore a current of the storm's cathartic liquids, those liquids streaming down his brow and cheeks, over his full dark lips, down his throat and over his breast and down, down over his belly. Another white cotton dress-shirt, those same blue jeans, those boots. His wet hair: ochre, vanilla, unbrushed lupine fur. Borderless eyes. My heart, that shadowgraph. The long silence between us was suffused by hues too subtle to describe.

Wiping rainwater from his brow: 'You are unreasonable.'

'Am I,' I said.

He shook his head. 'You are unreasonable.'

I only looked at him in reply.

'When it pleases you,' he said, 'you demand silence. Otherwise, you want the kind of eloquence found only in the mouths of those whose art it is to use words to disguise their thoughts.'

'Do I,' I said.

He shook his head. 'You are unreasonable.'

'I am too tired and too ill,' I said, 'to sound intelligent. The floor is yours.'

'You want to be impressed?' he asked.

'Why not?' I countered. 'Are you capable of anything else?'

He smiled. 'If I didn't know you better –'

'What would you do?' I asked. 'What would you *do*?'

In shadow, his observant eyes were cold and that one scar had deepened to a wound. 'What would I do?' he asked. 'I'd submit to your inability to establish anything beyond your sense of alienation.'

'Don't project,' I slowly said.

'Is there an option?' he asked.

Torched pause. 'I always sensed that you were cruel.'

The brief lull in the storm was broken by a resonating boom and cracking of the sky into a thousand glittering pieces which dissolved, in their decline, to rain.

Wiping that rainwater from his brow: 'What do you want from me?'

'The impossible,' I slowly said. 'Reason.'

'Reason as defined by you,' he said.

I watched the storm's cathartic liquids trickle in between his lips. 'Perhaps you are a little too accustomed to women who believe you to be superior,' I said.

'Transpose knowledge where there was belief,' he said, 'and you may have an argument.'

'Or perhaps not,' I said.

In shadow, his observant eyes were cold and that one scar had deepened to a wound and bled the storm's cathartic liquids. 'Admittedly,' he slowly said, 'I was not subjected to communist indoctrination and therefore the concept of female equality is very new.'

'I obviously don't fit the bill.'

'Too strong for my stomach,' he said.

Said with a smile: 'I always sensed that you were cruel.'

There was another resonating boom and then again, that cracking of the sky into a thousand pieces which dissolved, in their decline, to glittering rain.

Slowly wiping his scarred brow: 'What do you *want* from me??'

I watched the storm's cathartic liquids trickle in between his lips. The air was sweet with the perfume of flowers – campanulate bluebells, radiate daisies, spathiate lilies, their milky innerness stained only by golden pistillary powders. The stare we then exchanged was so direct, congested, in it a flicker of what may or may not have been an inexplicable anger, absorbent, in itself a duel. And without meaning to, I wept. In tears, protein. In tears, necessity. He tremblingly inhaled and then walked through that glittering rain and in it, so embraced me.

27

Those gutters pulsed like arteries. We drove in half-light across the Harbour Bridge, over sullied malachite waters and rocking ferries, under an unrolling canopy of cloud, through the narrow byways of the financial district and to the city centre. Gabriel paused the car to allow a swarm of glistening and versicoloured umbrellas to cross the road on hurried legs.

Watching a thread of rain undulate restlessly on the windscreen: 'Vulnerability increases the production of endorphins.'

'Meaning?' he absentmindedly asked.

'Meaning,' I mechanically explained, 'that when vulnerable, we are so drugged by the chemicals released by the anticipation of pain that our ability to both make and act upon decisions is seriously impaired.'

Gabriel seemed hypnotized by a child – blown chestnut ringlets, absent front teeth, a pinafore – who battled with the sudden gale for her umbrella.

'Meaning?' he again asked.

'Meaning,' I gently answered, 'that vulnerability is thus antithetical to human survival.'

The child with no front teeth had been appropriated by her mother or bustling female guardian and bundled into a restaurant. 'Would you agree,' he asked, rapidly turning his face away, 'that magic appeals to man because it gives him the illusion of control?'

'I would,' I said.

'Then have you never considered vulnerability to be the kind of magic which creates the illusion of control necessary to the maintenance of health, physiological or otherwise?'

I looked at him. 'Meaning?'

'Meaning,' he gently answered, 'that the perceived nature and outcome of vulnerability is no more than a matter of conditioning. The only variable is fear.'

Through a slow smile: 'You are a stubborn man.'

'If only intractability were the real problem,' he said.

'And what would you say the real problem is?' I asked.

'We both love games,' he darkly said, 'and that will be our downfall.'

Parked near the Great Synagogue (in which, I had been told, above the Torah and eternal light and Magen David, was a concave ceiling ornamented with a golden multitude of stars). Before us, all the green that is Hyde Park. On most nights of the year, the trees were lit by miniscule white bulbs, hanging like pearls amongst the boughs. Gabriel walked me down Elizabeth Street – past the porphyry and wet flags of grand hotels, past the inclines of subterranean car-parks, past the doorways of glamorous restaurants – and stopped outside the powerbrokers' block known as the Hanover. Topped by sandstone capstones, the two fronting masonry gateposts. The acroteria had been planted with ivy, which in that mournful light was the colour of blood. There were two black spear-pointed gates, stone pillars flanking the front doors, carved sandstone voussoirs.

Gabriel smiled and glanced at me. 'No need to feign approval. It's just a *pied-à-terre.*'

A dappled marble foyer and throughout it, our echoes. Frosted glass, aureate light and on the walls, a set of Queen Anne Chester County Paladine seal-matrices. Felt faint. Menstrual cramps spliced and respliced my pelvis and I tremblingly inhaled. Behind us on the marble floors, two scintillant and distinct trails of water. On the nineteenth level, an oak-panelled passageway leading to the door marked with the number six. Behind the sixth door of Bluebeard's domain, Judith discovered an achromatic sea: his tears. How many tears could there be in a sea? Front door unlocked. Gabriel flicked a switch. A hallway of closed doors.

'What were you expecting?' he asked.

'Wasn't expecting anything,' I said.

'You must have been expecting something.'

'I was expecting nothing,' I replied.

Slowly, he looked at me. 'You almost got it.'

Torched pause. 'Whenever I feel I am beginning to trust you,' I said, 'you make me doubt my instincts.'

'You've never trusted me, Angelica,' he said, 'only my ability to legitimize your frustrations.'

'Elegantly put,' I said, 'but incorrect.'

His smile was paradoxically self-deprecating. 'Don't lie to me; I know your voice.'

'That was delivered in a mildly threatening tone,' I slowly said.

Holding my gaze, unreadable: 'I know your voice.'

The intensity with which he looked at me did stop my heart. We both loved games, and that would be our downfall. He suddenly stepped back. Tight little exhalation. That brown muscular throat, so tensed. My awareness of him was an entity in itself and brilliantly eyed.

He opened one of the doors and with a false decisiveness, said: 'I'll light the fire.'

28

Within, the walls were draped with watered crimson silk; on the floor, Persian carpets had been placed with Euclidean precision. On the wall, one of Magritte's many masterpieces – a man in black immobilized by white lunar authority, and that Xanadu, incongruous against the giltwood side-table upon which the neoprene wetsuit lay prone. Three deep cranberry-coloured sofas heaped with *tapisserie* cushions. A wall of books: economics, military history, surgery, theology, cosmogony, psychopathology, philosophy, the higher sciences, gardening, gemstones, sports. Opened to its ex libris plate designed by Ernest Shepard, a first edition of *Winnie the Pooh*. Eclectic tastes. The chimney piece was crowded with empty photograph frames and to its right, a glass vitrine. Inlaid on the marble top of the low gilt table in the centre of the room, images of courting doves and columbines and scattered across it: keys and coins, a telephone, a sheet of dates and calculations.

'A contract note,' I said, turning it over in my hand. 'So you're a commodities man.'

Crouching by the hearth and still wet from the rain,

Gabriel smiled. 'That note you're holding belongs to one of my clients.'

Crushing in his fists torn strips of newspaper, he then nudged them in between the stack of logs. Fragrance of wood. That spitting match. Narrow blue flames sprang from the blackening crackle of newsprint, all the world's affairs reduced to ash. He remained crouching and stared into the fire, that dress-shirt adhering to his back in emphatic patches.

I watched him for a time and still he did not move. There was a beauty in his form that was indescribable. Torched pause. Unfastened the seven buttons of my shirt. Shivering, I sat down on one of the three cranberry-coloured sofas and listened to the flames. A minute spoon-shaped insect with a tortoiseshell casing and working feelers explored my navel and it then entangled itself within the fine pale hairs.

'The Garden of Eden was in Mesopotamia,' I absently said, 'between the rivers Tigris and Euphrates.'

'Meaning?' he asked as he stared into the fire.

'Nothing,' I answered.

'Stream of consciousness?' he asked.

'Stream of consciousness,' I said.

'A mere *non sequitur*?' he asked.

'A mere *non sequitur*,' I said.

'Agreement?' he asked, laughing. 'Are you feeling ill?'

'I'm due to bleed.'

'Red in tooth and claw?'

'Just due to bleed,' I said.

In his eyes – gold, chrysoprase and jet: one of the two colours outside the chromatic scale and the most intimate. His pause. And then: 'What do you want?'

Eased myself back into those cushions. 'Sometimes,' I heard myself say, 'I think that all I want is to feel loved, utterly loved. Sometimes I feel as if the absence of such love could kill me.'

The long silence between us was suffused by hues too subtle to describe.

'You speak of being loved,' he said, 'but not loving.'

'That's right,' I said. 'Exactly right.'

Torched pause. 'Cracked vessels hold no water,' he said.

Slowly closing my eyes and listening to the appetite of flames: 'An interesting analogy.'

'A little bug is crawling into your navel,' he remarked.

'Stream of consciousness?' I asked.

'A mere *non sequitur*,' he said.

'Cracked vessels hold no water,' I repeated.

'That's right,' he said. 'That is exactly right.'

'Meaning?' I asked.

'Nothing,' he said.

'Don't lie to me; I know your voice,' I said. 'Now tell me what you mean.'

'Ask your commodities broker,' he answered.

'Too volatile a market. Risk has never been my area,' I said. 'Explain.'

'Why risk has never been your area?' he asked. 'You have been badly hurt.'

Opened my eyes to look at him. 'That wasn't the question,' I said.

He smiled. 'It was the correct answer.'

'Before the world betrayed you,' I so slowly said, 'you must have experienced some feeling; arrogance is not genetic. Of course, I could be wrong.'

That heightened smile. 'You can be venomous,' he said.

Closing my eyes and listening to the appetite of flames: 'What do you fear?'

'Only you, Angelica,' he said. 'Only you. I'm going to shower. Join me when you want to.'

Opened my eyes and watched the insect dissolve into shadow.

29

His flesh was *peau de soie* through the white steam. Standing with his back to the door, he had not heard me enter. I absorbed him slowly with my eyes. The water beat against his throat. His head was thrown back and his arms were folded across his breast. Those massive thighs apart and thickly between them, golden pashm and the underhang of his testes and heavy sex. Stretched out my hand to wipe the water from his brow and he languidly turned. My every want, my every need: the world had been reduced for me to my hunger for him, the appetite of flames and to that storm, that summer storm, its essence in my home, marrow.

Followed his burning look down to my sex.

A rivulet of blood was brightly coursing down my thigh, forking over my calf and then dissolving in the pelting water to a mist. Gabriel grasped my shoulders and brought my mouth to his in one unfolding kiss. Pulling his lips from mine, he again looked down and slowly ran a finger up through the red rivulet and returned that finger to my mouth. He coloured and again coloured my lips with my warm blood, and then thickly eased his finger between them. Closing my eyes, the water hot against my face, I suckled: intoxicated, I had been possessed. A lifetime passed. Steadying himself upon my hips, he slowly dropped to his knees and licked that rivulet to its glistening source, his broad throat working as he sucked. The steam around us was no more than breath; it was as if we were stranded in a god's mouth; I heard and heard again the pounding of a pagan heart; our prayers to him were recited by our flesh.

My knees were trembling and I sank back against that tiled vermilion wall. Water against my face, filling my mouth. With his left hand, Gabriel gripped my hip and with the other, parted my buttocks and suddenly pushed his thumb into my darkness and then twisted it and then withdrew. My cry filled the room and still drinking from my sex, he turned away and gasped with blood-smeared mouth for air. Water against his face, against his tongue. Those madder-stained incisors and their truth. I came against his lips with a lost cry and slid – wet light, bright sound – to those unsteady tiles, my head bursting with stars destroyed before the birth of Christ. With blood-smeared lips, he rose to kiss me and in that instant, all was mist: my hands trembled against his shoulders, my spine was curved, my sex was offered – so open, so glistening – to him. A lifetime passed. Audible: only our breathing, only the hiss of that water. He pulled his thumb from me and wiped it slowly over his tongue, watched as I purred, and then shifted his huge muscular body over mine. Squatting, his soft and heavy testes swinging in the steam, one hand tightly on the base of his gorged cock, he began to rub its peeling nub over my vulva, sinking that cock within me and then pulling it out.

Intoxicated, I had been possessed.

And then his truth: he hauled my hips up and pushed me down over his cock. Magma through me, and its slur. Water against my face, filling my mouth. I turned away and brightly gasped for air. Gabriel's eyes were steady on the motion of his sex: blood-streaked and slippery with oils, its piston-momentum so slow and so thick, evincing from me cries and then bright gasps. My every want, my every need: all the world had been reduced for me to my hunger for him, the appetite of flames and to that storm, that summer storm, its essence in my home, marrow. Still squatting and firmly gripping my hips, he increased the speed of his rhythm and watched with a carnivorous interest as my breasts heavily swung. Water against my face, filling my mouth. My cunt clung to him as a mouth clings to a teat. Ferociously, his blood-streaked cock pulled from me and plunged deeply within me, and again.

Through his clenched teeth: 'I'm going to come, Angelica – I'm going to come.'

I wrenched myself away and pushed him back and was upon him, unrestrained. Rapidly slid his pulsing cock into my mouth. So thickly sucked. Membrane against swelling membrane and his gasp. My hands splayed on his thighs, I let him feel. Essence of blood, essence of cunt: my mouth was overflowing with his want, his every need. His breath escaped in yielding exhalations and with one trembling hand, he stroked my cheek. Turning my mouth, I then kissed his fingertips, each phalange, his wet palm.

'Come here,' he whispered without opening his eyes.

I climbed his breast. Still sitting on his haunches, he pressed his mouth to mine in a soft kiss. That water trickled down our brows and in between our lips. His milks were fertile on my tongue. With one trembling hand, he stroked my cheek, my mouth, my throat, my aching breasts. He stroked my breasts. Opened his eyes. And suddenly, he dipped his head and took one of my thickening nipples between his lips: so slowly suckled, that reddening nipple was by his tongue lapped, flicked and wiredrawn. My every nerve was fed electric information and my cunt contracted, an oiled fist. I heard sharp catches in his breath.

Around us both, that steaming water and those glistening vermilion tiles.

Sitting with my thighs spread over his lap, I slipped my fingers down around his cock and massaged it and massaged it and slowly, it began to gorge in my soft grip. So suckled, that reddening nipple was by his tongue lapped, flicked and wiredrawn. I traced the circular oiled nub of his sex with my fingers, slowly peeled that foreskin from its membrane as I would have a peach. Waited a breathless instant and then heavily sat down upon his cock. He curved his pelvis into me and gripped my thighs. I took him by the hair and face to face, we kissed in shifts – my tongue slipping between his parted lips, my mouth dragging wetly over his cheek, his breath unsteady heat against my throat.

All control lost.

I ground against him viciously, in search of my own gouging come: that evanescent thing he owned, that cavern within which I found myself, that lamp alive with blood. Grunting, he curved his pelvis into me and gripped my hips. My thighs were wide apart and I so fucked him: with my full weight, his cock thickening within my thickened sex, that hot water pelting against us both. I fucked ferociously, I fucked until I felt the full swell of oblivion pour into one excruciating cry: tearing my mouth from his, I fucked – my head thrown back, my wet back arched – that come-momentum disgorged by me in a cry, and his own synchronous disclosure.

30

A lifetime passed. The fire was still richly burning. The room was somnolently warm. Reflected flames expanded and contracted in the glass of that vitrine and visible through them, the vulture-headdress of Queen Nefertary sculpted in miniature. The rain was beating steadily against each window-pane and muffled by long velvet drapes. Gabriel was asleep on a sofa, his breathing even, fragrant, low.

We both love games, and that will be our downfall.

I observed him from the sofa facing that fire. My hair was held back by the ribbon he had found tied around the box of Belgian chocolates on the third tier of his refrigerator. His breast surged slowly and subsided, surged slowly and subsided. With his brown arms behind his broad-jawed head, he evinced from me feelings too subtle in hue to describe. The complexity of a stimulus is directly proportionate to the memory's struggle to retain it, but he was no longer simply an external to be observed: in part, I felt him issue from within me.

Beauty. Traced the outline of his body with a glance – curved matter, the silence of lines, inflexibility and its textures. The fire crackled, spat and firmly burned. Queen Nefertary was visible through the reflected flames. Swallowed by the slowest yawn, I traced his ilia and heavy loins, the pasturage of his smooth breathing skin. The room was somnolently warm. His breast surged slowly and subsided, surged slowly and subsided. Lay back on those tapestried cushions and imagined his intestines as Anthias schooling on a reef, his appendix as bubble coral in the Red Sea. I imagined his kidneys as soft tulip-shaped coral polyps, his great lungs as billowing Caribbean marine greenery, his heart cushioned by Scarlet Gorgonia – sentient flora, and its liquid suspiration – off the primitive Belau Islands.

The fire crackled, spat and firmly burned.

I closed my eyes.

31

An hour or so later: the sleepy disorder of his kiss. Outside a gale levelled the world. Blood on my thighs. 'You'd better wash,' he said. In that vermilion-tiled bathroom, the water ran, a liquid pinkness, in my hands. Returned to him with a fresh sex. Kneeling by the low giltwood table with a magnum of champagne between two of the images of courting doves, he glanced up.

'*Le Maître d'Ecole*,' I slowly said, 'painted in 1954. Wasn't it part of a private collection in Geneva?'

'Not any more,' he said, grasping the base of the bottle with one hand and with the other, stripping the printed foil.

My thinking pause. 'The figures for which Magritte is best remembered are those who are mesmerized by the New Moon. Their backs are to us, but we intuit the expression in their eyes. All lunar imagery symbolizes the mother. Magritte's mother suicided when he was a boy of twelve. The impact of *Le Maître d'Ecole* lies in its echo of every man's wish: to return to the safety of his mother.'

Gabriel stopped to look at me, that look direct, congested, in it a flicker of what may or may not have been an inexplicable anger, absorbent, in itself a duel. 'An interesting analysis,' he softly said, and aimed the bottle at the furthest corner of the room.

With his strong thumb, he dislodged the cork and with a moistened hollow pop, it shot against the wall, careened and soundly rolled across the carpet. Indifferent to the damage, he stemmed the flow of the champagne with his full lips and eyed me carefully over the bottle's mouth. The pads of his fingers were oddly vegetable against the crystal of the two flutes, but I remembered them animal within my mouth, their salt male taste.

Lifting his glass to me whilst sucking his left thumb of spilled champagne: 'To all our games.'

I placed my glass upon the marble inlay of that low giltwood table and folded my hands. The fire crackled, spat and firmly burned.

Sipped his champagne. Rapidly licked his lips and cleared his throat. His frown was so sardonic. 'You're not drinking,' he remarked.

Drily: 'Perceptive.'

He took another sip and then rested his glass directly between us. 'Wrong toast?'

'Poor taste,' I answered. 'But you were aware of that.'

With a paradoxically self-deprecating smile: 'Forgive me.' Turned his face to stare into the fire and then – slowly, as if formulating a new strategy or redefining an attack – brought his look to me in a bright liquid arc: from those flames to my eyes, he had masked his every thought. 'I haven't told you much about myself, have I?' he asked.

I watched his face.

'Angelica,' he said with false decisiveness, 'I've entertained a lot of women over the years – a *lot* of women. Does that bother you?'

I did not speak, but watched his face.

He took another sip of his champagne. Torched pause. 'A liberal diagnostician,' he surmised. 'An open-minded woman of categorical sensibilities. Impressed. I am impressed.' He drummed two of his fingers on the edge of that table, and then: 'But there was something unsuitable about each one of them. And so I find myself alone. I have no-one to care for me, Angelica – no-one at all.'

I did not speak, but watched his face.

Leaning toward his glass, he closed his lips over the sweating rim, and then with his two thumbs and index fingers, tipped that cold champagne into his mouth. Slowly sat back. Those perilously intelligent chrysoprase eyes. 'No-one to care for me, Angelica,' he said after a pause. 'Now, don't you think that's sad?'

My hands still folded in my lap: 'There's a certain organic rhythm to your aggression.'

He was amused. Another sip. And then, as if to himself: 'Organic rhythm. I like that.' His pause. 'Organic rhythm.'

'You give with one hand,' I hesitatingly explained, 'and then take with the other.'

'And what do I do with the other four?' he asked through another sip.

'Patently obvious,' I said. 'Relentless and commendably dedicated self-pollution.'

His laughter was unexpected and profound 'Elegantly put,' he conceded with a nod. 'Elegantly put. But I digress. Angelica, what do you gain from seeing me?'

I did not speak, but watched his face.

'I can't be the only man in your life. You're a beautiful woman, brilliant, admittedly exhausting – but even that has a certain charm. So why spend time with a man who gives you nothing but trouble?'

I did not speak, but watched his face.

'Because,' he continued, 'I cannot give you what you need

207

or you deserve. In your heart you know that, as do I. There can be no future for us in any significant sense. We have nothing in common, and there is no room in my life for another person, none at all. Are you in love with me, or are you in it for the sex?' Sipped his champagne slowly and observed me with those intelligent green eyes.

Again, that paradoxically self-deprecating smile. 'No comment. Very well. I understand. You never show your hand too early in the game.' His pause. 'Let me put it this way: if you just want the sex, everything will be perfect for a set period of time. Understood? But if you are in love with me, everything must stop. It has to stop because one of us will get hurt and I can tell you now, it won't be me.'

'You can be venomous,' I said.

His heightened smile. 'Venomous?'

Torched pause. 'You make love with your body, and then annihilate your lover verbally.'

He whistled. 'My girl Freud.'

'You damage those you love until they are too damaged to love you.'

Sipped more of his champagne. Drummed two of his fingers on the edge of the table, and then, so solemnly: 'I damage those I love. And how would you know that? You've never seen me with anyone else.'

'You can be venomous,' I said.

Dismissively: 'Never analyze me, Angelica. You will find no-one but yourself in your conclusions.'

Torched pause. 'Gabriel,' I asked, holding his gaze, 'what do you gain from seeing me?'

Again, that whistle. 'You're a real player, aren't you?'

'Surely,' I slowly said, 'I can't be the only woman in your life. You're a beautiful man, brilliant, admittedly exhausting – but even that has a certain charm. So why spend time with a woman who gives you nothing but trouble?'

The cast of his broad jaw was suddenly determined. 'A real player,' he murmured.

'Because,' I continued, 'I cannot give you what you need or you deserve. In your heart you know that, as do I. There can be no future for us in any significant sense. We have nothing in common, and there is no room in my life for another person, none at all. Are you in love with me, or are you in it for the sex?'

His laughter was unexpected and profound. 'I never show my hand too early in the game,' he said, 'because I've never liked to lose.'

That shadowgraph, my heart. 'Why are you so aggressive with me?' I asked. 'What have I done to threaten you?'

Those perilously intelligent chrysoprase eyes instantly froze. His inhalation. Placing that glass between us on the marble inlay of that giltwood table, he simply said: 'You have told no-one I'm your lover.'

Stared into that fire and slowly shook my head.

'And why?' he asked.

Torched pause. 'And you?' I asked. 'Have you told anyone?'

His smile was paradoxically self-deprecating. 'No,' he answered.

My smile was slow. The fire crackled, spat and firmly burned.

'What have I done to threaten you?' I again asked.

Torched pause. 'You've never expressed interest in my profession,' he said.

'I'm not interviewing you for a position,' I said.

He closed his eyes. 'I think you are.'

I did not speak, but watched his face.

He slowly sipped his cold champagne. 'Do you know what I do?'

'Don't care.'

Smiling: 'Don't care?'

'Should I?'

That fire crackled, spat and firmly burned. Gabriel eased back against the sofa and inhaled.

'You never answered my question,' I said. 'What have I done to threaten you?'

Those perilously intelligent chrysoprase eyes deepened in hue and then he smiled. 'You're quite daunting,' he said.

'And in what way?' I asked.

'In every way,' he said.

'I don't think I've ever met a man more in need of love,' I said.

His laughter was unexpected and profound. 'I'm very demanding,' he slowly said.

'That may be so,' I said, 'but it doesn't change the fact that you're in need of love.'

Sipped more of his cold champagne and stared for a moment into his glass. And then: 'How would you know what I need?' he asked.

'Perceptive,' I replied. 'I evaluate quickly.'

'That way you can miss too many subtleties,' he said.

Torched pause. 'It has been an effective system.'

'So,' he said, observing me over the rim of his near-emptied glass, 'describe the woman I need.'

'A woman who wants to be controlled,' I answered. 'You would find it difficult to understand a relationship in terms of anything but domination and submission. Nonetheless, cool and intelligent. Socially clean. Willing to defer to your superior abilities.'

'A Nietzschean *übermensch*,' he continued with that false warmth and a smile, 'a blue-eyed blonde. High cheekbones. Got to have those cheekbones. A Pilgrim princess or an English equestrienne? Bronzed horsewoman's torso, that would be imperative. Consummate hostess. Pristine fingernails.'

'Moneyed,' I added.

'Irrelevant,' he said. 'Wealthy enough for both of us.'

'I see,' I said. And then: 'Right pedigree.'

'Not buying a dog,' he said as he refilled his glass.

'Oh, I don't know,' I said. 'You may as well be. I'm familiar with men such as yourself.'

Smiling: 'Familiar?'

'Familiar,' I said.

'You know,' he remarked, 'I knew the first minute I saw you that you were dangerous.'

Watching his face: 'Dangerous? And in what way?'

'Dangerous,' he said, sipping his cold champagne, 'period.'

My smile was slow. 'Oh, not as dangerous as those white slopes,' I said.

His pause. And then: 'What makes you think I ski?'

'Part of the socio-economic fantasy,' I answered. 'You're no iconoclast. The trappings of the upper classes are painfully important to you. They give you the illusion of security. Man as a tribal animal, all that. Belonging is obviously something you never knew in youth. And now, for you not to conform would be to die.'

'To die?' he softly asked.

'Klosters, Aspen, groomed black and blue runs, cross-country trails, perhaps a spot of XCD, drinking *glühwein* with executive royalty, trading back country tips with the chairmen of merchant banks. A lifetime squandered –'

'Your father was the chairman of a merchant bank,' he said.

My mouth, so suddenly dry. 'You and your kind think of yourselves as daredevils and cowboys: cheaters of fate. The stupidity of those around you is an insult, not a disability. For one to win, another has to lose.'

His look was so direct, congested, in it a flicker of what may or may not have been anger. 'Your father was murdered,' he said, 'and you have always felt the child you were was murdered with him.'

That pause of mine and its violence.

'Can't say I like to ski,' I managed. 'I tried and tried and tried again. On one occasion, I slid beneath the platform of a chalet and was discovered by my instructor with one thigh wrapped around my neck. It then occurred to me that the risks involved were not counterbalanced by the pleasures.'

'I knew your father,' he murmured.

I looked at him. 'So what?'

He watched my face.

'So what?' I again asked. 'Am I supposed to be touched or impressed?'

He did not speak, but watched my face.

'What do you know of loss?' That shadowgraph, my heart. 'Your life is no more than a story I have heard a thousand times before. Shall I recite it? You earn a surrealistic amount of money. You are a powderhound, a rider, a fixture at racing events. You own landscaped properties. Your suits are tailored in London. You have had many women and you have been the one to leave. No children, if only because they would require more attention than you are prepared to pay. High conformity quotient, active intellect, predatory nature, insurmountable defence mechanisms: standard alpha male. Authoritarian father. Distant mother. A certain kind of responsibility excites you: either an only child or the eldest. You experience difficulty submitting to authority of any description. A leader, without doubt. You function on too many levels simultaneously. This is useful in matters of negotiation, as multi-dimensional analysis expands the retentive powers of the memory. Always that edge over adversaries, Gabriel.' Brief pause. 'Low boredom threshold. Calculating. You use activity to escape feeling. The tension you experience when you stop moving is only the tension that has been there all along. Sleeping problems? Highly intuitive. Shrewd, competitive, enclosed within yourself. Shall I continue?'

Smiling: 'Am I so transparent?'

'A picture window,' I remarked.

Smiling: 'Your acuity either humbles or humiliates me, I'm not sure which.'

Torched pause. 'You're mocking me.'

'Perhaps,' he slowly said. 'Perhaps. What were those words you used? High conformity quotient, active intellect, predatory nature, insurmountable defence mechanisms. Standard alpha male.' His falsely exasperated sigh.

'Only the truth,' I said.

His pause and then, whilst observing me over the rim of his glass: 'Understood, understood, I appreciate your most informed perspective. One thing I don't understand: given that you consider my life so contemptible, why spend time with me?'

That vulture-headdress of Queen Nefertary was visible through the reflected flames.

'There is something to be learned from every man,' I said.

'Interesting spin,' he commented. And then: 'Egocentric? Emotionally inaccessible? Defensively cruel?'

Cold shrug. 'Goes without saying.'

'I meant,' he said with a slow smile, 'you.'

Caught unawares. And then, with grace: 'Quick on your feet.'

He shrugged. 'Authoritarian father. Distant and pretentious mother. I felt emotionally excluded as a child, and thus am self-destructively self-sufficient, self-deceiving, self-polluting and self-pleasuring. Just self, self, self.'

'You can keep up with me,' I said. 'I'm impressed.'

His laughter was profound and unexpected. 'You think I'm keeping up with you? A curious perspective.'

'In what way curious?' I asked.

His look was so direct, congested, in it a flicker of what may or may not have been anger. 'I see it differently,' he said.

Smiling: 'Explain.'

Sipping his cold champagne: 'Have you never considered that I may be slowing down in order that you can keep up with me?'

I did not speak, but watched his face.

'Now, to digress. I have decided that I have grieved long enough,' he said with false alacrity.

'For your integrity?' I asked.

His laughter was profound and unexpected. 'For the standard of my skiing,' he replied. 'Haven't performed as well as I would have liked on the slopes these last few years.'

'Crushing,' I said. 'You must have lost face.'

That gale outside had quietened.

'And my wife,' he murmured with the slowest smile.

'Don't understand,' I said.

'And my wife,' he again said.

Torched pause. 'Divorced?'

'Oh, no,' he said with that paradoxically self-deprecating smile, 'I am renowned for my fine eye. When I choose, it is always after much deliberation.'

'Don't understand,' I said.

The fire crackled, spat and firmly burned.

'Widowed,' he explained without expression through another sip of his champagne.

I did not speak, but watched his face.

Staring into that fire and mechanically, in the lowest tone: 'Colloid cyst in the third ventricle. Blocks off the fluid passage, causing hydrocephalus. We were –' and here he tremblingly inhaled, 'we were skiing in Utah. Champagne powder, waist deep, weightless.' Again, that pause. 'She suddenly collapsed.'

He drummed two of his fingers on the edge of the table and again sipped from his glass. 'She had been complaining of headaches in the morning for three or so weeks – of course, neither of us paid any attention. Her gynaecologist suggested they were caused by the stress of pregnancy. And then, dead wife. Dead wife and child.'

I could not speak, but watched his face.

He slowly rubbed his eyes. 'I'm tired,' he whispered. 'You've exhausted me.'

32

The newness of the day had rinsed the room of *volupté*, returning each hue to its piety and illuminating a glass cylinder of chysanthemums, every dense stalk converting simple water to the complex maintenance of bloom. And previously unnoticed: a full-bellied vase of dying out-of-season poppies, the two dozen stems stiffening to a mid-point and then collapsing, dehydrated in their distance from the viscid water. The petals of these woeful poppy-cups were frayed and hung like crumpled tissue-paper parachutes, the colour intensified at each crenellated petal-lip. So dejected, those pistils. Certain furred fat buds would never fully open, their strangely mammalian contours partially split, exposing in turn the gauzy saffron, brassy redlead and the smudged tongue-pink of each half-hidden bloom. They reminded me of sweat-soaked ballgowns tossed over the rails of Regency chairs – worn of their glamour, already transforming. The scent of these flowers was unusual to me, never sweet, oddly acrid, a fierce sharp fragrance suspended in the memory and unanswerable. I held one particularly wrinkled petal to the light: the lime flare at its base faded into an afternoon of crimson, used and spectacularly veined, so old, but still retaining its ability to transform light into a kind of beautifully occult experience.

Vehuiah is one of the eight seraphim of the cabala, and governs those first pale golden rays of sun. I had tugged the heavy drapes aside and was standing with both my palms flattened against one of the window sills, gazing out at the day. Spireless St Mary's Cathedral rose through the brilliant

214

foliage of the park, over which there sailed a single pigeon. Motion of flight and implied freedom: exhilaration.

Behind me, Gabriel murmured in his sleep. With his muscular arms behind his broad-jawed head, he shifted almost imperceptibly.

So softly called my lover's name.

With a grunt, he levered himself up and blinked at me over the sofa's hard upholstered back. Peripheral awareness strengthened by expectation. His expression suggested a dream in which he had been winged. That hair: ochre, vanilla, unbrushed lupine fur. Volume of shoulder.

'What's wrong?' he asked, spreading his powerful fingers over his throat and loudly yawning.

'The angel of tears dwells in the Fourth Heaven,' I said.

Squinting at me, his mouth still distorted by that yawn, he asked: 'What's his name?'

The calling of a man's name has been known to rouse him from a coma.

'Sandalphon,' I quietly replied.

Closing his eyes and raising his brows and again yawning: 'What time is it?'

'Eight o'clock,' I answered. 'Time to get up.'

Rubbing his breast: 'Eight o'clock? Did you say eight o'clock?'

Smiling: 'Time to get up.'

'Right,' he said, and unseeingly stood and then luxuriantly stretched. 'Eight o'clock. Time to get up.'

33

In that black car: rushed radiance of the season through all four of the lowered windows, blown warm torpor, champagne light. I was so stirred by Gabriel's thighs, by his male fragrance, by his voice. Before me, deliquescent reflections on the windscreen – melting insubstantial and elliptical distortions of the two of us into a glassy and blue-tinted universe. The landscape glimmered. We had left the city and were travelling south through rural and semirural land. His entertaining anecdotes. Malibu Point, a solid nine-footer, that stacked dawn-streaked horizon, moonlight slides and dumped on take-off, legendary carves. The surf breaks along the Santa Barbara County coastline between Gaviota and Point Conception. Margaret River in high June, a wilderness of silver and abyssal black. Intently listening, I watched garish scintillas burning on the bonnets of oncoming vehicles and intently listening, so loved his tone, his warm dark tone, the familiarity with which he spoke to me, his profile, that determined jaw.

'Where are you taking me?' I asked, holding back with one hand the sudden spray of wind-blown hair over my lips.

'My farm,' he answered. 'I'm taking you down to my farm.'

'Size of the farm?' I asked.

His laughter was unexpected and profound. 'Five thousand acres,' he replied.

Smiling: 'Anything less than a thousand acres is a farm, and any more is an estate.'

Behind his sunglasses, I knew his eyes to be gold, chrysoprase and jet: one of the two colours outside the chromatic scale and the most intimate. We passed a small plantation of bruise-violet plum trees and pyramidal pears. Doves cooed from roadside boxes as a man loaded his truck.

Glancing at me: 'Do you ride?'

'My father,' I slowly answered, 'was one of the few polo players in the world with a ten-goal handicap, and twice single-handedly won his team the Cowdray Gold Cup. I do ride, yes. Dressage used to be of some interest.'

'Like fencing, dressage was a military art,' he commented, drumming two of his fingers on the steering wheel. 'The power to inspire fear has always held a certain cachet.'

As he continued to extemporize, my mind's eye seized upon an image of him fevered in a white hospital bed – sighing with pain, his pupils dilated with morphine, perspiring and blindly reaching for my hand. I felt my heart contract and then expand with grief; suddenly through me, an inexplicable sadness and warm forgiving love; from that white hospital bed, he weakly grasped my hand and pressed it to his lips and then the reverie dissolved. I was staring out of the window at the awkward rockery fronting an ugly plasterboard house and then at a deep ditch of pampas grass, its tufted big blond tassels humming with a multiplicity of insects.

'I created the farm from nothing,' he was saying, 'from brown paddocks. Basalt land. I gradually bought up all the surrounding farms until I had five thousand acres. Very serious money. I had the earth brought in and oversaw all the landscaping, everything.'

'A Nietzschean *übermensch*,' I said, 'I am impressed.'

'Just eccentric and *ipso facto* boring,' he replied.

'Quixotic Gabriel.'

'Never romantic and chivalrous to the disregard of the material,' he said. 'I'm a pragmatist at heart.'

The countryside revealed itself in swells of green, gunmetal blues, yellows and wild bright reds. Broad-domed trees lined the nubbly road down which we were driving, a road jay-walked by a sexagenarian dressed in loud checks. That mental image of Gabriel in hospital still disconcerted me, and I wondered at its source. From a field, the discord of a tractor.

'My toy,' he said.

I had not been listening. 'What's your toy?'

'The farm.'

'Big toy,' I commented, and then rapidly tapped my temple. 'My toy's in here.'

'Big toy,' he said, his laughter unexpected and profound. And then: 'The house is a crappy little place, but serves its purpose.'

In the hazy distance and atop a hill littered with columnar and fastigiate trees, a philosopher's candy-striped mansion high above which slowly blew the fraying threads of a white cloud. It was the bluest day. The car seemed fixed to the end of an invisible spoke which was fixed to the axle of the dreaming jewelled horizon. Within me, all the indolence of all the circular or eternally revolving.

I lit a cigarette and deeply inhaled. The smoke was torn from my lips by the rush of hot air from the window. 'The great themes of life,' I lazily said, 'are becoming increasingly difficult to discern. There are too many distractions. It's almost as if man has relinquished faith in all life's mysteries, and tried to reinstate in himself some sense of certainty through the tangible. But – and here it is, the logistical difficulty you have been waiting for – that which is created to compensate for a lack of faith teaches man of nothing but his need to believe in that which is greater than himself: self-perpetuating complexity and ultimately, only a waste of time.'

We passed a bank of brilliant honeysuckle, and its perfume was haunting and true.

'Man finds himself only in nature, for that is his blueprint,' I continued, drawing from that cigarette. 'All human beings become dysfunctional in artificial landscapes. Why? Because man is free to dream only when convinced of a power greater than himself. Think of the awe experienced by those who witness whales at play: this is the awe of realization that there is a greater hand at work. To perceive oneself as the supreme authority is a responsibility too onerous for the frail human psyche, and thus it buckles with exhaustion and despair. Children and artists dream freely because they openly acknowledge powerlessness. I am reminded of an acquaintance of mine, a famous architect infamous for his atheistic views. This godless man designs only glass skyscrapers that reach ever-higher into the sky; his architecture prays for him whilst he denies his deep need for a god.' Leaning forward, I stubbed my cigarette out in the black ashtray of the car.

Gabriel drove steadily through a wall of sunlight and then said: 'Go on.'

I glanced at him. 'We look out of our windows into windows framing others looking into the windows framing us. Our civilization is one designed by Maurits Cornelius Escher. Those illimitless stairwells, that infinity of self-perpetuating detail, repetition as its own philosophy. I wonder if he knew he was predicting the future.'

That glance of his, so green, so torched.

Through another cigarette, I said: 'Magritte, too, had his back to us or paper bags over our heads, and all Picasso did was refute natural alignment. Real individualism and emotional identity are greater threats to our society than Nazism ever was. Our time is one of the unnatural, which is why man is suffering. Remember Spielberg's extraterrestrial? He was loved by all of us because his plea was universal. A home may be many things, but every man desires to return to it.'

An apple orchard to our left and high in one of its round trees and up a splintered ladder, a shirtless man extending a bright pair of secateurs. Two quarrelsome magpies at each other fiercely croaked. By the green creek or stream to our right, the surreal vividness of a mature Chinese Weeping Willow, its linear-lanceolate leaves drifting like hands in the shimmering water. Stubbing my cigarette out in the black ashtray of the car, I watched some speckled goats behind us deliberately stonewall their minder, just a boy, and he burst into tears.

34

Ordered two foaming cups of white coffee, two heaped plates of scrambled eggs, fried halved tomatoes, bacon and beef sausages, four slices of palatably buttered toast and two exaggeratedly cornute chocolate croissants. We had been seated at an artificially aged table covered with an ironed linen tablecloth on which was: an unattractive pepper shaker, a porcelain salt cellar, a dainty vase of dying daisies, a pristine ashtray and a pink paper menu slotted between two scratched perspex sheets which were clipped by a scratched perspex stand. The tinted front window overlooked dusty Main Street and its creased bored sunbrowned pedestrians. The bank's faded sapwood plaque was in that still air motionless. A child fought with its sibling in the back seat of a parked stationwagon. Slowly ate my croissant with my fingers (Gabriel dissected his quickly with knife and fork). Leaning on one elbow, that knife loose in his hand, resolutely staring at my face, he chewed his mouthful, swallowed and then said through half a smile: 'You have chocolate on the tip of your nose, Angelica.'

own a series of labyrithine byways and russet dirt
roads, past great Box Elders and Ghost Gums shedding their papery bark, past mossy ponds which at
night resonated with the haunting chorus of sad frogs, past
the warm pink nebula of a *Rosea flore pleno*, past inflamed
liquidambars, jasmine and laburnum, past paddocks in
which lonely geldings grazed, we travelled higher and higher
into the hills until we reached tall wooden gates hinged to
granite gate piers. Between two of the pickets, a single
cobweb glittered. The gate closed and locked behind us, we
travelled for another ten or fifteen minutes until the house
could be clearly seen.

Gabriel dipped his head and squinted at the property.
'Eighteen-inch load-bearing brick walls set on stone walls
reaching two feet into the earth,' he said. 'Exquisite Oregon
timberwork in the ceilings.'

Parked the Bentley in a haze of dust – flakes of dried blood,
powdered bloodstone – and climbed out into that heat. Salt-
scented sweat-stains spread over Gabriel's shirt. Rotating
sprinklers shot at a remarkable velocity slender, sun-accentu-
ated streams of water out onto the tended lawns. Cyathiform
flowers spilled over the edge of an antique stone urn.
Climbing the walls of the salmony-pink bricked house,
clusters of swollen unfolding Cloth of Gold roses, their
fragrance a delirium. Beyond the sounds of spitting water and
carnivorous native birds and the lowing of cattle, an absolute
silence. His shoes made a dry scraping sound on the gravel as
he walked to the front door. Sweating and swatting at flies, I
followed him.

The front door opened into a wide and wax-scented
hallway. Stepped over that threshold and into a deep pool of
cool dark greenish light. It took a minute or so for our eyes to
adjust to that marine interior. On the wall, a long rack

bunched with oilskin coats, roughly waxed Barbours, char-coal-grey hacking jackets, dressage whips, short crops with flappers, panama hats, baseball caps, velvet-covered hunting caps, two silk top hats and three golfing umbrellas.

'You obviously entertain a lot of guests,' I quietly remarked.

Behind those sunglasses, his eyes were shadows. 'Used to,' he answered.

Silently led me through unlit corridors. Doors left ajar revealed unlit and richly furnished rooms, scattered with vases in which an abundance of roses, carnations and glowingly blue hydrangeas had been arranged. Surprise of light. The room in which we stopped overlooked the breadth of the luminous landscape. Slowly walked to the glass doors and gingerly opened them. In the far distance, the sun-softened curvature of hills. Ten feet away and at the base of a stone flight of steps, an elegant parterre, its balustrade marking the point at which the rest of the world began. Bordered by a coloured gravel path, the box-hedged beds, and everywhere manicured curlicues of delicate blooms and more of those antique urns overflowing with cyathiform flowers. Aloof from the central pool beneath him, a beautiful bronze sculpture of the god Apollo.

'Still water is a liar,' Gabriel said. 'It creates the illusion of movement by reflecting the ever-changing sky.'

I turned to face him for a moment. 'A lie is a deliberate distortion of the truth and not an inescapable condition. It is the nature of still water to reflect.'

Resolutely staring at my face and with a tight little exhalation, he suddenly gestured to his lower right. 'Perfectly restored late Victorian pit houses, hotbed, fig and orchid houses. We grow melons, persimmons, peaches, black and white grapes, nectarines, figs, cooking plums and cooking pears, rhubarb, tomatoes, cucumbers, beetroot, flowers for the house.'

As I looked out: 'Why are you so insecure? You have this need to prove yourself to me time and again. Your dedication to display is only another means of avoiding communication.'

'Those starved of love,' he slowly answered, 'feel they must compensate for what they believe to be their essentially unlovable natures with dedicated displays of potency, dominion, skill and daring. I only feel I'm as good as my last performance on the Cannonball Run. I am my estate and my share portfolio and my Bentley Continental R. I oscillate between depression and inappropriate grandiosity. My self-esteem is founded on the opinions of others. When I am alone, I don't know who I am.' Behind those sunglasses, his eyes were shadows. And then that laughter, so unexpected and profound.

'The wit,' I said.

Smiling: 'Go put on a hunting cap and boots. You'll find a pair that fits you in the third room to your left down the hallway.'

When I returned, he was standing with his hands on his hips, staring out at that luminous landscape. The fall of his shadow was distorted by the carved chest and bowl of outrageously vivid hydrangeas behind him. The sleeves of his white shirt had been pushed to the elbow, and the strong light enriched the colour of his polo boots to amber. As he heard me enter the room, he turned around. 'That's mine,' he said with consternation and surprise.

Uneasily: 'But you told me to –'

'I don't mean that,' he said. 'You're wearing my hunting cap. Did none of the others fit?'

Confused by his agitation, I stepped back. 'I tried them all on, but –'

'You must have an uncommonly large head,' he said. Tight little exhalation. And then: 'You're the first woman to –'

'To what?' I asked.

'To wear my hunting cap,' he said, and paused. Suddenly, he looked away from me and gathered the keys from the table on which he had thrown them. 'Let's go,' he said, and walked so quickly through those unlit halls that I bruised my hip in my efforts to keep up with him.

The journey to his stables was thirty-seven voluptuously full Lombardy Poplars long. Again, the vehicle stopped in a haze of dust. A paddock faced the stables and restlessly pacing its fenced length and breadth, a glossy-flanked bay mare with tightly plaited mane and lapping water, her big grizzled beau.

Gabriel made an affectionate low clicking sound as he slowly approached the stables. 'Ares,' he whispered to the horse in the first stall. The horse, an intimidatingly muscular jet-coloured beast, responded by pawing the ground and snorting and extending its silky black muzzle to be stroked. Turning to me: 'My god of war. A Hannoverian. One shift of weight, and he changes direction. He's genuine, so genuine – aren't you, my boy? Cost me more than that pair of George III perfume burners on the table in the drawing room. It may be vulgar to discuss money, but this god of war is a beloved monster of high maintenance.' He rhythmically caressed the horse's wither and again it snorted, pawed the ground, and regarded him with that love of which only animals and children are capable: unwavering and innocent, profound.

The white beauty in the second stall was tractable but less a devotee of Gabriel's manipulative charm; she masticated clover hay whilst watching me with mild interest. 'Nice round appearance to her rump,' he said, 'and a marginally lower tail carriage than usual. You have to watch for weakness in the hindquarters with these Pure Arabians. A pretty mare. Ares has always been in love with her. She's yours.'

'Her name?' I asked, walking towards the stall.

'Psyche,' he answered without looking at me. 'German. Came complete with computerized records of the performance details of the sire and dam. Periodically strikes attitudes, but otherwise reliable.'

With my left hand shading my brow, I examined both animals through the light: 'Four horses in all. One bay, one black, one white, one grizzled.'

'Eight more in the other paddocks,' he said. 'But four here.'

The air was lanolin against my skin. 'The Four Spirits of Heaven take the guise of horses: one bay, one black, one white, one grizzled,' I remarked.

'Meaning?' he asked.

'Nothing,' I said. 'An observation.'

Glancing at me: 'Stream of consciousness?'

'A mere *non sequitur*,' I said.

His pause was heavy with unarticulated questions and again, he made that affectionate low clicking sound at his Warmblood. And then: 'I'll saddle them up.'

36

Saddled and stroked, the horses allowed themselves to be led. I grasped the Pure Arabian's pommel and quickly kicked up; Gabriel mounted his Warmblood. Lightly kicking its flanks, he led the way out into that luminous and perfumed landscape. He rode with an erect back, those reins easily gathered by his left hand, and stooped from his saddle only to lift the latches of the many wooden gates.

Behind us, that avenue skirted by those Lombardy Poplars, and crowning a hill in the distance, the phantasm of the house and its phantasmagoric roses.

We rode through fields of blue cattle. Their tender ears were clipped by numbered tags and their pelts shimmered in the light. Before us, a prospect designed and executed by an unknown hand. There was also that silence to consider, and the serene heat. Gabriel suddenly spurred his horse and vanished down the hillside at a gallop. I watched him for a moment and then heedlessly pursued him, my sex slamming down hard onto the leather, my breasts heavily rising and then falling, the balls of my feet weightless in the stirrups. Exhilarating chase, that liberation from premeditation and structured expression: being in its purest form.

Gabriel was waiting for me by the edge of that bluish bushland, his broad chest heaving and his throat and temples and defined forearms glistening with perspiration. Exhaling hot lungfuls of air and light-headed with the sheer release of the pursuit, I cantered up to him on my sweat-lathered mare. 'Your cheeks are flushed,' he slowly said, turning into the bush.

Virgin territory: pyres of fragrant bark strips and great graceful trees, native flowers postmodernist in form and scent, shape-shifting clouds of pin-prick insects and leaves that shattered like slivers of Venetian glass. Bunched clumps of blue-black berries hung from frail reptile-yellow stalks. Smooth mottled trunks. A gum was dying in the poisonous embrace of squirming spitfires. Trees bled sap that was no more than liquefied rubies. A certain haunting music. That gliding of an introverted serpent into copsewood. Spaced caws and sweeter trilling. The rhapsodic glottal call of an azure-tinged baby kookaburra. Wild doves with outspread wings, their sheen that of black pearls. That canopy of vines created a subaqueous ambience.

Hoof beat, heart thud.

Like carp milling at the surface of water, the twisted richly crimson blooms of Wilson's Grevillea. Odalisque heat. A creeper foaming with star-shaped flowers brushed its tendrils against my cheeks and lips and nacreous eyelids. The aromatic eucalyptus family: *maculata, mannifera, papuana, torquata, viminalis, woodwardii.* A dragonfly so dipped into moist shade, an iridescent biplane. Stagnant pondwater brimmed with spawn. A branch swollen at the socket, its five red-green leaves the fingers and thumb of an arboreal hand. That rotting log infested with woodlice. The apple-coloured air. Pie-slices of dull porous stone unearthed or sinking into dirt. Fungoid blisters flourishing on a skewed stump. That sweat running in rivulets between my breasts.

Heart thud, hoof beat.

The Warmblood trotted to a stop, tore at the undergrowth with its big teeth, and my horse followed suit; there was the easy and liquid-thick sound of two horses chewing, and then that of vegetation powerfully ripped from its white roots.

'When I was a girl,' I said, snapping a piece of honeycomb from a low bough, 'I believed in men like you.'

Caught in a filtered shaft of sunlight, Gabriel slowly stretched and looked at me. Amused green eyes. And then his laughter, unexpected and profound.

37

A bay window overlooking a pale river of Italian lavender. I had showered and was sprawled on the chaise longue (one sallow silk-skinned foot dangling over the seat-rail), reading a slim green-jacketed volume on toleration. Gabriel was still sweat-stained from the ride and wearing polo boots which in the sunlight were enriched to amber. Now framed by the doorway and with his back to the kitchen, each hand on its respective doorjamb and with his chin tilted, his square-jawed face was streaked with sweat. That scar showed up untarnished. 'I'm going to leave you for an hour. Things to do.'

I did not speak, but loved his face.

An hour passed. A dream of priests and superimposed, the slam of a carved cedar door and then the amber leather of Gabriel's boots on the parquetry and polished floorboards (interpolated, the hush as he stepped over any number of soft handwoven rugs). Opened my eyes. He was standing with his hands behind him on the crest-rail of a dining-chair, staring at me. That sweat-streaked face, so absolutely beautiful. I slowly closed my eyes for what I knew to be a year. Reopened them. The light was lilac, and the colour of the lavender had deepened to sea-blue. I was about to speak, but instead slowly exhaled the words and then they were forgotten. I closed my eyes for what I knew to be a year. Reopened them. Described to me in childhood: a paranormal apparition at the foot of a girl's bed. 'It was a shadow,' she explained, 'but a shadow paler than the night.'

And this was Gabriel to me in that darkening room.

Corolla, calyx, onyx spurs. Narcotic depths, dreaming in foam. He was still standing there, seemingly no more than an aggregate of 'simplified visual schemata', but too real. Loose image scree: our kiss, that one slow tongue unfolding and his foreskin peeling back like the skin of a sweet peach – exposed, his peach-sweet glans and then his cock softly within my mouth. From the dim pond, the hollow and hypnotic baritone of a great frog.

38

My thighs were wet in that warm, pulsing dusk and deep between them, my liquefied centre. That shirt of his I wore was half-unbuttoned and had ridden high over my belly, high over my bony hips, the left one bruised, tenderly bruised. Gabriel's eyes travelled from my sex to my sleep-heavy mouth. I was still bleeding, but my cervix had been padded with clean unbleached cotton. Such air, no longer apple-coloured but tinged with desire – an altogether different temperature, an altogether different hue. He slowly walked towards me and stood there in the darkness. I heard the liquid trickle of his zipper and then closed my eyes.

Trawling those depths, dreaming of games.

He balanced his left hand on the backrest and with the other, grasped his cock. That scent of sweat intoxicated me. I spread my thighs further apart. With sleepy fingers, I pulled that blood-drenched cotton from its source and then laid it on the cool floor. The stain remaining would suggest a murder. Reopened my eyes. Gabriel moved his left knee up against my buttocks and murmured words that dissolved into the evening.

Outside, those stars, those limpid stars.

39

The pauropod with whom I lived was absent the following morning. None of her trademark shower-steam on the bathroom mirror, no prolonged gurkings at dawn. Threw back the sheets. Miserably hot. An hour's sticky sleep. In me, the suffering of every symbolist. The sky was white (baked of its pigment). A Dali day: gold pocket-watches melted over the fence palings and birds screeched, their plumage richly burning. There was the suggestion of a limbless torso on the lawn, its arms and legs torn by a violet tiger. The tarmac on the roads would already be bubbling: liquorice streets. This light was brutal, it was toxic, and the ash from the bushfires it caused would wash up on every shore – chunks of charred wood, papery blacks.

Two hours later: I sat stewing before the many mirrors of the hair salon, my hair in a Cellophane cap beneath a monstrous dryer, listlessly waiting for the 'deep conditioning treatment' to take effect. The manicurist interrupted. 'Compliments of the management,' she muttered as she dumped her little basket on the mirror-ledge and sat beside me, a big parabolic farm-girl with a surf-white corkscrew perm, pungent come-thick lip-gloss, dressed in pressed black polyester slacks and an urgent sweater, her plump and squarish breasts halved by a tiny brassiere, the pockets of her rich thigh flesh distorting the neat pleat of her pants. She held my hand and studied it as if it were the Koran, her eyes moving knowingly over each pore. Her thighs were a good way apart. Her hips were tremendous, fecund. Her belly was rounded and pounded, frustrated, at that bursting zipper. Two inches long and seemingly cut from Plexiglass, her fingernails were architectural structures, weapons, Dada artworks, and she explained, as she examined my hand with convexed fingers (ever-careful not to damage those frightening claws), that her nails were the latest in acrylic and that she could perform the same juju on me, all I had to do was ask. I did not ask. Once she had soaked and filed and filed and buffed my chiselled hands, she applied frankincense and myrrh to my cuticles, with pursed lips clipped the superfluous skin, and then began to massage each birdlike bone – kneading, kneading, kneading with a drug-slow passion before thickly masturbating each of my fingers – up and down and down and up, in time to the sleazy clatter of her bangles, those oils she used making suck-show sounds as she fucked my knuckles with her pliant white and lubricated hand. Earnestly gazing at my palm, this sexual automaton finished servicing me by tickling my hands with those bizarre arousing fingernails, slowly biting her moist bottom lip and with a set of catlike movements, returning her equipment to its basket. With declining interest: 'That's it, then.'

Perspiring commuters on the station platform. Open air, a Blyton sky. Yellow-beaked Indian mynah birds bounced on black telegraph cables. That girl in red, a leatherette briefcase between her coltish legs, desultorily chewing gum: *ker-pop, ker-pop*. The lenience of early evening. A man heavily fanning himself with a trade journal, his knees apart, leaning forward on the newly painted bench, that fat area between his socks and crumpled trouser-legs freckled and furred, sadly turning every minute to the tunnel for a train. Klaxon song, the indigestion of engines, blue fumes. I leaned against the fencing and stared at those gleaming railway tracks, my hair perfumed by chemicals. Considered, as I lit a cigarette, the design of my Questar catadioptric telescope. Considered, as I inhaled smoke, the fact that I would not be returning to work until late January. Considered, as I exhaled smoke, the words of a doctor in the *British Medical Journal*: 'The foreskin is as important to the penis as the eyelid is to the eye.' By the wilting flowerbed to my right, a woman elbowing her friend as an attractive prospect sauntered past and then her smile: mean-IQ lewdness. In February 1987, Supernova 1987A burst open in the Large Magellanic Cloud. Gabriel, Gabriel, Gabriel: the hippocampus, in which memories are stored, is said to be shaped like a seahorse. My seahorse lover. Arriving with a loud electric purr, one of the new trains christened Tangara.

Brine had come, seen, conquered and again left. Her catbox scent was everywhere, as were those 'little feminine touches' (taffeta flowers, tulle-concealed toilet-lid closed). Left on my answering machine, a rambling message from Amedeo. Our mother and stepfather had borrowed the Bossu pile in Lake Forest for the Christmas season and I was invited to their annual orgy. The ticket would be couriered to me. Flight QS 11 would leave at 3.45 p.m. on 21 December from Kingsford Smith and fly non-stop to LA International, where I would board flight QS 305 at 1.09 p.m. for hard Chicago. First class, 1K. I would be arriving at O'Hare at 7.13 p.m. local time. He would be there to pick me up. I was to bring cold-weather clothes: the windy city was a morgue. He was wrecked, up all night with a whore – gift from a pal, incredible. And, right – before he forgot: he was engaged. Thumper, his fiancée, would be at the airport with him. 'I'm outta here,' he said. 'The market's moving, gotta go.'

A private girl, I had always kept my fractures and elisions to myself. That night I walked for an hour until I reached Beulah Street Wharf. Two proud apartment blocks from the Prime Minister's Kirribilli residence, it swayed and creaked in darkness with drunken old fishermen who only dropped their reels to drop their pants and glitteringly urinate into the harbour. These vampires vanished before dawn, leaving a view blind to their pollution. It was one or three o'clock in the morning and for once I was alone, and stood on that rocking wharf and stared at the six white ears of the sinking Opera House – just there, like anything else.

40

Brine was at home, celebrating her forty-thousandth birthday with five of her girlfriends. Clustered around a nasty cake baked in the shape of the tumescent male genital (and decorated with twenty-one matching candles), the party exploded into an atonal chorus of 'Happy Birthday' as I entered the room. Out of courtesy, I remained until their song had finished and the foreskins of the candles had trickled to pink tears of wax. Caroline was pissed and flushed and as close as she would ever be to real happiness – serenaded by her fellow witches, fêted by unwrapped black twelve-inch dildoes, teddy bears in frilled pinafores and 'joke' books featuring anthropomorphized cartoon penises, her mouth stuffed with a piece of candy cock. Hooting with delight, she clapped and clapped and threw her head back (exhibiting her metallic upper molars, the shag-pile of her smoker's tongue and ferny nostrils).

There was a strange line at the base of her neck, a line demarcating a complete change of skin-tint: it was as if an orange head had been sewn onto the baggy body of a ghostly freckled ageing nondescript blonde (she frequently forgot to apply her artificial tanning lotion below the shoulder). She would be jumping on her broom tomorrow (vacation with Mandi, of the leopardskin-print brassieres and unavoidable overbite) and tonight was her big occasion. Ever sensitive to social demands, she had very seriously dressed for it: a clinging polyester slip emblazoned with grotesque appliquéd hearts, jangling plastic earrings and around her throat, a dog chain anchored by her Christian name in diamanté cursive (from Brenda, with love). Her best friend Sally (she of the Long Slow Comfortable Screws and wattled cleavage) shouted: '*Speech! Speech!*' and I, understanding what was to follow (a prolonged and sentimental monologue interrupted by wine spillages, drunkenly proffered washcloths, cake-crumbs sprayed across the tablecloth in crazed cackling), acknowledged the lot of them with a flaking smile and escaped through the back door and out into the darkness.

Still in my backless black dress and sheer black stockings (dull dinner with legal animals and duller spouses), I removed my heels and settled with a sigh into the grass. Myself again, estranged from the racket of fatuous rituals. Leaned back on my palms and arched my back, legs crossed at the ankle, soothed by the crackle of crickets. Watched the fireflies kindle those languid passionfruit vines and exhaled as if relieving myself of all the universe.

The sky was smalt, a gully pluvial with stars, and this diffuse eternal light made it possible for me to distinguish the silhouette of each jacaranda frond, evolved as they were (or so it seemed to me) for this one moment: such natural perfection was godly in an epoch of force. Above me, the blueprint for the ceiling of Grand Central Terminal's main concourse. The air was a balm. From a shadowy enclave of leaves, a sharply etched black bird lowered his beak to snap an insect from its twig, this motion as clean as a gunshot, his round eye mimicking the moon's circumference. Centuries of men believed birds to symbolize angels, and this angel raised both wings in a gesture of territorial assertion, scattering other birds from their seclusion. Above me, Venus was preparing for its conjunction with the Sun, a signal for the priests of Ancient Egypt to have their kings embalmed for burial.

My slowing breath was so assimilated by the heat, and with me, only the thought of Gabriel: my ache for him stretched out like a hand to that smalt sky and imperceptibly dissolved, leaving a burning trail of stars.

41

The night's blue scope was indistinct through those half-opened windows. Steadily shimmering, the celestial river Eridanus. Untiring Chaldean priests had charted the same stellar bodies six thousand years ago. Their careful perseverance may have been a legacy of paganism: before the advent of that compassionate avatar we call Christ, man had to shape – not memorize – a moral and ethical framework for himself through available natural means. I lit a cigarette and watched its tip hiss and subside against the cut-out black of my unsteady fingers. Gabriel's face so suddenly before me and then I felt dismembered as I recalled his eyes filtered by sun – its light working unearthly greens to the corneal surface, a human history retained within those pupils. I wondered whether it were true that powerful affection generates itself within the astral body before pouring down into the live field of its object, a phial of liquid gentleness, imagine; spiritualists have always described felt affection as a roseate light – the idiom of the soul translated into the body's vernacular. And this is love.

42

A blast from the past, as they so assonantly say: a childhood playmate was in town from India. His father had been stationed in Milan, where our glamorous parents pleasanted each other and exchanged waltzing partners and political gossip at high-level functions. I recall my father once describing my friend's mother as 'a dugong sunning itself on the shores of a Schiaparelli sea', but it was a jovial comment, kilned in the lung and not the heart, he was just being cute. The two couples had been friendly, if violently different; my father had never been a conservative thinker. Intellectually, he was a wild man – swinging from one philosophical vine to the next. The Tarzan of transcendental idealism! His generous nature was never threatened by exposure to the unfamiliar as early love had consolidated his internal sense of security.

In contrast, my friend's retired parents now pruned their scentless roses and sipped exotic bitter teas in the gardens of their stately stucco villa in Point Piper, leaving the house only to dine at the Royal Prince Edward Yacht Club or the mansions of their cronies, paralysed by protocol and enduring – with the hideous uncomplaining consistency of cult victims – each cheerless blow and cold constriction of their socio-economic status.

Cain-Duprès was the eldest of four unusually handsome brothers, and seven years my senior. After reading *Siddhartha* at the age of twenty-one he had escaped to Calcutta, where he lived a golden life of idleness and meditated every evening on a mat, invoking slowly stripping glendoveers. Hesse's gloomy humanism and ascetic immaterialism had provided my friend with an alternative to those family traditions of composure, chitchat and croquet. Robed in saffron, he pretended to study translations of the original tantric texts and nursed his kundalini, rarely masturbating or engaging in sexual intercourse.

It was, he acknowledged, a less than useless existence by Western standards.

Very occasionally he indulged in a little high-grade Persian Brown (a postprandial mixture of coffee and heroin) and dreamed of those cool blonde girls he once squired to formals, now cuckolded wives and zinc-deficient mothers. And that early ambition to be a polymath had long since been rejected; it was too late for him to revert to the traditions of his youth – the teachings of his Church, his schools, his lineage, all had been betrayed. Every third Christmas he conceded to some show of blood-duty and returned to his parents, bearing gifts of indigestible Indian sweets he had carelessly wrapped in greased paper. His mother, ever-careful not to reveal those feelings she felt were so vulgar, would flare her hands in a parody of surprise and cry: 'Why, how *lovely*, darling!' Cain-Duprès was hard to pin down, that was for certain; he relished his inaccessibility. I don't believe his parents were ever really happy to see him. They felt scorned, and secretly hoped that he would return to them a mess (emaciated, weeping, gagging to learn the restoration of antiques). The fact that he never did return led them to doubt their convictions, and this doubt further eroded their eroded lives.

They attempted to muffle this doubt with needlepoint and scones, solipsizing their traumata and baffling squadrons of specialists with their cluster-headaches and seemingly source-less physical pains. Their son remained indifferent. Like many of his well-born peers (myself included, possibly), he sought to define himself through his eccentricities rather than his achievements, eccentricities as paradoxically elitist as the high banking and law he so mocked. And there was no-one to pester him in India, no-one to remind him of that which he had relinquished or from which he had been saved, he could be as intractable as he liked.

Crisp knock. Opened the door. It was Cain-Duprès all right, but so altered – there was a new layer of sadness or wisdom over his charmingly vacuous grey eyes. Deeply etched lines had changed the impact of his features and he was punitively thin, each untaxed muscle visible beneath its film of skin. Around his neck, a silver symbol hanging from a simple chain and on his bony feet, fraying leather sandals. Predictable greetings and a long embrace. From the local grocery we bought a brown paper bag of cherries, figs and sour plums and walked down the hill to the harbour-fronted Primrose Park, where an amateur softball game was in progress.

He spat a pit into the water, the disturbance of its surface only temporary. 'I love the clarity of Sydney,' he said after a pause. 'Calcutta is so black.'

I was picturing Gabriel waist-deep in the glistering stillness, the density of his warm breast, his baseless eyes. My concentration had slipped through the net of the actual and was swimming out into the far blue possible, its fin sinking and rising, ever more distant.

'Calcutta was named for the goddess Kali Yuga,' Cain-Duprès said, plucking another cherry from the paper bag. 'She wore a belt of severed hands – not her own, I might add. In her left hand, she carried the severed head of a man; in her right, the blade with which he was decapitated. Do you know, these cherries are utterly heavenly.'

Skimming that warm breeze, a pelican or cockatoo and in the distance, the swell of applause.

'Her temple is painted black with scarlet fangs and within, her followers decapitate monkeys and pigs in her honour and then stick the poor creatures' heads on poles. The gutters there are always running with fresh blood.' His cultured voice had adopted the swayingly formal rhythms of Hindustani. 'Every number of years,' he continued, 'a group of baby girls with the correct markings on their hands and feet is left in the temple overnight; and the one who doesn't cry is chosen to incarnate Kali. A conditional honour. This child is treated with the reverence known only to kings until she bleeds. The instant she is cut or menstruates, she is cast out and immediately replaced.'

The sudden crack of a well-smacked softball. More indolent applause. A ladybird on my finger, and then she was gone. Recalled that Gabriel had a way of sometimes sitting with his broad brown back to me, his head lowered, a way of sometimes sitting with his face half-turned to me, those enduring eyes of his working my soul over his shoulder. He had a way of sometimes smiling, this smile fading from his lips but remaining in his glance, a luminous communion.

Cain-Duprès was plaiting clover-flowers with a deferential intensity. 'I have a child, you know,' he said, his voice low and controlled. 'An encounter with a Hindu girl – not a love affair, merely an ... encounter. She was left pregnant, but didn't tell me about the child until it was too late. The child is female. A little girl. It lives with an old couple – good people, but slum dwellers, surrounded by drugs and prostitution.'

Behind his head, the dazzling sky and suspended in it, the pellucid membrane of the moon.

'Her mother abandoned her. I don't know what to do.' Drawing his shoulderblades together, he dropped his chin and stared fixedly at that wreath of pink-and-white clover flowers in his weathered hands. 'I suppose I could have it adopted or give it to my parents – who, of course, know nothing of the whole horrendous episode – or I could take it back with me to Calcutta, which would be totally impossible.'

Looked up from that plaited wreath and then his fingers tore the thing apart and closed over the wrecked foliage. 'The world,' he said, raising his eyes to mine, 'has finally been brought to me and I just don't know what to do.'

Five silent minutes passed.

'Let's visit my parents,' he suddenly suggested. 'They'll be absolutely ecstatic to see you after all these years.'

43

The place was a museum – orthodox antiques, Home Counties hunting scenes, finicky chintz, biographies of Benjamin Britten, ivory netsuke, narcissi stiflingly arranged in powder-blue Chinese bowls, and upon every enamelled or waxed or scrupulously dusted surface, a faceted crystal vase of lilies. I drifted through this expertly arranged interior, an interior aesthetically rather than emotionally significant, deaf to the practised banality of that conversation behind me and overcome by the urge to exist purely within those contoured flowers. Their supernatural fragrance was no less than the recollection of a kiss, its lingering a white trial in itself.

Lady Cain-Duprès, surrounded by snuffling pug dogs who were fed grapes by the butler after their supper of grouse, grasped with her perfect fingers my thin arm and wistfully smiled. She had always been an attractive and patrician woman, at home amongst the histories of the *ancien régime* and all those Stygian bouquets. She was a champion of heritage and not culture; breeding was of more interest to her than polemical historicism. No longer the flamboyant dugong of my father's joke, she was dressed in a long and floating citrus shift, freshwater pearls and in the filtered lamplight, her imperious eyes were the colour of smoke. At her slender tended feet, the apricot-fawn pug named Banbury began to whimper and then sat back on its fat stunted haunches and openly wept. Its mistress elegantly dropped to stroke its jowls and coo, 'Banbury, darling – please don't cry; we have a *guest*.' To me, she said: 'He was given to me as a pup by a friend at Glyndebourne, you know. Terribly sensitive, and suffers horribly from nightmares.' There was a shuffling noise as her husband of a hundred years materialized from the library. 'Awake already, darling?' she asked without turning her head.

Sir Cain-Duprès nodded and resolutely approached the drinks cabinet. 'I had the most extraordinary dream,' he said as he crashed into a silver tray, causing the liquor decanters to delicately shiver. 'I was married to the Queen and dressed in morning dress and I was letting her out of her carriage, fancy that.'

His wife's smile was a kind of memory. 'Bless your heart, dear – it was only a dream.'

Without acknowledging me or his eldest son, he poured himself a good measure of oblivion and downed it in a single stinging gulp. Wife and heir began to discuss the merits of different gins. ('One has a picture of Queen Vic*toria* on the label. Queen Victoria! She probably never had a jigger of gin in her life, bless her heart!') I nodded and politely smiled and glanced around with gentle interest.

'I was so sorry to hear of your father,' Lady Cain-Duprès said as she laid a mother's hand upon my shoulder. 'We were all terribly upset.'

'It seems so long ago,' I said.

'It was,' she answered, slowly moving away. 'But he was *such* a wonderful man – so frightfully intelligent and so gifted, a different order to the rest of us. But what can one do? God moves in mysterious ways.'

'Has it been that many years?' Sir Cain-Duprès wondered out loud in response to some unarticulated calculation. 'Good Lord, this life! How quickly it passes, how quickly it passes.' And shaking his mottled head, he poured himself another stiff measure. 'It seems like only yesterday that your father and I were arguing the merits of the Arabic hareem.'

'There has been the most *fright*ful increase in local real estate prices since that awful tycoon bought the pink house on the hill,' his wife announced, reprimanding him with a hard look. 'And for *such* grotesqueries, you have no idea. *Mon*strous! Absolute *eye*sores festooned with cherubs and follies and Corinthian columns and Spanish archways and God knows what.'

Nodding, I turned to a framed photograph of a young boy in tennis whites. 'Is that you?' I asked the vacant Cain-Duprès.

There was a crepitating silence as they all exchanged glances. Without the use of words, it had been decided that the mother would be responsible for the grim information and in preparation, she straightened her already military spine. 'No,' she answered, reaching for her son's unresponsive hand. 'No. That's Henry, his brother. He died four years ago.'

Those Wedgwood eyes of hers filled quickly and she inhaled and suffered a little, there in her overstuffed armchair. 'A heroin overdose,' she said. 'Be a dear and light a cigarette for me, won't you, Edward?' A talcumed pause. 'Henry had been an ... an addict for years, he read too many books, the silly boy. Those Decadents, you know, a lamentable influence.' Again, she paused. 'They really shouldn't *teach* that kind of thing, I don't care if it's relevant. We were so happy for him when he stopped taking drugs. Sebastian encouraged him to enroll in a fine arts course and he took up badminton ... but then his girlfriend – terribly ordinary, if you know what I mean – left him to marry his best friend, which was terribly cruel, unforgivable, really, and – well, he – he – he just couldn't *cope*; he was never able to cope with too much feeling, really, was he, Edward? That was just the way he was, poor thing; he'd always been like that, even as a little boy. Of course, he was so much younger than the others, a late child, all that. I don't know if he felt up to taking on the world. Charles, as you know, has done so well, and Timothy – well, Timothy excels at everything he does.' Here she inhaled her soured pride. 'Henry should have been pro*tected* from his feelings, not encouraged to express them ... we – we really should have pro*tected* him, Edward, I think.'

Her voice cracked as her husband handed her the burning cigarette. 'So,' she said, expelling the word with a mouthful of hot smoke, 'he took some heroin, and it – it was a bad batch, you know, cut with something horrible, and then he ... Henry died.'

44

Dinner in a bustling provincial French restaurant. The depressed Cain-Duprès and I were entertained by irritating dancing girls kicking their scarlet-gartered legs about and winking at the corpulent male patrons, and then a happy acrobat on a shining unicycle seamlessly wove his way between the tables. The cost of these entertainments added to the already monstrous price of what we both decided was a mediocre meal startled me, but Cain-Duprès shrugged. In this gutted mood, he drove me to a clifftop overlooking Bondi Beach, where we stood and stared at the horizon.

'You never told me Henry died,' I eventually said.

He slipped his hands into his pockets. 'I didn't, no,' he answered. 'Not mentioning it made it unreal.'

Beams of moonlight capped the distant waves. We stood and gazed at those ever-surging indistinct white rills of spume below, those rills so perfectly counterbalanced by the twinkling shorebound lights of the pavilion.

'Isn't it strange,' I said, 'to think that this black water leads to everywhere.'

'Except the past,' Cain-Duprès whispered, 'except the bloody past.'

45

Over the grainy grass, under the argentiferous trees, past the windsurfers and beachgirls mirrored in each other's sunglasses and past the evening paddlers of Balmoral Beach I walked, absorbed by the clanking and rocking of moored modest boats. The light was opal and the air was flaxen. Without, the world at its alchemical best; within, it was as if I were being rattled by some unknown hand to serve some unknown purpose – that of my future, perhaps: a cold breath-clouded glass. The light was opal and the air was warm and flaxen. That breeze through the leaves was silk evaporating on the skin.

Years ago, a certain man had whispered (burning, unforgivably) against my lips: 'You know those hot dark nights when you're driving in the country and some animal darts across the road and you swerve to miss it but you hit it anyway, and then the car skids into a tree and when you come to, the windscreen's shattered and there's steam rising from the engine and it stinks of blood and petrol and your forehead's gouged? Well, that's how you smell when you come, Angelica.'

Spread my white beachtowel across the sand as if preparing for some pantheistic lunar rite and, brushing the shore from my white knees, sat in its centre like a thing of bone. In Cain-Duprès' India, white is the colour of mourning and I sat there anxiously, as if attempting to dispel an unknown grief. Flags blew like tissues from the masts of boats, a car door slammed, the ocean rolled. At the turn of the century, the Theosophists had built a temple at the far end of the shore and all that remained of it were certain foundation stones in the form of a lower jaw over which the seas receded and then gushed. A beautiful youth emerged from the water in the briefest sealskin, his genital a suffocated flower. Plato believed that only those with the ardent nature of lovers were equipped to refine the most evolved philosophies. The elongated shadows of centaurs a way away from me slowly progressed with their strong shocking laughter. Tears brimming in me, coloured silver and ultramarine. A child named Tom was being naughty and his mother cried: 'Come *here*! Come *here*!' Those graceful gulls in downward arcs into the water and then back up again, as if magnetized by an invisible and perfectly circular rail. Cognitive pluralities were of no help. A noise behind me, perhaps caused by that child or its mother. Go to her, Tom, because before you know it, she will disappear.

Driftwood and thistle, white ash and columbine. He was beside me suddenly and I could not breathe.

'I've missed you,' he said softly. 'This place will now always remind me of you.'

The storm of wanting him had made me mute.

'I have a fever, feel,' he said, and offered me his brow.

Cunt-hot. My hand, still glowing from that touch.

'I've been so ill,' he said, 'I have been so ill.'

There was a lull in which a Persian bird lived, and its song.

'Come swim with me,' he said.

I looked at his broad face. 'All right,' I said, and levered myself with his arm.

With the burdened working legs of Atlas and our hands mechanically waving in that same semi-circular dance, we waded into and against the water, the concentric rings around each of us joining at the one trembling point so that we both were captured in the hollows of a liquid figure eight. My sex responded to his eyes and to his voice, that scented unguent. 'I was standing on the edge of that jetty,' he said, indicating with an angling of his head the setting, 'it was the darkest night. I was staring down at the water when a sudden radiance bloomed from the depths. It moved as slowly as a drunken sun, and I remember wondering if you had drowned and if this was your phosphorescent body rising from the silt to haunt me.' The evening air passed from my lungs to his, its properties forever altered. 'It was only a scuba diver and his torch.' And then, with an acute charge of emotion: 'I have missed you; I have been so ill.'

Wind over the promontory. Again, that surreal clanking. Again, that surreal rocking. Roused and again roused by his hot words, my soul.

'This water isn't clear,' I said, rippling my fingers over the surface, 'it frightens me.'

Tenderly smiling: 'Only fishies in there, little fishies.'

That undertow of blood and nerves. Such a forgiving sky. Gabriel suddenly dived, his biceps, thighs and calves knife-aligned, and punctured that bodyheat sea. It seemed an eternity before he resurfaced, shimmering and shaking that wet lupine hair, sweeping the ocean from his cheeks and thrumming temples with his palms.

'*Dive!*' he shouted. '*Dive!*'

I stared at him, inhaled, and plunged into that warm dream-green, working the journey with my forceful tail – a skinless lorelei, entranced. Ahead, the strangely pale unfocused columns of his legs. Above, his fevered want, his fevered need. I swam towards him with my hair flowing behind me like terror, and then rose – sliding up over his pelvis and belly and hard breast and without thinking, called him precious, I called him precious; and without thinking, closed my mouth over each of his brown nipples and then suckled him, uncaring of the possibility of being observed, no more than the sum of my passion, I drew deeply of his warmth. My hands grasping his hips, I felt – as I had felt in nightmares and stellar reveries – his sex swell poignantly against my ribs, and heard – as I had heard in nightmares and stellar reveries – his exhalation of shocked sexual pleasure, and so I suckled from him all the nutrients of trust.

Cradling my head with his brown hands, he spoke my name and spoke my name until it filled the air like muscadine and so seduced me.

I rested my chin against his chest, and looked up at him looking down at me, his face bestowing an intensity upon the world. And what thing was this? To have captured this one moment in a cameo and worn it close, between my breasts: a wish. I recalled my father telling me that the Chinese ancients, those masters of succinct mystical lore, believed that only artists possessed seven chambers of the heart – and in each ringing chamber, a star; and in each ringing chamber, a new future; and in each ringing chamber, chaomantic vigour.

'I can't think straight,' he said. 'My mind is scrambled. I feel as if I have betrayed some fundamental principle of mine, some law. The old ways don't seem right, I cannot fight it; all

I do is think of you, I think of you.' He closed his eyes and slowly shook his head. 'Angelica, you've somehow touched me and I don't know how it is or why it is that all I do is think of you.'

As those soundless clouds above softly exploded, I kissed him: salt and surrender, visceral desire.

'Gabriel,' I whispered, 'take me home.'

46

Supper untouched.
Upended the punnet of strawberries into the sink and with my hands, washed them in cold running water. Arranged them one by one in a porcelain bowl and carried it to the table. His expression was one I could not place. A stifling pause. He raised one of those bright and shining fruits to his lips and as if recalling a significant event from that time before he knew me, murmured: 'Wild strawberries.'

The room grew close, it seemed so dark and all I knew was Gabriel, his light so nebular, his force pure will. Spherically slow, his fingers pulled back the points of the strawberry's cap and with a watchmaker's precision he bit into it, his teeth slicing that sweetest pulp – it may have been my heart, who could have said – certainly, I was not aware of any difference. Drugged on the morphine of his scent and all the moment, I absorbed him with my gaze. He rolled the pulp over his tongue; between his right thumb and forefinger, he held what remained of that red fruit. There were multiplex erotic disturbances within me – levels of lavish arousal, winged indigos, relics, veils, baptismal waters: he was so beautiful to me, it was impossible. That silence lay between us like a waiting bed. Brine's opaque bulb began to flicker and to flicker until – with the blundering symbolism of a poor German art-film – it detonated with a hiss, and we were left in darkness.

'Angelica,' he said, and pressed my damp palm to his lips.

A single shaft of neon light bored through the kitchen window from the house next door, infusing the room with a sense of dreamlike permanence.

'I never knew,' he said, 'that it was possible to feel like this.' And then again, he pressed my damp palm to his lips and kissed and again kissed it until I was forced to swallow all my tears.

The apotropaic properties of vulnerability: still holding my hand, he slowly leaned forward and smudged his mouth against my own. Truth has an unforgettable impact. What my mind had conjured in secret moments, what my flesh had desired and my inner voice beseeched, what my ear had sought and spirit craved, this was too dangerous. I closed my eyes.

'Why do you want me?' I asked, maddened by his proximity.

'Because,' he answered, 'I never knew that it was possible to feel like this.'

Instinctively I dragged my lips over his cheeks, his eyelids and his brow; instinctively I licked him and then made mine the slippery innerspace of his spiced mouth. He suddenly embraced me and pulled me trembling over his broad thighs and as I straddled him, my sex was a kind of violence.

'I want it all,' he said, 'I want everything about you, I want everything.'

Rapture. Our kisses thickened, deepened, altered in hue and I knew somehow that he would be the only one to ever really take me. His fingers kneaded and so scorched my skin, scorched its texture and pigment and with it, sentience. He rubbed me to a soft moan; I was so stretched by his broad thighs. My hands on his shoulders, I relented as his fingers spread and spread my warm responsive cunt. That hiss of pleasure. That one shaft of neon light. With his free hand, he brought an apple from the bowl to my panties and slowly began to polish it against my shrouded sex, his other hand beneath the voile holding open my wet vulva. He said my name and said my name until it filled the air like muscadine and so seduced me.

'Angelica,' he said again, this time with what was almost pain.

That pause, heavy with fear.

And then: polishing that apple to a gloss, he pulled the

voile aside and pressed the fruit against my sticky cunt, holding it there before lifting it to my astonished lips and willing: 'Take a bite, Angelica.' I sank my teeth right through the sex-slicked skin and tasted myself salt over that sharp citric spurt. His breath had hoarsened and I felt the world, all the starred universe, and leaning forward, he began to eat that cunt-oiled fruit from my full mouth and as he did, he slid the length and breadth of two hot fingers in me and said: 'I want to own you here; this is to be my one domain.'

That cry of mine was sourceless and he shivered at its plea.

'I want it all,' he whispered as he slowly fucked me with his fingers, 'I want everything about you, I want everything.'

Our kisses grew more open-mouthed, they became open-hearted. The pale trajectory that was my body – that occult journey between pillars – was travelled by him and only him. I suddenly knew what it was to forfeit definition in favour of union: it was a willingness to be in the world, not of it; it was a willingness to be revealed. My cunt clutched at him and he so exhaled. I was of foam; I knew of no other home but this. That shadow of his head, a myth shifting against the wall. I had waited out my life for this, for him, for us. Knotting his fingers through my hair to gain a hold and with his other hand so deeply in me that I bucked involuntarily, he again kissed me and then threw his head back so that all I could see was his curving throat.

'That's it,' he eased, 'that's it.'

Unbidden imagery: that small boy screaming in a silver barber's chair, his mother cruel and wrenching still his head as the old butcher wielded his old razor; around them, perfumed talcs and bottled lotions, blue postcards from the postmarked past, so many mirrors and the floor a dead meadow of golden hair. Songs of innocence, songs of concupiscence. The boy's mouth widened and the image then dissolved, a plume of mist.

Gabriel was still cradling my head as I convulsed over his knees, his fingers still within those folds, his fingers webbed by my sex-silks and so bewitched, I was all breasts and deliquescence. It was to die. It was to enter a white decade. To be so taken; to be his. Caught in that shaft of neon light, my breasts seemed molten. Gabriel stooped to suckle them, and it was all I could do to remember that we were distinct, we were not one; but even that knowledge was rapidly disintegrating. Cycle and epicycle, orb in orb. Telescoping from the moment through a tunnel to a greater consciousness, I breathed and breathed his want and nothing more. Such rapture. I was aware only of the burning points at which our flesh met and so merged. So suckling my nipples, turning each bud over and again in his wet mouth, his eyes half-closed and his fingers owning me in their slow sliding, he roused in me a supple trust.

'The other room,' he murmured, my nipple further thickening between his lips.

He stood, my thighs clenching his naked waist. With one hand cupping my skull and the other moist against my spine, he carried me into the bedroom. I was suspended – or so it seemed – between a tremor and the alchemy of true desire. Through spume: I was of foam. I knew of no other home but this. A moth was flickering amongst the lunar motes, its head bisected by a noble marking. Gabriel laid me on the bed. My long white dress fell in light halves on either side of me, exposing the known wholeness of my skin.

The scent of cunt, the scent of sweat.

He paused above me, trapped for an instant in his expression of illuminated awe, looking down at me as if I were a jewel once coveted behind a pane of glass and now his: his features registered a soft amazement and calculation. Suddenly dipping his mouth to kiss me, he crushed the heatfield of his belly to my pliant curves. Such rapture. He was ruthless in essence and pinpointed that instant in which I would or could submit completely. The intimacy between us had developed its own field of vision, it was animate and clawed. I felt the response of every nerve – those bright harmonic fibres, these conveyors of melodic impulse: I could have sworn I heard their song.

Tilting his broad face, he pressed his mouth to my wrists. His shoulders dropped as he slipped his pants to his ankles and kicked them onto the floor. Behind him, in the cheval-glass: my vulva and poised over it, the beast-breadth of his haunches and his back, his genital a density in shadow. Slowly moving down the bed, he took my feet into his hands and delicately kissed them – each toe, the transverse arches, the insteps, my soft soles. I curved and curled and so uncoiled. Love is a force: it can be warfare or new life.

'To have you like this always,' he said, kissing and again kissing my salt flesh.

A way away from me, that moth twisted itself outside in the darkness, its wings assimilated by the night. There was the slow shift of his weight, I heard it; my skin was now both voice and ear. He lapped and nipped my inner thighs, indenting that softness, and then shouldered his way between my legs and with both hands, lifted my buttocks from the bed and sucked my sex as I had sucked those swollen figs at Primrose Park: rapture. I arched and jacked myself against him, further spreading my spread thighs. It was to die. It was to enter a white decade.

My mouth was opened to the reddest rose.

I ground hard against his flattened tongue, begging him to pierce me with his fingers and as he did, I came – this time against his lips, disorganized and so deranged: this was a realm in which all barriers had been forbidden. In each, the echo of the other – a yield of real discovery. Academic lore holds that only through geometry can man isolate the Divine mind, but I saw it differently: this was a trance, a trance of nerves and pores, corpuscles, simple nuclei. 'Angelica,' he said, his chin resting upon my belly, 'I've seen the dark star of your life; I've been within you; I've seen you lose your cold perception of yourself; I've known you pared to bestial stratum, plenum, lovely stuff; I understand better than anyone the great oeuvre of your heart.'

Fever of want. I wiped his broad brow of hot sweat and said his name and said his name until it filled the air like muscadine and so seduced him. His face in shadow was all gold and chrysoprase and jet: one of the two colours outside the chromatic scale and the most intimate. My expectations may have been improbable, but he met each one. When he gently ordered me to turn onto my belly, I obeyed. Life to me in that moment was no more than a series of equipollent actions and counteractions. I could hear his knees over the sheets and sensed him position himself behind me as that cicada named the Black Prince made himself exclusive to the night. My palms were flat upon the sheets, my sex was hot, matted and wet. My thoughts were of the ocean, dragging its low hem across the shore, all memory of life within its dissolving and prismatic folds.

Pressing my narrow back to his broad chest, he kissed the wet nape of my neck. Between my thighs, the slow encroachment of his pelvis, the round head of his sex against my own. I spread my legs further to offer him complete dominion. And with a firm moist shove, he partially entered me and with an inhalation, held himself swollen and still. 'Lift your cunt to me,' he said, his words darkness against my throat, 'lift it up hard.' Closing my eyes, I then backed into him and screamed.

Visions of water-lilies, those impervious white cups, supported by the tension of a pond's green surface.

Lost within each other and eternally connected by this loss, we moved only in unison: there was too much of him in me to recall that which was myself. We filled each other and we filled each other, therein finding a serenity of which we had only dreamt. Swaying, that night, and perfumed by unimaginable flowers. I no longer knew where I had been, I only knew my runic pulse and his, mechanically slamming so deeply within me. Dream-fragments, wishes, the religions of a stranger star. There was a metaphysical obsession with our synthesis at work here – mollient destiny, the perfection of our coupling.

Escalibor, proffered by angels.

Around me, the summer hung like cigarette smoke in the air and the lunar pallor of the furniture infused the room with radiance. Such beauty. In the corner on the floor, a pair of European evening shoes: one on its side, the other at an angle, and such a tense black sheen to each spiked heel. There was a single bitten peach upon the sill. Outside on the cement there was a litter of frangipani, their throats offered to a lycanthropic god. Gabriel was entering me so powerfully that I began to come and come again, cored so voluptuously, almost dismayed by my own candour. His hand was slow over my belly and then slower to that tangled sweat-soaked sexual fur, to my bruised full labia: with his fingers, he felt and felt again his thickness slipping in and slipping out.

Such rapture.

I came and came again with rented gasps; he thrust himself far into my viscidity, my substancelessness. There was the

248

moon, anthropomorphized as a woman in the lands between the tropics of Capricorn and Cancer. There was the fragrance of the oils secreted by my glands – attar of roses, chypre, Prussian woodsmoke – a fragrance which he inhaled and which so transformed him. I could only submit. Left: only the achromatism of delirium. And then he bore within me, he bore within me as if he wished only to part my soul.

'Your cunt,' he grunted, 'nearly kills me; I can't live without it; it won't let me be.'

I softened every limb and allowed his substantial sex to overwhelm me. My cunt so suckled his sliding cock, its rhythms were attuned to mine, my concentration was intense – I could no longer be distracted: I was aware of him and only him. A sudden spasm shocked me as he bit my throat and crushed my body to his own with one hard arm. My thighs so spread and his palm fiercely palpated my wet flesh. I was soundless as he staked himself within me. Blindness. To hear his moan as he discharged his silk, his milk, the fluid web in which I had been captured. His shuddering, prolonged. The *deus otiosus* had been released in his every exhalation. Blindness.

Overcome, I sank my face into the pillows. A hair of Gabriel's on my tongue. Turning my face, I met his lips – a kiss lost in its own dark wilderness. Felt sexual insularity can serve the purpose of psychic replenishment. We kissed again, passing the night from mouth to glutted mouth, by now functioning exclusively on instinct. He peeled himself from me to sit back on his haunches and I felt him spread – with careful trembling fingers – the sticky lips of my soft sex. As he unplugged himself, his semen trickled audibly: a rich gush of the future, prostaglandins, real nephology.

'You make love with your soul,' he said, 'and I have never known anything like it. Before it was a matter of flesh and its arousal, and I now feel as if I come with my heart through my head; in that instant, reality dissolves and there is only you.'

Wrapped in each other's arms we fell asleep. At some transparent hour of the morning, I awoke; from the window to the left, I could see Sirius – the star at the tip of Canis Major's muzzle – working above the ever-distant stellar hare: Sirius, that star treasured by Isis, fiercely burning, still pursuant after all these years. All the surrounding sky was an impossible blue-black.

Gabriel's eyelids vibrated in his sleep. With my eyes, I loved his soft rich hair, its unique colours. His temple pulsed. With every breath, his mystery. I loved the lush pulp of his mouth. I loved his throat. I loved the dense curvature of his collarbone and the dell at its big base. There was an active discipline about his form. Hauled, my soul from its pearled caul. I loved that lightly tarred soft hiss of fur down to his sex, and then the dormant sex itself – its flushed and precious tissue, the foreskin crumpled up against his thigh, a rose, a rose collapsed. His massive legs lay loose, one of his feet extending over the ticking. Silently, I so loved him.

> *Liquefactions:*
>
> *A holocaust's stench.*
> *Our bodies packed together*
> *for the drained –*
> *the drained reservoir.*
>
> *The human pelvis makes a chair,*
> *a candelabrum lit*
> *by tapers made of our thin skins.*
>
> *Of our thin skins a taper lit*
> *to find the staircase:*
>
> *You go first, I follow.*

47

Perhaps as a result of my excesses, I had been extemporizing in my sleep and reawoke in the difficult middle of a grand and sweeping thought. These grand and sweeping thoughts of mine were gorgeously arrayed by the subconscious; lit by some great source, their concavities and feminine convexities commanded the attention of my inner eye – exciting it with certainties, fresh theories, those banks of memory easily accessed by the dream-agent. There were times I awoke on the tail of some truth and instead of rousing my body, my consciousness would stumble backwards, frantic to retrieve the scope of sleep's perception. In all attempts to retain such insight, I muddled myself: ideas flew from me like static. I was quite capable of literally reverberating with confusion. The mind has a swift, silent, unflagging pace, and its journey is never linear.

Those two old rodents from the flat upstairs were out with their blue mohair throw and picnic basket. Having resigned from her position as a salesgirl in a stationery shop (where, pinned to her garish uniform, she had worn a Daffy Duck badge and officiously presided over the classification of ball-point pens) to join a small PR firm, Fay Fergusson (who claimed aristocratic Norwegian ancestry) was sprawling on the aforementioned mohair throw. Her flatmate, Tiffany Clutterbuck, was pegging her sad clothes to the clothesline and humming.

Fergusson was north to my south and engrossed in the latest of a score of novels by a popular cod-faced harridan. Her unfortunate aspect was further aggravated by her abbreviated garb: a single strip of crochetwork, knotted at each hip and then lost forever more in the folds of her raw fundament. On either side of this strip, her buttocks sagged like bags of mud; above it, her back was a carpet of fat; below it, her thighs – ample hams, one marred (or made peculiarly erotic) by a purple bruise, spectacular in its dimpled yellow setting. Between her legs, a rotting thicket (its flora African and nothing like the powdery Scandinavian bloom of her scalp). The sexual pragmatism of this girl was truly spellbinding.

Of the two, Clutterbuck (a secretary of unknown ancestry) was the more inhibited, and stood with her face to the sun and five pegs in her mouth, primly clad in what looked like a butchershop awning, her shoulders sprinkled with scurf. The Brine telegraph may have regularly relayed news of her sexual orientation, but Clutterbuck was (to the point of putting a gun in her mouth, God help her) exclusively heterosexual. I knew that she worshipped at the shrine of the white picket fence. She dreamed of lawns, she dreamed of prams, she dreamed of creamed corn and a husband who provided and provided and then vanished like a sprite into the day. And she wanted a baby as other people want a new kitchen appliance. She justified this ambition with the usual pap about 'biological clocks' (a theory with enough of a scientific sheen to generally deter further examination). Bored and frustrated, she sought a man upon whom she could blame this boredom and frustration. She was also lonely and eager for more salubrious lodgings.

Reality is always the wheel on which hopes are hopelessly broken.

Cumbersome and indifferent to the world's aesthetic judgments, Fergusson rolled heavily onto her back. Her exposed breasts were interestingly formed: they grew outwards and upwards from the sides of her wide torso like two cornets. The aureolas were considerable and fringed by fine black hairs. She tugged at one, grimaced, spat *fuck fuck fuck*, then let it stay. Every gesture of hers was designed to draw attention to her femaleness and was effective in this way. She gloated over her Willendorf appeal. Her nipples glowed like ox-eye daisies. The flexure of her belly suggested mighty chugging pink intestines. She reached over to unscrew a fat tub's lid and dug from it a greasy fingerful. Slowly, with a doubled chin, her lower lip touching her septum and her eyelashes almost resting on her full cheeks, she began to rub her nipples with banana butter – hoping, she said as she challenged her pal with a glance, that those unsightly strap marks would fade and tan a carcinogenic brown.

Clutterbuck clucked; appalled by this display, she energetically resumed her pegging.

48

Naked in the kitchen, stirring the sugar into my cup of coffee, studying the orphaned cobweb Brine's hygiene putsch had missed, I began to think of my mother. In an instant, the room seemed to expand and absorb all sound in this expansion. My sudden inward focus intercepted my brain's instructions to my hands and I knocked the cup over.

Coffee flooded the laminated benchtop, seeped beneath each labelled jar – beneath the rosemary and seasoned steak salt and the bearded basil. The fact that Brine rarely cooked made the existence of these jars baffling. My theory was that they were just another ruse to snag a husband, to dupe some fool into believing she was a first division catch. But Brine was no hausfrau who gratefully smiled as she rinsed the lettuce, her eyes never suffused with love as she reglazed the Hot Cross Buns; she was a razorback, and liked to charge. She convinced herself and most of the unfortunates around her that she had a flair for 'curtain blew cue scene,' but I had seen the hostility with which she dusted the cooking implements – she had never really liked them.

Witness the recent evening on which she was stood up by her date, a liquidator who had promised her the earth. Once she had stormed home, she attempted to fry two eggs for dinner and had cracked the shells so viciously against the pan that the yolks exploded all over her white silk-jersey cocktail frock. This was a moment of real grief for her and wailing, she dropped her head into the crook of her arm atop the active stove and almost incinerated her small brain. I sat back in my chair and watched the splitting tip of her ponytail rapidly char and then, aware that she could not see me, commented that I could 'smell something burning'. She immediately flipped her head back, screamed, and began to flay her skull with a decorative oven mitt. 'Is there anything I can do?' I asked her with concern, my hand still on the newspaper before me. Deaf to all offers of assistance in her panic, she continued to dance around the kitchen screeching: '*Me head's on fire! Me head's on fire!*'

Understandably then, such culinary episodes were rare. The street-barrow majolica and supermarket willow-pattern china, the freeze-dried chives and pots of gourmet Le Gastronome de l'Ile de France 'Old Fashioned Grainy' mustard, the coordinated jars and country-feel plaques ('This is Caroline's kitchen!'), these were just props.

It took me a quarter of an hour to finish mopping up the coffee. Were Brine to turn on me, I wanted the cause to be more substantial than adhesive brown stains on the counter. Reset the kettle, returned to thoughts of my mother. Never an ethical or moral vigilante, she was a European lady of the old school – decorous, *molto raffinata*, precise in her intractability. These behavioural tricks had been passed on through generations of such women; a taxidermist would only have to dine with them a single night to understand how to arrange their chins and limbs for his display-case. She and her kind knew how to listen, when to speak, how to consume, what to retain and, most importantly, how to make an entrance and when it was gracious to leave. A proletarian eternity would otherwise be necessary to discover and apply the basic rules.

My mother knew all of horses, she was well versed in finance, knew her politics, she was familiar with good wines. The best discussion of such things requires finesse, if not a touch of genius; misunderstood or partially appropriated, they become the hallmark of the parvenu. By feigning weakness, she found herself surrounded by the strong. By feigning indecision, she was absolved by others of responsibility. By feigning hurt, she became the feebly protesting subject of extreme attention. Such Florentine instincts were valued in this blatant era, if only for their rarity.

The kettle shuddered and began to whistle. I switched it off, poured the steaming water carefully into my cup, stirred it and walked back into the bedroom, my thoughts a tortuous and tortured retrospective. Clutterbuck and Fergusson were tearing chicken wings apart with their teeth and fingers in the garden, and their conversation had progressed (they were discussing fabric swatches).

Still naked, I tied my hair back and began to search through a pile of papers for a photograph of my mother in all her glory. Finding one, I stopped and held it up to the sunlight. Her smile was really unforgettable. It levered the slow-moving corners of her eyes and effortlessly seduced. Drugs and alcohol only enforced its universal charm. And I remembered her at black-tie events, her laughter oxygenated by Dom Pérignon, that laughter enslaving every potentate with its erotic rhythms. Little children in Third World countries would stare up at her wonderstruck, too reverent to ask for anything. My mother was the only person I had ever known who was not mobbed by cripples or leprous beggars when she visited Bombay or Bangladesh; they drew right back from her, amazed and hushed. To those who did not understand its intent, it was a delectable smile – comprehensively acquisitive, sexual, detached. It was the smile on the face of elitism, and had nothing to do with happiness. Profitably aware of its inferred rights and privileges, she could summon it as quickly as a gunslinger draws his gun.

To meet her again after all these years: a sobering prospect. I never knew what to expect. With her, change was a constant; she was always refining her body and face. Once a month, she had fat transferred from her slim golden hips to her cheeks by injection. Amedeo had written to me that she no longer frowned (her dermatologist injected her with Botox, a neurotoxin that paralyses the offending muscle): my mother had always preferred beauty to the expression of emotion. Her scalp was dotted with the one-centimetre incisions necessary for endoscopic face-lifts – she had them performed by her favourite cranio-facial surgeon (the flattering Otto Scarlotti) at the Wellington in London. Such appeal required very serious upkeep. Any changes in me were unlikely to affect her. I could have grown a trunk or antlers and she would remain undistracted from her account of the pedicurist's expertise. It was as if she literally could not *see* me, it was as if I were invisible or magically eliminated from her field of vision by some corneal anomaly. She had always had difficulty meeting my eyes. The level of her look would drop just below my brows and there it would stay – unflinching, infusibly blue. On the noteworthy occasions that our eyes had met, she had immediately looked away, embarrassed, somehow affronted, invidious. She really stiffened: it was as if she had been ambushed.

Ambushed is right. To have read the expression in my eyes would have been to acknowledge my emotions (I am unusually informative in this way). An unforgivable assault on her falsity. Her inner world was one of graphite monuments, her charm the rainbow caused by clouds of crystallized ice, that ice refracting moonlight far above the earth. This illusory amplitude did not allow for the responsibilities of motherhood.

I did not exist to her except in theory, the Daughter Theory, a theory once put to her by my now theoretical father. To illustrate: an old family movie shows me as an infant chasing pigeons in the park. In the foreground and with her back to me stands my mother, very impressive in crushed and tailored oatmeal linens, with a broad straw hat over her ash-blonde braid, faultlessly beautiful and sexually smiling at my father (whose joy communicates itself to the viewer in the manner of all heartfelt feeling). Not once during this documentary does my mother touch me or approach me or in any way behave as if we are related. My father may have subconsciously perceived this indifference and overcompensated, not realizing that this would cause me to be further punished by her for distracting him from the worship of his most demanding idol. He had always been blinded by her ice-crystal charm.

It was difficult to construct her image solely from memory. Somehow the bits of her slotted together badly and the result was only distortion, although her voice was always very clear. Every unrequited lover becomes a litanist. I used to spend hours caressing her clothes: the mutton-sleeved white chiffon blouse spotted with black velvet and worn unbuttoned to the waist; those thin metallic evening gowns which seemed to liquefy her every curve; those rare exotic furs – lynx, tiger, leopard, baby seal – furs which she had professionally refrigerated every summer; the dreamy handmade lingerie, mostly transparent, heartstoppingly erotic; the custom-made heels in colours corresponding to every imaginable gradation of mood – frost, fuchsine, crocus, *rose du Barry*; the hats, some tied with inflexible satin bows and others decorated with fluttering flowers – all these *accoutrements* were more my mother to me than the woman herself.

The hues of certain silks can still move me to tears.

At some point during my unhappy adolescence she entered my bedroom and, as they say in the fashion industry, 'turned on a dime'. She was modelling an imposing neo-pilgrim number to be approved by me. Silenced by her severe beauty, I felt incapable of the usual verbal ardour and so merely nodded – inadequate, distanced by her performance, so aching for her love. This silence of mine offended her, and she retaliated by ignoring me for a week. She was not above such psychologically destructive games. I remember begging for her attention; I remember my frantically polite knocks on her locked morning-room door; I remember quaking as I plucked at her sleeve to alert her to some news I thought would interest her and having her knock my hand off with a swift elevation of her elbow. Gastric tension, that nervous gauze of wishfulness – I remember it all.

<h1 style="text-align:center">49</h1>

Interspersed amongst these thoughts and recollections was some reading about the Franciscans and Ockhamists and their post-Aristotelian physics. I kept to myself in these moods because I felt I might have cracked if I shared the unpredictable black intimacy, it all might have been too much. By five in the afternoon, Clutterbuck and Fergusson had burped their way through their luncheon and were supine on the blanket and snoring like trains, their pale fat faces frying in the sun. The noosphere could not have been enlivened by their contribution. Bulbous flies converged upon the *disjecta membra* – grey chips, chicken-bone splints, yellowing slops of mayonnaise, dry crumbs and rinds. High in the jacaranda tree, an adult magpie was arranging a rat's corpse in the fork of a branch. Once its catch was safely balanced and mostly obscured by leaves, the crow began to peck at the rat-guts, programmed by evolution and insistent, the occasional scrap of rat fur blowily floating to the grass. Appropriately enough, one of these fur scraps floated into Clutterbuck's near-bottomless oesophagus and she coughed in her sleep and so swallowed it, smacking her lips.

I was having trouble concentrating on anything and returned to bed. Fell asleep: the last thing I remember before Brine came belting in was Kepler's mother explaining to me the understanding of acceleration, motion and momentum in fourteenth-century Paris.

My bedroom door hit the wall and I sprang awake, quickly pulling the sheet over my sweating nakedness. The first notes of consciousness are rarely so badly played. Brine was back, and no fictional mélange of undesirable characteristics could have been more astoundingly packaged. Her hair had been permed and framed her face like spinifex. Her eyebrows had been obliterated by the sun. She had gained weight: her adored vinyl shorts (the pair with an appliquéd handprint on each buttock) cruelly segregated her labia. A bandana flattened her loose breasts and her feet were strapped into skyscraper clogs. Her toenails were painted silver. Her fingernails were chewed. A blood-soaked plaster was diagonally arranged over a razor-cut on her shin. The batwing flesh of her upper arms vibrated as she wept, this weeping siphoned from some greater repository of pure misery.

I could not have said with any certainty whether I was dreaming or whether she really was standing there, sobbing in my doorway. The fact that she had turned to me in this, her time of cardboard woe, could simply have been indicative of her sinister opportunism – perhaps Mandi and Bambi and Kelli (and their similarly suffixed sisters) were too hungover or busy fellating drunken strangers to lend her their frequently pierced ears, or perhaps she was merely being impulsive. Either way, she was standing before me: my new friend in need.

With an agility that startled me, she lunged onto my bed. I had been trained by my upbringing to calmly deal with the bizarre and so watched her pound and pound her fists against my mattress and listened to her curse her god, her stars, her confounded luck. She had been 'comtinplating' suicide. Fresh geysers of self-pity, tears. After five or six minutes of this melodrama, she hoisted herself onto her elbows and fixed my kneecaps with a melting expression of sorrow. It transpired that she had had a fling (surprise, surprise). She really thought it had been love. A corporate type, he was so intelligent that he could do long divisions in his head and could even (even!) move his bowels on demand. Another round of snivelling. He had promised to call (he lied). Their love together had been beautiful, a once-in-a-lifetime thing, the air between them vibrated with butterflies. *Nello spirito del risparmio*: Fast Jack had left her with a keepsake she was unlikely to forget – 'the gift', he had written in the note she now tugged from her reluctant hip pocket, 'that keeps on giving' (Brine had missed his sarcastic inference and wasted hours searching for his address or a lottery ticket beneath the shrink-wrapped hotel mattress and decorative conch shells on the cane dresser).

Controlling myself, I expressed sympathy for her predicament, sympathy I even managed to tinge with some sincerity. Humane impulses make themselves known in any number of ways. But the wretched whore would never get it right, no matter how formidable her efforts. That suggestion of gauntness about her cheekbones spoke of doom.

50

Brine's new monomaniacal interest in genital lesions soon drove me from the flat and to an associate of my mother's, who was opening an exhibition. Iggy Lowenstein ran Perspective, a chic art gallery situated between the headquarters of a corrupt whitegoods corporation and the famously named Paine, Malaise & Toombes, a mostly female law firm known as PMT. The gallery was a really beautiful edifice in the Bauhaus style, its architectural restraint a contrast to its proprietor's ballistic nature. Lowenstein loved such paradoxes. In his twice-divorced forties, he was Einstein-haired and with a heavy pear-shaped face, sharp little teeth, and the eyes of a mongoose working behind Viennese spectacles. His hands were completely feminine – poreless and satiny and seemingly without cartilege, they deliquesced in handshake. These girl-hands of his disturbed me, made me wary: they were incapable of a good solid grip.

And this was Iggy all over.

He was renowned for oozing out of contractual loopholes and for slapping ugly writs against his enemies. Certain people were soothed by the thought of boiling him in hot oil. A man who had never concerned himself with popularity, who had worn the nickname 'Funnelweb' since high school, he had no time for injuries. He had once been quoted on the front page of a national newspaper: 'Like I give a fuck what people think. Descartes had it ass-up. It should have been *je suis, donc je suis*. Fuck *opin*ion. I wipe my ass with *opin*ion.' This tough street-talk served the same purpose that spines and the colours black and yellow serve in the bestial kingdom: it was a warning, and substantially backed. My generally anti-semitic mother was one of the few with whom he could hold enlightened conversations. She liked his girl-hands and his legal wars, his lowbrow soul and high-class investments – they clicked, shared giggles, discussed most everything from fetlocks to Eurobonds, hair extensions to double options, sexual gossip to political upheavals. He was *un menefreghista*, and she loved him for it. My mother wasn't bothered by his quirks because in her mind, power was always easy to forgive (and besides, he endeared himself to her by remembering to send birthday cards in which her age had been forgotten). Aldo was never jealous of their intimacy as he thought Iggy a pear-faced joke, a 'pussy Jew'. Sometimes I thought he almost liked him.

The gallery was packed with socially muscular types – media freaks, the aimless rich, merchant bankers eager to appear cultured, leggy beauties open to exploitation, retired politicians, hungry journalists – and Lowenstein was in his element, courting the moneyed and baiting the press in his embroidered black kimono coat by the front desk. I was careful to avoid him and steered clear of those who would have wished to engage me in artificially animated repartee. Instead I did what no-one at such functions would ever have dreamed of doing: I actually looked at the paintings.

Iggy was legendary for exhibiting atrocious trash. He nursed a grievance against talent, it was the one thing that could really make him cry. His early life had been overshadowed by the brilliance of his older brother Saul, whose achievements in the field of molecular biology had wiped Iggy's dollar skills right off their parents' map. The Lowensteins were educated old-world people, and disdainful of the pursuit of lucre. When his brother walked off with the Nobel Prize, Iggy had a heart attack and spent a fortnight in intensive care, pale and weak and bawling like a baby on the hour. To avenge himself, he made a point of only promoting mediocre work – he was out to undermine the aristocracy of genius, and this destruction was always executed with a poker face. He was particularly proud of having exhibited the work of an English artist who had created a self-portrait from eight pints of his frozen blood. Aware of his machinations and their origins, he privately excused himself with the justification that 'the balls of art should hang on the ground'. The only place where the balls of art hung were his walls.

Somewhere in the chattering crowd was his new 'find' – probably female, possibly Chinese, undoubtedly tanked, predominantly schizophrenic and subsisting on government grants and the investments of collectors suffering from goitrous cretinism. The work was comically terrible. Lowenstein was clearing his throat by the lectern and the room hummed to a stop. In a gruff brown voice, he introduced the Minister for the Arts who in turn introduced the 'Chairperson of the Visual Arts and Crafts Board', a culture vulture who wore her dress as a table wears its tablecloth. Her garnet earrings rattled as she bounced onto the podium. She nodded at Lowenstein, stroked the beginnings of a not unflattering moustache, and beamed at her cringing snaggle-toothed academic midget of a husband.

With a life-or-death ferocity, she gripped the sides of the lectern. Her pause was ominous. 'In a 1982 gouache,' she began, 'a gouache entitled *This! Little! Piggy! Is! Too! Sick! To! Go! To! Market!*, Uma Nieuwenhuizen-Wingwang depicts the familiar therianthropic "self" which appears in all her work. Here she is analysing the contents of "another"' (with every quotation mark, she made little rabbit-ears with her fingers) '– drawn as an acephalous porcine torso with lactating teats – at its trotters, an overturned basket of bananas. The analysis of the "self" – in particular, the artist's own – is her primary theme.' She deeply breathed, and her bosom rose as powerfully as a squall. 'Of equal thematic weight has been her investigation into the act and meaning of painting. In the seventies, she explored farmyard imagery from childhood following conceptualist and minimalist tenets. In the early eighties, she fragmented the structure of her imagery using sequins, prosthetic eyeballs, and a bottled foetus. By the middle of the decade she had transgressed – and very impressively, too, I might add – conventional painting techniques through the employment of varnished pork chops and a cultivated naivety in the depiction of words and images.'

With the carnivorous expediency of a lizard, her tongue flicked up over her lip and wiped her septum clean of perspiration. 'On the surface,' she intoned with renewed seriousness, 'all this appears to be the puerile work of a moron, and yet is under the *complete* –' (here she sexually eyed her cringing husband) '– control of an artist who has chosen to storm the barracks of conventional painting to dignify the widely ignored female predicament.' The audience uncertainly began to applaud and she silenced them with an eyebrow.

'The pig,' she continued in a corrective tone, 'the dog, the cat, the tampon – these recurring subject/objects are imbued by her with a dark spirituality in the manner that uncivilized tribes empower their fetishes. In Nieuwenhuizen-Wingwang's obsessive narcissism, the dialogue is *never* exclusive. Her signature on the painting becomes an important part of the image, as though by practising the writing of her name she is somehow exploring her own identity as a woman living at the end of a millennium. The name "Uma Nieuwenhuizen-Wingwang" extends to cover all things in the world that can be "owned" –' (in her intensity, she misaimed her quoting rabbit-fingers and knocked Lowenstein's glasses to the floor) '– by the – *sorry* about that, Iggy, pet – by the artist.'

General laughter. Even the earnest chairperson allowed herself a chuckle. Lowenstein examined his spectacles for damage and then smiled, but his mongoose eyes were very dark as the chairperson resumed her sermon. 'In the large-scale work from 1987, *Doggy's? Gone? Done? A? Doodoo?*, the "holding environment" –' (Lowenstein twitched as her quoting rabbit-fingers reappeared) '– of domestication and the torments of aesthetic deprivation are made manifest.' She turned the page, and her chin almost disappeared into her bullfrog neck. '*Doggy's? Gone? Done? A? Doodoo?*, with its graphic images of physiological functions and predominance of browns and pus-yellows, presents the earthy physicality of owning pets, and has the same attention to detail and profound emotional impact of sleepy old Proust savouring that legendary madeleine.' Her broad forehead was glistening, and she stooped to gulp from the glass of firewater offered to her by old snaggle-tooth.

'In the current series of *$Piggy$Wiggy$Doggy$Miaow$*,'

she authoritatively growled, 'the aspects of memory, fantasy and materiality coalesce. These purple woollen paintings, with the addition of fake-fur dog and cat tails and sanitary napkins soaked in tomato sauce, create a sensuousness which is then put into tension with the stark execution of the imagery and the corresponding texts. One sees the image of a dog with a tampon balanced on its nose and reads on the corresponding panel: *she cryed because she never had a dait on saterday nite*.' The masterpiece in question was suspended by slender silver chains on the wall behind her and she turned to it, widely gesturing as if to illustrate its creative breadth, and then buoyantly nodded to herself. 'Within these apparently incongruous images, within these words misspelt in the spirit of playfulness –' (in actuality, words misspelt in the spirit of dyslexia) '– the complex humanistic female microcosm in relation to the simplistic zoomorphic masculine macrocosm is exposed for our education and boundless appreciation. In closing, I would like to say that we should all be honoured to be privy to such intellectually challenging and emotionally affecting work, and on behalf of the Visual Arts and Crafts Board, I thank you all.'

She stepped down from the podium as if parting the Red Sea. The applause had pinked her cheeks and she gurgled '*thank* you, *thank* you' in response to every compliment. Lowenstein returned to the microphone glad, as he later said, 'to see the back of that flatulent walrus'. He smilingly waited for the cheers to abate before introducing the artist, a frail waxwork of a woman with dyed green hair down to her knees and shaking hands.

Uma Nieuwenhuizen-Wingwang, an exiled Manchurian who had exhibited at the Marlborough, Agnews and the National Gallery in Canberra, drew a number of difficult breaths, coiled and uncoiled a long lock of her hair around her thumb, and expressed her sorrow – haltingly, and with the threat of tears – that her husband could not share with her this most momentous of momentous moments. 'Jasper,' she whispered mistily as she gazed down at her bare skeletal feet, 'was the most beautiful human being. He hanged himself from the light fitting last year when he realized that all his life he had fought against the deep conviction that he should have been a woman.' Here Lowenstein glanced at her. Even he had his limits. 'It is a crime,' she said after a wavering pause, 'that art today is thought to be a discipline. Artists are not computers. Artists are not blow-dryers. Artists are not washing machines. Artists should not have to speak of their work in terms of craft, although craftspersons may speak of their work in terms of art.'

She paused to hissingly inhale. Her elegantly elongated eyes began to follow the locomotion of an invisible subject/object seemingly situated two or so metres above the audience. A few people looked up and began to worriedly murmur. Lowenstein quickly stepped forwards to whisper something in her ear and she suddenly blinked, shook her prehistoric fern-head, and frowned at the sheet before her. 'We must,' she causally continued, 'reconsider our definition of art to include the work of everyone – accountants, landscape gardeners, midwives, insurance salesmen, paleontologists, triathletes, prostitutes, fishmongers, greengrocers, acrobats, actuaries, sculptors who work with scrap metals, television presenters and the criminally insane. Within each of them, wee fairies and poltergeists and flames from the Eternal Torch.'

Consternation furrowed a number of brows. The Chairman of Sotheby's inclined his head towards his wife to mutter: 'She's fucking *crack*ers.'

Nieuwenhuizen-Wingwang's hands worked violently as she pursued her point. '*Cooking a curry is art!*' she cried. 'Lifting a box is art! The most important art of all is the ability to get out of bed in the morning and not slash one's wrists! In all its forms, art delineates the frontiers of our awareness: it is the last frontier, and a frontier without horizons but with many fences. We must train the horses of our vocabularies to *jump* over those fences. Without art, man is a shell ... although a shell is also art, in which case ... even *without* art ... man is *still* art, so ... art is fundamentally ... ines*capable*. It is omni*present*. It is *omni*fic. It is *omni*potent –' (the prefix excited her, but the horse of her vocabulary was stalling at the gate). 'We must remember this, and fight the good fight against the destructive concepts of "genius" and "talent", two words used solely to discredit truth and to support fascist elitist sophistry. The Marxists in the audience –'

(there were none) '– will know exactly what I mean. All categorization is a capitalist tool used to create difference. From difference, we grow competition. From competition, we grow dissonance. From dissonance, we grow war. Wherefore unity? As T.S. Eliot once asked: *Where are the eagles and the trumpets?* The eagles and the trumpets, ladies and gentlemen, are in our hearts. The *eagles* and the *trumpets*, ladies and gentlemen, are in our *hearts*.' Her fist audibly slammed against her breast. 'Doeg the Edomite saw the son of Jesse coming to Nob. Hundreds of years later, we were told that the eagle had landed. Does the wind of the wing of madness break the bough? The answer, my friend, is blowing in that wind. May God preserve you all. Goodnight.'

Needless to say, I dematerialized before (as I read in the newspapers the following morning) Nieuwenhuizen-Wing-wang succumbed to a cheerfully spectacular schizophrenic fit (during which she seized the flaps of Lowenstein's kimono coat and dragged him around the floor with that strength attributed only to the supernatural and the insane). The strain and surprise of this development caused his dicky heart to fibrillate, and both artist and agent were spirited away to different wards of the same hospital by a screaming ambulance. As a result of these inadvertent entertainments every painting on show at Perspective was sold, and had it not been for the beta-blockers Lowenstein was so diligently sucking, this news would have finally buried him.

BOOK THREE

THE BESTIARY

I

I was quiet on the aeroplane, depleted by uncertainties and possibilities, feverish in my confusion. My consciousness was that of all great bodies of water: the focus shifted in great waves towards a single point, building momentum, gathering force to expend its motion in a sibilant dispersion in which small stars of light flickered and were extinguished. The urgency of too many foci somehow weakened me, distracted that potent momentum and its potent effect, made it so all I wished to do was sleep. Escape was in itself a kind of sleep.

I rested my head against the cold oval of the window and stared at the aircraft's great silvery wing, vaguely aware of murmuring voices and of the confining lap-click of metallic seatbelts, comforted by the familiar rumblings of the craft, by the neo-infancy imposed by its limitations – to be fed on cue; to be entertained, cajoled, indulged; to be attended to without question; to be left still, suddenly liberated from a world in which relentless activity was effectively the only acceptable mode of being. There is a quality of timelessness about long flights, a sense of existing in the vacuum of purest reflection. Any dulling of the senses requires a shifting of focus from the external to the internal, hence the frequent flyer's weightless reveries.

A frank deep cough bothered my thoughts and so I turned. Reginald Liverlily, host of the high-rating *Rise and Shine* programme, was busy squeezing himself into the plush mauve air-armchair beside me after fifteen fruitless minutes spent searching for his seat in business class. Known for his homogenized charm and easy witlessness, known for the women's magazine centrespreads in which he posed with his poultry-thighs apart and pelvis tilted (the effect one of promoting his groin), known for his nuclear tan and ham-fisted visits to the bedsides of hospitalized children (a captive

269

audience), he was the most ridiculous and dedicated of the small band of local celebrities.

He coughed again, glanced at me, winningly shrugged.

The craft began to shudder down the runway as its staff stood at the head of each aisle and perfunctorily pointed to the television screens upon which fat bit-actors blew into the bright pipes of their safety jackets and clamped perforated oxygen masks over their cheeks. Liverlily cocked his empty head to my shoulder in a manner that suggested intimacy and said in a chuckling *sotto voce*: 'I've seen these safety routines so many hundreds of times that I could escape from a burning zeppelin in my sleep.' There were no difficulties in eliminating him from my awareness – he was not the type to appropriate attention without force. He became soul-savingly absorbed in the in-flight publication, I returned to the cold oval of the window, and it was as if a screen as fine as a lover's lie had automatically materialized between us: sudden strangers. Deliberate distance has its own sentience.

Outside, the gaseous gold sunlight sewed the chaste veil of blue with apples and coins and dragons made of cloud-stuff. Vaporous tapestry. Physicists believe it possible to tame this pristine ethereal wilderness through their mathematical interpretations and tourniquet-formulae, but the nature of a thing dictates the nature of its enquiry. Applied mathematics, by definition, pivots on the principles of qualification, quantification and progression – processes antithetical to any understanding of the metaphysical. Attempted apprehension of the intangible and its workings serves the same purpose that a night-light serves to a nyctophobic child: it is an attempt to illuminate, to alleviate fears and to gain control over that which, by its very mystery, exerts the fantastic power of the unpredictable. In their refusal to invest meaning in anything but their own efforts to discover order, pragmatists are cowards. The concept of respecting unknowability undermines the Western mind's confidence in itself as the Western mind equates acceptance of limitations with incompetence and failure. To even consider the possibility that meaning can be found in simple being is ridiculous to a mind whose efficacy depends upon its performance in the palaestra of logic. The problem? Logic relies upon specificity to function and specificity, by its very exiguity, further obscures the nature of meaning.

Elusiveness can be central to the effect of certain forces, and this is what the modern world denies. It is like a child in this way, stamping its philosophical foot in a tantrum. The observable was easy to describe as I looked out of my window – a star, a larval cloud – but I felt no need to qualify their impact on me with terminology that presupposed supreme power or expertise; in being, it was to me enough. And I could never recover from the sensation of looking up and up and up and never seeing even the suggestion of a conclusion. The truest liberty was that conferred by staring at the sky, it was sublime. Unusually tired by my thoughts, I still was experiencing a certain ease. There are special properties in every dialogue with the universe.

2

I must have dozed off, because the clatter of trays surprised me. Sat up. I had no appetite and refused my supper, but Liverlily rapidly consumed each perishable placed before him – the shrimp cocktail, the schnitzel, the mustardy salad, the fruit tartlet, the brown seed bun, the quince preserve, the crackers and cheeses, the four foaming beers. Just watching him eat made me so sleepy that I dozed off again, only to awaken when all the lights had been dimmed and we were flying in darkness through a prairie of stars.

The slow dreaming breathing of the passengers combined with the steady air-conditioning and engine-purr to form a strange celestial nocturne.

Slowly shifted my pale weight against the window until my cheek was cool against the clear. The rhythm of Liverlily's breathing had subtly changed. My own soft sigh. The craft was ploughing through cloud to soar into an infinity of soundless indigo. I opened my eyes and looked out at the moon. The friction of the earth's tides was causing the distance between the earth and moon to increase by a finger

every passing year. Again, that otherness. With the implausible celerity of the imagination, Gabriel's features were by me
superimposed over the surface of the moon, that stern
Hellenic area. In that moment I saw him eternal, I saw him
stilled, I saw him as I felt him – that is to say, superimposed
over my heart. His dense essence seeped through me and left
its mark, indelible. Sometimes it takes the truth of want to
pass a flame from that mythical torch which so obsessed the
fern-haired Uma.

At the thought of him: a sudden flow of blood throughout
my body, a flow effacing any logic, a quizzical thrill of
nerves, desire. His face and his words came to me unbidden,
the memory of them was promiscuous, it was taxing and
difficult to deal with such emotional mutiny. In a way, I
would have preferred the spiritual autonomy of despair or
loneliness – states in which I could be blessed with a certain
melancholy grace. Desire is the sweetest scent in hell, where it
permeates the walls of each impossible labyrinth and drives
its prisoners insane.

3

Empowered by such dreams, I felt much like myself
again. Spatial concepts fascinated me, they could hold
me spellbound for hours. I would sprawl on the rug in
my father's study, my stockinged feet swaying so idly in the
air, poring over encyclopaedic volumes as my tongue tapped
against my palate. Motion, I deduced, was wholly dependent
upon otherness. And this otherness was really interesting, if
only because it seemed to be antithetical to my father's 'all is
water' doctrine. I remember standing by the railings of
London's Hyde Park one cold white afternoon, studying the
line of trees on the horizon. I was not alone – Speakers'
Corner was nearby and quacking with maniacs and camera-
festooned tourists, but somehow I managed to block out the
mayhem. This was not difficult: all I had to do was siphon
my focus until it was as if I were nothing but an intellectual
beam. Thus isolated, I marvelled at the concept of distance

and at the motion required to cover that distance and at the energy necessary to create that motion. Seemingly three different concepts, but really only one: they were all tributaries of the one and boundless sea. My clever father, I decided, was right. His interest in financial fluctuations and upsurges was only a front for an unusually enlightened soul.

These were satisfying thoughts, and responsible for the jump-sparks in my feeling eyes during those years. I never really shared them with anybody. It was enough that they made me happy, for I loved to brood. Musings of this nature made me realize that I was an animated property – that is to say, anima expressed through tangibility, the word made flesh. Many believed that the atomic was synonymous with 'that which exists', but I knew with a certainty which electrified me that there was another kind of existence, and it was this existence that interested me most of all.

The sky I was staring into from the humming craft was the same sky I had stared into as a child, the same sky I had shared with my father, with Gretl, with William, with however many lovers. In observing it, I am always reminded of all of them – it is as if their memory is a filament in the cobalt firmament, or the white energy of a new star.

This constancy was really something in itself, bewildering and bewilderingly stirring. To think that such a canopy could remain stable over Bacchic millennia of humanity. It was a reference point of absolute grandeur, indicative of nothing if not a higher heart. I never tired of gazing up at it, of the pretence of understanding it, of its transpersonal supremacy. There were nights I felt that simply by studying it, I knew something of what it must be to fly. The eyes of modern man are trained away from the ether, trained to concentrate on ephemera, one explanation for the emotional paucity of our civilization. In absorbing the ramifications of its mystery, those observing the sky are bestowed with strength, a strength unrelated to logic or to religion – the strength of the infinite, of the beautiful, of the eternal. Modern man will not accept this truth, and instead aims his every grief and wish at the lush, but ultimately inert earth, into which it lodges with a sickening finality.

4

The smog above Los Angeles shivered like skin as the craft plunged deeply into its vaporous lividity. From this layer of cloud – not the ninth, above which the Japanese Ancients believed that the god we understand to be the North Star, Polaris, resides – I could see nothing but the light of the sun fighting through fumes. Liverlily was impatient to land, and crankily chewed gum and swallowed beer bottles whole as he tapped a tattoo on his kneecaps and stared over my breasts and out of the window. The air-traffic congestion, Captain Ahab silkily informed us, would disrupt all schedules. We were one of the many silver loads of travellers circling the city. On hearing this, Liverlily gritted his teeth and began to gnaw on a swizzle-stick. When we were finally jolted by the craft's impact on the runway, he vigorously jerked his seatbelt apart, ready to vanish in a blur of denim and snakeskin and sterling silver, no doubt eager to fulfil some reconnaissance mission with some local roller-blading collagen-pumped barbell-queen. And I was of no use to anybody, really – jangled by the change in time-zones, dehydrated, somnolent and peripherally anxious in the way that the displaced are.

Forced to sprint through the terminal to catch the connecting flight to O'Hare, I twice tripped over my shoelaces, dropped my handbag, and crashed into an eclectic assortment of airport zombies. On arriving in Chicago, I was so dazed and hurried and preoccupied and the people around me were so unforgivably loud and big, that I began to feel assaulted by the uniformity of the modular environs, the tendons in my neck twisted or clamped, and stood: my soul lagging behind me, and waiting to have my passport approved by the yawning ground staff.

COMUNITA EUROPEA
REPUBBLICA ITALIANA
PASSAPORTO

(1) *COGNOME/ SURNAME/ NOM: BOTTICELLI.*

(2) *NOME/ GIVEN NAMES/ PRENOMS: ANGELICA ORNELLA CARLA.*

(3) *CITTADINANZA/ NATIONALITY/ NATIONALITE: ITALIANA.*

(4) *DATA DI NASCITA/ DATE OF BIRTH/ DATE DE NAISSANCE: 19/09/1965.*

(5) *SESSO/ SEX/ SEXE: F.*

(6) *LUOGO DI NASCITA/ PLACE OF BIRTH/ LIEU DE NAISSANCE: FIRENZE, ITALIA.*

(7) *AUTORITA/ AUTHORITY/ AUTORITE: CONS. GEN. D'ITALIA.*

(8) *RESIDENZA/ RESIDENCE/ DOMICILE: SYDNEY, AUSTRALIA.*

(9) *STATURA/ HEIGHT/ TAILLE: 1.67m.*

(10) *COLORE DEGLI OCCHI/ COLOUR OF EYES/ COULEUR DES YEUX: MARRONE.*

Such unsmiling categorization is only designed to facilitate modern ritualistic behaviour, ritualistic behaviour created to designate human rank. Spiritual progress is impeded by such absurd divisions and subdivisions, they are all ultimately absurd.

Once the wiseacre behind the perspex partition had decided that I was not a terrorist, drug-baron or arms-smuggler, I was permitted to step outside the sacred circle of Customs. The Chicago accent is an assault – broad and flat and hard, it is the voice of industry, the voice of money, both smoke and steel: the voice of determination and raw survival. I searched through it for my brother, who surprised me with a quick embrace. Widely smiling beside him: a tall healthy brown-skinned natural blonde rooted to the earth by Timberland boots never worn on anything but a man-made surface, her thin stretch leggings emphasizing the wonderfully defined musculature of her elongated calves and thighs, her hands deep in the pockets of her monumental down parka, her classic throat muffled by a plaid woollen scarf, her high-boned face enlivened by a snowfield flush and with a mouth like a magnolia flower. She looked like the tearaway daughter of the Statue of Liberty.

'Like, wow – Angelica,' she gushed as she accepted my

hand and shook it with a grip that nearly fractured the birdbones of my fingers, 'I have to say that it's *totally* great to meet you, really.'

5

Cultures which value intelligence and the temperance of wisdom promote the significance of the expressive face. Cultures which value youth and its velocity promote the significance of the expressive limb. And her legs said it all, they told me everything I had ever wanted to know about the culture of which I was a part and its deals. These were legs that just about encapsulated every advance of the twentieth century – *Zeitgeist* legs, legs that not only straddled my brother's thickening waist, but the principles of those two cities of the World and Heaven.

Margot 'Thumper' Hamilton-Knox was the youngest of six bombshell daughters of James 'The White Demon' Hamilton-Knox III and Clare Powell-Winchester (known to their children as Daddo and Momsy-Momsy.) Daddo was old money, a former Olympic skiing prince, society jet-boat racer and penguin-suit-about-town, a lifelong layabout now fond only of gin and golf, intellectually remaindered, sexually dead. His birthday party invitations featured commissioned caricatures of himself in one of many sporty locations (tennis court, mountain top, racetrack, on horseback, et cetera). The international grapevine dated his last erection as having occurred after a thrilling win at the Epsom Derby in 1975. Momsy-Momsy was a charity queen with a space-station bouffant and cherry-stem limbs, schooled in provincial French cuisine and tapestry, big on political propriety, eventing, chilled gooseberry fool and hormone replacement therapy. These were people to whom the word 'season' meant particular parties rather than the mythopoeic climate, people who drank themselves into polite stupors after supper to avoid the misery of communicating with each other, people who donated thumping sums to opera foundations and who coughed up countless thousands at boozy after-dinner auctions to attend private cocktail parties with a luminary or two from the more glamorous worlds of film or fashion, people who never wore pyjamas to the breakfast table and whose lobotomized daughters gravitated towards spiritually bankrupt high-rolling lost-boys like my poor damaged brother.

Alexander the Great's biggest crush was on Diogenes, the cynical iconoclastic philosopher who believed that the only currency worth having was that of virtue. Such a concept was so threatening as to provoke fits of hyperventilation from my brother and those with whom he associated. These days warriors do not admire profound intellectuals; they save their admiration for themselves as the self has become the only cult, and wisdom is no longer perceived to be a respectable life-choice. Amedeo had the bearing and monetary spoils of a warrior-suit, but this was only mimicry: his stance was betrayed by a diminutive vein over his left temple, a vein that fluttered with an anxious irregularity.

He had no concentration span, none at all. Antsy in his skin, he was unfamiliar to himself, diminished by conscious-ness, and his eyes were obscured by ignored despair. Despite the fact that he was an eighteen-carat player, despite his dazzling Roman profile and powerful Teutonic build, despite the athletic obeisance of his ravishingly legged and well-bred fiancée, he still managed to project a dangerous fragility. Thumper was, of course, oblivious to these subtleties. She was young, for one thing, and then there was her intelligence quotient to consider (a melodiously nominal affair). I noticed a peculiar sense of joylessness about them both, peculiar because they appeared to be happy (clowning like young lovers in an A-B ad, giving each other loud high-fives) but some essential spark was missing; sincerity had absented itself. Theirs were spirits distraught by their isolation.

'Let's blow this pop-stand,' my lock-jawed brother drawled, 'because I am *fuck*ing starving.'

With her intricate architecture, slender streeting, complicated fragrances and explosively hormonal temperament, New York is a feminine city – charming and compelling, vindictive and sly, secretive, so sexual. Chicago, on the other hand, is a big, impatient man of a town – all cement and breadth, metal and sweat, direct and bluntly unforgiving. I had never liked it enough to spend any amount of time there. Both the confrontational feel and sheets of mercilessly cold wind unsettled me. These were my thoughts as I sprawled in the black Range Rover's deep back seat, longing to sleep but remaining in that dragging state of semi-consciousness in which one is simultaneously aware of the need to rest and the demanding machinations of the external world. My brother's exchanges with his fiancée were just excruciating.

'The desirability of an object is inversely proportional to its availability,' he said.

'Oh, you are a total, *total* scream!' she cried.

They spoke at cross-purposes, powerfully dissimilar in everything but their worship of the trivial. Thumper was concerned with fashion, the sexual intrigues of her girl-friends, exfoliating masques, lipstick (matte vs. gloss), an upcoming sale at the Charivari boutique, the new Calvin Klein campaign and the effect of gravity on her physiognomy. My brother was obsessed by intermediate upmoves in long-term bull markets, an upcoming auction at Gin Lane in Southampton, rote algorithms, volatility in crude oil, the fact that 'Robertson' from 'Tiger' had moved into Hong Kong to do 'a major deal with Li', the altered menu at Coco Pazzo, racquetball and how he could fiddle his schedule next year to make the Queen's Cup at Windsor. Together they were like every other effectively but unhappily mated couple in history, they were people to whom love was no more than a case of *quid pro quo*.

A few light years of puling about the way in which she had been snubbed by Rose-Marie Oppenheimer at a Republican ball calmed Thumper, who then remembered my limp existence in the back seat. 'You know what Am-Am did to me on his birthday?' she musically asked. 'Like, I bought him this really really *really* rare CD, right? Like, they only had a hundred pressed? And he just left it on the table because he was, like, *totally* pissed about some dumb deal he'd done. So the next day I unwrapped it for him and said: *Look what the Birthday Fairy got you!* And you know what he did? He said: *Could this be a frisbee?* and sent it sailing off the balcony. Appa*rent*ly he wanted some dumb pair of Harry Winston cufflinks, like I *knew*, right? Like I'm a *mind* reader. I mean, talk about *moody*.'

This Blondie-and-Dagwood-go-to-Gstaad anecdote was related in the precious manner she had inherited from her mother. In the meantime, my brother grew preoccupied with the weather report on the radio and sharply increased the vehicle's speed.

We arrived in Lake Forest just as a blizzard was hitting. It could have been the end of the world. Gabriel's four horses would soon come galloping over the horizon. Major roads were in the process of being closed, meteorologists were panicking, trees were forced into the arms of telegraph wires, foolish campers were freezing to death in shallow caves (where their glassy-eyed corpses would be discovered a fortnight later). The wind was unlike any I had ever known – it was an entity, Olympian, much more than a force of nature: it was a message. The Range Rover stopped before two overblown fairytale-castle gates and Amedeo dropped his window to shout (through sleet, through snow) into a black receiver. The gates opened with a painful mechanical exactitude and then shudderingly closed behind us. Hailstones were slamming against the car, hailstones so big and viciously aimed that they caused Thumper to whimper and whine and grip her future husband's tensed and muscular arm. On either side of us, topiarian masterpieces – spiralling Common Box, high conical hedges, unearthly spheres. The palmately lobed leaves of the *Aceraceae* had browned to mulch beneath the slush. Difficult to see much else. The drive rose and sharply curved, rose and sharply curved.

Thumper nervously began humming the theme from *Beauty and the Beast* and my brother suddenly snapped and bellowed: 'Will you fucking *can* it??'

Her tears inspired no pity. Minutes later, we reached the mansion that a plastic used in surgery built. An awesome neo-Gothic horror had been designed to impress and intimidate – all snowy sloping dormers, icy parapets, eccentric oculus windows, chimneys, friezes and roof-cresting. A fixed system of architectural ochre lighting only emphasized the ominousness of the place by creating arching areas of shadow through the stressing of stripped branches. This was the summer house of the Bossu clan, industrialists from way, way back and members of the Fortune-500-based organization of my stepfather's 'closest friends'. Aldo had hired the place for the season and had equipped it with all the appropriate technology, mother's fine gowns and a bestiary of internationally significant guests.

Within, the mansion was as every other maintained mansion – emphatically impersonal in its perfection. I felt as if I had stepped out of the stained pages of Brine's penny dreadful and into those of a coffee-table book, on which ghosts are exorcized from photographs of their homes by lovingly angled golden reflectors. The place looked like a shrine to the deity of interior design: Home of the Tasteful Curtain Wand. The scale of its artifice dizzied me and I steadied myself against what Thumper confidently assured me was a nineteeth-century Louis XV escritoire. Every item and its placing told of twitching professional consideration (undoubtedly that of aimless and lightly educated rich men's wives or daughters) – the cabinets of singing crystal, the exotic artefacts ('conversation pieces' such as the shrunken Haitian head preserved behind glass, or the framed and bloodied blade of a Parisian guillotine), obscure leatherbound volumes, the collection of Victorian paperweights, the cherubs and Japanese scimitars, the grand archways, the criminally acquired Greek iconography.

In distancing man from his mundane humanity – a quality forged and refined by visceral difficulties – wealth can be dangerous. The very rich can be persuaded by luxury to forget humility and as a consequence, their affections are replaced by affectations and all feeling is exteriorized with an ever-increasing urgency.

To illustrate: I once attended a starry opening night (*Aida* conducted by Karajan in Salzburg, tickets courtesy of my unspeakable mother) with an English Wall Street émigré, a man who owned a brace of Georgian houses in London, a penthouse and shining yacht in Nice, and a villa in the Cayman Islands (where he had a mosaic of his face affixed to the bottom of the pool in order that he could dive through his reflection to his depiction, finding himself suspended in liquid somewhere in between). When in Hertfordshire, he sipped Earl Grey and swigged bitter, schooled point-to-pointers over sticks, shot pheasants and chattered to the Master of Foxhounds about the M11, the British Field Sports Society and the Square Mile. When in East Hampton, he sipped cranberry juice and swigged martinis, sunned his chest and baked for his neighbours pecan pies, played baseball and chattered to movie producers about the Long Island Expressway, the Pulitzer and Henry Kravis. He claimed his father had been the star of his time at Eton and then the Coldstream Guards, and that his mother had been photographed for magazine covers by Avedon and courted by several European princes. During the interval, this hero had turned to me with his white smile. 'You know,' he said, 'it's not at all true that I'm pretentious. My tastes are very simple ... every third Saturday afternoon. Why, I'm as happy with a pitchfork in my hand as I am with a Seurat.' This never-married ladies' man was known for qualifying his friends by citing the jet they were endorsing and his conquests by their sexual pedigrees. But he was only one of many, no less human than his economic peers.

Exhausted by the labour of humping my suitcases up the stairs, Amedeo stood gripping the banister, his hair blizzard-slicked. 'That's it,' he said, shaking his head, 'I'm fucked.' Mother was sick in bed, Aldo was in LA on business, mine was the last bedroom down the corridor on the left of the first landing, breakfast was at o8.oo hours sharp, he would see me in the morning. Thumper reflexively bounded up after him, an antelope in heat – long ponytail swinging, barrettes gleaming, thighs superbly flexing.

6

The cubic area of my room was the same as Brine's entire flat. A baroque affair, glinting and eerie, crimson and gilt, masterfully lit. I almost expected to find the corpse of a strangled houseguest nestling beneath the heavy coverlet (strangely embroidered with images of the Archangel Gabriel and the Virgin Mary). A fire was quietly burning in the black grate; above it, an elegantly decrepit and creepy twelfth-century kellion fresco of Saint Somebody, the fore and middle fingers of his right hand raised in a heavenly salute or blessing, a halo obscuring his black staring eyes. Welterweight drapes framed a broad bow window, a window overlooking what must have been princely gardens, its panes whorled with frost. I undressed and burrowed sheets. On the bedside table, a vellum note in s₁ *Darling, glad you could make it. Bacioni, a. ... Mamma.* I crumpled the note and aimed it at the fire, where it burst into a range of yellow sparks and sharp blue hisses. Sadness is simple; it is repression which becomes complex.

My sleep was fitful, I was buoyed and dumped by solid waves of jet-lag. I dreamed of Gabriel paralysed in a white hospital bed, drugged and perspiring, sighing with pain, his pupils dilated with morphine, the room darkening with afternoon. 'Two people came to visit me this morning,' he whispered, 'and I didn't know who they were.' In the dream and wearing white, I asked him: 'Do you know who I am?' He smiled with effort and swallowed. 'Of course I know who *you* are,' he replied.

I was awake at one and two and five and finally at six and lay there, my eyelashes still wet with tears, the rhythm of my heartbeat unpredictable, and gazed out of the window at the atrocious frigid morning. The wind was wolfish, hungry, it bayed through the rain. Menacing undertone. An oval mirror reflected me from one of the walls: long drowned, I was a ghost divining the direction of the current with her ever-rippling web of hair. The room seemed dazed, its cumber-some furnishings dragged the ambience to the floor and held it there until it was defeated. Demons or rats scratched at the immured pipes, and there were ponderous footsteps on the floor above me. I lit a cigarette and dreamed awhile, saddened somehow and still haunted by the image of Gabriel's suffering. In Sydney it would be twilight: on the vivid grasses of the northern foreshore there would be scattered petals of an intense violet; umbrella flowers would be swaying like the white rice-paper lanterns of old Chinese junks; vibrant algae would flatten with the tide's withdrawal and then swell; city lights would be dished, red and gold, through the harbour's deepening blue waves, and the air, that summer air would be perfumed with him, with him, with him.

For an hour I lay like that, smoking and thinking and staring out at a night that slowly vitrified into a glacial dawn. At seven-thirty, I walked over to that window and stood there, breathing a garden of vanishing camellias against the glass, my eyes closed, remembering my lover.

7

The breakfast table was laden with milk jugs and sugar bowls, slim silver flutes of labial orchids, big faceted jugs of fresh orange juice, and with respect for absent enemies, set for the Last Supper. Twelve places. I was, of course, the first to arrive (obedient and hypervigilant), and created collapsing sugar-crystal palaces on my bone china bread-and-butter plate until my brother (stretching, grunting, squinting) arrived with Thumper (smiling, brimming, preening). His throat was so marked with love-bites that from the collar up, he looked like a leopard. And she had that silky-glazed possessive look about her, and walked with an insolent swing.

Aldo, I was told, had flown from Chicago to LA, where he was to speak on Issues, Strategies and Tactics at a conference on Teaching and Training Business Ethics in the 1990s and

Beyond, and was scheduled to return on Christmas Eve. Better a live dog than a dead philosopher? Mother was 'far too ill' to socialize and would not be seen or spoken to by anyone with the exception of her sycophantic specialists. Amedeo did not know what was wrong with her because she had not told him; her communications with him were abrupt and via her private line. None of this was as surprising as it should have been.

The houseguests appeared in the following order: Bohumila (the aristocratic hound-eyed Slavic widow of a doctor well 'beneath' her), Jake Bilge (a leverage buy-out artist who had that morning organized the purchase of his first G-IV), Susie Corybantes (a dedicated British socialite who enjoyed a public *affaire de coeur* with a hipless female Labour MP and who believed herself bohemian because she had sported a mohican during the seventies), her husband Cecil (a balding crypto-Nazi and best-selling novelist), Shoshanna Gold (*née* Goldberg, a drawling, big-titted, chain-smoking, award-winning poet who studied demonography, megalanthropogeny and numismatology), her lover Xavier Allcock (a handsome alcoholic loafer and married to the heiress of the Swedenborg Funeral Homes fortune), and Null Bock (the German *übermodell* doped to the eyeballs on Selective Serotonin Reuptake Inhibitors and also divorced from Honoré de Souris, the newly gay magnate).

We greeted each other with the fake melting civility of strangers aware of each other's social, financial and intellectual clout, and as the aereated croissants and scrambled eggs and peach-fresh salmon were being served by the hunchbacked help (appropriately decked out in antebellum costumes), we exchanged *bons mots*, epigrams and extensively unfelt interest in each other's lives. Thumper outdid herself with a choking recital of her 'Why I Am a Republican' speech; Null was silent, all cheekbones and collarbone and gargantuan debauched invisibly lashed eyes; Shoshanna bitched in hash-black tones about her former husband, the civil litigator Darius Hoare, and how she was certain that he was artistically perverting their daughter, Sappho; Susie, who was convinced that her innate malice was fully disguised by her spoony courtesy, orated fragments of Shoshanna's best-known poem, 'Longing for Myself', which she then described as *'life*-changing – truly *life*-changing!'; Jake and Xavier downed six tumblers of brandy between them and berated one of the maids for not filling their water glasses before the guests had entered the room. The behaviour was predictable, but the line-up intrigued me. There was not a single person at the table who could keep a secret. Aldo obviously had news he wanted broadcast, and in every circle. Bohumila made him snore, rumour had it he'd nailed Null in one of the Trump Tower lifts, and he detested Cecil. But then again, his absence was telling. It was possible that he had simply allowed his pathologically dramatic wife to select their guests.

He was a fiercely busy man, after all.

Breakfast was a feast that degenerated into a drunken brunch. The issue of tampering with the body's chemistry was not relevant to these people. They would never understand that they were only expressing dissatisfaction with their reality by getting plastered; it was their way of life. Years may have passed. Eventually, the crowd dispersed – some to read, others to play billiards or boardgames or to watch as-yet unreleased movies in the private cinema, a few to half-heartedly mate. The weather was still hostile, it was ungovernable, no-one could escape the Gothic pile. I left for the most remote drawing room where, surrounded by watercolours of the common red poppy and woodbine, I sank into the quicksand of an armchair to stare into the fire. Those flames were active enough to engross me for hours.

A random memory, no doubt discharged by my melancholy: that train journey from Sydney to a city up the eastern coast, the reason for undertaking it forgotten, perhaps conveniently. Ever-unfolding, my dark past. I had dragged my luggage into the smoking car, a carriage which reeked of boiled toads and regurgitated mucus, armpits and unwashed feet. Sat with an emptied heart by one of the sunproofed finger-smudged windows. The graffiti on the seat in front of me concerned Candice and her availability to State Rail passengers. So slow and sulphurous, the journey took me through some of the most dispiritingly monotonous country-side in the world – mile upon mile of paraplegic gum and roasted brush, of stale earth and sandstone, of scarred serpents sliding beneath rock, and everything beneath a dry sky tainted green by that scalding glass.

At Wyong, I began to weep as I read the siding of a stationary coal-train:

NHBF
N1405
TARE 21   TONNES B
CAPACITY 41
EQUIVALENT LENGTH 1.9

The flap-top metal ashtray on the armrest was stuffed with cigarette butts. Stench of the lost, stench of the dead. The temperature was despotic. I could smell my moistness on the vandalized naugahyde. We passed more bushland, more hewn stone. We passed a dismal little hamlet named Wyee (my plaintive entreaty) and then a great factory or foundry on a hill – a crepuscular silver underworld twinkling with orange lights, smoke welling and welling from its tall steel chimneys, and everything distintegrated into twilight.

It must have been around two in the afternoon when the compact Bohumila cranked herself with a Carpathian Mountain grunt into the armchair next to mine. Her flesh was stained, her dull dark hair was roughly brushed, her lips were arid (she licked them constantly), and the diamonds on her short fat fingers would have been worth several millions. The Chanel couture she wore may have cost her close to fifty thousand dollars, but she carried herself like a knapsack packed with rocks. Passing me a plate, a napkin and some cutlery, she said in a low doped monotone: 'I am kitchen woman. Food is what I love. Here is food. You eat meat?'

Glanced down at the offal and then helplessly back at her.

'I am bored,' she said at me and not to me, 'so I make lunch for you. I am widow, your mother tell you? My husband, Stuart, was doctor. Six year ago he die of prostate cancer. Bob is boyfriend – not father of children, but boyfriend. Even so, I don't know. He do nothing romantic any more.'

She had a distinct, salty, thick, sexual body odour which,

when combined with the rectal aroma of the marinated offal, turned my stomach.

'Stuart was also king of chess,' she continued. 'Medals, medals, medals. Look what I did.' She lifted the singed corner of the chaff-bag blouse she wore beneath that perfect jacket. 'I make hole with iron. Ha. But I still wear.' With those oracular outer-space eyes, she referred to the shadowed ceiling. 'My husband always working. Working, working, working. I hate doctor bag so much I jump on it, because he married to bag and not Bohumila. Jump, I jump. But I not tell him because he be angry. Always alone, Bohumila. Stuart was building practice and I take the pills and am unhappiest for many years. And then Stuart die and I meet Bob.'

Sighing a golem sigh, she slowly rubbed her round brown neutral-stockinged knees. 'Bob is wonderful man when we meet. The best. But now? Ha.' She made a cut-throat gesture. Her hands were abnormally large and spatulate for such a compact frame – they were the hands of a peasant, hands that should have fed sows and gathered blood-streaked eggs. 'Now I don't know because there is nothing for a year. Bob is impotent. How good he was a lover, you should know. But now he not touch me.' Her pause was meaningless. 'Joe is oil baron. Billion assets. The big house on the bayou in Houston. Divorced the wife, blonde stick-woman. He ask me out, very nice man. I am woman with many need. My children hate Bob and want Joe. I take plate.'

She took plate, upon which was untouched offal.

My fastidiousness was of no consequence, I don't think she even noticed. The mood-regulating medications Bohumila religiously swallowed prevented both the acknowledgment of too much perception and the resultant agitation. Despite her Carpathian Mountain grunts and barnyard hands, she was the product of a world in which feeling is regarded as a criminal act. In such a world it is necessary to create penitentiaries for the heart, and psychoactive drugs are as effective a dentention centre as any. Pharmacists use the term 'half-life' to describe the sedimentary properties of drugs and their aftershocks, but the term is one that should be used to describe the actual effect of the drugs – a half-life, in that access to the full emotional spectrum is denied, in that the only feelings permitted by the drug are dulled or diluted or distorted in order that their expression conform with the moveable feast of normality.

Fiant pilulae et pereat mundus: let pills be distributed though the world perish.

Our civilization is based on such principles. The laboratory technicians we call our philosophers would have us believe that discontent has a viral or genetic basis, that misery is a 'disease' rather than a response to the unacceptable, that human emotion is no more than a kind of chemiluminescence: love as a bout of colic. And what scorifying stupidity. Bohumila certainly would never rock this ideological boat – she was a conformist and very willing to exist in a universe of blunted corners and dissolving faces, trickling sentiments and fragmented thoughts, a universe in which every colour thickened to dun and all shadows grew to be indistinct. Opinion, definition, exertion, passion – such overt expressions of human vitality were construed as attacks on the social order, and she wanted no part of that.

8

Her metamorphosis into an uncertain memory was effortless, and I was still there and staring into the fire when the sky had darkened and Bilge came swaying in, a seasick vole, the lapels of his Welsh & Jefferies suit – he owned no casual clothes – rich with cigar ash, his Turnbull & Asser shirt a paisley of egg and Peptobismol, playing an intestinal medley and muttering about the 'fuckin' load of shit' a Democratic candidate had spoken at the Wharton School of Business.

A perverse delight was taken by him in this emeritus rich-boy stance, he loved being a slob; it was something he cultivated, something he treasured, it was that which he most admired in himself. He would warmly chuckle at the spectacle of his naked physique in the mirror, relishing his body's sheer barbarity – the hanging flat fat bosoms, the puckered thigh flesh, the swinging belly, the terrier genital, and he thoroughly adored the mercenary chaos of his face.

His whole life was a protest against Daddy. This brilliant remote authoritarian father of his had been a surgeon, externally precise but internally an archetypal Kokoschka, and he had ruined Bilge's childhood with his irrational demands and *pur sang* cruelty. To the day, Bilge could not visit a hospital without being deafened by the punitive fury of his pulse. Father and son despised each other with a ferocity that could bear no contact and as the mother had died of an ovarian tumour in Bilge's second year, there was no intermediary. It was a war.

The laces of his scuffed Lobb's shoes were loose and disconsolately dragged behind his dragging feet. The tail of his shirt was crumpled and hung in bunches over his big buttocks. He smiled his flinty smile and tunelessly sang: '*Ta-ake me out to the ballgame, ta-ake me out to the park ...*' Narrowed those smart yellow eyes. 'Peanuts and cracker-jacks?'

My glance was vacant.

'*You*,' he said with intense emphasis, 'really are the spittin' image of your father. In a female kind of way.'

'My father was murdered years ago,' I remarked.

He flopped onto the sofa, jocular, indifferent, kicked his feet up, swallowed a belch, lit a cigar, took a smacking swig from the brandy bottle he was clutching and then slammed it down on the coromandel, ebony and ivory marquetry. 'Oh, man,' he said, attempting some emotion, '*bum*mer.'

Again glanced at him and returned my attention to the fire.

He toyed with the florid bulb of his nose for a time, hummed more of his ballgame song, and suddenly began to snicker. 'Guy at work,' he said, shaking his head and lopsidedly grinning, 'guy at work had this Trophy Girlfriend – some kind of intellectual, broke, divorced, ass like a fuckin' tennis ball, and *seriously* connected. Way perfect. So they were datin', right? He had all the inside information he would ever need on her. She was gorgeous, fucked like a pornstar, knew how to talk. They ate at San Pietro's, they got along just great. True love. So for the first time in his miserable fuckin' life, this guy was thinkin' marriage, kids, a dog, the works, you name it. No more bims, no more coke, no more horseshit. Came up to me in the men's room and says he's plannin' on callin' their first kid Franklin – after the mint, right? Problem: he's an ED and used to callin' the shots, right? Ten years of tellin' a zoo of MBAs what to do and how to do it and it gets to be a habit. The guy just has to win. He knew she'd spent five years sweatin' it over some fuckin' thesis on whatever and felt she had the edge. He needs the fight, right? So what does he do? He pays some ghost to write a financial saga for him. The usual blockbuster shit: innocent hick banker gets screwed by Big Smoke assholes, turns into a hard-nosed player, meets this brainy, stacked *naif*, they fall in love, he shakes the bullshit, they end up happy ever after in Brattleboro or Montauk, who the fuck remembers. This piece of shit is published, hits number one, they make a movie from the book, the guy is a complete celeb. He won. The Trophy Girlfriend blows a fuse and gets knocked up by some museum piece at Yale. The guy finds out in a meeting, he starts hysterically screaming and vomits all over the floor. Never recovered. Still in Silver Hill. End of story.'

He leaned over to grasp the remote control and with an impatient flick of his wrist, activated the television. As he reviewed each channel's offering, he chewed his cigar, its priapic tip bristling with embers. 'CNN, I love it ...' he commented as gruesome images of some Third World military conflagration dominated the wide screen. A man with limited time for the opinions of others, he lowered the volume of the reporter's cloying concern.

And then, like the lonely lush at the counter of the all-night bar: 'Pal's kid, right? A lawyer. This kid was being shafted up the ass by one of the partners, but thought that he was on top of the game as he'd come from a place where they played bigger and harder.' Here he snickered so viciously that he began to cough, and spat all over my lap and flinching legs. 'Kid thought that the assholes he worked for were transparent. He was up for consideration as a partner in July, and wasn't going to jump for the bait as he thought they were only testin' him. Couldn't apply to the Bar until September and so sat tight. He wasn't going to let them rain on *his* parade. A pal of his had gone against a partner's wishes and been sacked, but his pal had only shot the bullets whereas the kid had made them. The punchline?'

Bilge smiled as he watched an emaciated African baby slowly die in a dingy haze of heat and faeces and gorged flies. 'The kid is dumped, gets shitfaced on Tequila Slammers, drives the Porsche into a wall and ends up in a fuckin' *wheel*chair.' He laughed so long and hard that one of his shirt-buttons popped, exposing an elliptical gash of fur and his protuberant pink navel.

Bilge was a killer and very much at home with my stepfather. They shared a deep respect, that deep respect shared by familiars. Both were amoral strategists, intellectually exceptional and like that man who stopped by the side of a highway to neatly hack off his son's head, devoid of conscience. Each regularly had a number of blackjack tables at the MGM Grand Casino cleared in the witching hours of the morning to place millions on consecutive bets – this was not industry practice, but exceptions were made in the cases of those highrollers known as 'whales'. And like Aldo, Bilge once a week ordered a whore or two or three (a baker's dozen for his birthday) from an upmarket brothel and had them suffer his humiliations. This was a very important outlet for his frustrations. 'Why *pay* for it??' he once incredulously asked a curious associate of my brother's. 'Be*cause*, you asshole, then you get a fuckin' *re*fund if they don't per*form*.' He liked his hookers big-chested and big-assed, compliant, noisy, butter-fleshed, hookers with big hips to grip and who lustily sucked his champagne-cork cock. It really tickled him to have these bouncing megaphonic dolls escort him to white-tail events, where he could steer them into conversations with 'those fuckin' skull-faced Park Avenue witches'.

This was one of his means of sodomizing (as he often put it) the status quo.

And yet despite his taste for Breughel broads, I could tell by the manner in which he feigned euphonious enthrallment with Bock's few and heavily accented words that his ambition was to have her over the balustrade by the end of the week (and I could tell by her sticky little smiles and foxy walk that it was going to happen). The atmosphere around them both crackled with a special kind of internecine electricity. Aldo's experience of her had reportedly been mediocre, but I had heard that she had no such problems when her Hispanic mechanic fucked her from behind as she grunted against the emblem of her Ferrari Spider 348. She was wild, all right; bored and meretricious, on the edge of her leopardskin seat for a little excitment. Honoré may have had his sexual confusions, but he was at heart a pampered blue-chip boy – she referred to him as 'that big pretty girl'.

So Bilge and Bock were not such an unlikely couple. They had much in common. Bock had fucked most of Bilge's friends and associates; Bilge had stripped a number of Bock's acquaintances of assets. Both existed on a diet of Krug, cold sex and nicotine; both were late-night types, high-level nihilists. Honoré used to book the American at Sag Harbor for romantic marital weekends, but Bilge and Bock were just as happy in a parking lot. 'Nature,' Bilge answered when asked what it was that he enjoyed.

He eventually settled into a comfortable inebriation and pretty much forgot that I was there. This obliviousness suited my purposes. I was busy caving in to a grim funk, feeling broken and nailed, fantastically fragile. To have had Gabriel with me there, to have had him gentle me to serenity, and then to have been kissed by him – frail, blurred, impelled and giving: this was my wish. I could not say that I had the skills to be intimate, only the sad desire. Intimacy was something I had known for glimmering minutes: sometimes I felt that kindness actually had the potential to destroy me. A child breastfed on toxins can go into convulsions over a cupful of unpoisoned milk. And kindness was something I did not fully understand. It was a dream I had never dared articulate lest it be ridiculed or ripped into a thousand irreplaceable white pieces. All this again reminded me of my escort in Salzburg, perhaps because my brother mentioned reading his obituary in the *New York Times*, perhaps because he had once been tight with Georges Bossu, perhaps because he had come to symbolize my plight and that of those around me.

Some time after our operatic date it had been discovered that he was a fraud. He had been using a respected broking firm to launder major money through the gnomes, and was collared by the SEC. All was revoked or from him barred – the tax-exempt securities in the Cayman Islands, the Dutch Antilles, the Bahamas, sunny Lichtenstein; the support of the international network of high-flyers who had pledged their eternal allegiance to him; the 'love' of the many beauties who had sworn that their affections were inspired by his soul and not his fiscal reach; and worst of all, his sense of belonging. This crushed his heart, his beautiful black hair greyed overnight. The high-born equities genius with the Count-of-Monte-Cristo past had been exposed as an E3 printer's son by the name of Harold Crappe (and not Harry Villiers). It was so sad. The Villiers persona had been his coping mechanism, his way of distancing himself from Harold Crappe's griefs: Villiers was a man who had never known such mortal wounds. All this was of little interest to his former courtiers; as far as they were concerned, his lack of cash flow erased him. A socialite who had once overdosed on Thorazine because he would not marry her told the gossip columns: 'I always *said* that there was something suspect about that little man.'

Poor Harold Crappe had left it all too late, life turned on him. People can be damaged to the degree where they cease risking the equilibrium life has left them. Crappe hid behind his hero Villiers; I hid behind silence. Those who relinquish their responsibilities to the heart and let convention dictate their behaviour wake to find themselves the hollow men: they have paid for the perks of conformity with their very lives. This evolution is documented in the eye – in a child, always active with starbursts of feeling; in an adult, often clouded or blank with resignation or hard spite. Villiers' eyes eluded contact. He was terrified of being known. I should have understood more of him that night after the performance. 'You know,' he suddenly whispered, 'I have fallen in love three times in my life and each time they left me. I *plead*ed with them not to go; I *begg*ed them. It didn't make one scrap of difference. I can no longer risk myself, Angelica; I have been ruined. There is nothing left of me except the act, nothing at all.' His jaw then tightened and he looked away.

Parting such painted veils is never easy. To be truly close to another is to reveal one's catastrophically magical internal world – the fluent rapids, rootless and translucent vines, wild umbral grasslands rippled by the hot diseased sirocco, those canyons fertile with serpents, extinct birds, the deep repositories of fallen stars. That one peninsula of vulnerably suspiring flowers.

9

Bilge was contentedly snarling and farting in his slack-mouthed sleep when my brother crashed into the room. '*Thumper*,' he breathlessly said, 'I don't know what the fuck to *do* – I think she's *dy*ing!'

Up the main staircase three steps at a time, we were propelled by all the energies of dread. The bedroom he and his future wife shared was on the third landing, down a high-ceilinged corridor lined with prune-hued Victorian portraits of the ancestors of the dowager who had sold them to Bossu. Amedeo was gasping as he shouldered open the door. I followed him expecting nothing, expecting everything. And there, in the ringing centre of a dazzling rug, bathed in an aesthetically arousing pool of limpid lamplight, mermaid-nude but for a pair of pink silk-tissue panties girlishly garnished with cerise rosettes, hair foaming like the milk I had poured over my bran flakes at breakfast, lay thumping Thumper, well overcome by the demands of her exacting epilepsy. Like any respectable anthropologist, I automatically registered every detail of her condition. Always my first response to the unexpected, childhood habit. And the comely patient? Her long tanned hands were crippled up against each long tanned cheekbone; she was baring her teeth, a rabid effect; her eye-sockets were marshy; frothy sputum bubbled from her mouth; she jerked and jerked and stiffly twisted, an impaired sexual machine. The two of them had, I guessed, snorted too much cocaine. And on the table: the glinting credit card, the dusty mirror, bright clutch of car-keys and a purse bleeding dead presidents.

'I couldn't be*lieve* it!' Amedeo was shouting. 'She – she – she just *fell* and then – then – she – she s-s-started –'

'She's not dying,' I said, 'she's having an epileptic fit.'

'What the fuck should we *do*?' he cried.

'Don't know,' I said, 'I can't remember.'

And reluctantly, afraid but still retaining my apparent composure, I looked up from Thumper's impenitent aureolae and into the dark blue spills of Amedeo's eyes. 'You shouldn't –' The jagged words caught in my throat, and then I managed to unhook them. 'You shouldn't squander what you've been left.'

A bank of mist languidly lifted from the high jewelled crest of an imposing mountain. Thumper began blinking and hoisted herself onto her coltish elbows. Smudged expression of confusion, blood-speckled sputum on her chin. Her croaks were for water. Tears prettily rolled down her freckled nose. Pink silk-tissue gusset of her panties damp, her sinewed thighs apart, ribs heaving, and then her heavy head cranked up. More tears, those sick exhausted waters of the heart. My brother's leap into the en suite for a glass. Was he planning to drink those tears of hers? And I, the stunned and substance-less queen of a dream, slid through the shadowed sea to answer the suddenly audible telephone. It was my mother. Theatrically hoarse, dictatorial and in that, strangely seductive.

'*Amedeo!* I'm trying to *sleep*!' she hissed. 'What are you *doing* in there with that –'

'It's me,' I said as I watched Thumper press her mouth to the glass. Droplets of water spattered her gleaming breasts; a rivulet trickled down between them.

Her voice had halted and I listened to her wheeze. My sympathy would be expected. I remained silent.

'Angelica?' she asked.

'What's wrong with you?' I blandly interrupted as Thumper shakingly accepted my brother's embrace.

Outside, a pitiless immortal gale was gradually destroying all the universe.

'What's wrong with me?' Stalling for time. 'What's wrong with me is not – it's nothing. *Non c'entra. Passerà. Si continua.*' She again wheezed. 'I'm tired now. Tell your brother to be quiet.'

'Am I going to see you?'

Her pause was light. 'When Aldo comes back,' she answered.

I replaced the receiver, stepped over the Hippocratic tableau of my brother cradling his crumpled Cresta Run cutie in his arms, past the *psyché* in which the ghost of me was waveringly reflected and into the bathroom, where I splashed my face with frigid water and then stood staring into the sink, both hands resting on the rim, that frigid water in drops falling onto the curving porcelain.

10

Dyspeptic and repulsive, the people my mother had invited to her overheated house of feigned cheer were prostrated in the master loafing room, their cheeks blazing with too many liqueurs and the reflected firelight. There is a certain kind of suppressed hysteria that passes for socializing. Stocky little Susie (who had confided in Bock that 'Ceccie *loves* a finger up the arsehole but I just can't bear poo beneath my fingernails,') had finished circulating old love letters from her MP. (Shoshanna: 'Were they written on real House of Commons notepaper? The one with the *portcullis* motif?') Susie was reclining on the sofa in a map-of-the-world kaftan, shod in chlorophyll-green mules, the eye of the beholder distracted from her girth by the lurch of her *décolletage*, one capable brown arm behind her head, the other resting on her husband's sloping shoulder. Her square face was clean of make-up, her crisp coppery bob was swept back by a Chanel band, and she was casing the otherwise infatuated Bilge with her spectacularly large light laughing eyes.

'You *are* a poppet, Jake!' she was crooning as I faded in. 'I swear to *God* you are the most thoroughly evil man I have ever, *ever* met!'

Bilge chuckled forbiddingly from his winged armchair as he eased his glance like a hand over Bock's skirt and in between her thighs.

Cecil glared at his wife. 'You are im*mense*ly unkind,' he

scolded. 'Here am I, feeling like a *to*tal wreckage, and all you can do is play verbal footsie with that pugilistic microbe.'

'*Gladia*torial microbe, you great hulkin' queer,' Bilge burped. 'Get it right for once, will you?'

Fat burning logs spat black ash and asthmatic sparks, cosily cracked, slipped heavily within the watched circle of fire, illuminated the French tapestry depicting an inferno of grotesques.

'Do you know,' Cecil appealed to his adventurous wife, 'that Roger faxed me that review this morning? Do you know that it des*troy*ed me? I was *utter*ly distraught. It was just too, too awful. That man is an assassin.'

Densely enigmatic behind her silver pall of smoke, the husky-voiced Shoshanna (she of the grimy bitten fingernails, Dead Sea eyes and bacon-rind complexion) enquired: 'Which assassin do you mean, Cecil? Andy Bates or Bandy Andersen?'

The laconic Allcock, until now obscured by his lover's satanic mass of hair, waved a tumbler of whiskey. 'Babel,' he offered, 'Abu Babel. Quite a guy, quite a guy. Wrote a bunch of think-pieces on the death of literature. Really quite a skilled –'

Cecil cut in with unexpectedly overt savagery. His knuckles were on show and he shook his wife's hand from his shoulder. 'How can you even *think* of referring to that pustule as "skilled"? Have you heard his polytechnic nasal? Have you seen his shoes? Have you met his boyfriend, that courtier who wraps himself in greased paper for black-tie functions? I have to say I thought more of you, Allcock.'

Susie clucked. 'Cec has been *down* on himself.'

'Surely he's not *that* supple?' (Bilge.)

'I mean dep*ress*ed, you wretch,' she laughed and then, turning to her husband: '*Pooooooookie* – sweetie, snookums, darlingest, darlingest boy of mine – *pleeeeeeeease* don't get upset; you'll spoil my evening.' Parking her glass on the floor, she proceeded to lift the corners of her mouth with her index fingers and implored, '*Do* smile – now *there's* a munchkin. You *knooow* why Simbel –'

'Babel, darling, not Simbel,' Cecil said.

'*Babel*, darling, *sorry*,' she continued. 'You *knooooooow* why he wrote that horrid thing. Why, he was *greeeeeeeeen* with jealousy, the poor chap. You should feel *sorry* for him, Cec, not hurt; that's what he *wanted* you to feel. My dear, he is completely bald and I have never been able to stand men with no hair behind their ears; they look as if they're listening too hard. And besides, darling, he's envious because you're related to Prince *Charles* and he's just some dreadful Turkish –'

'Egyptian, darling, not Turkish,' Cecil said.

'*Egyptian*, darling, *sorry*,' she deeply breathed. 'He's just some horrible old Egyptian loofah smoker –'

'Hookah, darling, not loofah,' Cecil said.

Susie miaowed. 'Stop correcting me, Cecil, because it drives me *maaaaaaad*. Where was I? Oh, yes. The revolting old Turk had his novel rejected by *thirty* different publishers and here you are, an absolute star.'

'Thirty?' Shoshanna asked. The cigarette in her mouth nicely thickened her words. 'What was it called?'

Cute Susie pulled a face. '*Hammer and Tongs*,' she answered. 'Some neo-conceptualist piece of claptrap about the marriage of a hammer and a pair of tongs. Can you imagine? It was the joke of the Frankfurt book fair. Seraphina told me that Quentin Swill unzipped his trousers and actually *peed* on the manuscript in front of Edwin Hughes. Hughes was furious, of course; told Swill he'd never sell him another book, not that Swill cared. He passed out in some editorial director's lap ten minutes later. But the most *interest*ing thing about Babel – (and here she leaned forward and almost purred) – is *not* common knowledge.'

Cecil turned to her. 'What's not common knowledge, darling?'

'No, I can't, I really can't,' Susie said, pretending to be flustered. 'I just can't.'

'Darling, please don't be absurd,' Cecil said.

Susie opened her mouth and then firmly shut it. Waving her hands before her face, she repeated: 'No. No. I really can't. *Too* wicked. *Much* too cruel.'

'Let us not be *Christers*, darling.' Cecil's expression was one of disgust.

Susie's eyes filled. '*Don't* be unpleasant, Cec – there really isn't any need.' She paused. Tugged at the polar regions of her map-of-the-world kaftan. 'Well, *all* right.' She paused again and when she spoke, her voice was smooth and beautifully malicious. 'Joaquin was on a yacht with Babel off the Cap d'Antibes, and they were both *very* squiffy. Heavy drinkers, you understand. Babel told him that in his university days he'd made ends meet as an escort, no pun intended. Said that most of his clients were seropositive, but that the sex he practised was safe as houses. Joaquin just couldn't believe that the clients had been so honest, and Babel said it wasn't a matter of honesty – he claimed he could *smell* it on them. The scent of AIDS, he said, is that of *death*. Justified his behaviour by telling Joaquin that he brought love – *love!* – into their lives, but the truth is that he's mad. *Sev*eral sandwiches short of a picnic.' Here she proudly exhaled. 'So *there*. I told you it was wicked.'

Cecil was gazing at his wife with a deadly kind of fascination. 'Truly?'

'Of *course!*' she replied, affronted. 'When have I *ever* lied?'

'That piece of information will come in more useful than you could *poss*ibly imagine,' he slowly said, his versicoloured eyes narrowed behind his spectacles. 'Fabulous gossip. Best I've heard all year.'

'Oh, darling,' Susie dismissively said, 'there's *far* better material doing the rounds. If you spent more time with me you'd hear it all. Don't you know who his last lover was?'

'Before that awful greased-paper man?' Cecil asked.

Susie nodded. 'Absolutely.' And as she smiled: 'Chat Cornfield.'

'Isn't he married?' (Shoshanna.)

'Lavender marriage,' Susie explained. 'Bishop's purple. He was caught in a Texan bathhouse in 1981 and his agents had to pay a *for*tune to cover it up.'

'Say,' the bored Bilge commented as he indicated the shrunken Haitian head, 'that's some conversation piece.'

Allcock blearily looked up. 'That's no conversation piece, that's my *wife*.'

Shoshanna's hooded eyes closed and she mirthlessly smiled. 'Sometimes,' she murmured, 'I almost can't believe the things I hear.'

'Referring to me?' her lover asked.

And with her eyes still closed, 'I was referring to Susie.'

This surprised the socialite, who rapidly blinked and flushed with guilt. 'And what have I done wrong?'

'You kill,' Shoshanna whispered, 'with words.'

'But I *swear*,' she cried, 'that everything I said was true.'

'Your veracity is not something I'm calling into question,' Shoshanna said. 'Your motivations are what interest me.'

'Motiv*ations*?' Cecil stiffened. 'And pray tell what "motivations" lurked behind your butchery – and in *Vanity Fair*, of all places – of your former boyfriend's book of poems?'

This question and the tone in which it was asked aggravated the proud and jungly Gold. 'Kiss my squirrel, pal. What you refer to as "poems", others would see as the stylistically tortuous meanderings of a mediocre mind.'

'Alliteration 101,' Cecil said. 'The "meanderings of a mediocre mind". I like it, I like it. Keep going in that direction and next time you won't have to perform cunnilingus on the judges to win the Alice Faye di Castanoglia Award.'

'Hey,' Shoshanna retorted, 'at least I didn't drive my partner to homosexuality.'

'Well, I'll be *darned*!' Cecil exclaimed in a cornpone accent. 'I never for a moment suspected that your former husband wasn't a *wo*man.'

Inspired, Bilge began to sing: '*My name is Sam, I don't give a damn – I'd rather be a black than a poor white man.*'

Susie was strangely ashamed of having triggered such discord. 'Don't *fret* so, Cecil. Shoshanna's just being clever. *Every*body loves you; *every*body thinks you are ri*dic*ulously talented. Why, just the other day Mathias rang spe*cific*ally to say that he just could not *believe* that anybody sooooooo lovely could be so *brilli*ant.'

Shooting his wife a mossy look: 'Really, darling? That was sweet of him, don't you think?'

'And what about Emma's review in the *Atlantic*?' she continued. 'Did anyone see it? She described *Orion Plunges Prone* as one of the finest novels of the century. She called it a "dazzling *tour de force*".'

Shoshanna cupped her hand to grimly light another cigarette. 'Did she also call it a *pièce de résistance*? Did she refer to your *Weltanschauung*? Was the exercise a *coup de grâce*?'

'Oh, *fuck* off, *fuck* off.' Cecil's lip curled. 'Go back to the projects or wherever the dickens you're from, you appalling woman.'

Bilge shifted his flanks. '*Ceccie*,' he teased, 'I hear that you were recently hospitalized for acute depression on discoverin' that the au pair had misplaced your rattle.'

'*Jaaaaaaaaaaaaaake* ...' Susie frowned. 'There's *no* need to be so cruel.'

Cecil's aggression dissolved with a self-gratifying recollection. 'I trust that everyone's aware that Herod King is painting my portrait?'

'Which face?' Bilge asked.

'I think,' Shoshanna colourlessly said, 'that I'm dying of alcohol poisoning. All I seem to do these days is drink.'

'And drink and drink and *drink*,' her lover drawled. 'And drink and drink and drink and drink.'

'And *fuck*,' Bock added with a glossy show of calf.

'And *fuck* and drink and fuck!' Susie squealed.

'And *fuck* and drink and suck!' the ribald Allcock roared.

'And plagiarize,' Cecil muttered.

'Pardon me?' Smoke curled from the corners of Shoshanna's downcast mouth.

'*Ceccie* just accused you of being a plagiarist,' Bilge burred, enjoying the trouble.

This was too much for the psychically overburdened Shoshanna, who sat up and cried: 'Oh, give me a *break*, you guys! I mean, I have been *really* sick for weeks now; I have just returned from a *four*-month international lecture tour; my first husband has just proposed to a woman young enough to be my daughter; my daughter is fucking a guy old enough to be my father; and to top it all off, those venal little assholes at the IRS have decided to investigate me. So I feel like *shit*, OK?? So get off my *back*, all right?? Quit ragging my ass.' She clamped her arms over her bulging breasts and bit the filter of her cigarette, infuriated.

Allcock cleared his throat. 'Where's Bohumila?'

'Doin' backstroke in the bayou, baby,' Bilge yawned.

'Sleepies,' Susie answered, dropping her right cheek into her open palm in an illustrative gesture and smiling. 'She said the blizzard makes her tired.'

'*That* boring old card-carrying member of the undead!'

Cecil shuddered. 'Who *cares* where she is as long as she's not here? She smells, I promise you, like an abattoir in midsummer. It is *thorough*ly intolerable. The Bubonic Plague had nothing on old Boohoo. With what *does* she wash? The hides of freshly slaughtered sheep?'

'Don't let's be unkind now, darling,' his wife reprimanded. 'Boohoo can't help the way she smells. She's frightfully hygienic. It's just her *genes*.'

This racially damning analysis caused Bilge to guffaw so violently that he slid down the armchair until his back was flattened against the seat and his knees were at right angles and shaking. Gripping the rippling tarpaulin of his belly, he honked and brayed and coughed, his dewlap dancing, his sloppy feet stamping the floor.

'Her *genes*!' he kept repeating. 'Her fuckin' *genes*!'

The blank Bock sipped her wine as she watched him back and spit, uncertain of the response expected of her. After a catwalk model's pause, she ventured forth: 'Are you all right, Jake?'

'Her fuckin' *genes*!' Bilge was in a spasm, unendurably amused. I had never seen him so delighted. His open laugh was raucous, but very natural. The fly of his trousers snapped as he bucked and shook and hooted, and after one particularly forceful convulsion, his sturdy little genital flipped out and shivered against its backdrop of pinstriped Italian wool.

Bock stared at it and without moving, said: 'Jake, your cock's hanging out.'

Long indifferent to social niceties, Bilge continued hacking and slapping his thighs.

Cecil drew his big tubular legs up, repelled by the display. 'When's Aldo turning up? Haven't seen him since the Punic Wars.'

'Aldo,' his wife answered sternly, struggling not to giggle at Bilge's antics, 'is in LA on business.'

'Aldo's *al*ways away on business.' Allcock stifled a fluttering blue yawn. 'That man is surgically attached to his briefcase. God only knows what's in it.'

Shoshanna blew a mouthful of smoke through her words. 'Why, what else, Xavier? Human hearts.'

From the pure black of my diseased dreams to the virginity of winter morning. I knew it was snowing before I opened my eyes; snow brings a special kind of silence. It absorbs the static of the world and intensifies the impact of the particular over the universal. The very absence of colour in a frozen landscape is soon oppressive. Much like the pitch of a moonless night, the white of snowfall has the effect of the *caput mortuum* – the Death's Head, or at least its imprint on the mask obscuring all vitality. Frustrated by the lack of stimulus, the human retina becomes fully active in search of a focal point, in search of a justification for its existence. That which can move must, or it withers. Not so complicated. A sense of reality depends upon associative potential, and that with which I could identify in this environment (stifled momentum) only consolidated my radical sense of isolation. That one golden crocus, so insignificant in the organic maelstrom of spring, demands real reverence in winter; its hue becomes a form of anarchy or assertion of hope in what seems to be a hopeless situation.

Heavy snowfall also brings with it the possibility – however improbable, however skewed – that the universe will never be the same again. Perhaps it would snow like this forever, until the world had grown a carapace of ice and what the Pythagoreans understood to be the Divine nature of hierarchical geometric order was exposed as the daydream of an impossible mathematician. Were that to happen, my heart, too, would congeal – a ruby trapped in hard arctic translucence and in it, the image of my one desire.

Over breakfast, I could only stare and again stare at the magnetic Bock. Eight in the morning and this towering glamorous skeleton was ready for a cover shoot. Her belladonna eyes were slow to blink, the lashes glutted black, those lids patiently shaded. The naturally cloudy pallor of her skin faintly shimmered. That pretty bow-lipped mouth of hers (as ever, hanging open) had been painted a cocksucker red. Her peroxide bob was artfully ruffled, all stiff curled strands, a hanging basket of fried albumen. And her garb? A violet Lycra catsuit, a three-strand South Sea pearl necklace (valued at two and a half million US dollars), a pink Minnie Mouse watch and silver spike-heeled transparent plastic knee-high Lagerfeld boots.

The only time I ever witnessed any suggestion of embarrassment in her behaviour was when these Apollo 13 boots of hers steamed up with sweat: she blushed and wiggled each boot's metallic piping, patted the side seams, banged her heel against the rand. 'Golly!' she said, for once uncomfortable with her conspicuousness. She was so stoned that it would not have surprised me had she doffed a tasselled lampshade or appeared naked but for a bow-tie and green rubber flippers. Bilge was still loaded from the previous evening and not equipped to register the eccentricity of her outfit; all that interested him was the way in which it clarified her ambit.

The vignette filed and eggs digested, I decided to explore the place. Figured that if I couldn't lucidly think or feel, I would keep moving – fight or flight, as those evolutionary cheerleaders cry. And so I walked up and down the staircases, through endless corridors, listened to shreds of conversations, to the strains of Chopin's *Sternenregen Etude*, Op. 25 No. 1, walked into tens of useless little rooms storing a multitude of useless little things, this useless littleness a patrician statement in itself.

Orgiastic wealth was implicit in every detail – detail which demanded a considerable investment of energy and education and subsequently possible finesse, an investment which indicated a disdain for the fundamental only made possible by its surplus. The fragile teacups, the brittle relics, the frail upholstery and shattery glass: this was a world of little things and little ways, their delicacy presupposing their protection. I mused with interest on the coarseness of those for whom protection had never been an option. My slippered footfall was inaudible. There were few defined shadows in the gloom. The sound of my breath was startling, as was the lisp of my soft skirt against my stockinged thigh. Hollow-cheeked air, a sunken tomb. Now that the wind had retreated or exhausted itself, there was only the echo of its force, an echo visible in that destruction obscured by tenderly drifting beautiful indifferent flakes of snow.

Shoshanna's voice (a dying marine animal) swam towards me from the depths of a hall. 'I don't understand,' she was saying, 'I really don't understand.'

The sound of her withdrew into its own vacuum.

Again, the snow's dense silence and its bite, felt even through the externally thick insulation. Crept down that hall, a dislocated spy in black. Made myself insubstantial by the doorway of a room throbbing with clocks. Subjective time had long ago surrendered to the imposition of the objective, or collective subjective experience; every one of these ticking mechanisms had been built to establish an absolute beyond man's perception of duration. I remember turning to the Sainsbury's clock not long after my father's death and noticing that the hands had been removed for cleaning or repair of some description; I remember standing there motionless in the pavement crush, just staring at this timeless clock and thinking that no more appropriate a metaphor for death existed. Shoshanna's voice resurfaced.

'I've gotta hear the *truth* from you, Xavier – please tell me the truth; we used to tell each other everything. Don't tell me you've forgotten the pact we made. Don't let me down, honey – not now ... not now ... not after all these years, honey, please don't. I don't want us to be like this, Xavier.'

Each word was flattened – as if spoken through her fingers, as if spoken through defeated tears.

I stared at the monogrammed black velvet slippers William had ordered for me, slippers that were tattered but still adored. Their black tips rested on the edge of a pale fan of lamplight from the door behind which the last act of Gold's romantic drama was being played. I could picture her slumped on the bed, suddenly round-backed, suddenly a woman scorned one time too many, that nightmare hair of hers suddenly obviously dyed, flat bags beneath her eyes, braless and with a belly like a sackful of dead mice. And Xavier? He would be standing with his long lean soft-waisted back to her, his hips somehow womanly, arms defiantly folded, those cupreous eyes of his clicking open, clicking shut, clicking with calculations. Gold could be a formidable bitch, egocentric and wilful and childish, but she was kind in her overbearing way and not without compassion. Allcock, on the other hand, was an exploitative and opportunistic animal and when he finally spoke, it was with loathing.

'It is *over*.' He enunciated every word. '*Over*. Finished, you got me? Over and out, Shoshanna – it's history. I don't *want* this fucking shit and I don't *need* it, you understand? I don't give a *fuck* about you any more, I'm beyond interest. It's been five years now and I don't want to know about it any more. You're a fucking *plague*, Shoshanna. No-one gets out of an affair with you *alive*. Look at what you did to that poor asshole Darius! The guy gets the shakes when he hears your *name*. Look at your screwed-up daughter! I'm not going to fall into that trap, I'm getting out of this *intact*. One piece, you understand? *One piece*.'

The fact that Gold remained in the room after this attack indicated that she was no longer confident of her appeal or her importance. She had been a honeypot in her youth, a sexual pest, a princess – feted, fondled, feared. Now she was a role model, a pioneer, a queen of sorts, but unwilling to renounce her irresponsibility. Allcock was a monster, but he was not illogical. He was tired of being her last connection to The Land of Fuck. He had never been her plaything and he had never been her partner; the definitions had been blurred. Their relationship had been a thing of networking and hashish, orgies, health farms, facial peels, aromatherapy, body wraps, five-star restaurants, Concorde flights, poetry readings, standing ovations, ponderous speeches, hangovers, loud fights in hotel suites, demolished beds, cocaine, broken plates, parties that concluded the following week, award-giving ceremonies, promiscuities, gossip, lies, reunions, *paparazzi*, an abortion. And now it was all over. Allcock had found himself a bigger fish and Gold was being strong-armed by destiny to accept loneliness and shed all of her illusions.

'How do you think I *feel*?' she cried with the despair of the irrelevant. 'How do you think I fucking *feel*?? I'm forty-five years *old*! I mean, this whole situation strikes me as – strikes me as – I mean, it's ludicrous, Xavier! It's so – it's Jackie Collins! This is not real life! I mean, I have done more for you than anybody can *believe*! I mean, are you *crazy*? Are you fucking *crazy*? Annabelle *Wilde*??' Here she began to (furiously, piteously) sob. 'I'm forty-five years old and I want a *part*ner! I mean, how do you think it looked when Suzy published that stuff about you screwing a twenty-two-year-old?? Do you realize the repercussions that had on my public *im*age? I mean, my whole – my whole *career* has been based on – I just cannot comprehend why you would – I mean, this is just television, it's not happening. I mean, I cannot believe you – you de*meaned* me in that fashion for a – well, let's be straight here, Xavier – for a – for a fucking *bimbo* ... I mean, give me a *break*! Leave me for, you know, Diane Sawyer or Barbara Walters or Barbara Taylor Bradford or, you know, a woman of *sub*stance – I mean, fuck a *nov*elist or a – a – a respected *pain*ter or Hillary Clin—Rodham Clinton, or – or – I mean, Xavier, not a *bimbo* ... God, this can't be *ha*ppening, this can't be *ha*ppening.' Violently, she hiccoughed. 'I mean, an under*graduate*, Xavier? I mean, I should be grateful it wasn't a – a *lap* dancer or an understudy for – for Melrose *Place*.'

Deeply impressed, I nodded to myself as I leaned against the doorjamb, eyes open but actively unseeing. That on which I was eavesdropping was engrossing stuff – predictable enough, but still engrossing. Every clock (there were seven) in the room behind me began to chime and I jumped. The Swiss monstrosity on the wall to my right not only chimed, but put on a show: as the toothed cylinder within it rotated to the tune of 'Edelweiss', a little wooden shepherd stammered out, his staff upheld like that lantern (in which a star fearlessly shone) brandished by the tarot's Hermit, and he was followed by his little wooden sheep, the little wooden sheep-face painted with a thoughtful smile. The two managed eleven rounds of their circuit before retreating behind snapping wooden shutters. Even Gold and Allcock were shocked into silence by the cacophony. And then his reply.

'You narcissistic *cunt*,' he scoffed. 'The only thing that figures in your universe is your fucking reputation. That's all that really matters, isn't it? Your public image. You know, I don't know what I ever found appealing about you, what ever made me think –' His pause was abrupt. And then: 'Blow your patronizing bullshit out your ass. I'm sick and fucking tired of your neuroses. I don't give a shit about your reputation. I want to feel I can breathe again. You suffocate people – you eat their *air*. We've got a couple more days of this charade and then it's *over*, you got me? It is *over*.'

Her tears were those of desperation. The decreasing pace of age is only ever the counter-pull of the past against the future, of experience against hope. Her dream was up for the guillotine, and she was grieving in the only way she knew how: hysterically.

'Xavier, honey –' she begged, '*please* ... just give me another chance, give me another chance ... let's try again ... I'll double – I'll double my appointments with the shrink; I'll kick the smoking; I'll have a chin-tuck; I won't – *please*, darling, *please* don't leave me – it's been five – it's been five *years*! Th-th-think of every – honey, everything we've *been* through together, think of all the – all the – you *fuck*ing bastard! You can't leave *me*! Who the hell do you think you *are*?? I was a Nobel *nom*inee! I'm an international *cele*brity! You should feel *privi*leged! You should be *grate*ful! How dare you –'

'Dream on, Shoshanna, dream on.' And with these words, he left her.

As he opened their bedroom door, I jumped behind a shelf and waited there, my heartbeat louder to me than any mechanized ticking in the room. Gold did not follow her determined rake but instead howled like a frustrated carnivore and then positioned herself in the doorway and screamed: 'You have *broken* my heart!'

This last statement was too agonizing for her, all manner of emotions were unearthed, too many, and she continued through long shaking sobs. 'You could have done *any*thing and I still would have loved you! You have *killed* me! You have *mur*dered me! You are a *fucking* bastard! You used to come over to my duplex and tell me that you'd never been happier! Five years! Five *years*, you bastard! I gave you *every*thing! I was prepared to give you a child! And this is what I get??! *This* is what I get??! You have *killed* me! I am an artist and you have *killed* me! I will *never* forgive you!'

The girl who had inspired the feelings which caused this rift was the only child of Rupert Wilde, the billionaire whose interests ranged from missile technology to publishing.

Annabelle Wilde was fresh and freckled, spoilt and beamy, a talented equestrienne who studied art history at Columbia. Gold was not wrong in sneering at her intellectual capacities, but was wrong in assuming that intellectual capacities made for wholesome love. So Annabelle was a moron. Big deal. She was also a sweetheart and attentive to the needs of those she loved. Her father may have been congenitally ruthless, but he was a pushover for his daughter, as was his dim and doting wife: her wish was their command. And she was gaspingly in love with Xavier; she wanted him as she had never wanted anyone or anything before. He would leave his wife for her. This radical action would be spurred by arithmetic and not distracted passion. In market parlance, the Wilde fortune ate the Swedenborg's lunch, and Xavier (charming floppy-fringed twinkly eyed gigolo that he was) liked money better than love. The concept of a soulmate was less interesting to him than a palace in Marrakesh. Of course, Annabelle was unaware of this. She was devoted to the suave old leech.

Her father was less susceptible to his winking patter. He knew a slimebag when he saw one. And so he had Allcock's weaknesses delivered to him in a plain brown envelope – not just the 'accidental' collision that became the subject of an inquiry by the Hurlingham Polo Association, but a little tax evasion here, a little involvement with insider trading there, a little photographic evidence of bisexuality here, a little information of unacknowledged offspring in Costa Rica there. Wilde called his future son-in-law to his office and delicately let him know that not only would he never inherit a red bean, but if he stepped out of line in any way at all, he would be destroyed. Effectively, Xavier would be an employee of Wilde International, answerable to the boss. 'And if I hear that you've been chasing skirt,' Wilde murmured with a hard-eyed smile, 'I won't just have you put away, I'll have you *disappear*.'

What other option did the handsome charmer have? He was forced to eat his hat, and made certain that his marriage was a joyous one. It was not the worst of situations.

12

None of the houseguests was too active in the afternoon; each was busy digesting his seared salmon (served with herb-scented *crème fraîche*), brick-thick *torte*, vodka, port, further excesses. Once Gold had buried herself beneath a pile of blankets in the bedroom where she could claw her face in peace, I crept back out into the hall. Returned to my own gilt-crimson room where I lay on the sofa, one leg hooked over the ornate crest-rail, the other balanced on the armrest. Stultifying, that quiet. I was left to my sad stumbling obsessions – my father, Gabriel, the state of my world – compulsively taking, as one remarkable intellect put it, my own emotional temperature.

13

Years may have passed. Resumed my exploration. More busts, more pasteurized portraits, more upholstered velvet loveseats and strange isolated chairs, more butterfly tables, pedestals, more priceless curios, more rugs. Discovered a capacious nursery or playroom – wood-panelled, empty-smelling, lit by the desolate late silver light of this late silver season. At the far end of the room, a Broadwood cottage piano. On the shelves to my immediate left, hundreds of illustrated children's books, demonic porcelain dolls, old Pomona toys, Steiff teddy bears.

Sudden nostalgia for my childhood flashed through me, leaving the colour blue, the colour gold.

A magisterial Victorian rocking horse had been placed in the middle of the room (no doubt conforming to some designer's system of symmetry); the reins and saddle had been fashioned from carmine calfskin, and the mane and tail could only have been made from human hair – the texture was too pliant, too familiar to my touch. Such locks, pre-Raphaelite, Gretl's perhaps. Palpated the convex eyes, the hard ledged lids, the alert carved ears. Climbed on in my short cashmere skirt, black stockings, monogrammed slippers, with two swinging plaits. That giving carmine saddle in between my thighs. My feet arched against the stirrups' tread. Shivered. Began to rock the stallion, one hand gathering the reins, the other entwined in the voluptuous cherry mane. Consoled myself with the hypnotic senselessness of the backwards and forwards of the wooden creature. Scratched with a penknife on its throat: the name Gabriel. Carl Jung would have appreciated that one. Noticed a corresponding cut on the muscular hypothenar of my left hand, cuneiform writing in congealed dull blood. Must have cut myself on an unkind thought.

The motion of the toy was ocean, lulling, sugar blue. This was the midpoint of infinity as I understood it – right here and now, on the wooden back of a rocking horse, bathed in the nacreous afterglow of storm. Heard, as if submerged in a dream, the door opening. Glanced up. Xavier. Xavier with a bourbon swagger to his strut. Xavier gracefully dishevelled, smiling, cowlick in its place over his calculating eyes. He shut the door with theatrical care and turned around.

His features had the compelling plasticity of a film star's and this was his main means of seduction. Women starved of the connection implicit in romance were enchanted by his lively face – enchanted in the medieval sense, in the sense of being bewitched. Western men are trained to conceal rather than reveal their feelings; expressiveness is the first casualty of corporate life. All A-1 money studs know better than to show their hands. Their fossilized features dominate boardrooms, make the covers of investors' periodicals, sometimes even star on banknotes. These are marks of having succeeded in our culture, badges of honour. And their sacrifice? Not just sweat or tears, but their ability to communicate their feelings. Most women find themselves confronted by Easter Island statues across the dinner table, they labour to make conversation, they struggle to love.

This being the case, it was no miracle that Xavier was such a hit. His active countenance both responded to his subject and encouraged a response. Through this responsiveness, women were made to feel that they impacted on his life, that they exerted enough sexual or intellectual potency to actually effect a change in him. Who wants to bill and coo at a brick wall? Smart Xavier worked on improving his persuasive aspect. Naturally mobile, his features were conditioned to express the most subtle feelings, the most frangible emotions: their alignment could articulate a thought more eloquently than any lexicon. I had witnessed a number of these fantastic looks, but one in particular had remained with me. It had been directed at the wife of a major multinational's executive chairman at a cocktail party and it unhinged the poor woman, caused her to spill her champagne down the scalloped gold lace of her gown, I watched her pant with wet frustration and desire.

And what a performance! In comparison, Karajan's *Aida* was a flop. With a millesimal widening of his eyes (which expressed his wish for increased visual absorption of his subject), with a slight tightening of his underjaw (which pinched his mouth, indicating conscious restraint), with a stiffening of his neck (which betrayed the conflicts that this restraint aroused in him), and cramming his mind with images of market crashes, prison cells and sexually transmitted diseases (which filled his eyes with an agonized pathos), Xavier succeeded in securing her eternal support (and thus the certainty of her coaxing her husband to cooperate with any scheme, however harebrained). With one lightning-quick look, he told her that although what had transpired between them could never come to anything, she would reign over his heart forevermore. The intricate premeditation behind this glance and its faultless execution were, if viewed outside a moral framework, real things of beauty. He was the best that I had ever seen.

Of course, he wasn't always that refined.

Sometimes he could be vaudevillian, an embarrassing idiot, stupidly winding his right index finger an inch away from his temple to signify a feeble mind; grimacing as he slashed a hand across his throat to warn of trouble; manipulating an invisible penis and rolling those salacious eyes of his to level one he thought pretentious (from him, a pretty rich conclusion). At such times, he really looked ridiculous – like Little

Lord Fauntleroy at forty, a bad jester, a flashy operator. But generally he was amazing, from the buff of his black patent-leather pumps to the loose black bow of his dinner tie. Hardened society witches rediscovered their chastity in his presence, they even blushed. His fluid expressions were as much of a disguise as a poker king's inscrutability, but far less obvious. With the exception of the intuitive, who would have suspected him? Xavier's truest feelings (anger, shame, inferiority) were too prettily wrapped. They flickered like the shadows of rapidly blown clouds across his eyes, the rest of his face solely controlled by his sharp mind. It takes a lot of early trauma to develop such manipulative aptitude.

His lazy movements suggested only a connoisseur. This would have driven Gold, who equated skilfully engineered erotic crises with true love, bananas. No wonder she had tried to scratch her face off! I was surprised she hadn't stabbed herself with a cheese knife through the heart. The police could have found her in the bathroom, lying in a pool of her own unrequited bile. Xavier had never been the Martha Stewart woman's poison. He attracted thorough-breds, sophisticates, very worldly broads. It was not difficult to see why. His eyes dawdled over my thighs. And then again, that sly embroidered smile, that American ease, his left hand deep in his trouser pocket, his right hand confidently slung over his hip. And what a swinger.

'I don't think,' he said with an amused curve to his voice, 'that we've ever engaged in anything approaching a proper conversation. Which –' (warm exhalation) '– is kind of a shame, really, because you look as if you'd have a lot to say.'

What poise! What clarity! What dreamy *savoir-faire*! I smiled and twirled a long stray lock of hair around my finger, rocked that restive horse.

Between a whisper and a sigh: 'I don't, but it's kind of you to think I do.'

He moved towards me with the speed of a Komodo Dragon. Stood so close that I could smell the alcohol breathed by his pores. Hollowed his long palm over the horse's snorting muzzle; stroked it with a lingering obsessiveness. Heaved his chest (brief heave) and looked me in the eye. This look was the chef's special, and I let myself be overcome. *Vraiment ravissant*, as my mother would say. His timing was not good, it was superb: reptilian, instinctive, beyond intelligence. He had ensured that the ambush would be devastating by avoiding my eyes until that moment. The gravity of it all! I felt as if he had just told me that he was carrying our child.

'You're a siren, aren't you,' he said (not asked). 'You lure that bunch of sailors to their deaths. And,' he added, 'what a way to go. That smile of yours is *lethal*.'

I was enjoying myself. Said nothing.

Xavier's hand was now idling on the white star painted on my stallion's brow. His posture suggested an archaic measure of emotional intensity. 'You were with that Grieve guy for a while, weren't you? Anyone since?'

This really made me laugh. I was delighted. Nodded. Rocked that restive horse. Waited.

He swept his head to the side, his thick and beautifully cut auburn-blond hair reflecting winter from the window. In that hair, several silver strands, some stripped of all pigment.

'You know something,' he said (not asked), 'you have the *greatest* laugh I've ever heard.'

I was accustomed to suppressing every instinct and as a consequence, the revulsion was not difficult to mask.

'I'm in love for the first time in my life,' I said. 'It's an interesting sensation.'

This information did not faze him, did not deter him, did not affect him in any way that I could see.

'What's love,' he said (not asked), his fingertips still idling on that one white painted star, their tracings reflecting the circular nature of his computations.

'Something that can only be expressed through metaphor,' I replied.

'So, only schizophrenics, primitives and poets speak love's language. Has Sho subjected you to one of her killer disquisitions? They're generally a hit with college crowds. If you follow that line of reasoning, the only people qualified to translate that language into one accessible to the proletariat are literary critics, anthropologists and shrinks. That's all it amounts to, I hate to say. To cap: you're telling me that literary critics, anthropologists and shrinks are closest to God?' His laughter transformed his face, infused in it real innocence. 'Love belongs to copywriters,' he said through

314

this laughter. 'They patented it *years* ago.'

I rubbed those carmine reins between my thumb and forefinger. 'It must be exhausting to permanently sacrifice experience to theory.'

This comment caused him to neatly re-evaluate me. 'Swing *low*,' he remarked with a smile. 'So tell me, this –' (lightly iridescent glance) '– handsome prince of yours – has he ever had a heart attack?'

I looked at him with curiosity. 'Why, no.'

'Well, then,' he said, using his impeccably shaped brows, 'obviously he's not *doing* it right.'

Sweet, I had to hand it to him. It was a parry I had not expected. 'Either that,' I answered, 'or he's not a coked-out ageing alcoholic.'

'Well played,' he conceded and smiled again, and used that boyish cowlick to effect, but the shadow of a cloud flickered across his eyes.

The fur-lined cape of silence. That rocking of the horse, its raw dry creak. Outside, it was still thickly snowing and the sky was stained with night. My pulse soaring in preparation – beat by beat, its count a panic. In moments of fear, the large muscles of the body are saturated with blood, facilitating a rapid escape. Simultaneously: the arc of his throat towards me, impression of sin, of porous skin, cindery hair, the gust of his decaying breath, his swift moist palms over my thighs. The Steiff teddy bear on the shelf opposite me had lost one of its eyes, the other dangled from a fraying thread. Some kind of bird flew into one of the windows, cracked its beak against the glass, then broke its neck or altered its dark winged trajectory. Xavier's mouth assaulting mine. Fungal, his brown tongue. I did not flinch as I would have years ago as I was now far too controlled. Those neurotransmitters named catecholamines flooded through me.

I shifted marginally and teasingly whispered (our eyelashes almost enmeshed, our lips a shiver from each other): 'If you don't take your hands off me, I will destroy any chance you have of snaring Wilde. Am I making myself clear?'

Like a puppet snapped of its long strings, he jolted back.

That single moment, savoured by me as if it were a tremendously unique achievement. Age confers power, no question. His real face rose – as if from turgid depths – to the surface of the present. And what a difference! Truth always ages the career liar. Those cupreous eyes of his were clicking, clicking, clicking, but did not reach a useful conclusion. It was as if he had been forced from the safety of his eel-green nebula to hard scrutiny (all mine, all mine). I dug my feet into the stirrups, rocked that horse until its unoiled mechanisms neighed, with casual eyes surveyed my quarry. Whore, the whore. He had stiffened, all right. Soldiered right up.

'Understood?' I leaned forward, those tender carmine reins melting within my fists, giddied by the proof intoxicant of my own anger. 'Understood? It doesn't work with me, Allcock, and it never will. I know you like I know myself. Now get out of this room before I have you thrown – and I *mean* thrown – off the grounds. You understand? *Now*.'

My heart was in my hand. This expression belongs to the desert states of great America and it perfectly expressed that which I was feeling. Xavier did not turn away but stepped backwards to the door, never once averting the amazed admiring wrath of his hard stare, his gait that of a precise Russian nobleman. How elegant his clothes were and how depraved his face. His system may not have processed booze efficiently, but my words certainly had. Before closing the door he looked at me as if I were the first true thing that he had ever seen, and then he vanished – the blurred turn of the doorknob the last vestige of his presence. My will dissolved as suddenly as I had been left alone.

I was demolished.

The scroll unrolled itself for me by way of explanation: Aldo had always suffered from profound insomnia and paced the halls all night, every night of my life with him, damned to his own bleak incubus. There are times even now when I pity him. But then again, but then again. Looking back, I realize that it was really something to be raised with such terror. The maturing of my brain's prefrontal circuitry was premature. I remember his predator's tread, doors opening and closing, lights activated and then killed, cigar smoke curling from the crack beneath his study door, the fumes of secret sacrificial pyres. My brother and I were always accessible to him as there were no locks on our doors. This in itself made for a certain hypervigilance. Aldo had let me know of his proclivities, and he was unpredictable. A wealth of devastating possibilities was implied by his behaviour, it was all reinforced by his few words. Subtext was one of his many specialties, he was a man of unclean talents, shadowed skills. His methods of controlling me were simple but effective – the thermal sense of pit vipers was also his: the only thing he had to do was set those eyes of his upon my mouth, upon my breasts, and I was transformed into the most obedient of girls, hysterical in my efforts not to provoke him, not to displease him, not to unleash the ordinary atrocities suggested by his look. I knew better than to question him as I had seen those postcards from the inverse universe of the abused, I had read their scrawled black sentiments. Three of my schoolfriends were long dead by their own hands. Gretl was one.

14

Back to the future: that night I sat by the window and stared out at the cold inorganic landscape. Its clarity was independent of the world, it was indifferent. I sat there for hours, wrapped in a heavy belted woollen dressing gown, my knees to my breasts and behind my eyes, a mist – the room around me in absolute darkness. The only place where I could freely play was within those glowing parameters of an idea and nowhere else. Nowhere else.

15

The first festive sound to reach me that black Christmas day was a bellow. It was impassioned, operatic, as resonant as a prize cello. And who else could have been responsible for such music? Aldo had arrived. Glanced at the clock: a bright green five, two zeros. Again, that bellowing. Pluto, god of the underworld, on discovering that Proserpine had fled. Avoiding difficult emotions is a profession in itself and this profession no longer interested me. Aldo's bellowing grew louder. He was baying for my brother. The other guests were safely tucked away in other wings, insulated from his lunacy. My stepfather's pet obsession had always been with what he saw as indolence (that is to say, any timetable that did not correlate with his). To him, it was an absolute justification for torture.

One unforgettable Saturday morning he had pounded into Amedeo's bedroom, lifted the sleeping boy from the bed by the cotton collar of his Peter Rabbit pyjamas, and repeatedly slammed his head against the wall until the paintwork was syrupy with blood. My brother (later treated for a fractured skull at a fashionable private hospital) was in such a state of shock and pain that he could barely breathe; Aldo, on the other hand, was very vocal. The sound of his own voice was enormously important to him. If I recall correctly, his words that morning were along the following lines: 'You *fuck*ing asshole! You *fuck*ing prick! You stupid *fuck*ing pointless waste of space! It's ten o'clock in the *fuck*ing morning! Get off your *fuck*ing ass, you bag of shit!' (The emphatic rendering of the expletive 'fucking' reflected the effort required to smash my brother's skull against the wall.)

I don't believe Amedeo was ever again able to sleep soundly. There were times when he awoke in the middle of the night screaming and screaming with a voice neither of us recognized as his own. The excitation-patterns of abuse had been stamped into him for years.

On another colourful occasion, I surreptitiously called the police. When they arrived, I begged them to commit Aldo, I was hysterical, quartered by grief. The two young blue-shirted men were mortified – so kind, and so completely impotent. My mother's signature was required for him to be committed and so the whole deal fell through. She wasn't signing anything. Aldo knew this. Exuberant in his supremacy, he then delivered one of his most extraordinarily insane monologues to the two men (his eyes rolling back into his head, the bolts in his neck turning, hair sprouting from his palms, lightning forking so dramatically in the background, a raven perched on each of his hunched shoulders, et cetera).

Mother stood and gazed at all of us with minimal recognition, a deliriously and deliberately vacuous monster. She was dressed, I think, in lemon chiffon. New jewels, the usual four-inch-heeled mules. Her son's blood was on the wall (and on the tables, sinks, doors and her husband's hands), but this was irrelevant. Unpleasant truths had no place in her life. Reality was such a bore and anyway, it was nothing to do with her, nothing at all: it wasn't really happening, it was a dream. Her denial mechanism reduced all hate-crimes to a trick of light.

'*Amedeo!*' Aldo screaming, and what lungs he had. God let him have a stroke, God let him disappear. '*Amedeo! Vieni ad aiutarmi con queste borse! Mi senti?! Adesso! Spicciati!*'

The bellows had become intolerable. Sound has the incredible power to resurrect the past and all of its authoritative associations. Ran out onto the landing and there he was, the grim old devil, still yellow and black, a thing of toxicity, surrounded by bursting luggage (stuffed with handmade shirts and pornography, no doubt. I had seen the covers of his snuff videos, I had seen his magazines). There are many to whom such sacrilege is pivotal to sexual excitement. He paused to squint as I leaned over the banister. Slight smile. His big shoulders bulked up the cut of his big expensive overcoat. Hands in pockets, stomach strong, those big old legs apart.

'It's five o'clock in the morning,' I said. 'Amedeo's asleep. Get one of the men to help you with your bags.'

His look was telling. Again, that slight smile and the patronizing inclination of his head. His gracious message? 'Go back to bed and mind your own fucking business.'

At those words, my heart hardened – in it, the essence of strategy, will, impure coagulating poisons. I walked down the staircase, walked straight past him, walked down two halls, through the kitchen, through five rooms in pitch to find the help. They were obsequious, my two flunkies, preposterously impressed by my stepfather's standing (he had been featured on the cover of *Time* a week or so beforehand). And what an example to his fellow men! That much black money gives any beast real stature. Returned with my two goons to his displeasure but did not care, I really wished him dead and for the first time in my life, ostentatiously ignored him. It was as if the memory of Gabriel had strengthened me, had given me some colour. I then left to find my brother.

Inside his room, the air was close with marijuana smoke and sexual sweat. The scent reminded me of a childhood associate's family mansion, in which her titled parents regularly stayed up all night to share dope and cocaine with their eldest children and their friends (I believe that on one particularly debauched evening, the father ravished his daughter's best friend and the mother retired to the bathroom to fuck the best friend's boyfriend under the sink). Thumper stirred, blinked open one amazed and beautiful eye, whispered something about 'the labrador', a labrador who then retrieved her reverie. My brother lay in a medicated heap away from her, increasingly a stranger to me.

Shook his hot shoulder.

'Let me sleep,' he thickly said.

Again, I shook him. 'Aldo's here,' I whispered, 'you'd better get up. He'll want to see you soon enough.'

He shifted, muttered, ceased responding – again, too many drugs.

'Wake *up*, will you?' I harshly said. 'He's *back*. Aldo is back.'

I was at the breakfast table an hour before any of the others, pressed by destiny and thus depressed, chain-smoking cigarettes and wildly trying to devise a system of logic with which I could make sense of my situation. No luck. Fortune was often nothing but a dead monkey in my life. My goal was not to eliminate my suffering, but to learn to convert said suffering into the force of a greater understanding and tenderness, real tenderness.

Around me, the gymnastic bustling of the nineteen-year-old maid, a slattern trained by night-school professors to serve all food from the guests' left and water and wine from the right, to remove the first course with her left hand whilst substituting a warm plate with her right, to never touch the water glasses she filled and to catch spillage with one of the many fifteen-inch-square napkins, to obey the orders communicated by her employers' eyes. She was chatty, this mercenary girl, eager to make my acquaintance, a displaced hillbilly, pretty, log-legged, spiritually trashed. Told me her drunken father used to come home at four in the morning and threaten to decapitate the lot of them with an axe. Told me her drunken mother had a problem with gambling, that she couldn't save a cent. Told me her drunken husband liked her to wear a scarlet garter belt when he took her by 'thuh back door'.

Her breasts had a nice bounce to them, she wore heeled shoes.

Alabama kiss-curls and sly cheap green eyes. Told me she had a 'big man' on the side who had guaranteed (cross her weatherboard heart and hope to die) to make her a 'big star'. Told me that my stepfather was a real gentleman and nothing like that George Bow-Sue who treated her like chickenshit. Set the table, worked those jugs. Glanced at me quickly and with hostile envious interest. At close range, her brown kidglove complexion was very coarse, there were deep pits in her cheeks, the skin around her chin was scarred. I lit another cigarette and listened to her carefully. She was proud of the coloured piece of glass on the ring finger of her right hand, waved it around, testily referred to it, as if impatient for the fulfilment of its promise.

I was not overwhelmed. The ring was Aldo's signature, he gave it to all his lower-drawer floozies. Tacky jeweller was his way of paying for clumsy Southern-fried fellatio. He liked to compensate for all the sexual acts performed upon him – this ensured that they were perceived as transactions and not in any way as expressions of feeling. I had seen him act the concerned patriarch with the desperate waitresses he employed. It was an effective routine and appealed to their sad meretricious instincts. And this Miss Kiss-Curl was no socialist; her sly cheap eyes negotiated. The mistresses with whom my stepfather impressed his circle were her antitheses – impeccable women, cognizant of behavioural expectations and fine literature, majestic masochists and smart, a world away from this bumpkin.

16

When Aldo finally took his rightful place at the head of the table, his guests sharpened up, even Bilge scooped his face from the floor: feudal vassalage. There were greetings, there were gracious smiles, fluttering hands, there were his magniloquent words. With ravishing and killing charm, he explained that as his adored wife was feeling better, she would be making her first appearance that evening. He thanked them all for their support, their warmth, their gifts, their thoughts, their dear concern. Neither he nor his indisposed spouse, he confessed, would forget such humane generosity.

The peeved Bock sighed and pushed her poached eggs to the edge of her plate with a fork as he spoke. When he finished, she abandoned her cutlery and stared into space, her thoughts in their own lightless void. Bilge and my brother launched into a discussion about hell traders and scalpers, shareholders and the merchant bank about to list, their open mouths full, nodding and expansively gesturing, temporarily absorbed. The silent Shoshanna stabbed at her sausages and watched with burning eyes her former lover argue the case for the removal of jackets (if not ties) at the Henley Royal Regatta with the stuffy Cecil, who would moo and then bluster: 'Good God, Allcock! You must be joking!'

Aldo was monopolizing the (limited) attention of his future stepdaughter-in-law, a stepdaughter-in-law I could see he planned to seduce, a stepdaughter-in-law who laughed at his jokes with the brilliant ease of the unexploited.

Beside me, Susie was lecturing Bohumila. 'Darling,' she stage-whispered, 'you have abs*olutely* *nooooooooooo* idea how *awful* she was being to me! It was out*rage*ous! Kept going on and on and on about her bloody job until I was about to go stark staring *maaaaaaaaad*. What could I do? I simply *had* to defend myself.'

Here she touched her fleshy collarbone with her two chins in a lopsided shrug. 'And so I said: Francesca, Chessie, darling, really – you have absolutely *nooooooooo* idea how much hard work is involved in being a socialite. No idea at *all*, the absurd creature! I mean, one labours at it like a *black* man! *Hours* of work – on the hair, the face, the body, the nails, the wardrobe, the wit, taking care of the properties, keeping track of the children, keeping track of the husband, catering to one's inner needs, organizing dinner parties – and *don't* get me started on the *night*mare of dinner parties! – the seating arrangements, the floral arrangements, the food, the service, synchronizing the guests' schedules – really, darling, it's just *bi*lious! I swear it'll send me to an early grave. So it's hardly as if I sit at home all day twiddling my *thumbs*. I mean, I *wish* I did something as simple as a "job." And do you think this made one iota of difference to her? Absolutely not. She continued with this re*puls*ively superior attitude, on and on and on and on, as if sitting at a computer terminal all day were the last word in humanitarian contribution! Have you ever *heard* of anything so ri*dic*ulous?' She bit her lip and tapped her fingernails against the perfectly golden casing of a bread roll. 'Isn't that right, Ceccie, darling heart?'

Her husband looked perplexed. 'What was that?'

'About Chessie.'

He pushed his spectacles up the bridge of his nose with a slow finger. 'What about Chessie?'

'Last month, Cec, don't be so obtuse.'

'Darling,' he winced, 'I've been involved in a ludicrous debate with Allcock for the past half-hour. I don't know what you're on about.'

Susie snorted with impatience. 'Oh, for God's *sake*, Cecil – *Chessie*! At Yolande's house! When she went on and on and on and on about her bloody –'

'Job. Righto. Yes, I know what you're banging on about. Dreadful woman.' And with this, he returned to Allcock and his voluptuary's manifesto.

'There, I told you so,' Susie primly said. 'Cecil was there; he heard it all; every grisly word; nearly made him sick. But then, what do you expect? The woman has a *chronic* drinking problem – husband knocks her about, you see. Bruises the size of dessert plates all over her body – Min said she saw them when they undressed for a sauna at Champney's. I mean, it's all rather tragic. *And* he sleeps with all her friends – why, he even made an improper suggestion to *me* once, not that I succumbed, of course. Not at *all* my type; can't abide those brooding Continentals. Far too ponderous for me, thank you so much. One must be charitable, but the truth is simply that Chessie's a re*mar*kably bitter woman.' She passed a forkful of kedgeree into her rosebud mouth. 'Do you know she once confessed to Harriet that the only thing that made her life worthwhile was her collection of houses?' Here she paused and politely chewed, that coppery bob rhythmically swinging. 'So much for her bloody *job*.'

Bohumila's dark divorced eyes never once left the Georgian salt cellar. The atmosphere around her was a drugged forcefield, difficult to endure. She laid her cutlery down and suddenly looked at me. I don't think she had listened to a word Susie had said. Her heavy hair had been pulled back into an unforgiving chignon. She wore thick gold earrings, a gold crucifix, that blinding flotilla of diamond rings. With a single gesture, she dismissed Susie from her consciousness. This was an orogenetic process, one with which I was anxiously familiar; inaccessible mountain ranges could be made to spring between two parties in an instant. Bohumila may have been chemically distorted, but she was not stupid. A certain animal intelligence flickered behind her oilcloth eyes. And again, her fascination was with me.

'There is a man around you,' she said. 'You were together in another life. Soldier, he was the soldier. You were in white, I see you. You left him to go to the other camp. Field hospital? I am not sure. He never found out what happened to you and he was killed. It was a tragedy. His love for you was a passion.' She held my concentration with her compelling powers, in a voice without emotion. 'He had nobody to love but you and you left him. That is why you are together now, to correct the past. In him there is still anger towards you, but also the passion.'

Like the jet of a fountain, Susie rose from her seat. 'Darling *heart*!' she cried. 'You never told me you were *psychic*!'

'Who's psychic?' This was Thumper.

Susie clutched with long filed blood-coloured fingernails at Bohumila's arm. 'You must must must *must* tell me my future! I simply have to *know*! Will I ever fall in love again?'

Her husband affected a certain appropriate disapproval. 'Darling, *really*.'

'Oh, *pleeeeeeeeeeeeease*!' Susie persisted, her hands pressed together in supplication, pulling a repellently infantile face. 'You *can't* not read me! Why, I'm practically made of *per*spex! That's what the Queen Mother's clairvoyant said – he told me I was an open *book*.'

'Is Bohumila psychic?' Thumper was very animated and oblivious to my stepfather's irritation, to the hand he had ominously placed on her exposed thigh.

The expressionless Slav sighed. Susie had commanded the attention of the whole party, the only role in which she felt truly comfortable: centre stage. Even Bilge and my brother were listening. I felt light-headed, so distressed, a certain nausea had overwhelmed me. With unheard murmurs, I excused myself and ran upstairs, where I was sick.

17

Left at the table on my return: Aldo, Bilge, my poor crushed brother. The light from the bay windows was refracted by ice crystals, new to human eyes. The men were indifferent to me as I entered, they were incandescent with their own concerns. Discussed, money: the topic altered all their features, imparted an desperate quality, changed the temperature. The atmosphere was intense with the unspoken – each man had a substantial silent agenda. My stepfather's cigar smoke disintegrated slowly. His drug was that of pride, testosterone; his bloodstream was unfamiliar with the gluco-corticoids of the submissive.

Amedeo was leaning forward in his chair, the tendons in his throat uncomfortably apparent. 'We can sell the French operation at one point three billion,' he said through a dry cough, 'which means that we could meet all criteria with extra if we bid a hundred and twelve.'

Bilge, from the bowels of hell by way of Arkansas, steepled his capable fingers. This was a serious signal; he was engaged;

his eyes were newly bright, cold, hooded. 'We have a buyer for the French section who would pay *big*.'

My stepfather's contribution was a gunshot. 'What sort of bid price on existing stock?'

I watched my brother as he forced himself to become the only person he felt the world could accept. 'Hundred and seven, maybe hundred and twelve.'

There was a pause as each of them considered the possibilities.

Shaking his head, Bilge slowly smiled. 'So *why*,' he asked, 'are we *sittin'* here? Why the fuck aren't we out there buying up existing *stock*?'

I cleared my throat, if only to reassure myself that I was real.

Aldo rested his tongue on his upper lip as he looked at me. This was the aristocracy of violence, implied and actual. 'Let's go upstairs.'

Bilge shrugged. They all stood, linked by the same expression. My brother studiously avoided meeting my eyes and their troubled message. Aldo was the first to cross the room, his gait deliberate and suggestive – the motion of some pitiless carnivore. It is said that empathy acts as a buffer to cruelty, and that it is a quality lacking in psychopaths. With his hand on the doorjamb: 'Christmas fucking Eve, Angelica. Give it up, will you?'

They left their ugly laughter behind them and it seemed to increase in volume until it was as if I had been deafened by my own shame. I sat there with all the half-emptied plates, all the half-emptied glasses, left at an angle to the table as the chairs had been.

I could not shake my brother from my thoughts. It can be said that deeply traumatized children grow to be adults who live in the minefield of their own extreme emotions. *Plus ça change*. During his childhood, I often visited Amedeo in hospital (if my mother's explanations to the clinicians were to be believed, my brother was incorrigibly clumsy). He was, as ever, in traction. Predators invariably attack those whose behaviour is conspicuous, and my brother had never been a compliant youth or man.

As he was unable to effectively feed himself, I passed him

the small silver bowl of consommé from the tray and offered to help him. Of course he refused; we were raised to mistrust offers of assistance, taught to be suspicious of the motivations that may have lain behind them. Awkwardly, he began to spoon the broth into his mouth. My hands were twisting in my lap as I watched him, it is so difficult to witness the suffering of one you love. The morphine or its synthetic substitute had made him groggy; his hand shook a little and he spilled some consommé onto the sheet. It was at this point that I had one of the few true glimpses into his internal world: his demeanour flipped from stoicism to an absolute, unnerving panic.

'I've made a *mess*! I've made a *mess*!' Cowering, he stared at me, his breathing gashed. 'The – the – the *sheet*! I've made a *mess*! I've m-m-made –'

'It's all right – it's nothing,' I quickly whispered. 'It's just a little stain; no-one will notice; it's just a little stain; it doesn't matter.'

And with these words, I took the bowl from him and then cradled his head as he sobbed and sobbed against my breast. I could feel the shallow dents in his skull where Aldo had brutalized him and I wept, I wept for both of us.

This helplessness was a freight we had to bear every day of our lives.

Aldo had this effect on people, he was bad news, a catalyst. To be around him was to feature in the daydreams of a blue-ribbon psychotic and no-one, but no-one, was ever the same again. Once the spiral arms of his paranoia had embraced you, you were suddenly possessed, you were his property. Certain minds are capable of exerting such witchcraft; certain fantasies can be a form of real abduction. These were realities that strengthened him. What aperitif is more intoxicating than innocence? His universe was one of unnecessary complexity, one in which all was refashioned to justify his every behavioural excess. It was insanity and it was unbridled. There was no pattern to it and there was no plan. And perhaps it was this very lack of logic that rendered this madness so persuasive: the dominion of passion! the dominion of will! His victims were always too busy trying to understand his actions to refute them with any eloquent

327

conviction. Who argues with a storm? And to what end? They were seduced, swept off their feet by his audacity, irrevocably tainted. He had the black ability to pervert the purest thought. Through his rage he made himself a god and a god who wanted sacrifice.

Said psychopath was in the study with Bilge and Amedeo, a study that had been equipped with five Sun terminals (running Reuters or Bloomberg or Knight Ridder or CNN or charts or historicals, relevant feeds, the fiscal works). The money with which he was dealing ran in billions. 'The beauty of equities,' he liked to say, 'is that you can have a smorgasbord of high and low risk securities. Optimal entertainment; minimal boredom.' He was one of the few who had pulled out of the market a week before Black Friday (a lucky fluke: he had been securing a double-barrelled deal and required liquid funds). That dark day he watched conglomerates dissolve, he received news of all the suicides and bankruptcies of those thought to be invincible, he was astonished at his prescience. When he had finished celebrating, he sat down to the share price index and laughed himself into a fit of hiccoughing. He just could not believe his luck. It was now possible for him to buy back his old portfolio and still have enough left over to credibly bid for South America. The words he spoke to his broker the following week were quoted in the financial pages of newspapers the wide world over: 'Let's go *shopping*.'

Impressive, but an exception.

Aldo's successes were generally premeditated. Most of the big league players were on his team. A crooked company-analyst-cum-journalist for the *Wall Street Journal* regularly rang him through a voice scrambler to unload insider ken. Aldo was an information addict, he needed its immediacy to feel alive and in this way, he was a true man of his times. His facsimile machines spewed news all night and day, his pager vibrated, his mobile trilled. The newspapers which landed on his stoop each morning were a matter of poundage. There are those who mistake information for intelligence, but not my smarter stepfather; he knew information for what it was. Power, clean power. Aldo preferred his information cold and free of human context. His whole system was geared to function at the highest speed. Any decrease damaged his expensive engine; he began to grunt, to give off sparks, leak oil, to stall: he blocked the traffic. This busyness of his was pathological and necessary to the safety of those around him. It stopped him feeling anything but his own accelerated momentum. *Out of my way.*

Ferociously angry people whose intelligence demands a semblance of propriety compulsively accumulate velocity, ideas, things, people. Denial of their demands kickstarts their mania, their infinite rage. To illustrate: one of Aldo's peers was in a huff because he had tripped over his shoelace in front of some serious investors. This was the living end for him, total humiliation. His reaction? He would be on the next flight to Monaco, where he could vent his spleen on the gaming tables and then jet off to the Corviglia Club, the exclusivity of which reinforced his sense of relevance. This huff of his was considerable. Why did he refuse to be driven to the airport in a limousine? 'Because any asshole can hire a limousine.' He wanted a pterodactyl, he wanted a magic carpet, he wanted a Stealth Bomber, but notice was short. Got his PA to call the local helicopter company. Was told that as the risks were too high, clients could not be flown at night. He offered them twenty, thirty, forty, fifty K. No dice. Only owners were permitted to be flown at night. This was a very sexy challenge, very juicy, it really got him hard. The clock was ticking. 'How much?' was his question. The answer? One point five million. The going rate for a helicopter was one point five million. One point five million to get to the airport while New York City hospital staff were turning away the dying for want of funding. One point five million to get to the airport while most major First World cities were breaking under the weight of their poverty. One point five million pissed up against the wall and that was it, essentially – the Great Wall of China had nothing on his ego. The deal was finalized by the time he stepped out of his bubblebath and into a fresh rompersuit.

Out of my way.

18

The afternoon was an illness. I was restless with memories of my one love. I could still taste him with my swelling vulva, he haunted and would always haunt my blood. With my want I reconstructed him and then projected him so that my fingertips could sink right through the beauty of his face. The mirage is a function of any desert. His name was enough: at the thought of it I became a kind of cannibal, an artist in a phaeton drawn by furies. I was spread over the hake of my own longing. Recollections of him filled my mouth. The language of love is liquid – the eye speaks in tears, the nipple seeps milk, the cunt pulses glucose, the skin sighs sweat. I recalled the way his tongue sometimes caught in the syllabic trap of my round name. I recalled the desired invasions of his hands, those slow fingers, that big silken sex. An illness, that long afternoon.

19

It was cocktail hour on the *Titanic*. Aldo, Bilge and Amedeo were still following the journey of sunlight (and concomitant journey of the currency inspired by the star's form and colour) around the world – the sixteen trillion dollars exchanged in futures and their dangerous derivatives every day were all that openly interested them; the rest of the party congregated in the room in which the shrunken Haitian head was so gruesomely featured. Any minute now, my mother would undoubtedly indulge herself with a grand entrance (and stand, framed by an arch or doorway and absorbing every wave of light). I remained in the shadows, clad in the usual funereal robes.

Bohumila was slumped in a chair by the far window, looking out into the night for a self not even she could clearly remember. Twinkie Princess Thumper was in kitten pink, with pearls and pleats and plaits *à la Parisienne*. In miniature and tinkling from the gold charm bracelet blow-torched to her wrist: a handsome horse, a set of skis, the key to her secret castle, a tennis racquet, a lilliputian yacht, the letter M, a lock in the shape of a heart, a quilted handbag, an unsheathed lipstick, a hockey puck, a Gucci loafer and her latex diaphragm (just kidding). This trinket provided her with hours of amusement; it was a game every cerebral cell of hers could play. I had watched her study it, rolling each charm between her fingers, wonderingly rattling it, watching it slide up and down the tawny satin of her arm. When my brother could no longer stomach her sugared wittering he would redirect her attention to the bracelet, aware that she would lose herself within its many mysteries. Susie was being given a tour of the marvel.

'*Sweeeeeeeeeeeet!*' she exclaimed, her eyes ingenuous. 'And *who* gave you this adorable W?'

Thumper was pleased to be granted the rare opportunity to correct a senior. 'It's not a *W*,' she said, 'it's an *M*.'

In a show of delight, Susie pressed her palms togather and I noticed that her fingernails curved backwards like bamboo splints. 'Darling,' she urged, 'I shall simply *die* if you don't tell me what it *stands* for.'

Her husband's contribution was sardonic, and from behind an ironed newspaper: 'Moron? Mar-a-Lago? Mediocrity, perhaps? Money market? Minnie Mouse? Myxomatosis?'

'Cecil ...' Susie warningly purred.

'It could stand for *Mundus*, dearest,' he added. 'Or perhaps Thumper here is a budding alchemist, and wanted the symbol for mercury dancing from her wrist.'

'You'd better stop there, darling, before your brain implodes.' Susie's look was a deathblow. A woman of vicious social ambitions, she knew that any daughter of Clare Powell-Winchester-Hamilton-Knox had to be oiled, and lovingly.

Thumper was not confident of the offence she had taken at Cecil's suggestions and so reverted to the childhood habit of sucking on her hair. With her left plait in her mouth, she blinked at Susie and uncertainly explained, 'M stands for – M stands for *Margot* because – uh – because that's my real name.'

'Your real *name*! And to think I never *knew*!' Susie linked those splint-nailed fingers of hers and smiled with her entire body.

Cecil gagged. 'Surely,' he said, 'you didn't think that Jim Knox named his daughter after a *rabbit*? Of *course* the girl has a name, Susannah!'

'Darling,' his wife evenly said, '*if* you don't stop being so foul I shall become dreadfully cross.' She forced her body back into its smile. 'Now what do you think of *that*, Xavier? M stands for Margot!'

The wrecked Allcock, who fifteen minutes earlier had finished sodomizing Bock in the library, raised his eyebrows as if wonderfully surprised. Bock, who could not sit down without suffering, who had expressionlessly asked him to hit her, hurt her, to treat her with contempt, leaned with her back and one long foot against the wall and smoked a black post-coital cigarillo. I had seen all their shenanigans from the carelessly half-open door. Bock was thinking of Bilge, I knew; her eyes wandered, in them was almost an expression of interest, and she sighed. She had not been satisfied by Allcock. He didn't care.

'I don't think M stands for Margot at *all*,' Susie declared. 'I think M stands for *mar*vellous, you darling girl!'

'Oh, for God's *sake*!' Clearly repelled, Cecil slammed the newspaper down on his knees. '*Must* you, Susannah? *Must* you?'

'Pay no attention to the festering toad,' his wife breezily said. 'I should never let him out of his box.' Like Aldo, Susie was a slave to her limbic system; she often told friends that the only reason she had never given birth was for fear of being tempted to eat her offspring, however charmingly they may have been dressed.

In drowsy tones and from the nucleus of her blue nimbus, Bock commented: 'In the library there is leopardskin all over the ceiling and the walls. I have never seen it before. Ostrichskin, yes – at the Savages' house; but the leopardskin, never. I wonder if the butterflies eat it.'

'I think you mean moths,' Shoshanna said.

Allcock smiled to himself and savoured his Scotch.

'Mariella is just *the* last word in style,' Susie decided.

'Oh, don't be ridiculous, Susannah – the entire concept is utterly sick-making,' Cecil said. 'Imagine if the beast had *eczema*.'

'You *can't* be such a bore, Ceccie – I think it sounds divine. And Mariella is a visionary, really. Her taste is faultless. Didn't you see –'

'I can't say that a room draped in skin blows the wind up *my* skirt.' This was Shoshanna as she walked to the window, where she stood with her back – prematurely stooped, a bookworm's back – to the others. In the black waters of the pane, the blurred reflections of her hurting eyes and Bohumila, who was unnervingly still. 'I mean, call me old-fashioned, but the hide of a once-sentient being is not my idea of decor.'

'It never ceases to amaze me that Jews believe all roads lead to Nazism,' Cecil wonderingly said. 'You must ac*cept* that their interior designers had a certain genius, Shoshanna. From an environmental standpoint, recycling the dead is a remarkably sound practice. What else are the stiffs going to do but take up valuable space? I certainly wouldn't object to Susannah metamorphosing into a lampshade. Could be quite cosy. And given the weight you've gained, darling, I'm sure we could stretch you out to a smashing three-seater sofa and two matching footstools. A marquise for my eightieth wouldn't be out of the question, would it, darling? You'd do that for me, Susannah, I *know* you would.'

Bock suddenly uttered a guttural cry. 'There was this ... *man* who used to follow me,' she said to no-one in particular and for no reason, 'and wait outside the apartment with – oh, God – chocolates and roses and then I went to – to Monaco, and he followed me and ... he told me he knew this great nightclub where – it was very bizarre! I've never *been* so stoned! And in the car I began to freak out totally – I was *very* stoned – and we ended up in this nightclub with – with doors coming out of the floor and – um, people wearing the spacesuits or something like those mans from outer space, the walls ... the walls – you know, sliding into each other and I was – I was naked with the silver dust on my breasts, so I – I asked this guy how much for getting in and he said fifteen million francs or twenty or something, and I looked in the crocodile bag and gave him all the money because I was so stoned and also because I did not understand the money ... and of course it turned out to be ten thousand dollars or something, and then he went to jail.'

Allcock worriedly glanced at the drugged Bock and announced: 'Evangeline Bruce had a lot of complimentary things to say about you, Susie. I was seated next to her at Newt Gingrich's. Kay Graham was there with –'

And then, just as everybody had forgotten why they had been summoned, my mother appeared.

The silence was disturbed only by the sclerotic cracks and sputters of many burning logs. In that moment, we could all have been mistaken for waxworks: the initial impact of surprise is always to petrify. Allcock choked on his Scotch and Thumper winced. Shoshanna darkly inhaled. Susie's tone was uncharacteristically sincere.

'My *God*!' she breathed. 'My *God*! What has *happened* to you?!'

It was probably my mother's grandest entrance, her very best. She was a queen. Framed by the unsuspecting doorway, cocooned in fuchsia or crimson and cadmium silks, her *maquillage* a masterpiece, her *bijouterie* sublime, she worked the hot and gluttonous tints of the firelight like the angriest of futurists: she seemed to swim before our eyes, at once an inert thing and a pandemonium. The uncontrollably young Thumper blundered into tears and then into the astounded Susie's arms.

'It's so kind of you all to come,' my mother whispered. 'I am so sorry to have been such a recluse, but as you can see ...' She gestured and then extended her frail arm to Allcock, who leaped up to help her to an armchair.

Still with her laddered-stockinged leg at an acute angle to the wall, Bock observed the proceedings with fascination – the same elementary fascination a cat develops for a leaf: fascination discrete from evolved comprehension, artless and instinctive, borne of nothing more than the subject's consciousness of the object's difference to that which surrounds him. Physics and the single girl. Such a level of intensity is the crowning ritualistic goal of every religion but can also be very secular stuff, kitchen sink opera. And it was true, the girl was given dimension by her concentration; her great debauched invisibly lashed eyes seemed somehow solidified by the very act of vision – they could have been two crystal balls in which the history of another, less exotic, woman could be seen.

Cecil and Shoshanna were merely dumbfounded, their circuitry had blown. The primitive and witchy Slav was inscrutable (no change in demeanour, none at all, only the customary torpidity of her countenance). I was having trouble breathing and my hands were shaking and my knees almost collapsed beneath me but above all, I was destroyed by admiration. Mother, there has never been another like you. Yours was flair, it was real talent. The blood that crawled and screeched in her veins had never been classified. To elicit such genuine surprise from frauds and imbeciles is generally the prerogative of presidents and serial killers. She was a diva. With elegant difficulty, she turned her head (that torsion of silk). 'Where is Aldo?' she asked Cecil.

His answer was halting. 'Upstairs, I believe.'

To Susie, who was robotically soothing the racked Thumper: 'Would you be so kind, darling?'

Once Susie had unlatched Thumper's arms from her own and hurried upstairs, my mother gently smiled. There was an arch suggestion in this gentleness, more than a shrewd black comic touch, she would not have missed this for the world. Those black pupils of hers disgorged malevolence. Leaning over, she laid her hand on Cecil's knee.

'Darling Cecil,' she managed, 'you look so handsome. Such a handsome man! *Vraiment ravissant.* Susannah is so fortunate.'

The poor man manfully swallowed and clamped his ample hand over her slender one. Every fascist is a sentimentalist at heart. This was a moment of stagedoor affection, relished by all. My mother inhaled, closed her eyes, opened them, again closed them, extravagantly exhaled and then, after a glaucous pause, delivered another floating smile. In that instant – because of my roiling heart, perhaps – she looked to me like a woman I had never known, a photograph I had once seen, a child's depiction of its home, a dream, a lie, my only truth. She was dying. My mother was dying. Everything she was, everything she could have been, everything she should have been, everything she never was – it all would be cremated with her. I would be left with nothing but my unmet needs and memories.

> *My tower of pearl, my eyeless siren,*
> *wrecked on the jags of the stars of Orion.*

There was little left of her aside from jewels and silks, that appetite for pity. I think she had been waiting for this moment all her life. She didn't seem to mind that beauty had betrayed her, that it had disappeared – she understood that each thing had its price and that life was no different. It occurred to me that she may have left her face behind at a function, left it behind as another would have forgotten an umbrella or an overcoat, that perhaps she had simply misplaced it. There was also the possibility that she had always looked like this but no-one had ever noticed. Who could have discerned a single feature beneath that mask? Her flesh had dissolved, leaving only its superb Teutonic scaffolding. If nothing else, the Germans have always deeply understood the aesthetics of structure and its relation to efficacy. The universe's empathy could slide down those cheekbones of hers for all eternity and never be absorbed. She was impervious, hers was a closed bespoke ecology.

Not long after her marriage to Thoth she had taken to fainting. Examined by the best doctors, pawed and bled and neatly punctured, measured and weighed, consoled and questioned, she was diagnosed as severely anaemic. The solution was not complicated – a ferrous sulphate supplement once or twice a day. One particularly daring specialist suggested that she ingest some food with her daily gallon of champagne and semen. But, lo: she did not alter her hooker's diet and that clear glass jar of poppy-red pills forever sat unopened on her bathroom shelf. She was far too busy enjoying her romantic fits. Mother! Following a series of dramatic mishaps, she assigned me the task of supervising her showers. This involved me nervously perching on a stool outside the Roman recess and watching as she luxuriously fondled herself. In retrospect, I am surprised she did not give the job to my brother.

I was forced to witness her richly soaping her ripe brown

nipples, her long thighs, that perfect fluffy golden cunt. There were times when she would turn to me and delicately spread her labia, meticulous in the quest for hygiene. Her glance at such moments was no more than a rapier plunged deeply into molasses. And then, confident of her psychic conquest, confident of her fantastically perverse effect, she would ask me pretty please to scrub her lightly freckled shoulders and strong lean spine. *A little lower, darling ... proprio lì, ecco – proprio lì ... ancora ... now to the left ... à gauche, chéri ... just there ... a little harder, would you, darling?* It was only when this pornographic show was over that she allowed herself to stagger and to ooze (dyed lashes fluttering) onto the tiles: my melting mother. This was, of course, my cue to leap into the steaming waterfall, wrestle with her slick wet size, grapple with the bags of her big breasts, my hands slipping into her warm waxed armpits, one balancing kneecap in her swampy crotch, grunting and gasping and gripping, manouevring her in order that I could (with my third hand) sprinkle her face with cold water from the tap that I had (with my fourth hand) turned. It was a real adventure, *dolce Dio*.

When the excitement of the shower-slumping palled, when it all became one awful bore, she took to fainting in the kitchen, swooning in mirrored foyers during opening night parties, she took to falling face first into her vichyssoise, she slowly toppled from chairs, she collapsed into the brawny arms of African dignitaries and Eastern Bloc dictators, she made certain she was always lavished with attention. And now this, her capitulation to time. The physiological process of dying is all about disintegration, diminishment, the lessening of the apparent. Death governs the interior and its currency is the unseen. In its denial of the senses, it redirects human attention and returns it to its origins: soft conclusions, peeled emotions, needs.

Suddenly I realized my mother was talking and struggled to listen (as if I had been trapped beneath the hard telluric crust) to her clarifications. Precise terminology can be used by high-level individuals as the cosh with which they pulpify their enemies. Malignant. Marrow. Myeloma. Perhaps these were the words for which that M dangling from Thumper's bracelet stood.

My thoughts rose in a sudden upsweep, a flock of

blackbirds synchronized to form a live celestial arrowhead. I just could not get over it, it did not fit. For years it seemed to me as if my life had been defined by death. What new invariable could I possibly find in sadness? To have lost everyone who ever meant a thing to me – now that was hard, now that was gruelling. To see, and be by protocol denied open reaction to, all the remaining scraps and collops of my mother's body – now that was difficult, now that was pain. Her body: my old playground, that perfumed address. It was a killing realization; I could have cut myself in half. There were my tears, so muted as to be inaudible in the high wild clamour of concern. There was Aldo's cheerful greeting as he entered. Following him: my brother, Bilge, the baleful Susie.

20

Our widower-to-be was radiant, his cup was foaming, he looked like a million bucks. Looming bereavement suited him. He strode over to my mother and squashed the remnants of her face between his hands. '*Pussy*,' he coochy-cooed, 'I didn't realize you were coming down so *early*.' Their wet kiss was a public first. It had taken a malignant tumour to get him to express affection or its squirming substitute in public, but that was fine by her; she could not have been happier. And that was it – my mother almost looked contented. She was triumphant; at last, she had won. They kissed again. This kiss was hard unfelt bestial intense repulsive – even Allcock averted his eyes. My brother, wiped of pigment, left the room; he had never been allowed to develop the skills required for such profound confrontation, he only knew how to escape. I alone fully appreciated what they were doing, I alone fully appreciated the finer points of their charade. Above all, it was avarice in motion.

Her green and growing fortune would soon be added to his, he would get everything – the stocks and shares, the properties, the blunt cash, everything. This was the nature of the will he had so generously helped her draft. Black Friday all over again and the man could not believe his luck. What prescience! It was the only quality of his before which I stood in awe. He should have set up shop as a clairvoyant. Aldo really had an instinct for survival, a second sense, the paranormal ability to filter the future through the dense mesh of the present. For all his madness, he was a brilliant logistician in matters of everyday life. Scaring everyone to death was also useful, it was a coveted power in the world.

My mother pulled away from him with fey adoring grotesque grace and then caressed his cheek. 'My darling husband,' she whispered, 'always by my side.' Here she obscurely sighed, coughed up sputum laced with blood, and again sighed. 'When you reach a certain age,' she told the amazed assembled as she gazed at her amazing mate, 'all that is left to live for is romantic love.'

They were both oblivious to my presence. This was nothing new, nothing about which to stew, it was business as usual. And they were very wrapped up in themselves, after all. This exclusivity of perception was a relief; it removed certain weights (performance, praise, *politesse*) from my shoulders. Impending death is much like the first flush of real infatuation in its demand for an obsessive and highly coloured solipsism. Neither of them could keep their hands off each other, their groping was a community affair – one minute longer and he would have been on the brink of a coronary embolism, his middle finger to the knuckle in her tight blonde cunt (as it always had been in the good old days, when the two of them would fog the Maserati's windscreen by Mrs Macquarie's Chair at X-rated midnight). Observation is a trance and a trance to which I am susceptible. It is easier in the short term to analyse than to feel; gaining insight is less agonizing than losing one's heart. I watched Aldo remember to switch his expression from one of glee to a more appropriately tenebrous tenderness as he asked my mother how she felt. The way in which she welcomed his overt perfidy was breathtaking. No work of fiction could have been more bizarre. *Buon Natale, Angelica.*

If my mother's appearance was any indicator, Aldo would soon be the most eligible ape in the financial zoo. There were women who had been waiting to snare the animal for years – why, even that lovely North European princess fell to pieces when seated next to him at supper. His tumescence was legendary, it was so glamorous, it compared magnificently to that of his corrupt stuffed-shirt peers (the wives of whom were climbing their ostrichskin walls for want of a little active primitivism). The paradox alone was exciting to them: a thick blue-collar cock attached to a white-collar icon. And not only would he be the season's prize, the real catch of the day, but he would be more intimidatingly wealthy than he already was. Those long centuries of Vorstellung-Savoia industry, most of my father's earnest honest careful work – it all would belong to him. Oh, he must have felt a thrill when the prognosis was announced; he must have air-punched like a hero in the privacy of his own suite. Jubilation! Vindication! Malignancy, that one-way ticket to Elysium!

Everything of which he had ever dreamed would soon be his. The moral and spiritual paucity of these dreams did not concern him, he had no stake in the intangible (which he referred to as 'that crap'). By his definition, he would be a free man in an enslaved world and that, to him, was the ultimate – a visible reinforcement of his methods by modern civilization, applause translated into dollars, a reward for a job well done. He was so happy that he could deny my mother nothing. Hell, let the little woman have her Gloria Swanson moment, let her have every wreath in the whole fucking world! If she didn't die of cancer, he would suffocate her with flowers!

At her funeral he would spout tears like a fire hydrant, he would drain his capacious nose into a silk handkerchief, it all would be so moving. Soothed by his floozies, vibrating with the agony (and it was deep, and it was merciless) of having it all, taking business calls in the car tailing the hearse, ensuring that the news cameras filmed him from his best angle, emitting one dark piercing cry as his newly inflexible wife was wheeled into the ovens, Aldo would establish himself as a tragic figure of some international note. Suburban matrons married to bombastic bores would write him moist letters of condolence. To the quivering microphone he would whisper: 'I feel as if I never want to see another human being again. My life is over. I'm throwing the towel in. I owe that woman everything – she was the one who taught me how to live for love. Before our marriage, I was nothing but a tragic old playboy. That's all I have to say.'

Such full-bodied quotes ensured that his indecently rapid remarriage was favourably covered by the press: BILLION-AIRE WIDOWER FINDS LOVE WITH TEENAGE PRIN-CESS! These headlines conferred status, they were very hot PR. He was forced to set the dogs on the *paparazzi*. The rest of his life really began with the wake (champagne, cocaine, a battalion of beautiful whores). Every paper ascribed his deranged aspect the following morning to grief but, as he wearily told one associate, the truth of the matter was that 'fucking so much young snatch all night can really knock the living shit out of a guy'.

<h1 style="text-align:center">21</h1>

Before I was aware of my actions, I had left the party and was scaling the stairs to my mother's bedroom. I would wait for her there; she would be enervated by the company and its racket soon enough. The suite she had been assigned ordinarily belonged to Mariella (she of the ostrich-skin walls and uterine prolapse, a wreck of a woman who spent her life with her head down the toilet, violently retching). Lit a shaking cigarette. The wall facing the deathbed was mirrored. The other three were *trompe l'oeil*, executed with real genius, very striking. Over the bed was a depiction of Medea standing before the altars she had erected to Hecate and to Hebe, hair streaming and dressed in a robe, in the process of sacrificing a black sheep and beside her, the flaming twigs she would dip into the ovine blood after thrice circling those two altars. Beneath her raised left hand, a three-dimensional bedside table loaded with medications.

Everywhere, the sweet mephitic stench of sickness.

The long cloud-white dramatically dragging drapes had been drawn, their full sashes almost feminine in form – two indolent mulatto odalisques, each wrapped around her cloud-white column. Twenty feet above the bed, a dome surmounting the tester. The *passementerie* had been made in the Le Puy convents of another age and on the bed's ormolu mounts were designs of poppies, those flowers of sleep. I lit another cigarette, the second of what seemed to be a thousand. In the facing mirror and through reflected smoke, my jade-tinged reflection mimicked my every action, however inconsequential. Meticulous actor! I was the victim of another's hex: my flesh seemed to evaporate, leaving only my heart in its articulated prison. The wind suddenly rose. Leafless branches at each window scratched, tearing as they did at the night, at the very weft of my soul. Mine was a state of clarity in which I felt interpreted through what was almost an ecclesiastical composure. Any minute now I might just crack, I could just fold, I knew I had to keep extremely still for fear of real abstraction. The strength to defer gratification is a gift one gives oneself. In contrast to an old wish, this new one: I wished for nothing but a complete abdication of control – just once, just for a lenitive instant, to be liberated from all inhibitions and still be acceptable to that intractable cold judge of self.

To have confronted my mother with all fury and all grief, with love and all longing, with truth: that was ambition. In a dream another mother reigned, a mother in whom an image of me was cherished. For my real mother to admit to abuse, neglect, anger was unthinkable. What did she have to gain from the austerity of guilt? Her life would not be concluded in ashes and sackcloth. I knew she would never change if only because she lacked the desire and without desire, there is nothing, nothing at all. This in itself was a component of her charm – she was intractable, a seraphic bitch. My mother was subject to surface disturbances but inwardly unmoved by all.

Amongst those reflections in the mirrored wall, the sly cut of a door. Walked up and pressed my fingertips against it, my breath a reverie of flames over the polished glass. That slice of mirror fell open to a high, wide closet. Stepped inside. Stood there in the suffering darkness and inhaled the so-familiar aromata of my mother's clothes – wool, and its benign suggestion; satin, and its inguinal promise; cotton, and its purity. Over these rapturous fabrics I let my fingers drift. Stared beyond the walls and far into an eternity in which the palest of regrets fluttered like swallowtail pennants. Medieval sensibilities at best. As a child I had (in stolen moments, in the hush of aroused solitude) sifted through my mother's laundry basket, through the dewed panties, the gossamer camisoles, through the whispering silks of her slips and stockings and fine *negligees* – inhaling her through each weightless piece, moulding their fragrance to my open mouth, in search of her even then. Connection of any description is always an ecstasy. And secreted between my tongue and palate even now, her natural scent distilled to a taste – the scent beneath the jasmine and the sickness and the cigarettes, the scent beneath her life-experience: it was the fragrance of transparency, of a girl whom I had never known but only sensed, of inviolate nothingness.

Mother!

I fell to my knees, my face against the hem of her prodigious Inaugural Ball gown, breathing her in as I would have oxygen, my head a star incinerated, wrenching myself apart with tears, with love, with tears. There was in me more than a sea to be expelled.

22

At some point I must have returned to the bed for that was where I found myself when the door opened. I dared not turn around and instead glanced behind me in the mirror. My mother was alone and poised with difficulty, her dry decrepit hand closing around the doorknob. Noise of her breathing. The intensity of the expression in her eyes was coruscating. Between us: ships carrying unknown cargo, the dead air prefacing a cyclone. Dark, darker, darkest – the claustrophobia of anxiety. For a giddy instant, I felt as if I had been scooped from the shell of self and into that spirivalve universe in which my father dipped and eddied.

And then, as I returned to myself with a jolt, my mother – with stringent diction, a certain inelasticity – asked: 'What are you doing in my room? I'm tired; I must sleep.'

It was all I could do to remember to breathe and even then, I had to think about it, I really had to concentrate: I had been rendered dumb by the essential functions of humanity. Her proximity was stunning.

The violence in my five-word plea: 'I want to talk. *Please.*'

Cleansed of contrived coyness and all courtesy, her voice was faint. 'To *talk?*' Hoarse emphasis. 'To talk? You must be joking. I'm exhausted.' The energy required for such distinct articulation drained her and she paled, then steadied herself against the backrail blazonry of a chair. Her eyes, when she redirected them to me, effused black light. 'Go to bed,' she said. 'Leave me alone.'

The silks she wore made their own elegy known as she began to cross the room.

What new daemon could I implore for strength? What deposed gods could I consult? In the ruins of my love for her, the poetry of final surrender. This was my last opportunity to express myself to her and I was mute. Intercepted, my intentions and subsequent actions.

Mother – that synonym for inner government, for that perspective which I sought to alter time and again. My every word was in my throat as I watched her strain to breathe, as I watched her submit to a cough that almost quartered her. Hotly flooding through me: a sudden terrible despairing and pellucid pity. There was the sensation that these actual emotions were greater than the identity who experienced them and with this, terror. I was intimidated, I was afraid. In the end, her power over me was too complete. Even now, even now as she disappeared before me, diluted to a nauseating cordial, reduced to this plain human fate, no more than a bolt of shot silk and a shudder, even now the very thought of her controlled me and she knew it. Dressed for the occasion in the crimson tunic of battle, her sharp shoulders only marginally softened by her cadmium wrap, she was prepared. Subduing enemies without a show of force was an art it took others a lifetime to master.

And there I was, blood of her blood, flesh of her flesh, convinced that I had felt everything only to be completely stupefied by newness, a disaster, and as my knees dissolved, I heard myself moan: '*Mamma ... mamma ... vieni qui ...*'

All my life I had loved her from afar, an awed beast in the

344

thrall of light, of wind, of an indomitable natural force – for that was how Mother was taught to me. Following her in half-remembered dreams, I loved her secretly, and even the sorrow and contempt and madness of loss she roused in me were no more than the pure weight of the heart. The nature of things as they are in themselves: transcendent knowledge, that cellular truth. She had always fooled the world. I was alone in perceiving the regret in her every word, her every glance, in discerning her delicacy. I was the only one who knew of those dim corners in which the webs of all her dreams hung tattered, the only one, and that was why she hated me.

'*Sei sorda?*' She was gasping, grasping that backrail, enraged, backing away as if from a monster. 'Are you deaf? *Leave!* Leave me alone! I am not feeling well, I have to *sleep!*'

There was blood on her lips and when I saw it, when I saw how it had stained her tongue, when I understood its ineluctable significance, I began to cry – if not for her, then for myself, then for my hopes of reconciliation. It had all been so futile. My every effort, my every emotion: futile.

'Leave me *alone!*' That gasp, wrought from her guts. 'Get *out!*'

My tears only repelled her but I still moved towards her with my arms outstretched, it was instinctive. How can I explain my state? How can I explain the wretchedness of understanding that I never had and never would have her? Such shame, the simplest monomania. The sound from my throat was one I had not heard since childhood. Trauma can be a gauge of love. I gathered her up in my arms, gathered up this snarling, malevolent, invidious spirit and held her as if she were all the world to me.

She struggled both with my embrace and with her own frustrated tears. 'Get *away* from me!' Her voice was breaking. 'I feel *nothing* for you! Get *away* from me!'

Sobbing as if to exorcize myself of pain, I pressed my lips to her high forehead, to her smooth and doctored skin. In effect, I was taking her against her will, but exacting moral distinctions were no longer relevant. It was no more a rape than her distortion of my reality; it was no more a rape than her abuse of my trust. And my needs in that moment were awesome, their magnitude outruled all sense. Her rejection of

345

me may have been my history, but I would not have it be my present: it was my turn to impose my will. Let me hold her if only to know that once – just once – I had succeeded in asserting myself with her, to know that I had in me the fire to demand. Mine was force and so was hers, but better that than unfelt acquiescence, better that than the unsaid. I preferred her fight. Let her struggle! For the first time, I would let her lose. Anything on earth but her indifference. Face to face for once, we were at war, united only by our differences. Debility did not detract from her display: her teeth were bared, she was contorted, her thorax fattened with a tempest that had never had a thing to do with me.

'I *loved* you,' I fiercely said, each of her jerking wrists gripped by my hands, 'I *loved* you, and you never cared.'

23

I will never forget her eyes in that moment: they seemed to fill with colour, it was as if black India ink had been poured into her blue blue irises, poured until those irises appeared to overflow, until they were so forcefully tinted that the emotions expressed by them were secondary to their impact – startling, as surreal as she essentially was to herself – and in that impact, they became the act of looking and it was through this act that I was transformed; no longer tangible to her, I was exclusively a symbol, no more than a table or a chair, any old thing. To have seen me as anything more would have been to annihilate her sense of sexual supremacy, it would have been to acknowledge her own hurts, and she addressed me as such, without interest in communication, those eyes attentive insofar as I could somehow reflect some winning attribute of hers; she really knew me as an adjunct and never, ever as anything more.

And through my embrace and its implicit assertion of identity, she understood that she was finished. This was the end. Her mirror, so to speak, had cracked. I was engulfed by her sudden expression of helplessness – in it, every loss, the damage, all the goods she had renounced, the triviality of her existence, it was as if she had cried: *Lord, what have I done? What have I done?* And she slipped from my arms like that pure weight to the floor, her head loosened, leaving a breath in the shape of a word to me. At my feet were her porcelain bones, wet silk, a pavé diamond ring, the light husk of a witch. All behavioural affectations impressed on the young by their elders only serve to make the truth of death repugnant. Propriety and pride were no longer relevant, they belonged to an antiquated syllabus. My mother, a woman who lived only for decorum, now lay in sour pool of her own urine. The dead are followers of Genet; it is the living who love Byron.

Decades may have passed but they were not white, no.

I stood and stared with broken recognition at her crumpled little corpse. My slippers were damp with her emissions. The wind outside gnawed at the panes. Her mouth and eyes were open. It had been Christmas for a good ten minutes, and then I could not stop stobbing. Police, an ambulance, discord. Aldo's truculence. My brother's anguish and its cessation with an injection of some sedative. I was in bed by four, extinguished. Susie in the corridor: 'How *aw*ful! How *awwwwwwful!*' Those telephones ringing and ringing throughout the dawn. *Buon Natale, Angelica.* Gabriel had gone, he was nowhere. Only the absence of dreams kept me going.

I awoke late that afternoon, having missed all the action. Amedeo had smashed all the priceless Bossu crystal. Untethered by medication and his grief, he had placed every glass on the main dining-room table and then systematically aimed them, one by one, at the vibrant family portrait (in which Georges Bossu, a sexagenarian closet transvestite, embraced with zeal the thirty-year-old wife he so openly detested, the two of them decoratively flanked by his gaga children – one heroin-addicted, the other permanently under observation for extreme suicidal tendencies – by two different women, both of these women dedicated drunks and professional former wives; the lot of them remarkably natty in hacking jackets and jodhpurs, a wicker picnic basket overflowing with glazed hams and maraschino cherries in the foreground, a fictive pop-eyed bulldog scowling in the background, and all this set in the Aberdeen green lands of the portraitist's lame imagination).

Alerted to the scene by the ubiquitous and insatiable Susie, Aldo was 'forced to defend' himself by nearly choking my brother in a headlock. The predictable ugliness followed. Amedeo broke loose to scream, *'you killed her! you've killed all of us, you bastard! you killed her!'* and then attempted to slash Aldo's throat with the jagged remnants of a brandy snifter. My stepfather was momentarily distracted by the sight of his own blood, but quickly decked his nemesis (who managed to sever an artery as he skidded into the heap of shattered crystal).

Both men survived to fight other wars.

Aldo suffered a few stitches and was left with a wound easily disguised by a scarf. When Amedeo was hospitalized, it was Thumper who required sedation. And Susie, who had watched these proceedings with the usual mixture of jaunty *Schadenfreude* and hyperbolical horror, actually swooned (but only when she was certain that the performance was well and truly over). The rest of the household thankfully remained asleep.

24

Saltbox mansions, robber-baron ghosts.

Lake Forest that Christmas was a real wonderland of twinkling lights and fir trees Nietzschean in their symmetry. The grand Academy was a city of stone and snow. At Deerpath and Oakwood, sleeping City Hall. There were displays of elite stranglers' gloves behind Marshall Field's windows. Notices posted around Market Square. The Lake Forest Woman's Club was to meet at Francine Latrine's house on Old Elm Road to discuss Act Four of *La Bayadère*, in which the Indian prince Solor is haunted by the spirit of Nikiya, the most beautiful of all the dancers of the Temple. On 25 February, the Lake Forest Symphony Benefit would take place. The First Midwest Bank had been supporting people and activities in the Lake County area for over eighty-five years. All insomniacs were welcome at the Sleep Disorders Centre of the only local hospital. The Wenban Funeral Home Ltd specialized in family monuments and markers. My mother's ghost, deliberating over tombs and the tombeau. A commitment to excellence in youth athletics was the hallmark of the Lake Forest Athletic Club. Above a photograph of an unthreateningly bland and balanced family, the legend: WHAT KEEPS THIS FAMILY CLOSE TO HOME? (The native newspaper.)

I wandered with Aftiel, the Angel of Twilight, those curvilinear tree-lined streets. My soft black boots left imprints in that virgin powder. Dim world and darkening. The debris of maples too weak for the storm. A graphite-eyed boy walking what at first appeared to be a cat and then revealed itself as a coiffed ormolu terrier. The heartbeat-rapid hopping of a sparrow or its sister. Mammalian roadkill, far too cold to bleed. Death dismisses the individual in favour of the general, it only trades in departicularization. Those gableboards loaded with snow. A civic elm, denuded. Nativity scenes and perhaps Jacobean tragedies were being re-enacted before exhilarating fires. With my every step, she again slipped from my arms and from my arms into the past. The streetlights flickered and then glowed, casting a shifting steeple far behind me.

That last breath of hers left to me in the shape of a word. Parallel consciousness. After an hour, I reached those steps which led down to the beach. It seemed like such a long way down, there were so many shadows through which to pass. My breath, cirrus. My hand a blind man's on the rail. That awkward step from overripe and rotting wood into a field of thigh-deep snow. I waded through the colour white. The water before me was indistinguishable from the horizon. It was all night out there, levelled. Around me: fresh sharp cracks of spindrift ice, the spume's chattering hiss, a sliding tile-smooth inland sea. Distinct and without parallax, each star.

When I was very young, my father would sit me on his lap and hold a set of antique constellation cards to the heavens and explain to me, in that burnished murmur I still hear in dreams, each star's myth and meaning. With an inclination of his head and an extended steady hand, he introduced to me the Lynx and Telescopium Herschilii, Boötes Canes Venatici, Coma Berenices and Quadrans Muralis, Hercules and the Corona Borealis, Lacerta, Cygnus, Lyra, Vulpecula, Anser and Pegasus – the winged horse I made mine in fantasy. On his muzzle, the star Enir; on his wing, the Saddle Star, Markab; on his forelimb, Scheat; below his breast, Andromeda, known to the superstitious Ancients as Sirrah vel Alpheratz. My Pegasus, son of Poseidon and Medusa, activator of the Muses' fount of inspiration, bearer of Divine lightning. '*Lo vedi lì, il cavallone?*' my father would ask, one index finger to the crowing and ecstatic sky, and I would gaze up and up and up, my eyes absorbent, learning to listen, learning to see. The sensibility he taught me was that of the eternal. And in that sky he loved, a beauty there long before me and long after me – a beauty belonging not to man, but to the universe: impossible to alter or own.

So many years had passed and there I was, still gazing up and up and up, still learning to listen, still learning to see, still abiding by the memory of my rare father. How human could he seem to me? I had never had the opportunity to align the reality of him to my ideal; he both lived and died between the notes of those hymns I composed for him: substanceless man.

The hollow wind had turned and was now blowing towards me great black sheets of water – those high cracking ice-capped waves: hoarfrost in between my lashes, cold crystal honeycomb melting on my lips. If souls were hued, then mine was pale. Like illness, sadness was something I had always borne in solitude. Certain natures accommodate too easily to mourning – natures accustomed to unequivocal emotional expenditure with no returns; it then only becomes a matter of focal adjustment to squander the sum of one's consciousness on another's absence. Self-abnegation, self-defeat. A permanent hunger.

I was tired of grief. No longer fixated by the unresolved, I wanted to let it go, let it all go. Would the world end if I left the past behind? The difficulty most had with perceiving higher dimensions had never been mine; the division between linear thinking and geometric visualization of forms was not an obstacle to me. I closed my eyes and considered the water, I considered the wind. Visible above me, the bright lunar crater Aristarchus – famous for its mists and hazes suggestive of volcanic activity: phenomenal transience. That bitter temperature. End of the world.

25

The unexpected pressure of a hand upon my arm caused me to cry out in fright. Such shock is astigmatic: blurred white dunes, that area of beach illuminated by a single alienating spotlight, my hand in motion, its naked fingers defensively outstretched, the waning moon, a man in black stepping quickly backwards into a cloud of snow. My ultra-violet pulse. The bold explodent of a wave splitting against a rock. So chilled, I stared. His shoulders were scintillant with cold dissolving crystals.

> *I have only ever loved*
> *one –*

Eerily illuminated by that single alienating spotlight and with an ashen voice, he said: 'I – I left as soon as I ... could.' I had never before known him to stammer. 'It's taken me hours to – to *find* you; nobody knew where you had gone. A child with – a child with a dog said – thank *God* I asked him, I thought you may have – he said he'd seen you ... walking down towards the beach, I was so – I was so ...' Another pause. 'Angelica, I'm here.'

> *my heart is a neophyte*
> *before him, and sung*

'I somehow cut my hand,' he said, looking at me with apprehension, with desire, with a grief I had never before seen. 'I don't know how.' He raised the muscular hypothenar of his left hand. Cuneiform writing in congealed dull blood.

I turned away from him, that last word of hers breathed to me, never to be articulated. Stared blindly at the blind horizon. There was in me no energy for explanation or dissent. From my arms and from my arms she slipped into my history. I had a sudden mental image of myself as luminous and almost laughed, and almost wept, I could have screamed. And that was it: the dead who, through their absence or inaccessibility to the senses, remind the tangible of their subordination to the unseen.

of ether and ether
of orb and plasma
of chyle and vulva

'If you ... were married for seven ... years ... as I was ...' Shivered and coughed. 'If you met the person and there – there were so many *years* ... shared by the two of you, however ... however difficult some of them may have been, to – to – to *lose* that person is ...' he swallowed before continuing, 'unlike – unlike anything you have ... ever known ... it is as if you were the one to ...' his voice flattened, '*die*. It is – it is a *terrible* thing to – to *cope* with the – to cope with the ... loss, not only of that person, but of what they symbolized, which could – which could – which may have been ... *love* ... and to allow yourself to be put into a position where that kind of – where that kind of loss can again occur is very ... difficult.'

is he
to the morning.

And then: 'There was no *time*, Angelica ... no *time* for me to prepare ... it takes *time* to – to prepare yourself for ... death ... there was no *time* for – for me – I – the – the – the things – everything I wanted to say was – she – she ... just was *gone* ... gone ... it was bewilder— bewildering ... it was ... I went through ... I went through a period – a process, I suppose a nat— natural process, a normal process of not ... *believing*

352

that she had gone, it didn't sink in ... I would find myself wishing that – it was impossible to under*stand* – you *hope* ... you hope ...'

I am his in essence

He stopped his tears with a full exhalation. 'I couldn't – I – there were so many memories, too many memories and every *night*, every night, all night long, months of sleeplessness, of ... tears ... no sense, it made no ... sense ... I just could not understand *why*.' Inhaling, that inhalation graded like the steps leading from a dilapidated cellar to a deserted house, he continued. 'She died so *suddenly* ... and why she – why she – why she – why our *child* ... our child ... had – had to ... go with her was ... something I could not understand. I was left with nothing. Nothing. I was left with nothing but my guilt. You can't – you can't imagine what it is to – to outlive the one person you ever loved. It is a punishment unrivalled in this world.'

as the sect of the Prodigal
draws to itself

'I didn't really want to – to – I couldn't confront the – the finality of death ... I wasn't brave, I was scared, I couldn't ... it was ... I just couldn't ... *do* it ... it was something I ... buried, something I – I lost myself in my – in my work.' And softly, so softly, he whispered, 'If you – if – if you *love* someone ... if you truly *love* ... them ... it is impossible to surrender that love ... willingly. Do you understand what I am saying?'

the madrigal cloudburst.

As I listened, I felt disembodied; it was the cold, perhaps, perhaps the shaking peaks and troughs of his dark voice; my head seemed to expand to a balloon; that breath left in the shape of a word by her to me; again, she slipped from my arms and from my arms into my psyche; perhaps it was the cold, perhaps it was his voice; I knew I could forever love him. Driftwood and thistle, white ash and columbine. In the fifteenth century, the Cardinal Bishop of Tusculum estimated there to be over a million angels walking the earth and Gabriel was the most beautiful – Gabriel, who governed the full moon. Sparks of snow were whipped into the light's unsentimental realm. The lake was loud. That neon imbued every shattered floe with primacy.

Memories transcend me:
at every turn,

'In – in a way I stopped living when they ... died. I was so *angry*.' His determination fractured on the word and I could hear his suffering. 'I was so *angry* ... I needed to know *why* ... *why* ... *why* ... because if you were raised – if you were raised to believe in the immutability of reason, if you were raised to believe in logical conclusions, in cause and – and effect, in *assertion*, for God's sake – in *action* ... if you had faith in these principles; if you invested your *trust* ... why is it ... why would someone like – why someone – someone so – she was so young, Angelica, she was so young ... you have to picture it, you have to picture it: I flew to the States with my future and returned only with my past.'

a vault of beauty imperceptible

'I just could not understand *why*,' he said, and then a brutal cough doubled him: liquefied pith, the black reverberations of a virus. 'And so I – so I locked it away inside me for ... years ... and replaced her with – I replaced her with – with my work ... I replaced her with professional responsibilities – chairman, president, director – I could not be *still*. I could not be still because the – the – the *pain* – the *pain* was too ... much. I *failed*, Angelica, I *failed* ... I wasn't strong, I couldn't take it, I collapsed ... I should have – I should have – I *failed*, Angelica, and that shame has crippled me.'

to the unwilling eye –

The wind literally screamed and words of his were lost within its turbulence. We were both violently shivering. The lake shifted and again shifted its volume, seeking dominion. I could no longer distinctly feel my limbs. The unseen force around us was enough to have ripped those glittering stars from the narcotic ether. That spotlight shot our shadows far before us, so that they were distorted by the sudden slope of buttes and deceptively shallow ditches. On the filigree brim of the shore, our shadows merged – a clean dihedral overlap – at the head, the effect being one of a freakish optical illusion or straight consanguinity.

> *friction,*
> *a caique bearing gold,*

'I went through a period of a year when ... when every morning I would wake – I would wake at two, at three ... *alone* ... in our bed with ... with the nursery – the decorated nursery – with the ... nursery ... still ... I could not face that room, I just locked – I locked the door and left it.' His breathing was so thick. 'I could not stop re*member*ing – the pain was – it was indescribable, it was – it was unlike any I have ever known ... and then the *anger* and frus*trat*ion and the *guilt*, the *guilt* ... it was as if – as if all I had left was my work. My work became my *life* ... it was the one remaining structure, the one structure that had not been destroyed.'

> *and seductions.*

His tender eyelids were feverishly tinged coral and opaline, the soft blooms of a bruise, and he coughed again – a spasm, his raw square hands cupped to his mouth, that spotlight gilding the delicate helix of his ear, his breath escaping in slow opaque whorls from in between his fingers. Through catarrh, he said: 'When – when I first met you, I was frightened because I didn't feel I – I couldn't – I didn't want to go back into my feelings because that was – that was where the *pain* was, do you understand? You *terrified* me – my feelings for you terrified me.'

> *He is of Babylon,*
> *the only one who makes me yearn*

From the purblind circumflex of the outer cantus, this

prospect: he was hunched against the winds, the hem of his black greatcoat rippling, his heavy arms folded across his breast, his chin to the socket of his left shoulder, his eyes tightly closed, that lush mouth parted, breathing drily. He was conserving what remained of him after his words. I looked back out at the horizon. Again, she slipped from my arms and from my arms into my memory. The Assyrian Phoenix, too, is born of its mother's carcass. When it has lived five hundred years, it gathers a pyre of spikenard, myrrh and cinnamon, and whilst inhaling the fumes or fragrances, draws its last breath only to resurrect in ash and aromata.

for the hand
of the Unspoken.

A massive wave suddenly burst open on the snow before us, sweeping our shadows back into the night, drenching us both with glacial water, its roar corroding. We both gasped and stumbled back into the drifts, wringing our hands, our cheeks smarting, fully involved with the stark moment, concussed into consciousness. I glanced at him only to be silenced by his face – exhausted but so beautiful, his hair sticking like syrup to his brow, his underlids livid, half-obscured by the angle of his head to that one light, those eyes of his communicating desolation, their expression hauling from me everything I had to give.

I gently said: 'Let's start again.'

Still shivering, he gazed at me. In vitreous rivulets, that lakewater down the silver incline of his scar. He shook his head free of the liquid, shook free a spray of diamonds. Despite the winds, a hush between us. He looked down to his right and then he raised those slow sea eyes – the trajectory of that look a liquid arc in which a lustrous sustenance flowed – to awe me with the red intensity of my response.

Torched pause. 'Stream of consciousness?'

'A mere *non sequitur*,' I answered.

I knew the echo of this moment would resound in me until I was prepared to renounce time, and perhaps even beyond that renunciation. Such pure desire. With an underwater lentor I leaned towards him and kissed him: softly, so softly, with an opened mouth. His breath was jagged, hot and bittersweet. Behind him, baseless indigo and its constellations. The conversion of mass to energy to light is the prerogative of every star. I lifted my right hand to his jaw and again kissed him, my soul diffusing into something greater. His every atom had been forged in a star and then released into the universe by the explosion of a supernova. In him: fragments of Hercules, Antares, Aquila, Draco, the river Eridanus, Serpens Cauda, Ursa Major, Pegasus. In him: the blood of Chaldean priests. In him: the firm stuff of eternity.

And there he was before me, and he filled me with wonder.